LA MAISON D██ ████████
ALL THE BEST FOR BRETAGNE.

Aww. No wonder Philippe had wanted his retirement party at the *Fest-Noz*, I realized. The whole town must have turned the festival into a celebration of Monsieur Vetault and his work.

Touched, I took out my phone to snap a photo. Then I swiveled in place, looking for more tributes to my mentor.

Philippe deserves this, I thought. He'd worked so long and so tirelessly. He'd shared his expertise and scrumptious *chocolate* with so many people.

I glanced toward the town square. Then, distracted by a furtive movement in the shadows, I squinted more purposefully in that direction.

Was that a man creeping through the park's tall trees?

As I watched, he dropped to his knees. His arm thrust downward. Something near him on the ground lurched sickeningly.

I glimpsed a shock of white hair and found myself running.

I wasn't sure what I planned to do. All I knew was that I recognized that white hair. That was *Philippe* on the ground.

Philippe!

Books by Colette London

Criminal Confections

Dangerously Dark

The Semi-Sweet Hereafter

Dead and Ganache

Published by Kensington Publishing Corp.

Dead
and Ganache

COLETTE
LONDON

KENSINGTON PUBLISHING CORP.
http://www.kensingtonbooks.com

KENSINGTON BOOKS are published by

Kensington Publishing Corp.
119 West 40th Street
New York, NY 10018

All Kensington Titles, Imprints, and Distributed Lines are available at special quantity discounts for bulk purchases for sales promotions, premiums, fund-raising, and educational or institutional use. Special book excerpts or customized printings can also be created to fit specific needs. For details, write or phone the office of the Kensington special sales manager: Kensington Publishing Corp., 119 West 40th Street, New York, NY 10018, attn: Special Sales Department, Phone: 1-800-221-2647.

Kensington and the K logo Reg. U.S. Pat & TM Off.

ISBN-13: 978-1-4967-1062-8
ISBN-10: 1-4967-1062-2
First Kensington Mass Market Edition: October 2017

eISBN-13: 978-1-4967-1063-5
eISBN-10: 1-4967-1063-0
First Kensington Electronic Edition: October 2017

10 9 8 7 6 5 4 3 2

Printed in the United States of America

To John Plumley, with all my love.

One

Have you ever tasted a dry, disappointing brownie? A flat, greasy chocolate-chip cookie? A chocolate cream pie that was neither creamy *nor* chocolaty? Me, too! The difference is, when *I* encounter less-than-stellar baked goods, candies, drinks, or treats, I have to fix them. And I always do. Because that's my job.

I'm a "chocolate whisperer" (the world's first!). That means that I specialize in *Theobroma cacao*—and everything that's made from it. My clients come to me (sometimes secretly) whenever they need to turn subpar chocolate goodies into culinary superstars.

Never heard of me? That's exactly the way my clients (and I) like it. See, I mostly work on a referral basis, troubleshooting chocolates on the QT for a carefully selected group of consultees. Sometimes that means developing new product lines for multi-national corporations. Sometimes it means creating chocolate ice creams, cheesecakes, or elaborately plated desserts for restaurateurs. Sometimes it means getting my hands dirty in the back-of-house at a local

mom-and-pop bakery, helping it compete with a rival
pâtisserie or encroaching fast-food chain.

I don't take jobs because they're lucrative. I take
them because they're challenging. Or interesting. Or
because someone really needs my help. I'm a soft
touch that way.

I just can't say no. Especially not when it comes to
sweet, heart-poundingly luscious chocolate, in all of
its myriad forms.

The bottom line is, if you have a favorite candy bar,
donut, or "house-crafted" chocolate dessert, there's a
good chance that I, Hayden Mundy Moore, worked
behind the scenes to improve it.

No matter what my assignment *du jour* happens to
be, I always succeed, too. That's (partly) because I
never quit. In the pursuit of chocolate excellence, I'm
indefatigable—if sometimes a teensy bit late delivering a consultation report. In my business, persistence
is a plus. Because, sometimes, coaxing out the best
from my favorite fermented fruit pod (aka the cocoa
bean) means multiple rounds of taste-testing. Sound
good? Sure, it does—the first twelve times. After that,
it's a job. Trust me.

Not that I'm complaining. I'm definitely not! I love
my clients. I love my work. And I *love* chocolate.
Melted, chopped, whipped into mousse or frozen into
gelato . . . it's all delicious. You think so, too? Then
hang tight, because I'm bound to have a few tips of
the trade to share with you—once we get to know one
another better, that is. Because while I might be tire-
less when it comes to truffles, I'm slightly less trusting
than I used to be these days. There's a good reason
for that, too.

See, my last few chocolate-whispering consultations
just happened to involve . . . *murder.* I know, it sounds

unbelievable. It did to me, too. Things got pretty crazy there for a while. But I'm hoping those days are behind me now.

In fact, I've put them behind me. *Miles* behind me. I'm nothing if not proactive when it comes to avoiding danger—at least most of the time. I'm not saying I literally ran from the last consultation-turned-deadly that I stumbled on in London, but once everything was sorted out, I was pretty happy to hop on a Eurostar train and head to France to visit my parents.

They're both experimental archaeologists, currently at work on a castle-rebuilding project in the Bourgogne-Franche-Comté region. Because of my mom, my dad, and my own sense of self-preservation, I happened to be in France during one of the best times to visit the Continent: early autumn.

I guess all the cool, crisp days and colorful changing leaves got to me, though. Because before I knew it, I had a case of back-to-school fever. At thirty, I'm well past the age of strapping on a backpack and boarding a school bus, but I had that expectant, clean-slate feeling, all the same. I was supposed to be lining up a new chocolate-whispering gig, but I was procrastinating. (If you knew me, you wouldn't be surprised by that.) I didn't want to risk running into trouble again.

That's why, when I received a message that my one-time chocolate-making mentor, Philippe Vetault, was retiring from his Brittany-based chocolaterie, I jumped at the chance to attend his *au revoir* party. I said goodbye to my mom and dad, grabbed my trusty crossbody bag, wheelie suitcase, and duffel, then boarded a TGV train to western France. Monsieur lived and worked in Saint-Malo, a walled seaside town full of quaint stone buildings, friendly people, and a genuine pirate's castle—all of which made being there about a million times better than sifting through the digital dossiers of potential chocolate-whispering clients.

Not that I could just disappear via high-speed train, of course. As a woman traveling the world solo, I have a system—one that involves regular check-ins with my "keeper," Travis Turner.

Officially, Travis is my financial advisor. He holds the purse strings to my inherited trust fund and makes sure I meet its (unusual) stipulations. He manages my travel arrangements and vets my consulting jobs, too. Aside from me, Travis is the one who decides whose chocolates will turn up next on my to-do list.

An inheritance sounds pretty chichi, but honestly, it's not. My trust fund has some serious strings attached. As much as I appreciated, and miss, my eccentric uncle Ross, who left me the means to travel and consult—and as much as I love my on-the-go life—it's missing some fairly standard amenities. Like a home of my own. A nearby group of friends. A routine, a future, a golden retriever. I'm happy traveling right now. But someday? We'll see.

Anyway, whenever I have a change of plans, Travis needs to be in the loop. That way, at least one other person knows whether I'm happily gridskipping to my next chocolate-whispering job or being mugged in a Milanese alleyway. Seated in a French train car as startlingly yellow fields of canola flowers flashed by my window, I dug out my cell phone and did what I had to do. What I (secretly) loved to do. Check in with Travis.

He answered on the second ring. "Hayden. It's about time."

His voice, deep and authoritative and undeniably

sexy, never failed to thrill me. I'd never met Travis—
not yet—but I'd spent plenty of time imagining what
he was like in person. Buttoned-up and suit-wearing
was my best guess. Tall. Organized. Supersmart.

Afraid of flying. More's the pity. Until I found an
excuse to show up in Seattle, where Travis was based,
we'd never meet.

"You used your credit card at Montparnasse train
station an hour ago," my financial advisor went on in a
pointed tone. "I was wondering when you'd call in to
tell me where you were headed."

After leaving my parents' rural work site, I'd changed
trains in Paris. "I missed talking to you, too, Travis."

"We agreed that you'd send me your itineraries
before you embarked on them." A pause. "Is the enforcer with you, at least?"

He meant Danny. Danny Jamieson, my oldest
friend and closest confidant. He and Travis had a long-
standing rivalry, sparked by the usual machismo (I
guessed). "The enforcer" was what Travis called Danny,
who evened out the playing field with "Harvard."

You can guess which fancy-pants school where my
keeper is an alumnus. You might also suppose that
Danny—who grew up in a gritty, wrong-side-of-the-
tracks neighborhood in L.A., where he still lives and
works—didn't go to college at all. But you'd be wrong.
Despite his criminal past, Danny has two university
degrees to accompany his bad attitude and love of
spicy food.

"No, Danny didn't come this time. This trip is personal, not business." For once, I wouldn't need my
buddy-turned-bodyguard. "I'm just going to a retirement party," I assured Travis. "Don't worry. Unless
kouign-amann is deadly, I'll be perfectly safe."

He humphed, not at all distracted by my wisecrack

about the famously buttery Breton pastry that was popular in Monsieur's neighborhood. Although its name literally means "cake-butter" in Breizh, the local dialect, it's similar to a caramelized pastry.

"Safe?" Travis sounded skeptical. But then, he often did. He preferred facts to assumptions. "I'll see about that. Details?"

I offered the usual—where I'd be staying, who would be there, when I'd be back. Then, "Monsieur Vetault is the reason I got into chocolate," I explained, watching a picturesque French village whoosh past the train window. "Without him, I never would have discovered my knack for working with cacao. Monsieur saw something in me—something special. I want to be there for him."

I was already feeling wistful about reuniting with my mentor. I'd been surprised—and a little sad—to learn Philippe was retiring. I'd spent a lot of time with him at his Saint-Malo shop, La Maison des Petits Bonheurs. My mentor was special. Kind, patient, and generous to a fault. Also, *brilliant* with chocolate.

I realized there was silence on the line. "Travis?"

I'd gone all soppy on him while reminiscing about Monsieur Vetault and my chocolate-whisperer origin story. Maybe my financial advisor wasn't the sentimental type. I wasn't sure.

I *was* sure that Travis knew about my chocolate-trainee past in Saint-Malo. He knew everything about everyone. Or he made sure he found out. Lately, I'd been relying on him for that ability.

"I'm here." He sounded distracted. Because he'd been thinking about how he'd helped me compile background on suspects while sleuthing? I'd never know. Predictably, Travis refocused immediately. "When you're finished there, you have a possible consultation in Las Vegas. Feeling like returning stateside?"

When he asked in that husky voice of his? You bet.

"Feeling like having me there?" I'd been abroad for a while now. "Maybe you can set up something in Seattle. There must be a chocolatier in Pike Place Market who needs my help."

"I'll let you know if anything turns up." If he was tempted to bring me to his 'hood, he didn't let on. Travis, I suspected, would make an excellent poker player. "Anything else for me?"

I couldn't help smiling. "Just a question." I cradled the phone and lowered my voice, as though the two of us were sharing an intimate, saucy phone call. "Tell me, Trav," I coaxed in my sultriest, most teasing tone. "What are you wearing right now?"

It was my habitual question to him. I could never resist trying to loosen up my famously straitlaced financial advisor.

His deep laughter was my reward, traveling the thousands of miles separating us. "Never change, Hayden. Have fun."

Then he ended our call and left me stymied. Again.

I still didn't know what my notoriously private financial advisor was like in person. Maybe I never would. But I'd be darned if I'd quit trying to find out—or if I'd start playing it straight on the phone with him. Teasing Travis was too much fun.

Despite knowing better, I had a *tiny* vocal-based crush on the man with the toe-tingling voice. Without knowing it, Travis had sparked my curiosity. That was a dangerous thing for a person with an inquisitive monkey-mind like mine. Even though Danny had done some reconnaissance on his rival, dropping bits and pieces like semi-sweet chocolate morsels, we both knew so little about Travis. He had a dog. He was a swimmer. He once raised guppies. He was a genius at finance, itineraries, and research. That's it.

My "keeper" didn't even have a social-media profile. Not anywhere. Not a photo, not a collection of 140-word observations, not a whisper about him on his company's "About Us" website page.

It was almost as though Travis was hiding something. But what? If I hadn't been so busy sleuthing (and perfecting chocolate) over the past few months, I'd have tried to find out.

My financial advisor was methodical. He was thoughtful. He was good at listening. Unlike me, Travis planned for everything.

Me? I like to leave room for serendipity. That means I try to take life as it comes: one taste at a time.

That's also the way you should eat chocolate. With 100 percent of your attention. If it's really good, quality cacao, it deserves no less. There's no other way to properly savor chocolate's silky texture, its complex flavor . . .

My stomach rumbled. My mouth watered, too. Whoops.

My brain had kicked off a chocolate-tasting party, and my taste buds wanted in on the action. Unfortunately, I was still several kilometers from my coastal destination. That meant my only options for a *goûter*—the traditional kids' afternoon snack in France—were prepackaged goodies from the TGV's dining car.

I'm no snob. I'm happy to enjoy a Reese's peanut butter cup or a prefab Oreo cookie when one is fresh and/or available. But when Monsieur's excellent hand-molded Breton chocolates were waiting at the other end of the line? I decided I'd hold tight.

When I arrived in Saint-Malo, I was glad I'd skipped the dubious temptations of cellophane-packaged train car treats.

The sun was out. The air was crisp. And Philippe had lost none of his expertise when it came to *le chocolat*. Standing in his personal *atelier*—his workshop— surrounded by chocolate-making equipment, I tasted dark chocolate tablettes and milk chocolate buttons filled with vanilla cream. I sampled a truffle studded with fresh crushed hazelnuts and a morsel spiked with liqueur.

My eyes widened as its heady, boozy flavor hit my tongue.

"*C'est si bon, oui?*" Philippe grinned, his face broadening beneath a shock of ever whitening hair. Beneath his chocolate-smudged white apron, his dark trousers and blue collared shirt were pristine. "You have not lost your feel for *le chocolat*, that is plain to see." My mentor seemed pleased. "*Tenez.* Try these."

He offered a tray of dazzlingly decorated chocolates. They appeared to be recently molded. I admired their shapes and colors, familiar with the cocoa-butter-based "paints" used to embellish their swirls and contours. I glanced up at Philippe's generous face. His countenance was more wrinkled than when I'd known him, and his posture was slightly less militarily erect. But his eyes were the same vivid blue they'd always been. They regarded me with the intelligence and verve I'd so admired.

"These are works of art, Monsieur. *Merci beaucoup.*"

I tried one. So did Philippe. He was no theorist, happy to devise amazing chocolates without ever indulging in them. Like me, Philippe Vetault loved chocolate—loved its smoothness, its sweetness, its complexity. His craft was a time-honored one, begun at the feet of his father and grandfather—who'd owned La Maison des Petits Bonheurs before him— and honed by further study and practice. Philippe had never been content to rest on his laurels. Even as his chocolaterie became more popular, he still strove to improve. To innovate. To keep up with new trends.

"But if I eat another bite, I'll spoil my dinner." I gave his hand a fond squeeze. His skin felt papery with wrinkles. "You know I would never risk ruining a wonderful French meal."

"Sometimes I think you are *française* at heart, Hayden." He beamed at me approvingly, proud of his heritage. "Except that your French still has not improved. Your accent? *Terrible!*"

Monsieur wagged his finger at me with stern disapproval, reminding me of the hours I'd spent at his side, scrubbing spoons and learning to make a couverture without seizing the chocolate. It was true that Philippe had seen something in me—some talent for tasting and developing chocolate that I still couldn't explain. But building that talent had taken work. Lots of it.

I apologized in my poorly accented French. Unlike chocolate, languages aren't something I have a particular affinity for. I understand and can get by in a variety of foreign tongues—French, Italian, Spanish, a smattering of Japanese and Mandarin—but for me, conversing with the locals during my travels usually involves a lot of hand gestures and hope. My method is to pantomime, smile, and offer a compliment whenever possible.

That's what I did then. "Your new atelier is beautiful."

We both gazed around the space, housed in a converted barn on the perfectly manicured grounds of the Vetault family's seventeenth-century château. I'd be sleeping in that château tonight and every night during my stay—something I hadn't done in the past, while working with Philippe. Then I'd been barely out of my teens (sometimes sulkily) globe-trotting with my parents. Now I was old enough to appreciate the atelier's ancient oak beams, pristine plastered walls, and shining open spaces.

"I needed it." Philippe turned away, busying himself with some old Breton chocolate molds. His hands shook slightly.

"Your shop was overrun with customers?" I guessed, remembering its cramped quarters where we'd worked together.

I'd rented a car—a compact Citroën with a standard transmission and a French-voiced GPS—near the train station. But my short route from the walled city of Saint-Malo to the château hadn't taken me past La Maison des Petits Bonheurs. Its name roughly (and aptly) translates to "The House of Small Pleasures."

Every one of Monsieur's chocolates was a miniature delight.

"*Oui*, something like that." Philippe glanced toward the barn's upstairs hayloft. I doubted it contained any hay these days. His gaze swerved to me, startling me with its . . . sadness? "I am glad you are here, Hayden. It has been too long."

Aww. I felt almost overcome with affection for

him. Thanks to Monsieur, I'd found my true calling. Without Philippe—without his exacting ways, his expertise, his inexplicable faith in me—I would never have discovered my gift for chocolate.

Any talent that can make people smile the way mine does is pretty wonderful, I'd say. I owed it all to Monsieur Vetault.

"It has." Smiling, I squeezed his hand again. Although we'd greeted each other with *les bises*—the expected French cheek kisses that were *de rigeur* in these parts—hugging my mentor was out of the question. To the French, an easy American-style hug was unthinkably intimate. "I'm so happy you're doing well. I can't imagine you retiring, though. What will you do? Fishing? Antiquing? Traveling?" I had another, likelier idea. "Spending time with *les petits-enfants?*"

At my French, he brightened. He also chuckled and shook his head. "Grandchildren? Not yet. Although my Nathalie is engaged."

Philippe mentioned that his daughter was busy working in Paris. Her arrival would be unavoidably delayed, he explained. I remembered her only as a young woman, about my age, who'd had more interest in the beaches and boys of Saint-Malo than in the family chocolate business. That long-ago summer, Nathalie Vetault had gotten *bronzée* (tanned). I'd gotten educated in chocolate varietals and molding techniques. I wasn't sorry.

I wondered if Nathalie would be taking over the family business after Philippe's retirement was official—in a few days, after his party. But before I could ask, my mentor took my arm gallantly in his and steered us both toward his atelier's door.

"But you will not want to spend your entire visit to Saint-Malo talking with an old man," Monsieur informed me. He waved outward. "You should go out! Explore the *centre-ville*! Have fun! You spent all your time working when you were here last."

"I was *learning*. And I was loving it."

Philippe gave an offhanded Gallic wave. "You were a natural talent. I gave you a direction to follow, nothing more."

That's where he was wrong. "You gave me *everything*."

I was grateful to him for it, too. But I didn't want to embarrass Philippe by being overly sentimental. His proud stance and upraised chin told me he didn't want to be fussed over.

"You can repay me with a dance at the *Fest-Noz* tonight. I will have a surprise announcement, but after that, I am yours."

A surprise announcement? I was intrigued. But I knew it would do no good to try wheedling the news from Monsieur before he was ready. He wouldn't crack. "Won't Madame Vetault object?"

"A Frenchwoman knows that loving is not possessing."

I grinned. "That's doesn't answer my question."

"It will be good for Hélène to see how much my young protégée appreciates me," Philippe stated. Chivalrously, he guided me out into the sea-scented air. "Sometimes wives forget."

I didn't see how anyone could *not* treasure my beloved, talented mentor. But I didn't know Hélène Vetault well. During that transformative summer, I'd only had eyes for chocolate.

Then, too, château Vetault had been a private residence at that time—one that I, as a mere trainee, had not been invited to visit. Given the French tendency toward formality, I wasn't surprised. It hadn't meant that the Vetaults were unfriendly—only that, to them, trust and closeness needed time to develop. In Brittany, as in the rest of France, there was value to be found in waiting—waiting for wine grapes, cheeses, formal parks and gardens, fine artwork, *and* relationships to all deepen with time.

As though acknowledging that, Philippe and I stood outside his atelier, gazing over the landscape. The areas surrounding the family château were all mani-cured in traditional French style, strict but lush, giving the appearance of many outdoor rooms bordered by hedges and topiaries, flowers and pergolas, dotted by fountains and ponds and tidy gravel paths. In the distance, the cliffs that supported the château gave way sharply to the sea. From our vantage point, though, the ocean appeared as harmless as a misty gray lake— one that was enormous and sounded like surf.

It was beautiful, that was for sure. But I couldn't wait to get inside the château, which had become a luxurious B&B while I'd been away. Somewhere up-stairs was a room with my name on it, sporting a grand four-poster bed, multiple tall, toile-curtained windows looking onto the gardens, and antique water taps reading *chaud* (hot) and *froid* (cold) in the tiled bath-room. I was looking forward to catching up on some non-chocolate-related, noncompulsory reading while I was visiting Saint-Malo this weekend.

Savoring a novel while in a French bubble bath? Yes, please!

"I would be honored to dance with you, Monsieur," I said.

"Flattery, bah!" Philippe squeezed my arm. Then, gruffly, he added, "*Allez!*" *Go!* He gestured outward.

"It will be dark soon. The *Fest-Noz* waits for no one. Especially not a pokey American."

He gave me a wink, reminding me that I'd discovered more than a precocious talent for chocolate that summer. I'd also uncovered a tendency toward procrastination. Monsieur knew that about me. He knew . . . but like my best friends, he loved me anyway.

On a rush of affection, I gave him a cheeky salute. "*Oui, chef!*" Yes, boss! "*Immédiatement, chef! Merci, chef!*"

"*À bientôt!*" See you soon.

Philippe patted down his chocolate-splattered apron and strolled inside his atelier to work. No wistfulness. No looking back. Straight ahead. That was my mentor. Practical and direct.

When I'd disappointed him with my chocolate-making efforts, I'd always known it. Monsieur had always been demanding; I'd always tried again. Something in Philippe had kindled an urgency in his trainees to do well. I hadn't been Monsieur Vetault's only protégée, but I was pretty sure I'd been the first. Until I'd wandered in, killing time while my parents delved into (yet another) experimental archaeological project, Philippe had never considered working with an outsider—someone beyond his village.

I liked to think I'd expanded *his* horizons, too.

Smiling to myself, I headed for my Citroën to grab my things. Almost everything I owned in the world came with me when I traveled—all of it fitting into two carry-on bags and a crossbody purse. Then I went to check in. It was time to meet my dance competition for the *Fest-Noz* later that night.

Inside, Madame Vetault was waiting for me.

Two

It was *l'heure d'apéro* (think cocktails and nibbles) by the time I made my way up the château's grand front steps and into its marble foyer. A crystal chandelier glimmered overhead; tasteful antique furnishings highlighted the house's symmetrical architecture and graceful mullioned windows. A low conversation came from somewhere in front of me, full of French sibilance.

That sound was one of the reasons the French language can be challenging, especially for the linguistically challenged like me. *La langue français* often joins its words—something called *enchaînement*—to improve its sound. Add in *liaison*—the practice of pronouncing the (usually) silent letters at the ends of certain words if they're followed by a vowel—and you have something that often sounds like a delightful, melodic, French mishmash.

Undaunted, I followed that sound past a sweeping stone staircase and a set of French doors, my trusty Converse sneakers silent against the finely detailed rugs. Honestly, in such plush surroundings, I felt a little out of place. In my line of work, I usually don't need to wear anything fancier than kitchen clogs and a chef's jacket, with a T-shirt and jeans underneath. Anything nicer gets destroyed in a professional kitchen.

I was underdressed for the occasion, but by the time I realized it, it was too late. I was just going to have to wing it. I slung my duffel higher on my shoulder, picked up my wheelie suitcase to avoid scuffing the floor, then turned a corner.

The French conversation I'd heard burbled to a stop.

Because it had been being conducted by *one* woman.

Caught midway through talking to herself, she brought herself up short. She peered at me through bespectacled eyes, her auburn hair twisted behind her head into what had probably once been an elegant chignon and was now (to put it politely) unkempt. With one hand, she held a wineglass full of red wine. With the other, she clutched a pencil, which she'd been using to press the buttons of an antiquated looking adding machine—the kind with a roll of paper spooling out of it. Travis would have loved it.

"*Bonsoir, Madame!*" I was surprised, but I wasn't a buffoon. I knew what was expected here. The French pride themselves on good manners. "*J'espère que je ne vous dérange pas, mais je—*"

I hope I'm not disturbing you, but I . . . didn't get to finish speaking in my halting French. The woman tossed away her pen with a careless gesture, then came at me with tipsy wobbliness.

That's right. Madame had been enjoying the cocktail hour while performing her old-timey bookkeeping. She was a bit drunk.

That explained the one-sided conversation I'd heard.

Oddly, it had sounded sort of . . . argumentative, though.

"Come in! Come in!" She set aside her wineglass—

clearly a last-minute decision, judging by the way she clanged that delicately stemmed goblet onto the counter. It fronted the nook she'd been standing in, which appeared to be an improvised front desk for the B&B portion of the château. "We have been expecting you!" she assured me in heavily accented English. "Your drive, it was good? The train? No strikes?" She noticed I wasn't answering and added, "Do not worry. Pfft! Your French does not matter!"

Her breath blasted me with fruity Beaujolais, pushed by her dismissive *pfft!* sound. *Do not worry. Your* terrible *French does not matter* was the implication. I could hardly take offense.

My French was subpar. I was the first to admit it.

Picking up her wine, she peered at me again. "Cat got your tongue?" A wild laugh. "Do not worry! I speak very good English!"

That was a relief. But I was puzzled. Was this really Hélène Vetault, my mentor's wife? Why had Monsieur not mentioned that his wife might have been knocking back *le vin* since lunchtime?

Maybe someone else was supposed to be checking me into the B&B. Maybe the Vetaults were merely family figureheads, who left the day-to-day running of the château's lodgings to someone else?

Surreptitiously, I sneaked a glance around. I glimpsed an entryway leading to a dining room edged by more French doors and a terrace, lit against the approaching sunset by golden lamps. I saw a passageway leading to an enormous sitting room, another hallway, and a multipaneled door nearby with a *privé* sign on it.

Private. The curious side of me wanted to open it.

Instead, I offered Madame Vetault a handshake.

"Thank you." I smiled at her. "I'm Hayden Mundy

Moore. Monsieur Vetault invited me to his retirement party."

"Of course, he did. Of course! You are the famous protégée! Everyone has heard of you." Warmly, she ignored my outstretched hand and leaned forward to offer me cheek kisses—air kisses, really. They left me inhaling her delicate perfume along with the tannic, fruity aromas of red wine. "Welcome to château Vetault!"

She threw out her arms, almost splashing us both with wine.

Unfazed, she gulped more wine. Conspiratorially, she leaned nearer. "*I* am Madame Vetault." She gave me a tipsy nod. "And *you* are our honored guest, Madame Mundy Moore."

"Please, call me Hayden."

"Unthinkable." Madame dismissed that idea with a pretty moue and a head shake—quintessentially French. Attractive and soft spoken despite her obvious tipsiness, she wore a ladylike navy dress in lightweight wool, paired with a scarf and slingback pumps. "Perhaps you would like some wine? Our dining room is closed this evening, because of the *Fest-Noz,* but I happen to have an open bottle at the front desk. It is *very* good."

I didn't doubt it. But because I'd eaten nothing but chocolates for hours, I politely declined. I was a lightweight, and I knew it. Danny often teased me about my low tolerance for alcohol, dating back to our days trawling Southern California dive bars together. All the same, we'd managed to knock back a few pints in some of those cozy British pubs recently.

"Are you sure?" Madame Vetault pressed, looking concerned.

"Yes, thank you." I glanced at that private door

behind her, still drawn to it. Sleuthing had changed me. Did I really prefer digging up secrets to savoring a nice Beaujolais? "That's very kind of you, but I should probably get ready for the *Fest-Noz*."

I'd experienced that time-honored nighttime festival when I'd been in Brittany years before. The *fête* (party) was unlike anything I've encountered in America. If I had to describe it, I'd liken it to a music fair crossed with Independence Day. Everyone in the village turns out to enjoy live music and traditional dancing, plus singing, food, drinks, fireworks displays, and more. Some party until midnight or later, for days at a time. The *Fest-Noz* was not at *all* lightweight. It was held in great affection by the local people, most of whom remembered attending as children.

For Monsieur's retirement, I would have expected a fancy celebratory dinner at the château, not a raucous French street festival. But Philippe hadn't explained the choice of venue, and I hadn't wanted to pry—not until we'd had more time together, at least. Maybe Philippe wanted to share his retirement *fête* with the entire village? He had lived there his whole life.

Hélène's gaze flicked over me. She gave a solemn nod.

"*Oui*. You will want to change before the celebration," she agreed after assessing my jeans, T-shirt, sneakers, and casual jacket. In moments, she'd gone to the front desk and produced an oversize key on a gilt fob, along with directions to my room. "It would not do justice to Monsieur Vetault *or* to the *patrimoine* if you arrived at the *fête* looking. . . ." She trailed off, giving a vague gesture of disapproval with her wineglass. "That way."

I wanted to defend myself and my ensemble (such as it was). But just as I opened my mouth, the château's front door opened, too. All thoughts of wardrobe and *patrimoine* (the vaunted French sense of heritage) dropped out of my mind as a troupe of noisy people spilled inside, chattering in rapid-fire French. At their head was one of those überchic French women with messy blond hair, effortlessly stylish clothes, and two men hanging on her every word. One of those men was prototypically tall, dark, and handsome; the other, compact and dressed worse than I was.

Behind them, a few more people crowded in. All I saw was my excuse to slip away from Madame Vetault's censorious drunken gaze.

I couldn't help being puzzled about her drinking while on duty. There was no doubt now that Hélène was manning the B&B's front desk, because she bustled over to greet the newcomers, trailing wine fumes and perfume and leaving me in the dust.

There was a story behind Hélène's drinking. I was sure of it. But for now, it was none of my business. That was enough for me—or at least, it would have to be. Just like that *privé* door.

When I told Danny about my newfound nosiness, he wouldn't be happy. But it wasn't possible to investigate murders and wind up unchanged, was it? All I could do was try to be careful.

And enjoy Monsieur's party tonight, of course. *Allez!*

As soon as I stepped into the village, I was swept away by the *Fest-Noz*. It was Glastonbury meets the Fourth of July (French style) in the best possible way, with a live *bagad*—a Breton band—playing bagpipes, bombards, and drums. There were groups of lively Saint-Malo residents dancing in circles, stamping and smiling. Children streaked past, their shining faces lit by the canopy of lights that had been strung from the eaves of one small village shop to the next. The sea-swept autumn air smelled full of incredible things to eat, from sweet apple cider to salted butter caramels to ham-and-cheese *galettes*. There were crumbly *palets bretons* (butter cookies), crunchy *frites* (fries), and more.

Naturally, I started with the food. I was *starving* after traveling, unpacking, and changing into a knee-length dress with flats and my most stylish jacket. My chocolates had long since worn off, so I tried a cheesy mushroom *galette* (basically, a savory crêpe) first. Then I chased it down with local apple cider served the traditional Breton way: in a small bowl, held cupped in both hands. *Voilà!* Dinner was served.

After that, I headed toward the town's biggest square, in search of Monsieur's party. It wasn't hard to spot. I glimpsed a long table full of chatting people, set with a tablecloth and lit by more of those glowing light strings overhead. If I wasn't mistaken, those were Philippe's family and friends, come to raise a toast and share a slice of rich *far breton* cake in his honor.

Hélène Vetault noticed me. She waved. I waved back.

With the loud music pushing me along, I trod past the *Fest-Noz* stalls, one of them undoubtedly representing Philippe's La Maison des Petits Bonheurs. I was curious which chocolates he'd have on offer, but I didn't want to stop. Not now, when I'd already spent time noshing on my improvised dinner. Other local shopkeepers sold everything from food to antiques to vivid blue-and-yellow Quimper pottery called *faience,* which was especially sought after by the English who took summer homes on Brittany's rocky coast.

Things didn't always go smoothly between the

locals and those British part-time residents, I'd heard. But at its heart—and despite its history of *corsairs* (pirates!)—Saint-Malo was a town driven by tourism. For tonight, at least, everyone inside its towering city walls seemed to be getting along famously.

I moved past another stall, struck by the realization that none of them bore logos or ads. There weren't paid spokespeople offering samples. There weren't *Fest-Noz* bikini models posing with attendees and taking pictures. There wasn't a Red Bull truck driving around the town square. The sugary crêpes didn't arrive bearing the golden arches of McDonald's (*McDo* to the French).

The resulting simplicity gave the whole *Fest-Noz* a sort of nostalgic glow. Being there was, in some ways, like stepping back in time—eating traditional foods, listening to traditional music, watching traditional dances that had been performed the same way for generations. I liked the Bretons' deep sense of history.

Passing the final vendor, I glanced to the left. That's when I saw it: the massive archway in the city wall leading to the *centre-ville* . . . and the huge, spotlit banner plastered atop it.

La Maison des Petits Bonheurs. All the best for Bretagne.

Aww. No wonder Philippe had wanted his retirement party at the *Fest-Noz*, I realized. The whole town must have turned the festival into a celebration of Monsieur Vetault and his work.

Touched, I took out my phone to snap a photo. Then I swiveled in place, looking for more tributes to my mentor.

Philippe deserves this, I thought. He'd worked so long and so tirelessly. He'd shared his expertise and his scrumptious *chocolat* with so many people. Maybe I'd overlooked another banner? Maybe, in the darkness,

I'd marched right past an engraved plaque, a bronze statue, a monsieur-size boxwood topiary in the park edging the square?

I glanced that way. Then, distracted by a furtive movement in the shadows, I squinted more purposefully in that direction.

Was that a man creeping through the park's tall trees?

As I watched, he dropped to his knees. His arm thrust downward. Something near him on the ground lurched sickeningly.

I glimpsed a shock of white hair and found myself running.

I wasn't sure what I planned to do. All I knew was that I recognized that white hair. That was *Philippe* on the ground.

Philippe! Enveloped in the park's chilly rows of hedges and chestnut trees, I knelt beside him, skinning both knees in my haste. I had the awful feeling I was already too late. The man I'd always called Monsieur—with great affection and respect—lay facedown on the ground, cold and motionless in the darkness.

A heart attack? Maybe a fall? Philippe was getting older . . .

The man I'd seen a moment ago stood nearby, gibbering to me in slurred, unintelligible French. He looked angry, his face contorted with rage as he stretched his trembling palm toward me. It appeared to be full of something—something that looked like a pool of melted chocolate.

Blood, I realized shakily. *That was blood.* I veered back, careful to keep one eye on that unknown man.

I didn't think he'd hurt me. But this park had been designed as a hideaway for the people of the *ville*—a place for lovers' assignations and secrets. I wasn't sure how much anyone at the *Fest-Noz* could see. I'd only noticed what I had because I'd been purposely, carefully looking.

Only to find *this*. Tears sprang to my eyes, blurring my view of the park, the ground, *Philippe*. Everything happened through a foggy haze. I had to focus.

I hauled in a breath. Not enough.

I couldn't believe this was happening. Not here. Not now.

More shouting from the distraught-looking Frenchman. I shook my head at him, then felt for a pulse. "*Je ne comprends pas.*"

I don't understand. I didn't understand, either. Not what the Frenchman was saying or doing. Not what he'd *been* doing. Not what had happened to dear Philippe, only yards away from the gaily decorated table that had been set for his retirement party.

I *knew* it was him. I didn't want it to be. For a moment, I tried to convince myself this was someone else—someone who'd wandered into the municipal park for a stroll. But I recognized his long apron, tied around his waist. His dark pants and blue collared shirt. His leather oxford shoes, still neatly laced and tied with twin bows—Philippe's quaint notion of "casual Friday."

I didn't recognize the *thing* sticking cruelly out of his back, though. It was obvious that's what had caused all the blood. Something long-handled and sharp . . . something deadly.

Oh no. No no no. Not Philippe.

"*Au secour!*" the other man screamed. He looked

about Philippe's age. Shorter. Louder. *"Aidez-moi! C'est Philippe!"*

He was calling for help. But I could have sworn I'd seen *him* standing over Philippe moments ago. I could have sworn I'd seen *him* thrusting something downward. The *thing? Oh, Philippe* . . .

I glanced behind me, toward the spot where Hélène had flagged me down earlier. I couldn't see her anymore. In her place were startled locals. People running. Confusion and concern.

I pressed harder on Philippe's neck, searching for a pulse. His skin already felt cold. I imagined it was turning paler, too.

Suddenly, I felt dizzy. I swayed on my knees, blinking back more tears. They swamped my vision anyway, partly obscuring the awful reality. *My mentor was dead.* Sweet, wonderful, demanding Philippe. He wouldn't ever make me redo a couverture again.

He wouldn't ever smile at me again. I couldn't stand it.

I would never be able to stand it. Why had I stayed away so long? That was all I could think about as more people came to help. They crowded around, shouting in emotional French. The *gendarmes* arrived, competently moving back the festivalgoers to reach Philippe. I blinked up at one *policière*, a tall brunette with a serious demeanor and an unequivocal air of authority.

She gave me an order in French. I understood enough of it.

Move away. She was telling me to leave Philippe's side.

I didn't want to. But her grave expression confirmed what I'd already suspected. Philippe was gone forever. One of the shopkeepers helped me to my feet, murmuring something soothing in French. I gave him a robotic *merci* and watched the proceedings.

It all happened with ruthless efficiency. Several officers erected a barricade around the ground where Philippe lay. Portable lights illuminated that awful space. Several gendarmes worked inside the cordoned-off area that held my mentor's body.

They were identifying evidence, I realized with a nauseatingly familiar feeling. Because this was a murder.

Without wanting to, I watched what the *policiers* were doing. I watched as they took statements from people nearby, as they lay out evidence tags, as they took photographs. I knew murder now.

I could help with this. If I could focus, I could help.

Forcing myself into alertness, I searched the people in the crowd. I still didn't see Hélène. That was probably for the best, though. The sight of her grief-stricken face would have dissolved what little concentration I'd mustered. I saw other sad faces, heard worried murmurs. I saw children being hurried away by their parents. I saw that even the *bagad*—the live band—had quit playing. Instead, the musicians had come to see the grisly scene.

I saw the man who'd loomed menacingly over Philippe, there in the deep shadows, in the moments before I'd rushed to him.

The village still shone with its festive light strings and decorations, but now the effect was macabre. Chilling. The moon had risen, but its light was muted. In the distance, ocean waves crashed against the craggy shoreline. It seemed miles away.

So did the girl I'd once been, learning at Monsieur's side.

I returned my attention to *the* man—to Angry Bloody Hands Man, as I thought of him now. He stood arguing with a different gendarme a few feet away, gesticulating as he spoke in fiery French. I made myself stare at him. I wanted to memorize his features, his movements, his face. I'd never forget his voice.

Au secours! C'est Philippe Vetault!

I transferred my attention to my mentor, determined to collect all the details I could. He lay on the park's cold dirt path with one arm outstretched, clutching something in his left hand. A scrap of paper? A business card? A receipt? From my vantage point, I couldn't tell. I wished I'd had the presence of mind to examine it as a possible clue, but I'd been too upset.

Feeling queasy, I watched as two *gendarmes* circled around Philippe's body, pointing and frowning as they discussed the murder weapon. That's what the *thing* had to be, wasn't it? I couldn't tell what it was, though, horribly sticking out of Philippe's back. Some kind of tool? With a wooden handle?

A spade, I guessed. Or another gardening implement. Maybe something used for woodworking. An awl? It wasn't a knife. The handle looked too rough-hewn for that—too round and too skinny. I've been in enough professional (and home) kitchens to recognize a knife when I see it. Philippe hadn't been killed by a knife.

But he *had* been stabbed in the back. That in itself spoke volumes, I thought. Had someone felt betrayed by my mentor?

"*Excusez-moi, Madame,*" a woman said. "*Je vous—*"

That no-nonsense voice ended my examination. I turned to see the *policière* I'd noticed earlier—the tall, severe brunette.

My expression had stopped her cold. She opened her mouth to regroup, but I shook my head. "*Parlez-vous anglais?*" I asked.

She nodded and continued in exemplary, if accented, English. "I am Mélanie Flamant, the officer in charge of this case." Her gaze probed mine. "You were the first to find Monsieur Vetault?"

"Not the first." I glanced at the angry man. He'd calmed down somewhat while talking with the police, but I still felt deeply suspicious of him. "Who is that?" I wanted to know.

Officer Flamant's mouth tightened. "I will be asking the questions tonight. If there is time, we will get to yours."

"He's a suspect, though, right?" I pushed. "I saw him over Monsieur Vetault's body. I saw him stab him!" I was sure I had.

The gruesome memory made me shiver. I felt woozy again.

Evidently, I looked just as bad as I felt, because Officer Flamant seemed concerned. She took my elbow and led me to a wrought-iron bench nearby. She sat me down on its chilly surface.

"First, please, your name." She waited expectantly.

I obliged. This was the point (usually) where someone in the police department told me, "Don't leave town, Ms. Mundy Moore."

"Tell me exactly what you saw," Officer Flamant said instead. "Start at the beginning. Step by step. Take your time."

She pulled out a notepad. A Moleskine exactly like mine—the one I use to compile to-do lists and make chocolatiering notes.

We were kindred spirits. This time, I'd have help when I tried to track down a killer. Because that's what I was going to have to do, I realized numbly. Philippe deserved every effort.

Determinedly, I nodded. I described everything in detail, from the moment I'd seen the banner dedicated to Philippe and his shop to the instant I'd glanced into the park's shadowy interior.

I hauled in a breath and made sure Officer Mélanie Flamant was listening closely. She was. I pointed at the short, angry, bloody-handed man, intending to make sure he did *not* get away.

"Then I saw *that man*," I said, "kill Philippe Vetault."

Three

You might think that, since I've been unfortunate enough to wind up front and center at a few murder cases recently, I would become inured to it all. You'd be wrong. I'm not at all inured.

I'm just as vulnerable now as I was the first time I stumbled across a dead body. Then, it had been at a chocolate-themed resort and spa near the bay in San Francisco. The victim? A friend who'd been working with me to troubleshoot problems at Lemaître Chocolates. That had been horrible—life-changing, in fact. This time, though, somehow things felt even worse.

This time, I'd lost a longtime friend. A mentor. Philippe.

I made my way back to the château, unsure where else to go. I was in no condition to wrangle transport back to the States on such short notice or to board a train to my parents'. Besides, I didn't want to bring my sadness to their doorstep.

I clutched the key to my *chambre* like a talisman, trodding up the ornate stone staircase without seeing much. The oil and watercolor paintings on the walls might as well not have existed. They, like the hand-loomed rugs, gilded lamps, and pieces of antique furniture, were just background to my awful reality.

Inside my quiet room, I dropped my key on the carved fireplace mantel. I eyed the empty hearth as I slipped out of my one pair of stylish flats, then crossed the room to stare out the tall windows, hugging my jacket against my midsection for warmth. I was still so cold. But that's my reaction, sometimes, to a crisis. I simply can't warm up. It would pass eventually. Like a craving for chocolate at midnight, I had to wait it out.

Around me, the château was silent. I'd passed a housekeeper on my way along the upstairs corridor, but she'd merely nodded and kept walking with an armful of fluffy towels. It seemed likely to me that she wasn't even aware of what had happened to Philippe.

It all seemed unbelievable to me, too. Still. Always.

I might be capable of attending a chocolate industry awards ceremony, parasailing with some Aussie friends, and then tromping through a cacao plantation to assess a harvest—all in the same week—but I'm still a human being, with all the frailties and faults that implies. I'm far from perfect. I'm often alone, too.

When push comes to shove, that's the price of my work—the price of my *ability* to work. Yes, I travel the world doing what I love to do. Yes, Uncle Ross left me with an all-the-chocolate-you-can-eat lifestyle. But it's not always a nonstop party.

Fortunately, I have a knack for making friends. People like opening up to me. I like meeting them. I enjoy getting to know everyone from taxi drivers to scuba divers, from chocolate moguls to dishwashers, from mechanics to bakers. Everywhere I go, I'm interested in finding out what people think, what they believe, what they hold dear, and what they prefer in their chocolates.

But that night, I was all by myself with my shock and grief.

I still couldn't believe Philippe was gone—especially not that way. Officer Mélanie Flamant had listened to my statement. She'd carefully noted every word. But she'd appeared distinctly skeptical when I'd pinpointed the angry man as Philippe's killer.

I'd seen that dubious look before. In San Francisco, in Portland—where I'd gone to celebrate a friend's bachelorette party and had wound up running a chocolate-after-dark tour while tracking down a murderer—and in London, too. What was going on?

Why did this keep happening to me? Why did I, ordinary Hayden Mundy Moore, feel compelled to embroil myself in trouble?

I ought to leave things to the professionals, I reminded myself as I crossed the room to switch on another lamp. Its glow brightened the walls—covered in delicate fabric, not wallpaper—and threw shadows behind the upholstered twin armchairs. I ought to mourn Philippe, yes, but then leave Saint-Malo for good.

I ought to . . . but I knew I wouldn't. The same thing that made me want to find out what was behind a door marked *privé* drove me to look for answers elsewhere, too. The same tenacity that I applied to my work with chocolate—tracking down solutions even when all seemed hopelessly chalky, dull, or flawed— gave me an edge when looking into a murder, I thought. By now, I recognized that about myself. In fact, I was almost proud of the way I'd managed to persevere during some difficult and unexpected times.

But this shocking tragedy involving Philippe. . . .

I had to leave matters with the *gendarmes.* Didn't I?

Even as I thought it, I could almost hear Danny laughing. My best pal knew I wouldn't be satisfied without answers.

I picked up my cell phone and dialed. It was late in France. Eight or nine hours earlier in L.A., depending on the season.

Time zones didn't matter. Danny answered on the first ring.

"What's up?" he asked. "Solve any murders without me?"

I almost crumpled right then. For a second, I couldn't speak. I could only gulp air as I gripped my phone. Hard.

"Hey." Danny's voice softened. "Hayden. Are you okay?"

Leave it to my oldest friend to somehow sense the truth.

I felt suddenly reluctant to say anything—to make Philippe's death even more real. I blinked back tears and settled on, "Why do you sound so far away?"

His voice had a tinny quality. A bad connection, maybe?

"I'm on speakerphone," Danny told me, his tone sharper now. There were reasons he could intimidate and subdue troublemakers on the red carpets of gala parties and premieres—his usual stomping grounds as a sought-after security expert. "There's no one listening. Tell me what's going on. It must be pretty late over there. Without my bad influence, you're in bed by eleven."

I cracked the ghost of a smile. He wasn't entirely wrong. In my work, I'm often up with the roosters. A *pâtisserie* starts baking treats ridiculously early, hours before dawn arrives.

I inhaled. "Tell me I can't investigate another murder." My eyes stung. I blinked fiercely. "It would be dumb, right?"

There was a long pause. Then, Danny said, "You can't investigate another murder. It would be criminally stupid."

"I said 'dumb.' It would be dumb."

"It's worse than that." Danny exhaled. Worriedly, I knew.

We'd temporarily parted ways after London. He'd planned to continue dating someone he'd met there. I'd planned to visit my mom and dad. We weren't joined at the hip, Danny and me.

His last words still lingered, though. He'd warned me, I recalled belatedly, not to nose into any more murder investigations. We both knew it wasn't safe. Even though I'd put Danny on semipermanent retainer (against Travis's better judgment) as an on-call bodyguard, he couldn't be with me 24/7. I didn't want him to be. We didn't have that kind of relationship.

I knew what he'd say next. He'd say he was on his way.

It was what Danny always said. What I relied on. No matter what happened or where it took place, Danny Jamieson always had my back. He would have protected me with his life. I believed it.

Just then, with a murderer somewhere in Saint-Malo, I was counting on it, too. *L'agent* Mélanie Flamant had duly questioned and then arrested Angry Bloody Hands Man. But her skepticism when I'd pinpointed him as Philippe's killer still bothered me. A lot.

"Hayden . . ." Danny sounded pained. "Don't get mixed up in anything. Whatever's going on, leave it to the professionals. You've been lucky so far, but sooner or later, that's gonna end."

Whoa. *That* was an unwanted change of pace.

"Hold on. Whatever happened to, 'I'm on my way'?"

"I can't come. Not this time."

Anger whooshed over me. Or was it fear? I couldn't tell.

"You mean, you won't. This is no time to teach me a lesson about snooping, Danny. Philippe Vetault is dead. My mentor!"

"I mean, I can't." Danny sounded terrifyingly resolute. "A bad guy popped me in the face on my last bodyguard job. I took him down—of course—but my eye is pretty messed up right now."

"So you're a little bruised! Big deal. You're tough, right?" He was the strongest, bravest, most capable person I knew. I couldn't accept that he was legitimately laid low. "Shake it off, okay? I'll ask Travis to arrange a flight. You can be here—"

"I had surgery for a detached retina yesterday. It'll heal up fine, but right now I'm immobilized. As in, facedown. Doctor's orders. That's why I've got you on speaker." Danny paused to inject a little lightness into his voice. "Do you know how hard it is to mainline tacos and beer while facedown? I'm reduced to smoothies and those disgusting green juice things. Ugh."

Despite everything, I laughed. "Knowing you, you have a gorgeous and dedicated on-call nurse to bring them to you."

His answering laughter spoke volumes. Danny had learned to make the best of things. Given his rough upbringing, he'd had to.

I pictured him recuperating, all six-feet-plus of his muscle-bound frame lounging on what my mind's eye insisted on imagining as a massage table. It didn't seem all that comfy.

I was worried. "Are you really okay? Does it hurt?"

"No more than your pity does." Danny swore. "There's a reason I didn't send out a PSA about this," he grumbled. "It's bad for my tough-guy image. I was hoping no one would find out."

With me, I doubted he was truly worried about his reputation. It seemed likelier something else was at work here.

"I won't tell Travis, if that's what you're worried about."

My buddy humphed. "Harvard probably has your phone bugged," he pointed out in an aggrieved voice. "Thought of that?"

"It would explain how Travis always knows where I am," I reflected. But I knew my financial advisor wouldn't stoop to listening in on my phone calls. From Travis's perspective, tracking my finances was more telling and less invasive. As a private man himself, Travis wouldn't have wanted to pry.

But he was a sore subject with Danny. When it came to the two of them, there was no reasoning with either one.

"I can't believe you didn't tell me you were injured," I protested, getting back to the important stuff. "Surgery? Danny! Next time, you're going to have to come clean from the get-go."

"That'll be the day."

"Do it for me," I urged. "Promise me. Okay?"

"Are you kidding? Everyone except my nurse thinks I'm taking a road trip to Tijuana this week. You already know too much."

Reality thudded back. "That's the name of my game lately."

Danny understood the reason for my altered tone

immediately. "Tell me what happened," he urged. "I can help from here."

"No, you can't." I was alone on this one. "Thanks, but—"

"My *brain* isn't on doctor-ordered bed rest," my buddy-turned-bodyguard interrupted testily. "Spill it, Hayden. Now."

"Thanks, Danny. But you're right. I should just sit this one out. There's already a suspect in police custody anyway." So what was I worried about? "I'll stay until Monsieur's memorial service and then I'll come home." Wherever that was. These days, who knew? "Travis has a job for me in Las Vegas. That might be fun, right? Showgirls for you, chocolate for me, winning all around."

Danny hadn't been my friend for years for nothing. He knew me. He proved it then, too. "I bet you already have suspects."

"Well, there *is* Angry Bloody Hands Man," I admitted. "He's obvious. Also, Hélène Vetault, Philippe's wife." In the past, investigating detectives had warned me that spouses always had to be considered suspects. "Aside from them, I'm not sure. Philippe was *so* kind. I can't imagine Monsieur having any real enemies."

Whoops. Danny had roped me into revealing too much. My need to know who, how, when, and why. It was the same need that drove me to perfect chocolate, even when solving problems with it became challenging. Through force of habit, I'd confided in him.

I stopped talking, irked and distraught at the same time.

What was I going to do without Danny? All on my own? If Angry Bloody Hands Man *hadn't* killed Philippe, then I'd need to start looking. But circumstances were putting a major crimp in my still-forming plans to (maybe) find out who, when, how, why.

Without Danny, investigating on my own would be foolhardy. Any reasonable person would have bowed out. By now, though, I'd moved beyond the reasonable stage. I'd changed too much.

"I've got this, Hayden," Danny assured me. "Long distance is better than nothing. For you, I'm always a phone call away."

His reassurance grounded me. To his credit, Danny didn't even crow about being right. But rather than convince me to forge ahead with more (inadvisable) amateur sleuthing, Danny's offer of long-distance help made me snap out of my daze of grief.

"Thanks, but I mean it. I'm not investigating this time."

He scoffed. "If you think I'm buying that—"

"You're going to have to." *Especially since you're too hurt to help me.* I knew that bothered him. I didn't want him to think he was letting me down. Hoping I sounded convincing, I added, "Listen, it's late here, and I need to get some sleep."

I could tell he didn't believe me about not looking into Philippe's death. I wasn't sure whether I believed me, either. Especially since my motivation at the moment was sparing Danny's feelings. He'd always hated being less than 100 percent.

"Call Travis," Danny urged. "He'll be your backup."

That brought me up short. He'd referred to his arch-nemesis as Travis. Not Harvard. Not the Human Calculator. *Travis.* Uh-oh.

This was serious. Even more serious, maybe, than the time the two of them had teamed up to "protect me" in Portland.

"I can't call Travis." We both knew the reason. My "keeper" was afraid to fly. He was phobic about it. We weren't sure why. "It will only make him feel bad about being unable to help."

Danny swore, belatedly reminded of Travis's condition. Then, "Fine. But be careful. Don't do anything I wouldn't do."

"That doesn't rule out much."

"Don't do anything I *would* do."

"Don't you want me to have any fun?"

His growl of frustration made me smile. Danny didn't know it, but his protectiveness made me feel a little better. I had lost Philippe. But I was going to make it through. I'd be okay.

"I want you to have exactly as much fun as is safe."

"Travis?" I joked. "Is that you? You *did* bug my phone!"

"Har, har. We both want you to get out of France alive."

"That makes three of us." I hugged my jacket close again, then glanced at the waiting four-poster bed. Suddenly, it looked pretty darn inviting. It had been a very long day. "I'll check in later. Oh, and *don't* tell Travis, okay? He'll only worry."

"He's going to find out," Danny warned. "He has his ways."

"I'll tell him tomorrow." *When I feel less like crying.* Travis's sympathetic demeanor—unlike Danny's take-charge stance—tended to bring out the waterworks with me. "Count on it."

"However you want to handle Harvard is up to you. It's none of my business." I knew Danny didn't understand my sight-unseen voice crush on my financial advisor. "Try to get some sleep."

I nodded, then realized I hadn't spoken. "I will."
I'll try.

And that's exactly what I did. *Try* to sleep. All the rest of the night . . . with very little success to show for it.

Morning came early in the French countryside—
la campagne. Although château Vetault was only a few kilometers from Saint-Malo, the house and grounds felt relatively isolated on that scenic clifftop. Traffic was sporadic, winding along the narrow country roads at an *escargot*'s pace. Neighboring houses were held at a distance due to the château's lush, extensive grounds.

It was a rooster that finally got me. I must have fallen fitfully asleep—dreaming of Breton music and blood—when that noisy bird started crowing. I wasn't sorry to see the night end.

I wasn't sure what the day had in store for me, but I had a few plans of my own. I wanted to offer my condolences to Hélène and to Nathalie, who I assumed would be coming home from Paris that day. I understood she'd been delayed by work and would have missed her father's retirement party altogether . . . if it had ever taken place. Then I wanted to drop by La Maison des Petits Bonheurs. It was possible I could help out. Philippe had always kept a small, trusted staff on hand in his chocolaterie. They would likely be overwhelmed today—if they were open at all.

They might be. The *Fest-Noz* had a daytime component, as well: the *Fest-Deiz*. No one would want to disappoint the remaining tourists or the locals who'd placed chocolate orders.

I crawled out of bed, caught sight of my brown,

shoulder-length, bedhead hair and hollow eyes, and wished I hadn't looked. I was still mourning Philippe. I had the tear-stained cheeks to show for it. But there was no rushing grief. Staying in bed all day wouldn't force out my sadness any faster. It wouldn't help anyone. Philippe wouldn't have wanted that. Neither did I.

I showered carefully in the tub—there wasn't a shower—using the ornate French-style handheld shower head. Doing so required a little dexterity, but I managed. Once you've navigated a squat toilet in Bangalore, learned to use a bidet in Bern, and had your personal bits delicately blown-dry by a robo-potty in Tokyo, you tended to take differences in bathroom amenities in stride.

Once dressed in my typical jeans and sneakers with a light gray sweater and jacket, I felt very much at loose ends. This was the part where Danny usually met me—where we reviewed the trouble I'd run into and made a plan to tackle it together.

I didn't intend to actively start sleuthing, of course. I'd promised myself as much late last night, especially given that the police already had a suspect in custody. But if the opportunity presented itself, if some new evidence turned up, I might . . .

Give it to the gendarmes, I reminded myself sternly. I was only hanging around to honor my mentor's memory at his funeral services and (maybe) lend a hand at his chocolaterie.

I certainly wouldn't need Danny's security-expert services for any of that. Especially since, at the château, all was . . . well, *noisy*, actually. What was all the ruckus outside?

I locked my room behind me, then stopped at one of the second-floor hallway windows to look. The source of all the hubbub was the same French guests who'd interrupted my check-in yesterday. As a group, they stood around the fountain at the formal garden's center, staring up into the morning sky.

Puzzled, I craned my neck to see better. All I glimpsed were puffy clouds in a serene canvas of blue—nothing to merit the shouting and pointing the chic blonde and her friends were doing.

I shrugged and kept going downstairs. If there was a *petit-dejeuner* (breakfast) to be had, I planned to partake. I wasn't particularly hungry, given the circumstances, but I'd be no help to anyone if I keeled over later. Plus, the B&B portion of the château was obviously still functioning. If the rowdy group was anything to go by, none of the guests were being asked to leave.

I'd almost expected a knock late last night, telling me to vacate my room and find elsewhere to toss and turn. Château Vetault was a family home, first and foremost; it would have been understandable if Hélène had wanted privacy to mourn Philippe.

But no knock had come, and as I reached the stairs, I caught a whiff of fresh coffee—maybe, I thought, *viennoiseries*, too. A basket of *pain au chocolat, croissants aux amandes*, and baguette slices with good Breton *beurre* (butter) and *confiture* (jam) would put some pep in my step—especially if those items were accompanied by the juice, sliced local fruit, and yogurt that typified a European-style start to the day. I don't tend to wake up ravenous, as a rule, but that morning my stomach growled.

Hélène was the first person I saw. *"Bonjour!"* she trilled.

Her smiling, jubilant demeanor startled me. In contrast to her appearance the evening before, today

Madame Vetault appeared tidy and chipper. Her auburn hair was wound into a topknot. Her pencil skirt and sleek sweater were matching in black on black.

The bespectacled widow Vetault was . . . downright dishy.

"*Bonjour*, Madame Vetault." I'd always enjoyed the French tradition of politeness. It insisted on personal greetings, whether you encountered a colleague at work, a waiter in a café, or a clerk in a shop. Today, that custom held new resonance.

Bonjour! Literally, "good day." That seemed unlikely.

"I'm so sorry about Monsieur Vetault," I said, stepping close enough that no one would overhear us. I didn't want to embarrass Hélène. "It's truly a tragedy. He'll be so missed."

"Indeed!" Madame Vetault's gaze met mine, held for one crazy overlong instant, then skittered away. She lifted the basket of pastries she'd been delivering to the dining room. "Well, life must go on, must it not? We cannot fight what fate has decreed."

I stood gobsmacked. I knew people sometimes spoke about a certain French tendency toward fatalism, but . . . this? On the day after losing her husband? I couldn't quite grasp it.

Hélène had to be in shock.

"Here. Let me take these for you." Gently, I eased the basket of flaky, buttery treats from her grasp. "I'll take them to the dining room myself. Is there anything else I can do?"

For a moment, Hélène looked lost. Everyone reacts differently to grief, I knew. Sadness strikes intermittently and ruthlessly. Maybe Hélène was relying on busyness to push it away?

If so, I was sorry I'd deprived her of her coping mechanism.

Before I could devise another approach, a whoop from outside jolted us both. Hélène and I started, then stared through the French doors. Beyond them, the blonde and her cohorts appeared to be taking selfies near some statuary. They posed with huge grins.

"Parisians," Hélène told me in an apologetic tone—as if that explained everything. "Here to film a series of music videos."

Nothing had ever seemed *less* necessary to me. "Is there anyone to intervene? Do you want me to ask them to leave?" I straightened. "If they're disturbing you, I'd be happy to do it."

I'm protective that way—always willing to champion the underdog. Particularly under circumstances like these.

"*Non.* No, of course not! They are paying a great deal for the privilege of shooting here. They are friends of my daughter."

Madame Vetault broke off, probably thinking of when Nathalie would arrive. At her woeful expression, I wanted to comfort her.

I was supposed to be considering Hélène Vetault an official suspect in Philippe's murder. Or would have been, if the police hadn't already had a suspect and I'd actually been snooping around to find out more. But I wasn't. So I didn't have to tamp down my natural instincts. I liked her. I felt sorry for her.

"Nathalie and I have met," I chatted into the forlorn gap that had fallen between us. "The summer Monsieur trained me."

Hélène brightened enormously. She actually squeezed my hand and smiled. It was a slightly manic smile, but still. Progress?

"Yes, I remember! You were Monsieur Vetault's favorite," she told me. "He could not stop talking about you! You must stay for the funeral, Madame Mundy Moore. It will be *beautiful*."

Her moody behavior gave me chills. It was odd, I won't lie.

"Of course, I'll stay. If you're sure you want me to."

"That is what Monsieur Vetault would have wanted, *n'est-ce pas?*" Hélène assured me. She shot a grievous glance at the noisy Parisians outside, then squared her shoulders. "The police tell me it will be a few days before we can have the memorial."

Because they needed time to perform an autopsy, I guessed. Time to gather evidence. Time to be sure about Angry Bloody Hands Man.

I nodded, feeling a lump rise in my throat. This was what death made us do—speak in normal tones about unthinkable things.

At that moment, I wasn't sure I'd make it to Philippe's service. I needed perspective. Answers. Both were in short supply. On the other hand, I mused, merely *speaking* with Officer Flamant wasn't off limits, was it? I could still ask questions.

"Do enjoy your breakfast!" Hélène nodded at the basket of pastries I was still woodenly holding. "I must get more coffee."

She whirled in her pumps and left me standing there while she bustled toward what I assumed was the château's kitchen.

The moment she left, it was as though a spell had broken.

Once again, I heard that rooster crow outside. I heard the Parisians laughing. I saw the yellow and orange flowers arranged on the antique sideboard near the dining room. I felt the cushy rug beneath my sneakers. Autumn air crept in from an open window someplace, raising goose bumps on my arms. The scents of coffee and perfume, floor wax and ripe apples, permeated the air.

Travis's voice, full and deep and authoritative, rang out.

Huh? Sure I was losing it, I listened harder. Maybe Hélène's temporary, grief-induced mania was catching. Or maybe—more sensibly—one of the other B&B guests who'd assembled in the dining room sounded a lot like my stateside financial advisor.

It wasn't unreasonable, I reminded myself. Lots of men had husky, sonorous voices. Lots of men sounded as if they could compute compound interest while simultaneously preparing their income taxes and figuring out how much to tip the delivery person who'd just arrived with their turkey-tomato sandwich on rye.

Besides, that voice I'd heard had been speaking French.

I shook my head to clear it, then headed into the dining room. My thoughts were on pastries and coffee—but my gaze landed on the man standing at the head of the long dining room table.

He was still speaking French, fluently and affably, with a smile and a presence that had drawn in all the other guests. They stood assembled around him, listening as he said something about his arrival having been delayed by *une grève* (a strike) on the railway coming in from Paris. Everyone nodded knowingly.

The women in the group appeared transfixed. The men stood with widened stances and lowered voices, laughing at the man's next anecdote—even as they seemed subtly to compete at appearing taller, smarter, funnier, and more admired by everyone else.

Only one man I knew could have engendered that response.

Our gazes met, and I knew. Somehow, this was Travis.

Four

I wish I could tell you I was delighted to finally see my financial advisor in person. But I couldn't. I mean, I *was* glad to see Travis, but I was also flummoxed, relieved, and hopelessly caught flat-footed. All at the same time.

My keeper, naturally enough, was not at a similar disadvantage. Travis had known he was coming. He also knew what I looked like. He kept my passport up to date and my credit cards paid off. He maintained my business presence and administered my income. He probably had a dossier on me six inches thick, with photos and fingerprints and a personality analysis inside it.

I had no such resources. Yet I was sure it was him.

What was he doing there? *How* had he come? He'd sworn to me that he'd never board a plane voluntarily. Had he been faking his avowed aviophobia all this time? Was he *not* afraid of flying?

Had Travis been *fibbing* to me for years?

I stared at him, silently baffled. Travis's supposed air-travel phobia had been the one thing *definitely* keeping us (at least in my mind) from being soul mates. From raising golden retrievers together. From hosting dinner parties with views of Puget Sound together and living happily ever after.

You know, *someday*. Not that I was wedded to the idea of romancing Travis (not at all), but a girl liked to daydream—especially during those long gaps in travel time, when jet lag hits hardest and not even the few keepsakes from home I carried could keep the loneliness at bay. All in theory, of course.

Only a few seconds had passed, but that was all it took. All my wildest imaginings spun around and then settled down again.

Travis must have felt my incredulity and confusion, because he quit talking in the midst of regaling his admirers with a story about recovering long-lost art. Or maybe getting away with art forgery? I couldn't tell.

My financial advisor's (surprisingly) fluent French fell away altogether, replaced by a quizzical look in my direction.

Quizzical? He had the nerve to look quizzically at *me?* I was supposed to be in Brittany. He was supposed to be . . . on the phone, where he belonged. It was all too much, all of a sudden.

I thumped down my basket of pastries and stormed out.

I'm not really a leave-in-a-huff kind of person. Generally, I liked to stick around and hammer things out. But it had been an upsetting trip so far. So I was pacing along the slate-tiled walkway outside the château when Travis caught up to me.

His tall frame was instantly recognizable (*by now,*

ha!), even from the corner of my eye. He rounded the
east side of the Vetaults' immense home-turned-B&B
and came nearer, dressed in the same perfectly fitted
charcoal suit and expensive shoes that I could have
(and had) predicted he'd prefer. He looked . . . nice.
Really nice. His hair was blond (as he'd told me
once), his shoulders broad, his demeanor perspica-
cious. I wasn't wild about *that* part.

I didn't want anyone to figure me out. Not even him.

"Hayden Mundy Moore." His throaty, soul-singer's
voice washed over me, just the way it always did. "We
meet at last."

His smile would have melted a lesser woman.
Not me.

"I guess we have one less thing to talk about now."
I gestured at his suit, shoes, and open-collar dress
shirt. I was surprised he'd omitted a tie. "Now I know
exactly what you're wearing."

He laughed. The sound was even better in person.

"That won't stop you asking me," he said. "I know
that."

He had me. "How do I even know you're you?" I
demanded, crankily squinting up at him. Way up. He
was as tall as Danny, but his features were more
chiseled. He wore glasses—professorial horn-rims.
He was undeniably good-looking. You know, in a
clean-cut, guy-next-door way. "Prove who you are, then
we'll talk."

He studied me. "You seem upset. What's wrong?"

"What's wrong?" I choked out a laugh, trying not to
bawl. I was feeling more on edge than usual. "How
can you ask that?"

"You're not happy to see me," Travis surmised. "I
knew there was a risk of that. Before you get upset, let
me explain."

"Before you explain, tell me how to feed a guppy."

My financial advisor frowned. Then, "With a micro-balance to measure the perfect amount of freeze-dried fish meal, shrimp meal, plankton, and daphnia. Do I pass? It's me, Hayden."

It *was* him. Travis had told me once about the guppies he'd had when he was seven—about how he'd accidentally overfed one before learning to use a sensitive scale to weigh fish food.

Only my keeper would have devised such a precise solution.

His arrival was . . . problematic. For all kinds of reasons.

"Come with me. Hurry up." After a furtive look around, I grabbed him. I hustled us both to Philippe's unused barn-turned-atelier, then shut the door behind us. In the gloom, I looked at Travis. "No one can know that we know one another. Got it?"

My definitive tone seemed to puzzle him. Travis gazed at me with absolute concentration for a few seconds. Then he concluded, "You're seeing someone. Someone here in Bretagne. That's fine, Hayden. I'm not here to sweep you off your feet."

"Try not to seem so amused by the idea, will you?"

"I'm here to keep you company, that's all," Travis forged on. "I'm tired of seeing you blunder into trouble on your own."

"*Blunder?* Wait a minute."

"Although I've reviewed Saint-Malo's crime rates and murder statistics, I was unable to assure myself that you would not have an opportunity to play detective again. So, just in case, here I am." He spread his arms and grinned. "Tada!"

Tada, indeed. He looked so pleased with himself.

I almost didn't have the heart to tell him what he obviously didn't know.

I was unable to assure myself that you would not have an opportunity to play detective again. That's what he'd said just now. Travis didn't know what had happened to Philippe Vetault.

He thought he was here in prevent-trouble mode. *Just in case,* he'd said. He'd probably hit the road soon after we'd spoken on the phone yesterday, mere moments after he'd discerned—down to the map coordinates—exactly where I was going to be.

Travis gave me a friendly glance. "You look . . . really awful."

"Gee, thanks." Why had those B&B guests admired him, again?

"More precisely, you look as though you haven't slept well." Travis took a few steps into the barn atelier, curiously glancing around himself as he did. Probably taking inventory, knowing him. "I blame Danny, of course." My financial advisor turned around. "Let me guess—he's still sleeping it off, right? You came down to get breakfast for you both? I know you said he wouldn't be here, but let's be real. Reason and history would suggest otherwise."

History? I was aghast. "Danny and I don't sleep together."

Did Travis know we once had? Probably, he did. Gulp.

Interestingly, though, he seemed to be unaware of at least one critical fact—my bodyguard buddy's travel-prohibiting eyeball injury. Travis wasn't here as an unwilling emergency backup. He wasn't here just because Danny was (forcibly) MIA in L.A.

"If that's true," Travis said, appearing wholly unconvinced that Danny and I weren't an item, "why is

Danny so competitive with me? I only have to look at him and he wants to punch me."

"Maybe you have that effect on people." I knew *my* voice-based ardor was cooling fast. *You look . . . really awful.* Humph.

"I've never seen any evidence to support that theory."

He had a point there, I grudgingly admitted to myself. I only had to remember his cadre of French admirers to believe it.

"Although there was one Frenchman back there who wouldn't quit arguing with me. A lot like the enforcer, in fact," Travis admitted. "If I said there were lost Renoirs stashed in Brittany's attics, just waiting to be rediscovered, he said they were worthless works by inferior artists."

Aha. The lost (or) forged art story. Score one for me.

"If I said the striking train workers had a point," Travis went on, looking slightly aggrieved, "he said they were lazy."

That made sense. As a nation, the French love to debate. About anything. They'll take any side, just to match wits.

"If I said that local dairy subsidies were problematic," Travis added, "he said they were a source of national pride."

"Well, you can't win 'em all." I made a face, obviously having misunderstood the ultra-entertaining nature of his dining room chitchat. "Where did you learn to speak French so well?"

Travis had the sense to look abashed. "Here in France. I lived in Amboise for two years during a study abroad program."

"You've *already* been to France?" I was purposely trying to sound outraged, but I was glad he'd brought up the subject. This way, I didn't have to interrogate him for personal reasons and risk revealing my (rapidly cooling) feelings. Now that Travis was there in person, he was too real to be daydream material. "What about your fear of flying? You're supposed to be phobic, remember?"

He gave me a steady look. "I overcame it. Yesterday."

"Sure, just like that," I cracked. "Easy-peasy."

Outside the barn, the Parisian filmmakers were still carrying away. Something buzzed nearby—probably gardening tools. I knew that maintaining a formal French garden took lots of work.

"No," Travis said. "Not just like that. But I did it."

For you, his expression said. But only for a nano-second.

Travis cleared his throat. I guessed that golden voice of his didn't come without a price. He probably had shares in a throat-lozenge company as insurance. "You should know that I'm paying myself travel expenses but no salary for this excursion," he clarified, his face impassive now. "It didn't seem equable."

Well. That sucked the (potential) sentimentality out of the situation. "Happy to finance your Francophile tendencies."

"Don't worry. You'll get your money's worth."

The way he said it made me believe him. I was still amazed that he'd actually gotten on a plane. On purpose. "I'd better."

"I don't have the enforcer's skill set, but I get by."

"You're going to have to." I didn't want to spoil Travis's dreams of an idyllic French holiday, but the time had arrived. "Because my mentor, Philippe Vetault, was murdered last night."

"Oh, Hayden." He stepped nearer, eyes full of commiseration.

I held up my palm, keeping Travis and his nice-guy shtick at bay. His sympathy only hardened my resolve.

Because if Travis was here with me, he was also—
inevitably—at risk. Right alongside me. That was the
way, I'd learned, amateur sleuthing tended to work.

At any time, I—or the people I cared about—could
be hurt.

That meant that my internal debate was over.
There was only one thing to do. "And I've just decided
to find out whodunit."

It was better to be proactive than to be caught off
guard, I reasoned. If (somehow) Angry Bloody Hands
Man *wasn't* the guilty party, then the killer would still
be out there ready to attack his (or her) next victim. I
couldn't let that happen, could I?

Travis nodded. "All right. I'm in." He rubbed his
hands together, then regarded me with certainty.
"First up, a plan."

I admired his go-get-'em spirit, but . . . "You're *not*
helping with this. Trust me. *This* is why I hurried us
both in here before anyone saw us together. It's not
because I'm dating a Breton."

If possible, I knew it would be better for Travis and
I *not* to be linked in the killer's mind. My sleuthing
sometimes ruffled feathers. "More important, you
don't know all the facts."

"Then tell me the facts." If he had a Moleskine, I
was sunk.

"It's not as easy as that," I protested. "You've never
done this before. *I* have. I know how it works—how it
always works. I never want to get involved, but I always
do. You don't have to."

"Actually, we both have a choice. We could leave
right now."

"Together? No way." I strove to sound breezy yet
sure. "*You* can get back on a plane if you want to, but
not with me. I'm a seasoned world traveler. I like to

stay light on my feet. I don't need your aviophobic panic attacks slowing me down."

I was joking, but Travis seemed undaunted.

"No problem," he said. "Because I'm not leaving."

"You're way too aboveboard for sneaking around," I tried.

"There's a lot you don't know about me."

He had a point. Still. . . . "I don't want you to get hurt."

"I don't want *you* to get hurt," my keeper countered. "If you think I'm leaving you here alone, you're crazy." His gaze burned into mine, suddenly intense. "Do you think I liked helping long distance while you muddled around chasing killers? Do you think I liked knowing *I'd* vetted those consultations where you got into trouble? Do you think I liked endangering you?" With calm vehemence, Travis shook his head. "Not again. Not this time."

I'd never thought of it that way. That explained a lot about what my financial advisor was doing there, seemingly on the spur of the moment. He must have been planning this since London.

"I never blamed you for any of that," I assured him. "No one could have known what would happen. You were very helpful."

Evidently, it occurred to me, Travis had been trying to manage my (unusual) situation for a while now. He'd been trying to mitigate my exposure to danger . . . with very limited success.

Now, apparently, it was time for the next step: him.

I knew he'd purposely chosen London for my last assignment because it was supposed to be ultra safe—especially murder-wise.

"It has to rankle, I guess, when your calculations

are so off," I commiserated, watching Travis pace around the barn.

"You have no idea." He sounded serious. *Super* serious.

"Sure, I do. I was always terrible at math," I quipped, thinking of my vagabond upbringing while traveling the world with my parents. My school days had been interestingly varied, to say the least. "Except when it came to chocolate-making, of course. Accuracy is essential. Monsieur always said, 'Measuring once? Good. Measuring Twice? Better. Measuring three times? Find work you like well enough to give your full attention to or throw out your horrible scale.' Naturally, he said it all in French, so it took me a while to work out the gist of it."

"Sounds like a guy I would have liked." Travis's sober gaze flicked to mine again. "Philippe deserves justice. I'm helping."

"I'm not even sure *I'm* helping," I argued, automatically trusting him to understand. "I've been going back and forth about all of this since last night, trying to decide what to do." I frowned at him. "I'm usually very decisive, but not this time."

His gaze softened. "Don't be too hard on yourself. It's likely you're still in shock. You were closer to Monsieur Vetault than any other victim. You haven't had much time to process all this."

He was right. "This *does* feel unlike the other times." I couldn't believe there'd been "other times" involving me and murder. It still seemed completely unreal to me that I'd helped apprehend a killer once, much less multiple times. I guessed I was still catching up to my new reality as a chocolate whisperer and (sometime) sleuth. "Leave it to you to clarify things."

I felt grateful for that, too. Travis might be just what I needed. All the same. . . . "But that's all the more reason I can't let you get hurt." I felt responsible for him now. "You're only here because of me. If something bad happened to you . . ."

"Whoa, whoa, whoa. I can take care of myself."

I scoffed. "No one needs stock advice around here, Travis."

"Don't let the glasses fool you. I'm multifaceted."

I wished I could believe him. I wished I could be sure that nothing bad would happen to him if he stayed in Saint-Malo.

Worryingly, though, Travis wore the same pugnacious, eager-beaver expression *I'd* probably sported in San Francisco at the chocolate-themed resort spa Maison LeMaître, after I'd encountered my first murder. I hadn't taken no for an answer when it came to looking into what had *really* happened then. Clearly, my financial advisor felt the same way now.

All right, then. If I couldn't make him flee to safety—and if Travis and I shared a need for answers—then our path was set.

"It's not going to be easy," I warned him.

"I hate easy. I live for excruciating levels of difficulty."

"It might get scary. What I saw last night . . ."

Affected me. I didn't have to say so. Travis knew.

He nodded. "All I ask is that you keep me in the loop."

That seemed reasonable. I agreed. "Of course, I will."

"About everything." He had the audacity to grin. "Starting now and continuing indefinitely. I want to know *everything*."

Everything? If Travis was expecting me to 'fess up to my voice crush, there was no way that was happening. I swore then and there to ignore whatever imaginary feelings I'd entertained about him—solely based on his voice—and behave like a grown-up.

"Fine." I pulled over the nearest stool and sat, then patted the seat closest to it. "Here are the facts as I know them."

I began with a brief (probably redundant) overview of my history with Philippe Vetault and closed with a moment-by-moment recounting of every awful thing that had happened last night.

Travis, to his credit, took the situation in stride. He pulled out a notebook—with a graphing grid, not lined paper—and wrote impressively legible notes as I spoke. He concentrated.

Then, "So your suspects are Hélène Vetault and the man you saw—the one who possibly attacked your mentor in the park," he said. "The first step is finding out who that man is."

"I was planning to go to the police station this morning."

"I'll do it. You'll be visiting the chocolaterie."

"*You'll* go to the police station?" I took a mental step backward. "But I usually do that part. Danny never wanted to."

I'd also explained about Danny's debilitating injury—then made my financial advisor swear to never reveal I'd told him.

"Danny had good reasons to avoid the police," Travis pointed out. We were both familiar with his shady background. "But *I've* never done jail time. I have no problem with it."

This was going to be weird, I could tell. But . . . good, too?

"Okay. I guess that means we have a plan of action."

"Yes, we do." Travis flipped shut his notebook. He stood, then regarded me from his much greater height. "I'm sorry about Philippe. I wish I'd met him." A pause. "Do you want a hug?"

I laughed. "If you're asking that, you haven't spent nearly enough time in France. You're not really a Francophile yet."

Steadfastly, Travis opened his arms. "Ask me if I care."

His message was plain. The *hug* was there if I wanted it.

"I'll pass." I headed for the door before I could change my mind. "Thanks, but what I really need is some *pain au chocolat.*"

Untroubled, my keeper followed me. "I'm an almond croissant guy, myself." His deep, sexy tone was not at all disappointed.

Didn't he *care* that I'd skipped out on his comforting hug?

It didn't matter. Feeling better already now that I had someone unequivocally on my side here in Brittany, I opened the barn atelier's door. Everything was going to be okay. I knew it.

I stepped outside and saw Hélène Vetault a few feet away in the château's garden, partly obscured by a hedge. It seemed she did *not* intend to mourn her husband at all unless her grief involved being locked in a passionate clinch with another man.

And that man? You can guess: it was Angry Bloody Hands Man.

Oh, la la la la. I definitely hadn't seen that coming.

Panicking, I shut the door. I almost collided with Travis.

"You'd better hurry to the police station," I said. "Because the gendarmes appear to have released Philippe's murderer and he's having a torrid affair with Philippe's wife, right outside."

Five

I parked my Citroën in a lot outside Saint-Malo's tall city walls, then made my way into the town. It was jarring to see something as modern as a parking lot with an automated pay system within sight of an actual medieval fortification, but I didn't have time to loll around in the brisk ocean breezes and ponder the situation too deeply. I had a chocolaterie to visit.

I headed straight for the Porte St-Vincent, the main entry into the city. It was one of the few passageways that cut into the seven-foot-thick walls encircling the *centre-ville*. High on its stone passage, that banner still hung in celebration of Philippe. I turned to admire it, then heaved a wistful sigh.

I hoped my mentor had seen that banner and *loved* it.

Forcibly shifting my attention, I studied the city walls and the stone stairs ascending to the ramparts. They would have made an excellent getaway route for Philippe's killer last night, I couldn't help thinking— close enough to be convenient, but high enough above the *Fest-Noz* to be out of sight of most onlookers— especially in the dark.

I shivered and kept going, following the narrow cobblestone streets into the heart of the old town. Here, the buildings crowded closely together, low roofed and made of pale local stone. In medieval times, they would have housed cobblers and butchers, blacksmiths and wheelwrights. Today, they offered up crêperies and sausage shops, souvenir sellers, and a few boutiques—many of them with blooming flowers planted in pots outside and all of them still tightly shuttered. Unlike America's 24/7 retail environment, stores in France tended to observe strict opening hours—generally from late morning to late afternoon—sometimes with a closure for *le déjeuner* (lunch), in between. I wanted to reach La Maison des Petits Bonheurs early.

Awash in a wave of nostalgia, I strode past a familiar Gothic church with stunning rose-colored glass windows, then a very old manor house with a round tower and a slate-tiled roof. Both looked exactly the same as I remembered from my days *en formation* (in training) to make chocolate with Philippe Vetault. In those days, I couldn't have known what awaited me as a chocolate whisperer, but I'd found the work fascinating anyway.

Rounding the next corner, I spied Monsieur's chocolaterie, snugly wedged in its longtime spot between two other businesses—a *magasin de confiture* (jam shop) and a tea salon. Like the other stores and cafés I'd passed, La Maison des Petits Bonheurs had closed its shutters for the night, obscuring the windows where ordinarily I would have seen jewel-like boxes of handmade chocolates. In that space, instead, was a gash of ugly black graffiti, scrawled on the shutters in profane street French.

I couldn't translate all of it. But I could absolutely make out the most prominent word: *traître*. Traitor.

Shocked, I stopped in *la rue*. This was not a rough *quartier* where "street art" was common or where petty crime was rampant. This was a peaceful, still sleepy part of town. From a distance, I could hear musicians tuning instruments for the *Fest-Deiz* later. Closer, two shopkeepers traded gossip as they shared *deux cafés* down the *rue*. But here at the chocolaterie, all was quiet—the better to absorb that unbelievable, hateful graffiti.

It had to have been painted there *before* Philippe had been killed last night. Nothing else made sense. That meant this was evidence. I dug out my cell phone and snapped a few pictures.

Had someone felt *betrayed* by Monsieur? It seemed impossible. Yet the proof was there in that black-painted word.

Traître. Traitor. But to whom? Or what?

"*Hé, hé! Arrêtez!*" Someone shouted. A man. He came at me in a torrent of angry-sounding French, but I only understood some of it. *Hey, stop that!* was roughly the idea. Plus some swearing.

Startled, I stepped back and lowered my phone.

Instantly, the man's demeanor changed. He'd been shaking his fist at me, but as soon as he saw my face he lowered his arm.

He gave me an untranslatable sound of dismay, mouth agape. "*Ah, Madame, excusez-moi! Je suis très désolé, mais je—*"

I'm sorry. He was apologizing for shouting at me. I didn't recognize him, but I did understand making a social gaffe.

I smiled and nodded. "*Pas de problème.*" No problem. There was no lasting harm done. He'd alarmed

me, that was all. I pocketed my phone, happy I'd
captured enough detail that the graffiti could serve as
evidence for me *and* the gendarmes.

Unfortunately, even though I'd responded to him
in French, my nonnative accent gave me away. Thanks
to my travels, I don't (quite) sound American, but I
positively don't sound French. The man angled his
head upon hearing me. He squinted as though trying
to categorize me, then gave me a definitive nod.

"I am sorry, *chouchou*." He rubbed his bald head,
then studied me from my Converse to my eyebrows
and back again. "I thought that you were someone
else." He spoke heavily accented English, but with the
usual French syntax. "You have hair like hers, only it
is your smile that is the much prettier one."

His frank perusal didn't surprise me. The French
have no compunction about staring, especially when
they're French *men*. Neither did his flirtatious tone.
Although he was dressed in baker's whites, with an
apron to shield his dark canvas pants and button-up
shirt, he probably figured there was always time for
friendly banter. Ordinarily, I feel the same. But
today? No.

"I'm sorry if I upset you," I said. "I was surprised
by this." I pointed at the graffiti. "Do you know what
happened?"

Gravely, he shook his head. "*Pas du tout.*" Not at all.
"I was inside all night and heard nothing." He gestured toward the chocolaterie's upstairs window. "My
mentor lets me stay here."

My mentor. Right. Philippe would have had other
trainees in the years since I'd studied chocolate-
making with him. All the same, it was odd hearing
someone else speak about him that way.

Monsieur was *my* mentor. He'd been special to *me*.

"I worked with Monsieur Vetault, as well," I told him. "I'm . . ."

"Hayden Mundy Moore, the famed protégée. *Je sais.*" I know. "Monsieur spoke often about you." Another flirtatious glance. "You are much prettier in person than in pictures, *chouchou.*"

I let that pet name pass. I had the uncomfortable feeling that's what he called the woman he'd mistaken me for. *Chouchou.* I wasn't sure, but it sounded like a term of endearment.

Philippe had been right about my shaky grasp of French.

"When I was here, the upstairs was a workroom." I supposed Philippe's barn-turned-atelier served that purpose now. I looked past the graffiti to the window again. "You live up there?"

"It is only temporary." He paused, looking uncomfortable. "I am Mathieu Camara. Monsieur did not mention me? Never?"

I shook my head, feeling awkward that Mathieu knew about me while I wasn't the least bit familiar with him. "I only arrived yesterday. Monsieur and I spent all our time tasting chocolate."

Mathieu's face brightened. With his strong features and burly build, he wasn't good looking—not exactly— but there's something to be said for Gallic charm. "That seems very much like Monsieur," he confided. "His work is an inspiration to me."

"Me, too. Monsieur was very special." We chatted for a few minutes about Philippe, his chocolates, his training methods, his love of a glass of red wine every afternoon. We lapsed into companionable silence. I heard a sniffle. Mathieu. Poor guy.

"We've lost him much too soon," I commiserated. Mathieu nodded, his eyes welling with tears.

He appeared to be only a few years older than me. He probably hadn't experienced much loss. He didn't appear to have anyone nearby to talk to, either. It seemed likely that he'd spent the night as sleeplessly as I had. I would have squeezed his hand to comfort him, but it would have been too forward.

Also, I didn't want to encourage his frisky side.

Instead, I changed the subject. "Has the shop expanded to allow upstairs living quarters? That must be an interesting place to live." The chocolaty smell alone would be heavenly. "I know construction is strictly controlled here, but—"

Mathieu held up his palm to stop me before I could ramble further about Saint-Malo's (understandable) prohibition against demolition or modification of its historic buildings. To think that I'd (mentally) made fun of Travis's dorky dining-room small talk earlier. I wasn't much better.

Strictly controlled construction? Really, Hayden?

"Would you like to come inside?" Mathieu asked.

I laughed, relieved not to have revealed my limited understanding of the historic town's building codes. "Yes, I would," I told him. "That would be wonderful. I came down to the chocolaterie to see if I could help you, in fact. With orders?"

Mathieu pursed his lips and made a doubtful sound. He'd quit looking quite so sad, though, so that was a victory. "I do not think that will be necessary. Thank you for your kindness."

"But I can help." I followed him to the shop's front door, unable to stop staring at that ugly graffiti. *Traître.* But how? "I'm pretty handy with a bucket and some cleaning rags, too."

We both glanced at the black paint marring the shutters.

"It will not be necessary for you to help. With anything."

"But I want to," I assured him, studying his profile. His eyes were dark, his brow creased, his shoulders stooped. He was clearly upset about losing Monsieur. "It might be best to leave the graffiti for the police," I remarked. "It may be evidence."

"*Les flics?*" The cops? Mathieu spat a profanity. He shook his head, then thumped inside the chocolaterie, leaving me to follow. "They will do nothing!" he said with an irate wave of his arm. Clearly, he was an impassioned man. "They had Monsieur Vetault's killer and already set him free. *That* is not justice."

We had that opinion in common, then. Interesting. No wonder Mathieu Camara was feeling overwrought this morning. He was upset that Angry Bloody Hands Man had been released from jail.

That made two of us. In Mathieu's wake, I ducked through the shop's low doorway, then stepped fully inside. Instantly, the familiar sweet scents of chocolate and its companion flavors—vanilla, caramel, fruit, and more—tantalized me. La Maison des Petits Bonheurs was exactly as I remembered it.

Except for Monsieur not smiling at me from the worktable near the back room, of course. I missed him.

"Then you don't think what happened was an accident? You think Monsieur was murdered?" I transferred my gaze from the rows of colorful, ribbon-wrapped chocolate boxes stacked on a display table. Wide-eyed, I added, "And *you* think—"

"Hubert Bernard did it." Mathieu snarled the name.

Exactly as I'd hoped he might when I purposely hesitated.

We'd definitely built a camaraderie now. Plus I was powered by *pain au chocolat* and two cups of coffee. I was on my game.

"I heard everything about what happened," the chocolatier went on while I committed the name *Hubert Bernard* to memory. "I heard there was a witness who saw Monsieur Bernard holding a weapon—someone who saw him attack Monsieur! It was him with no doubt."

I decided it would be prudent not to say *I* was the witness. Not if I wanted Mathieu to tell me any more. Even though he'd claimed to have spent the night at the shop, I doubted there was anyone who could corroborate that story or his innocence.

I had to be suspicious of everyone, I reminded myself, even though I liked Mathieu. Despite our rocky introduction, I felt sorry for him. It wasn't easy to lose someone like Monsieur.

"He was forever jealous of Monsieur Vetault," Mathieu told me, still talking about Hubert Bernard as he paced around the shop. "He'd gotten so much from Monsieur, but he wanted more."

Sure. "He'd gotten" Philippe's wife. "More? Like . . . ?"

Mathieu studied me, then shook his head. "This makes, for me, too much sadness to discuss it. It is done. Finished."

Hmm. Maybe that French fatalistic streak really was real. I wanted to know what Mathieu thought about Hubert Bernard—if he agreed he was having an affair with Hélène—but I wasn't sure how to broach the subject. If I was too pushy, I'd scare him away.

Unlike *l'agent* Mélanie Flamant, I didn't have a policière's badge. I didn't have the authority or experience that went with it. I couldn't compel Mathieu to answer any of my questions.

"Yes, you're right." I decided to try another tactic. "Monsieur wouldn't have wanted us to dwell on any of this," I reflected. "Especially not when he and Monsieur Bernard . . . ?"

Another intentional pause. As I'd hoped, Mathieu filled it.

"It does not matter that Monsieur Vetault and Monsieur Bernard were friends," he blurted. "Not even a friendship since childhood can be an answer for what happened last night. Nothing can."

Wow, this was easy. My sleuthing was improving.

"So you would say . . . ?" I nudged further.

Mathieu's annoyed glance was his only reply. "*Oui?*"

"That Monsieur Vetault was killed because . . . ?"

He lowered his brows. "You may have been my mentor's favorite, *chouchou*, but you are not mine." His face began to crumple. More tears. "I cannot believe you speak this way."

Uh-oh. I'd overstepped. Maybe I wasn't a genius sleuth after all. I'd have to try a different, subtler approach.

"It's only because I'm so angry at what happened to Monsieur Vetault," I backpedaled. That much was true, anyway. "I can tell that you miss him, too, so I thought maybe you would understand how I feel. Especially about this injustice."

Mathieu shot me a sideways glance. A heartbeat later, he said, "I do. *Faites-moi confiance. Je comprends.*" Trust me, I understand. He straightened, then wiped his hands on his apron in a businesslike fashion. "You want to clean? Really?"

"And make chocolate. Really," I promised, mentally putting on an apron and getting to work creating. "There's cocoa butter, cream, and sugar with my name on it in this place. Just tell me what your orders are for, and I'll be your sous-chef."

Mathieu's mouth quirked. "That would amuse Monsieur Vetault."

I didn't understand. "Why is that?"

"Because in his mind, you were no one's sous-chef."

He nodded at the paneled wall behind the chocolaterie's *caisse*—its checkout counter. I saw more chocolate boxes stacked on the shelves behind it, an old-fashioned till, a stack of La Maison des Petits Bonheurs business cards, and some ribbon.

"Is that a picture of *me*?" Astonished, I moved closer.

"Monsieur Vetault told everyone who came here about his protégée. He was very proud of you—of his famous chocolate whisperer."

I squinted at the photo—an old snap taken of me at a chocolate awards ceremony in Heidelberg. I hadn't yet begun taking on clients, but I *had* conquered my competition with a multilayered torte comprising three kinds of chocolate, caramel and vanilla buttercreams, hazelnut *feuilletine*, espresso cake layers, a mocha drizzle, and whipped vanilla chantilly cream.

"He asked me to search for your name on the Internet, so he could follow your work closely," Mathieu went on. "Whenever your name was in the news, Google found it and told him. The farther you went from here, the more you were missing to Monsieur."

Aww. *Monsieur* had missed me? He'd even followed

my career? Now *I* was going to cry. I blinked rapidly instead.

My heart still ached for my poor lost mentor, all the same.

"That was very kind of you," I managed to croak. "A little bit stalker-y and borderline creepy," I joked, "but kind."

Fortunately, Mathieu laughed. "I will delete if you want."

"No, no." I gave a blithe wave. "Let me believe I had a fan club once, however small." I peered at my photo. "Oh, look. This is cracked. Right here on the glass." I pointed. "I was going to offer to autograph it for you, celebrity style, but maybe not."

"I will get a new frame and then you can sign." He bustled over and took down my photo. He hugged it to his chest, looking discomfited. "This one must have fallen sometime. I fix it."

Something about his demeanor nagged at me. I tried to laugh it off. "You're making me think you *were* stalking me."

His eyes flew wider. He turned away. "*Jamais!*" Never. "I would not. I am . . . how does one say? . . . star struck by you. I did not think that I would ever meet you! Hayden Mundy Moore, traveling the world to fix chocolates. It is a dream."

"It's honestly not that glamorous," I demurred. "It's a lot like what you do here, actually. I make chocolates, that's all."

"*Oui!* You 'make chocolates' in New York, London, Shanghai, Sao Paulo, Rome, L.A." Mathieu broke off and shook his head at me. "Do not be modest, *chouchou*. You know you are talented."

I was embarrassed by his over-the-top praise, but I

drew the line at being self-effacing. I'm proud of what I'm capable of.

"I work very hard," I told him. "Just like you do. You must be very good at chocolate if Monsieur was willing to train you."

Mathieu offered an offhanded Gallic pout. "*Peut-être.*"

Maybe. "Not maybe! Definitely!" If he'd been someone I'd been consulting with or one of my chocolatiering buddies, I would have made it a point to build his confidence. "I can't wait to see what you can do." I looked around the shop. "What have you made? You said you didn't go to the *Fest-Noz*, so you must have been busy working last night instead. Right? So let's have it."

When I looked up from examining the array of chocolates in the shop's glass-front display case, Mathieu was staring at me.

"No, I did not attend the *Fest-Noz*. You are saying that, if I had gone, you believe I could have prevented what happened?"

I'd been hoping he would volunteer an alibi. No such luck.

"No, of course not. That's not what I was thinking at all."

"I would give *anything* for Monsieur Vetault to be here now." Mathieu set down the frame with my photo in it—gently, with dignity. I bet he had a light touch when rolling truffles. "He was like a father to me. I cannot believe he is gone so soon."

"I'm sorry, Monsieur Camara." I couldn't politely call him by his first name until he asked me to. "Please forgive me."

I guessed I didn't have my investigatory feet fully under me yet. I wanted to sleuth expertly, but solving a few murder cases (evidently) hadn't yet given me all the skills I needed.

I didn't want to upset anyone. Especially not someone who had been as close—or closer—to Monsieur as I had been.

"You'll be fine," I reassured Mathieu, trying to channel the comforting tone Travis always used with me. "Even without Monsieur Vetault. You can find another chocolaterie. Or start your own?"

It occurred to me that I didn't know what would happen to La Maison des Petits Bonheurs, now that Philippe was gone. Had he drawn up a will? Had he incorporated? His was one of the most successful small chocolateries in France, but I knew nothing about his business affairs. I did know that the chocolatierie had belonged to the Vetault family for three generations.

Maybe Nathalie Vetault would inherit the shop?

"Or maybe Madame Vetault will let you stay on and run the place?" I guessed, searching for more answers. "That might—"

Be nice, I'd been about to say. But Mathieu's rancorous look stopped me. He seemed . . . perturbed. About Nathalie? Or me?

I have a tendency toward motor mouth when cornered. I could see where it might rub someone like Mathieu the wrong way.

"Madame Vetault will have no more choice than I will about what happens to this place," Mathieu informed me.

I frowned in puzzlement. "Did Monsieur not have a will?"

"What Monsieur Vetault had was an agreement to merge with Poyet," Mathieu said. "You must be familiar with them, are you not?"

Poyet? I was staggered. *Everyone* knew Poyet. They were big. Successful. Synonymous with fine French chocolate. Their lineup was ever changing, ground-breakingly innovative, and eagerly covered in all the leading industry media. Their logoed packaging was iconic—a collector's item for the customers who packed their well-appointed boutiques in Paris and around the world.

I realized I was shaking my head. "No. Poyet was Monsieur's biggest rival. He would never have agreed to merge with them."

"Yet this is true." Mathieu raised his eyebrow. "I thought *you* would have known, of all the people. You are here." His pointed look left me uneasy. What was he implying? "Did you not wonder why Monsieur Vetault was retiring? It was not because he loved chocolate any less. It was because of Poyet. And Nathalie."

I noticed his slip—referring to Philippe's daughter by her first name—but I didn't remark on it. I was too busy boggling.

Maybe the Poyet merger had been Monsieur's "surprise announcement"? He'd never had a chance to reveal it that night.

"Monsieur never liked Poyet," I protested. "They were too Parisian, too exclusive, too expensive. You must be mistaken."

Yet Mathieu had a point. I *had* been surprised at Philippe's sudden retirement. But handing over his chocolaterie to *Poyet*?

An instant later, another interpretation occurred to me. When Philippe and I had chatted about Nathalie's grown-up life, he'd mentioned that his daughter had gotten engaged, hadn't he?

"Madame Vetault *and* Poyet? Which Poyet?" I asked.

Like La Maison des Petits Bonheurs, Poyet was a

privately held company. A family business. I was familiar with at least a few of the Poyets—by reputation, that is. The chocolate world was an insular one, full of gossip, competition, back-stabbing (usually *not* literally) and its own ever-changing hierarchy.

"The youngest son, Fabrice Poyet," Mathieu said, confirming my hunch. "He is engaged to marry Madame Vetault."

Just as I suspected. It was possible the wedding date had been Philippe's surprise announcement that night. It would have been like him to turn the spotlight away from himself. Besides, my mentor had always relished a surprise—whether that meant hidden raspberries piped into a molded white chocolate seashell or eleven scrumptious ganache-filled chocolates tucked inside a box intended for a customer who'd ordered ten. He'd always been generous. Generous enough to give his legacy to Fabrice Poyet?

If so, that would make Fabrice Poyet and Nathalie Vetault the Romeo and Juliet of the chocolate-making world, for sure. Their romance would bring together two respected chocolate dynasties and end decades' worth of comparison and competition.

Old world, meet new world. Till death do you part.

Except in this case, that bit had been literal—even before the merger had taken place. Poor Monsieur. Poor Nathalie.

"Poyet came to Saint-Malo and everything changed," Mathieu was saying—meaning, I assumed, that everything had changed when Fabrice Poyet met and fell in love with Nathalie Vetault. "Now it will change again, except I do not know how. I had hoped that the merger with Poyet would help me to move up in the chocolate world. To grow and travel in the way that *you* did. But now . . ." He shook his head and gave a disheartened, "Oh la la la la."

I understood. Contrary to cartoons and pop culture, "oh la la" is not a racy exclamation. It's not sexy or suggestive. It's more akin to "oh, no!" It's the kind of thing you'd say when you mislaid an earring . . . or lost the chance for a hoped-for promotion.

"With Monsieur Vetault gone, maybe the merger will not happen," Mathieu explained, all but erasing any motive he might have had for murder. "And me, I will have no chance with Poyet."

"Why not?" I needed to check with Travis about that merger.

"*Bof.*" Mathieu made an irked face. "Poyet wants . . . different from me, that is why not." He gestured irritably, searching for the words in English. "Poyet wants people like . . . you."

I felt singled out. Not favorably, either.

"The merger might still happen." I wasn't sure I wanted it to. I didn't like the idea of Philippe's shop changing—becoming just another branch of Poyet. "A few days from now, things will probably be clearer."

After Philippe's memorial. Surely Fabrice Poyet would arrive soon to support Nathalie. Maybe he would clarify business matters, too.

"What did everyone in Saint-Malo think of Poyet taking over La Maison des Petits Bonheurs?"

That's how it would go down. I had to be realistic. A power player like Poyet would not kowtow to a provincial chocolatier.

"No one knew. I overheard Monsieur Vetault discussing the merger with Monsieur Poyet one day." Mathieu frowned at me. "I would not have listened, but . . ." A shrug. "I was to be affected. I had to know."

That was understandable. Philippe's secrecy was

not. Unless he expected some kind of resistance. From Mathieu? The town?

"Of course, you listened," I soothed. As an inveterate eavesdropper myself these days, what else could I do? I wondered if Mathieu had expected to take over La Maison des Petits Bonheurs himself someday. "Then everyone thought that Philippe was retiring simply to take a break from making chocolate?"

Mathieu nodded. "Until now, I told no one. But it does not matter anymore." He pulled a galvanized bucket from the shop's back room and dropped a cleaning rag into it. "It is finished." Another shrug. "Also, what happens here does not matter to you."

"Of course it matters," I protested, feeling pinned by Mathieu's obvious disapproval. "I cared about Monsieur."

I was still trying to figure out why Philippe would have kept the merger a secret. Hélène must have known, even though she appeared to run the château and B&B, not the chocolaterie. She must have been aware that changes were coming. Also, Hubert Bernard could have known, if he and Monsieur had been friends.

Friends confided in one another, didn't they?

Humph. *Hubert Bernard* was the one who deserved the *traître* slur outside, I couldn't help thinking as I glanced toward the shop's entryway. Had Monsieur known about his wife's affair?

I hoped not. It would have been hurtful. I know the French are reputed to take love affairs in stride, but to what degree?

Plainly unconvinced that I'd cared about Monsieur as much as he had, Mathieu stared forlornly into his cleaning bucket. His shoulders slumped with sorrow. Then he looked up at me.

"Do you think truly that the graffiti is evidence?"

I nodded. "It might be. The police need all the information they can get. If someone had a grudge against Monsieur Vetault—"

"Half the townspeople had a grudge against him."

Now it was my turn to look uncertain. "I don't believe it."

"Is true." Mathieu shrugged and added soap to his bucket. "Monsieur Vetault angered people here by sponsoring the *Fest-Noz*."

Next to everything else I'd learned so far this morning, that sounded pretty inconsequential. "Sponsoring it?"

"*Oui.* His banner to advertise La Maison des Petits Bonheurs was like a crime to those who believe most in *la patrimoine.*" Mathieu glanced up from his bucket. "You know *la patrimoine?*"

I nodded. "France's cultural heritage. Its history and values and sense of tradition." All those things were deeply cherished here. They had been for centuries. "But how did Monsieur endanger *la patrimoine* just by sponsoring the festival?"

A derisive snort. "It is obvious you are not *française.*"

I waited, inhaling the chocolaty aromas inside the shop to boost my patience. It wasn't a technique, per se, but it worked for me. There was something about chocolate that was . . . perfect.

Mathieu finally relented. "There has been talk of sponsoring the *Fest-Noz* for a long time now. Every year, the shopkeepers discuss it," he clarified. "Every year, the old-timers say no. Leave the festival as it is—as it has always been. Sponsoring means advertising. It means profiting. It means putting business interests before neighbors and friends."

"It means ignoring *la patrimoine,*" I guessed. "Tradition."

Liberté. Egalité. Fraternité. The motto of the Republic.

Freedom. Equality. Brotherhood. That was France.

At Mathieu's nod, I still felt skeptical. "All that opposition, just because Monsieur Vetault wanted to celebrate his chocolaterie one last time before it became part of Poyet?"

Monsieur had placed that banner I'd seen, I realized belatedly. It hadn't been a display of congratulations from his friends and neighbors. It had been—to them—an act of defiance.

Mathieu gave me an impatient look. "Everyone agreed not to sponsor the *Fest-Noz.* Then Monsieur Vetault made his banner anyway. Doing so gave him an unfair advantage over all the others."

His tone suggested I should understand. "Who agreed?"

"Everyone. The shopkeepers. There is a club for them, where they meet and make decisions like this one. It is private."

That had been my next question. "How did you know I—"

"Outsiders are nosy. Pushy. They do not understand."

I probably did seem pushy, given all my questions. But Mathieu had seemed to need to talk to someone. Aside from which, he made that pronouncement so matter-of-factly that I couldn't take offense. "In some places, that's just typical behavior."

"Ah, but you are not 'some places.' You are in Saint-Malo."

I was beginning to wish I wasn't. "Who runs this club?"

But Mathieu wasn't prepared to disclose any more. "That is none of your business, *chouchou.*" He hefted his bucket. "Now it is time to clean the graffiti before anyone else sees it. It is a cowardly, shameful attack on Monsieur Vetault. I am to remove it."

It had crossed my mind that maybe Mathieu had scrawled that graffiti on the shutters. After all, he'd been there alone when most people had been away at the *Fest-Noz*. But he seemed genuinely distressed as I followed him outside to confront it.

We both frowned at it. "The police need to see this," I argued. Believe me, the irony wasn't lost on me. I, Hayden Mundy Moore, was actually championing going to the authorities first. This time, it made sense. "This graffiti is evidence."

It was evidence, at least, that a lot of shopkeepers in town had been angry with Monsieur. To someone, he was a *traître*.

That term made a lot more sense now that I had been reminded of *la patrimoine* and was aware of the antisponsorship agreement that had been in place among the local merchants.

No wonder none of the stalls had featured advertising. I'd noticed that last night but hadn't considered its significance beyond lending an old-fashioned ambiance to the proceedings.

Philippe may have given La Maison des Petits Bonheurs a tiny leg up on the local competition with that banner, but he hadn't deserved to die. He didn't deserve that graffiti, either.

I stepped up to the shutters and blocked them with my body, flinging my arms wide to (paradoxically) protect the graffiti.

"You can't wash this away," I said. "Not yet."

Mathieu actually laughed. Amusement lit up his stern face. His dark eyes sparkled at me. "You are a funny one, *chouchou*."

His use of that nickname sidetracked me for a second.

"Yeah, about that." I was getting less and less comfy with my unwanted pet name. "How about if you just call me Hayden?"

He took a long time to consider it. Then, "I will, if you will call me Mathieu. We protégés must stick together, *non*?"

"*Oui*, Mathieu. It's what M. Vetault would have wanted."

I meant it, too. So far, Mathieu seemed (mostly) like a friend in Saint-Malo. He hadn't exactly been welcoming at first, but he'd warmed up to me. Plus, we had chocolate in common.

"I still want to know what you made last night," I said.

"I still want to know what *you* can make," he returned, "with your extra super good chocolate whisperer abilities."

"I'll show you mine if you'll show me yours," I joked.

Mathieu looked absolutely baffled. I guess not everything translated perfectly. I peeled myself from the shutter.

"I mean, I'm looking forward to getting to know you."

"Ah. For me, too, as well." He nodded, then reached out to help steady me against the cobblestones. Mathieu seemed strong. *Really* strong. But his touch was chivalrous. "I am still not going to *les gendarmes*." He sighed. "It is a long walk there."

I gawked at him. "You don't want to report this graffiti because it's too much of a hike to the police station?"

He shrugged again. "You can still do it, if you want to."

Humph. He was feeling all kinds of generous, apparently.

"I will let you clean the graffiti after. It is my treat."

Aha. Now I understood. I'd been fooled. Mathieu had just Tom Sawyer-ed me into doing the onerous work he didn't want to do. He'd been one part informative, one part confrontational (just as Travis's dissenter had been that morning), and one part charming—adding up to one perfectly expectable Frenchman.

I should have known better than to take sad-eyed Mathieu Camara at face value. Now I wasn't sure what to believe about the things he'd told me. Was Mathieu a reliable source or not?

Not at all sure, I added him to my suspects list.

He'd worked closely with Monsieur, I rationalized, and he'd just proven himself to be unpredictable. Not to mention, I was far from knowing everything that had gone down in Saint-Malo. It was possible Mathieu had had reasons to want poor Philippe dead.

But uncovering them would have to wait for another time. I had the feeling I'd teased out all the information I was likely to get from Mathieu for now, and my day was just beginning.

I was off to the police station to report that graffiti.

Six

Reporting the graffiti scrawled on Monsieur's shop turned out to be anticlimactic. I followed the signs to the town's municipal buildings, wandering through twisty lanes and past more flower-bedecked businesses before reaching my destination. Once there, though, I learned that Mélanie Flamant was "not available." No matter how hard I pressed, I couldn't see her.

I half suspected the *policière* was dodging me. But that didn't make sense. I'd been a valuable witness last night. I'd had useful information. I'd *seen* Hubert Bernard attack Monsieur.

In fact, I couldn't *un-see* it. I truly wished I could.

Deciding to leave the *policière* in Travis's capable hands (as we'd agreed), I described the graffiti at Philippe's shop to a uniformed *gendarme*. I offered the photos I'd taken, too, but the officer on duty declined. He promised either to leave a message for *Madame l'agent* Flamant or to visit the scene himself. (I wasn't sure which, in my less-than-conversational French.)

Unhappy with the (seemingly) lackadaisical investigatory style of the local police, I retraced my steps to my Citroën.

Along the cobblestone streets, the businesses were starting to wake up. Shopkeepers opened their shutters and swept their stoops. A few watered pots full of flowers; others arranged storefront displays of goods in preparation for customers.

As a group, they looked harmless. Welcoming, even.

But I knew better. I cast a chary eye on every storekeeper, even as I returned their welcoming calls of "*Bonjour!*" Any one of them might be the mean-spirited person who'd painted that slur on La Maison des Petits Bonheurs, I knew. I imagined their so-called business "club" as a cabal of coconspirators, all of them determined to preserve the status quoi in Saint-Malo.

Maybe at any cost necessary. Maybe even murder.

I didn't see what was so wrong with a little publicity. Philippe's celebratory banner had been so under-stated that I'd mistaken it for an eight-foot-long CONGRATULATIONS! card. Despite Mathieu's world-weary *it's obvious* tone, I couldn't understand why it was such a big deal for Monsieur to have stepped away from the pack and given his chocolaterie extra attention.

I couldn't imagine Philippe giving his word that he wouldn't sponsor the *Fest-Noz* . . . and then doing so anyway. He'd always been a man of integrity. But I'd been gone for a while now. Maybe I didn't know Monsieur as well as I thought I did?

In an effort to dispel any youthful illusions I had about my mentor, I tried to imagine Monsieur Vetault promising to do something and then sneakily back-tracking on that promise.

I couldn't do it. Not that I was able to devote my full attention to the matter anyway, as I glimpsed two familiar-looking people sitting at a sidewalk café nearby.

Travis and Mélanie Flamant. They looked . . . intimate. Hmm.

Immediately, I veered in that direction. But my financial advisor caught my eye and gave me a subtle headshake. I ground to a stop next to a *boulangerie* (bakery), thrown for a loop by Travis's behavior. Was he warning me away from him and the *policière*?

If he was, I deduced, it was because he really *did* have things well in hand with the *gendarme*. The two of them appeared to be hitting it off famously. As I watched from the shadow of the *boulangerie*'s striped awning, Mélanie Flamant laughed. She touched Travis's suited forearm. She fluttered her eyelashes.

At least that's the way it seemed to me. If I hadn't known better, I'd have thought the two of them were having a rendezvous, not a fact-sharing meeting about Monsieur's murder.

Frustrated to be kept at arm's length, I signaled to Travis. He noticed. He shut me down with a pointed frown.

That was that, then. Maybe my keeper *was* having a coffee date with the police officer in charge of Philippe's case. Typically, Danny found a way to get lucky while investigating; maybe that was Travis's MO, too. He *was* undeniably appealing.

Me? I was perennially left stranded on the sideline.

Delivering Travis a "we'll talk about this later" look, I turned and headed for my car again. Three steps away, I thought better of it and ventured inside the *boulangerie* instead.

Hey, I was a professional. Inside would be *chaussons de pomme* (literally, "slippers of apple," but in fact delicious apple turnovers) or—better yet—rich brioche studded with chocolate. Taste-testing was an occupational duty, wasn't it?

Ten minutes and several *mercis* later, I was walking toward the Porte St-Vincente with a white waxed bakery bag containing one apple turnover and one chocolate brioche bun—plus a bonus croissant—when I noticed a plump redheaded woman on a ladder. She was busy taking *down* Philippe's banner. As I watched, she ripped away the final section. The whole thing tumbled to the ground in a heap of printed canvas and ineffaceable memories.

The dress-wearing redhead scowled at it, then brushed off her hands and climbed down from her ladder. I expected her to stomp on the banner. Or for the local "business club" members to start a bonfire with it. I wondered if taking down Philippe's sponsorship symbol was only the latest step in dismantling his memory—the last step in someone's (murderous) plan for revenge.

I didn't have the heart to watch anymore. Instead, I slipped through the gateway in the thick city walls and headed back to château Vetault, where I hoped to drown my sorrows in fresh French baked goods and maybe call Danny to check in, too.

If his role truly had been switched with Travis's, I thought as I climbed into my Citroën and maneuvered the stick shift out of the parking lot, then my best buddy-turned-bodyguard wouldn't warn me away from danger. Instead, he'd probably ask me for a car-rental receipt and a business plan.

If Danny actually discussed expenses, consultations, and overcoming procrastination with me, all bets were off. The world really would have gone topsy-turvy, and me right along with it.

"He's taking advantage of you," Danny told me. "You can't just let Harvard enjoy a paid vacation at your expense."

We'd been talking for ten minutes. Nine and a half of them had involved Travis, my best pal's arch nemesis. I'd tried to bring Danny up to speed on the morning's progress (such as it was), but he'd answered the phone with twelve hours' worth of pent-up grievances and opinions. Given his doctor-ordered retina-injury recuperation, Danny had nothing but time on his hands and he wanted to spend several minutes of it with me.

I couldn't take it. "A vacation is not what this is about, and you know it," I argued, pacing across my sunlit room at the château in exasperation. I figured Danny was probably irked at taking a backseat to Travis. Neither of us had expected my keeper to show up. "Anyway, I don't care about the money."

"You never do." I could practically feel Danny glowering over the phone. My inheritance—even with its strict condition that I travel six months out of every year to continue receiving stipends—was a sore spot with him. "That's why you're at risk."

He went on to outline several ways Travis could cheat me out of my trust fund. In detail. It was very well thought out.

But that's what you get when you pal around with a (former) expert thief. Danny knew all there was to know about picking locks, stealing intelligently, and doing what you had to do to survive. His jail time had come early and infrequently. Once he'd matured as a man, he'd learned to avoid being caught.

Then he'd gone on to university, met one Hayden Mundy Moore, and the rest was history. *Our* history. A part of my life I treasured. Danny kept me grounded. He kept me appreciative and aware. As long as he was around, I never took the easy way out.

But I sometimes took a detour to enjoy some chocolate.

I swallowed a nibble of the chocolate-covered caramel I'd found on my pillow (thanks, housekeeping!), then breathed in.

"Thanks for the heads-up, Danny, but I've got this."

I glanced at the note beside my pillow, written in elegant French cursive. *Bonne journée! Jeannette Farges, ménagère* (Have a nice day! Housekeeping.) Jeannette was probably the woman I'd seen with the stack of fluffy towels in the corridor last night.

So far, château Vetault had provided exemplary service. Jeannette—or her staff—had anticipated every luxurious need.

"Anyway, there are more important things than Travis to talk about," I reminded my bodyguard buddy. "For instance . . ."

I described my encounter with Hélène that morning and recounted her oddly high-spirited behavior. I broke down having glimpsed Hélène and Hubert in the château's formal garden. Then I told Danny about my arrival at La Maison des Petits Bonheurs, my awful graffiti sighting, and my mixed impressions of Mathieu.

"No, you can't trust him," Danny said in reply to my wondering aloud if Mathieu was as unreliable as he seemed. "You can't trust anyone. Not even Spreadsheet Superman himself."

He meant Travis, naturally. "I can trust *some* people."

Like him. I imagined Danny shaking his head. Given his newly reattached retina, that was probably verboten, though.

"You don't get it. You can't trust anyone. Ever. Especially not now, while you're sneaking around poking into murders."

Trust no one was his unofficial motto. Yet, "You trust me."

Silence. "You're different. Anyway, keep your guard up," Danny rushed to caution me. "It sounds as though this Mathieu guy is jealous of you. That makes him unpredictable."

Jealous? I laughed. Something had obviously been lost in translation. "Jealous? Of me? Come on, I don't think so."

"Mathieu probably sees you as a rival. Or did."

Before Philippe Vetault was killed. We both thought it.

"No." I dismissed the idea. "Mathieu is an accomplished chocolatier himself. The only trouble he's having now is trying to break out of the small-town chocolate-making mold. In France, that's not so tough. All kinds of small businesses thrive here."

"The tax situation is probably favorable," Danny said.

Huh? I frowned and cocked my head. "Did you just say . . ."

"Just watch your back," my security expert said. "Promise."

"I promise!" I always did. "But if you'd been there, you would have seen—Mathieu couldn't have been

more complimentary of me and my chocolate expertise. It was kind of embarrassing."

"Yet you believed him. That was step one."

"Danny! He was *nice.* He was sad. I felt sorry for him."

"Step two."

"Come on. You're *too* suspicious. He wasn't conning me."

Except he had, I remembered ruefully. About the
long walk to the police station and the work involved
in cleaning the graffiti. I still intended to go back and
finish that.

"That's what all the best conmen make you think,"
Danny reminded me in a gruff voice. "Trust me. I'd
know."

I was just glad he wasn't part of that life anymore. I
knew that Danny—ever loyal—was still in touch with
certain friends from the bad old days, though. Sometimes, that worried me.

"Anyway, Travis has my back." Time to change the
subject.

"Sure, he does," Danny groused. "You're his meal
ticket."

"What?" I stopped pacing. "That's cynical, even
for you."

"Truth hurts." My buddy sounded unrepentant.
"How do you think Harvard gets paid? If something
happens to you, his firm loses. Your big-bucks account
goes bye-bye. He needs you."

I didn't like thinking of my financial advisor this way.

"All the more reason for Travis to protect me,
right?"

Danny scoffed. "More like, the *only* reason. Why
do you think he's there? He's watching out for his
golden goose."

No. There was more than that between us. "He overcame his fear of flying to be here, remember? He volunteered to help me investigate Monsieur's death. He's put himself at risk."

"He was probably never afraid to fly. That's got to be a sympathy play," Danny argued. "And he's helping you investigate because that's what *you* want. You can bet it wasn't his idea."

I honestly couldn't remember which one of us had brought it up. But I was sure of one thing. "He was very insistent. Just like I was, back in San Francisco. Remember? I wouldn't take no for an answer when Adrienne died. Travis is the same way now."

"Then you have that in common," Danny observed.

"Yes." I smiled, feeling triumphant

"That's what Captain PowerPoint wants you to think. Oldest trick in the book: forge a bond, even if it's fake."

"Travis is not conning me, Danny." I wandered to the window and looked outside. The Parisian film crew had moved indoors, but one of the blonde's cohorts was standing near the fountain, looking glum. He was dark-haired. Good-looking. Charismatic. I'd have bet fifty euros that he was the French pop star. "You only think he is because that's what you would have done. Once."

"Just watch yourself," my buddy urged, unapologetic. "To me, you're more than a paycheck. But to Smarty-Pants, you're—"

"Could we just agree to call him Travis?" I stifled a sigh of frustration. "I realize it's hard for you to be out of commission, but try to find some perspective, okay? Mathieu Camara is not jealous of me, and Travis isn't a cold-hearted opportunist who's only here to maximize profits. He likes me!"

Danny offered a skeptical harrumph. "So do I."

That's what I thought all this was about. Privately, at least. It was the same old rivalry at work between Danny and Travis, being played out in a slightly different way. I knew Danny was unhappy being unable to help me this time, so he was nit-picking at Travis, who could. I figured he couldn't help assigning his own jealous feelings about my keeper to Mathieu Camara and his interactions with me, since we'd shared the same mentor—just the same way, coincidentally, that Danny and Travis shared me. Danny probably didn't even realize he was doing it.

Then, too, my friend never felt far from his criminal past. Maybe he never would. Naturally he assigned his own earlier motivations to others. Wasn't that the way everyone behaved?

For instance, I liked chocolate. I assumed everyone else did (of course). But my bodyguard buddy was the oddball exception to the rule—Danny didn't have a sweet tooth at all.

That didn't make me wrong about chocolate. Or Danny. It only made us different—just like Mathieu Camara and Travis were.

"You can't rule out motivated self-interest," Danny said.

"Is that like compound interest? You're really taking this role reversal between you and Travis seriously," I joked.

"Har har. Just remember who your friends are."

That was easy. "You," I said fondly. *And Travis*, I added.

Seemingly satisfied with that outcome, Danny quit

badgering me. He asked for copies of the photos I'd taken so far, including the few I'd snapped at the last minute of that redhead pulling down Monsieur's banner, then we talked awhile about Philippe, infidelity, and Saint-Malo. The town had a history of being the most rebellious and hard to control in all of France. It had been so bold that it had even defied Breton authority. I figured those details—and the local pirates—would appeal to Danny.

They did. But it wasn't all corsairs and rebels between us.

"I almost forgot—your pop-star video crew? They're working for Lucas Lefebvre," Danny told me. "I'll send you links to his social-media accounts, in case you're curious or you want to add him to your suspects list. I know you're all about the lists."

He was right. "It's as if you've known me a long time or something." I was kidding, but I couldn't keep the warmth out of my voice. I cared about Danny. "Also, bravo on the research."

"Hey, the Human Calculator isn't the only one who can work a computer." A pause. "My nurse is a big fan of Lefebvre."

Aha. I smiled. "I'll have to check him out. Thanks for the tip and the all-star support, Brainiac. I'll talk to you later."

At my new moniker for him, Danny laughed. He was still chuckling as we signed off. Moments later, my phone dinged. I opened Danny's message and clicked the links. Hubba hubba.

Lucas Lefebvre *was* the moody guy I'd seen in the château's garden. He was every bit as attractive as he'd seemed from afar, too. At least he was, if a quick scroll-through was any proof.

Well, I decided, maybe there was a teensy bit of room left on my suspects list. I had to be absolutely thorough, right?

It was time to introduce myself as a just-inducted member of the Lucas Lefebvre fan club. I double-checked my feminine allure (lip gloss and mascara, for the win!), shook out my hair, then took my sneakers-and-jeans self downstairs to the garden.

I should have known that taking three seconds to primp would cost me my opportunity to accidentally bump into Lucas Lefebvre. That's why I usually run so low maintenance. Who knew what I might be missing while laboriously applying eyeliner or concealer, or doing something beyond wash-and-wearing my hair? This time, though, even my minimal grooming routine hadn't delivered the goods. Lucas was already gone when I arrived.

Disappointed, I stopped beside the fountain. Its tinkling waters lent a certain calm to *le jardin* (the garden). So did the rows of still-green boxwood hedges, tidy symmetrical plantings of flowers, and nearby arbor full of long wisteria vines. Taken all together, the effect was beautiful. I could have lingered among the topiaries and gravel paths for quite some time.

But I had a pop star to track down and beguile, so I perked up and followed the nearest path into some trees. Once amid them, I felt miles away from the fountain. Tall hedges blocked it from view, creating the effect of a private outdoor room.

No wonder Hélène and Hubert had had their tryst in the garden. Even though their assignation spot was only a few meters from Monsieur's barn-atelier, they could have been secretly meeting there for weeks with no one the wiser.

I kept going, glancing down to admire a planting bed laid out in a classic fleur-de-lis pattern, like a carpet made of greenery. Impressive. I passed a modern art sculpture, then an ancient-looking bust. More flowers. No hunky Parisian pop star.

Maybe meeting Lucas wasn't in the cards today. But I hadn't become proficient at making chocolate by giving up, so I walked on. Birds chirped in the trees. In the distance, the blue sky arched overhead, empty except for a few wispy clouds. It occurred to me that I hadn't heard a single jet roar overhead—something I experienced with regularity in most places I went.

The peacefulness lulled me into slowing down. The garden deserved no less. Like the best chocolate, its wonders were only revealed to those who paid sufficient attention—those who noticed the tiny stream trickling alongside the piled-stone fence and the peephole trimmed into the hedges to provide a look backward, as if through a window. Intrigued, I looked in.

Someone else's face stared back at me.

With a yelp, I stumbled backward. I twisted my ankle. *Ouch.*

Not sure how bad the damage was, I quit moving. That's when *he* approached—the person on the other side of the hedge.

You're expecting me to say it was Lucas Lefebvre. That's the way it would have gone down in the movies, with the pop star noticing the chocolate expert in a meet-cute scenario involving a dainty injury, then music playing as he carried her to safety.

Except it wasn't Lucas Lefebvre. It was Hubert Bernard.

Angry Bloody Hands Man himself.

He gave a muttered exclamation and rounded the corner, carrying a wicked-looking set of gardening shears—the kind of thing a killer might opportunistically pick up in such a spot.

I widened my eyes and backed up farther, not even thinking about babying my ankle. It would be fine— *if* I escaped from this.

Had Hubert remembered me as the witness from last night? Had he followed me here? Had he waited until I was deep in the garden—where I'd already observed we wouldn't be seen—to attack?

I considered running. But I kept my head instead. Monsieur Bernard was an older man, probably sixty-five if not more. It seemed likely I could outmaneuver him, if necessary. Besides, I knew how to take care of myself, given my solo traveling past.

More than once, my patented anti-mugger move— battle tested on the streets of Barcelona and in San Francisco—had saved me.

"*Bonjour. Vous allez bien,* Madame?" Hubert asked.

He wanted to know if I was all right. *Yes and planning to stay that way,* I thought with a lift of my chin. I couldn't help seeing him as he'd been last night, murderously looming over my mentor. He wasn't going to get away with it, I vowed to myself.

"*Oui, merci.*" Warily, I eyed him, still alert for trouble.

As usual, my accent gave me away. "Ah, you speak English?" Hubert thumped his chest with his non-weapon-wielding hand. "Me, too." He seemed pleased by that. "You enjoy the gardens?"

I had to admit, he didn't *seem* threatening today. In

the clear light of another Breton autumn morning, Hubert Bernard seemed . . . well, miserable. Preoccupied. And a little shaky.

His wrinkled, shears-holding hand trembled. With eagerness to stab me? Surreptitiously, I tested my ankle. It held. Whew.

"*Ouai*." Yeah. "Very much." I examined him as we talked, taking in his grass-stained trousers and perspiration-creased shirt. Hubert wore a fisherman's cap similar to one Monsieur had been fond of wearing. Beneath it, his eyes were watery, his face lined with fatigue. Frankly, he looked dreadful. "Very nice."

It was a meager way to wind up a detailed conversation about the château's gardens, but it was the best I could come up with while simultaneously making mental notes about my number one suspect in Philippe's murder and staying ready to make a quick getaway, if necessary. I glimpsed Lucas Lefebvre passing down another gravel walkway and considered flagging him down.

Not yet. I needed to find out what I could from Hubert.

"I am pleased." Hubert gestured at the grounds with his shears, seeming less than committed to killing me with them. "I have been working these grounds since forty years, almost."

"Forty years?" I raised my brows. "With the Vetaults?"

"But of course!" His voice quavered, though, and his eyes turned a shade murkier. He pulled out a hanky and blew his nose. "*Merde. Désolé,* Madame. It has been a difficult time."

He was playing it innocent then, hmm? The nerve.

"Yes, I heard about Monsieur Vetault's sudden death." I could scarcely squeeze the words past my constricted throat. I thought I might bawl at any second. But this was important.

So far, Hubert hadn't seemed to recognize me. Either he was a masterful actor, or he somehow didn't remember last night.

"It's truly a tragedy," I said. "Had you known him long?"

"*Pour toujours.* Forever," Hubert told me in a dejected voice. Because he was sorry to have killed his friend? He blinked up at the sky, struggling to collect himself. "It does not seem possible that he is gone. When I heard the news this morning, it seemed that the light had gone from the sky."

Hold on a minute. "You heard . . . this morning?"

His gaze swiveled to me, suddenly sharp. "You have poor manners, Madame. This is enough talking. Please enjoy the garden." He straightened his shoulders. "*Bonne journée.*"

Hubert saluted me with his shears, then turned. As he did, a current of cold, oddly scented air passed between us.

I recognized that odor. Whiskey. Never my favorite.

Given that smell, Hubert's unsteady stance, and his bleary-eyed appearance, the conclusion seemed obvious. Hubert Bernard has been absolutely plastered last night at the *Fest-Noz*. And he seemed to be hungover today in a handily memory-erasing way.

It was all a little *too* convenient for my liking.

Hubert had already occupied the top spot on my suspects list, but he'd just cemented his position. Between his "memory loss," his affair with Hélène, and his presence at my mentor's death last night, I couldn't believe he was a free man today.

I needed to track down Travis and find out the reason.

Seated across from me at château Vetault's terraced outdoor dining area, Travis closed his eyes and moaned. "Mmm. Mmm."

His uninhibited, throaty rumble attracted all the attention you'd expect it would. My financial advisor lay his palms flat on the table—never in your lap in Europe, if you don't want to be rude—and went on savoring his last bite of chocolate mousse.

The diminutive silver spoon it had been served with sat alone in Travis's delicate dessert dish, which had been scraped impressively clean by my financial advisor. I'd say one thing for Travis. He knew when and how to prioritize thoroughness.

I liked that about him. I also liked his (apparent) love of sweets. When the château's pastry chef had wheeled over a cart full of desserts to conclude our leisurely lunch and invited us to make whatever selections we wished, Travis had taken charge.

In melodious, husky French, he'd ordered *almost* one of everything. A caramel apple tart with almond frangipane. Three clouds of mousse in dark, semi-sweet, and milk chocolate flavors. Butter cookies with sea salt. A custard of pistachio, cream, and thyme. A cake made with honey from the château's beehives. Mocha macarons. Not for us to share, either—for us to experience individually. Whether that was because my keeper knew and agreed with the unspoken French preference not to share dishes or because Travis simply had a lust for chocolate, I didn't know.

He saw me noticing and grinned. "Hey, we can expense it all, right?" He offered me a toast with his wineglass. "To generous old Uncle Ross, and all his lovable eccentricities."

I flashed back to Danny's insistence that I was nothing but a meal ticket to Travis and wished I hadn't. That wasn't fair.

I was the one who'd suggested lunch. Who wanted to sleuth on an empty stomach? Now, after several delightful dishes, we were ready to settle down with the cheese course, then coffee.

All in all, dining with Travis was a nice change of pace from Danny, who usually championed a street-vendor hot dog and beer as the answer to any lunch-related questions. My security expert preferred the salty and spicy side of the culinary spectrum. For Danny, the closer a meal was to incinerating his remaining taste buds, the better (and more memorable) it was.

In some ways, my oldest friend and I were utterly incompatible. Not that I intended to quit trying to win over Danny to the right (chocolaty) side of things, because I didn't.

Over a few delectable slivers of Breton cheese, I informed Travis of my morning's progress. I took my time describing Mathieu, Hubert, the redheaded woman, and (even) Lucas Lefebvre.

Then, because I wanted jealousy to be Danny's issue, not mine, I got around to the subject of Travis's cozy tête-à-tête with *l'agent* Flamant at the café in the *centre-ville*. I didn't want to seem as though it bothered me that my financial advisor had gotten up close and personal with the *policière*, because it didn't. If it bugged me at all, it was only because I never seemed to get *my* turn with a whirlwind on-the-road romance.

"So, how did things go with Mélanie Flamant?" I set

my fragile coffee cup in its saucer. "What did you find out?"

Silence. I glanced up to see Travis studiously avoiding my gaze. He looked at the yellow damask tablecloth, the view of the ocean beyond the château's garden, the other diners, the few morsels of cheese still remaining on his plate. He cleared his throat, then adjusted his glasses. A flush crept up his neck.

Travis, I deduced, was *embarrassed*. He *could* be ruffled.

"Or did the *policière* not want to discuss the case?" I persisted. "The two of you looked pretty chummy at the café."

As I should have expected, my keeper snapped out of it.

"Mélanie and I did hit it off quite well," he confided, his usual control firmly back in place. "As you would expect, I approached her with a few queries about you, your status as a witness, your security as a witness, and so on." Travis gave me a level look. "My company is indirectly in charge of your well-being. *I'm* in charge of it. I explained as much to Mélanie."

I didn't quite understand. "You 'queried' her? And somehow that resulted in the two of you playing footsie in a café?"

He compressed his mouth. "I needed to learn, as your financial advisor, what your status was. Vis-à-vis your leaving Saint-Malo, your future duties as a witness, and your safety."

I couldn't help grinning. "You sweet-talker, you."

"Especially in light of Hubert Bernard having been released," Travis continued doggedly. "Those were pertinent questions and could only be answered by *l'agent* Flamant."

"You mean Mélanie. Are you two *tutoyer*-ing already?"

Tutoyer sounds naughty. But it's simply the practice of moving from formal French terms of address to more familiar ones. Mathieu Camara and I were still *vouvoyer*-ing each other.

Travis shook his head. But he grinned back. It turned out he could take a little ribbing. That was good. For both of us.

"I had questions," he said. "Mélanie suggested addressing them over coffee at the café down the street. That's it."

"Oh, I doubt that's it." I leaned my chin in my hands to listen more closely, not caring if it was (slightly) rude to prop my elbows on the table. The terrace was emptying anyway.

"That's it for now," Travis clarified. He looked like the cat the who swallowed the canary. "We're having dinner later."

"Travis!" Why did the men in my life have all the luck?

Somewhere around here, I *had* to find Lucas Lefebvre.

"Forging a sense of camaraderie with her will help us."

I raised my eyebrow. "Is that what we're calling it?"

"I can't help it if Mélanie had a . . . strong reaction to me." Travis gazed longingly as the dessert cart came gliding by again. I didn't know how he stayed so fit while (apparently) subsisting on a steady diet of sugar, butter, and more sugar. On the other hand, I managed to keep things in line by only taking a few scrumptious bites of everything I wanted. "You can't tell me Danny doesn't hit it off with sources."

"'Hit it off'?" I gave a wry grin. "You could say that."

"Whereas I have other, smarter methods," my financial advisor informed me. "Effective, businesslike, proven methods."

"Does Mélanie know you're so analytical?"

"Of course she does. I've been nothing but above-board."

"I'd expect no less." But I still wished I could have been a fly on the wall when Mélanie Flamant suggested coffee. "So what you're saying is that Mélanie likes hot foreign guys?"

It took Travis a second to catch on that I meant him.

Then, "So what you're saying is that *I'm* a hot guy?"

Whoops. He had me. This time, it was my turn to pretend to be absorbed in the terrace's upscale furniture, bottles of chilled Breton apple cider, and politely efficient waitstaff.

It really was impressive how well-run the château was. I'd scarcely had to think about a glass of water before a full goblet had appeared. Everyone who'd taken care of us at lunch had been pleasant, skilled, and interested in our contentment.

Best of all, no one had batted an eye at all those desserts we'd ordered—not even when Travis had gone back for seconds on the chocolate mousse, and I'd dared to dip my spoon into his dish. That kind of discretion always earns a gold star from me.

Now, in response to Travis's "hot guy" inquiry, I shrugged. Pretending indifference to my keeper's good looks was an Oscar-worthy performance. "Mélanie must think so. Otherwise, how do you explain getting any information from her at all?"

"It's called 'interviewing a source.' It's a tactic I learned someplace . . ." My financial advisor snapped his fingers and grinned at me. "Oh yeah, at that fancy school I went to."

"Good going, Harvard." I toasted him with my coffee cup, then finished off my dark roast. "What did you find out? Are there any other leads? What was the murder weapon, anyway? I couldn't tell last night." I shuddered, remembering its lethal appearance. "Why was Hubert Bernard released already, and exactly what is wrong with the local *gendarmes*? Their approach to investigating is lazy at best, if you ask me."

I was still miffed that my tip about the graffiti at the chocolaterie hadn't been jumped on with a little more zeal.

"Leads? Yes." Travis drew in a deep breath. "But Mélanie wouldn't give me any details. Murder weapon? They're not sure what it is yet. Some type of multi-pronged metal implement."

It sounded like a gardening tool to me—one more black mark against Hubert. Somehow, I needed to see it. "And?"

"Hubert Bernard was only taken into custody last night because he was too drunk and distraught to get home safely," Travis told me. "Apparently it was a protective measure."

"Let me guess: it wasn't the first time."

"No." Travis already knew about the whiskey fumes I'd detected on Hubert earlier that morning; I'd told him the whole story. "Everyone knows Monsieur Bernard. They're convinced he wasn't the one who killed Philippe Vetault. Mélanie believes Hubert merely found your mentor a few minutes before you did."

I felt outraged. "Sure, found him and killed him!"

Travis raised his hands. "Calm down." He gave me a warning look, then glanced around the mostly empty terrace. "We have to be smart about this. I don't want to be overheard. If anyone realizes we're investigating, it will limit our options."

"Fine." Leave it to him to take the sensible approach. I'd already caved to Travis's insistence that we didn't need to hide our acquaintance. "What about the police force's ineptitude?"

"They're not inept," Travis disagreed, shaking his head. "They're under no obligation to tell you or me or anyone else what they're doing to investigate your mentor's death. In fact, it's better for the *gendarmes'* case if they say nothing. Let's not jump to conclusions before we have all the facts."

"But that's the best time to jump to conclusions," I pointed out, signing the lunch check with a flourish. "If you wait until all the facts are in, it's too late." I stood. "Let's go. We have a lot left to do. We're burning daylight. Oh, and do you think you can get a picture of the murder weapon for me? Maybe I can ID it." It had happened before, in London.

Given the esoteric nature of the weapon, recognizing it had made me a suspect then, but, you know . . . details. I was willing to risk it, if it would help bring Monsieur's killer to justice.

"You're moving on? Just like that?" Travis looked surprised. "You're not upset about Hubert being set free?"

"Of course, I'm upset," I told Travis, my tone softening. "But the good news is, if he's really in the clear, then that leaves all the rest of Saint-Malo open to suspicion." I rubbed together my palms. "There's a lot of sleuthing still to do."

But first, I had an idea about approaching Mathieu Camara again, so I could find out more from him about Philippe's daily life and any additional skirmishes he'd had with his neighbors.

All of them had to be considered suspects, too, right?

I'd already asked Travis to look into the Poyet-Vetault merger—its current status, details, and legalities.

But there was more to the situation than logistics and lawfulness. There were feelings, too, Mathieu's and those of the townspeople. I needed an in. Travis had Mélanie. I'd have to work with Mathieu.

Figuring out the truth about my mentor's life in Saint-Malo was going to require one thing, I'd decided. Chocolate.

Lots and *lots* of chocolate.

Seven

By the next morning, I'd enacted my nascent plan.
I was already in Monsieur's barn-atelier as the sun
came up, wide awake and caffeinated when Travis
finally knocked on the door.

I opened it with a smile. "Good! You got my note!"

I'd crept down the hallways with it like a kid breaking curfew last night and slipped it under his door. I'd
had to, because he'd been out with Mélanie while
I'd been brainstorming.

I hadn't realized until too late that I didn't have
Travis's personal phone number, only his office number
in Seattle. I intended to remedy that oversight soon.

"I had to run the château's gauntlet of scary-looking
Vetault ancestors staring at me from their oil paintings
to give you that note," I informed him. "You should
know that." His floor had different décor than mine.
Different marble busts, different rugs, different art.
"It was like something out of 'Scooby-Doo.' I half expected all the painted eyeballs to move."

"Ugh, you're so loud." My financial advisor groaned.
"Why?"

His pained expression made me laugh. "Let me guess:

You're still jet-lagged, but you didn't realize it because you never travel abroad. Also, French women enjoy a little wine with dinner?"

Being a few time zones ahead of (or behind) your stomach and brain doesn't tend to make overindulging go over very well. Take it from me. I've learned that the hard way. Now I (mostly) limit my excesses to chocolate—just as I was doing that day.

My financial advisor pocketed the note I'd left— the one saying he should meet me here bright and early this morning.

"There may have been some wine," he acknowledged.

"How much wine, Travis?" This was fun. "Tell me."

Another groan. "You're enjoying this."

"Enjoying you being less than perfect? You bet."

He stepped gingerly inside, wincing as though any sudden movements might jolt him out of his suit and open-collar shirt.

He seemed to have an infinite supply of dapper clothes. He wore them effectively, too, with no stuffy attitude. Given château Vetault's exemplary amenities, though, it was possible Jeannette or her minions provided overnight wash-and-press.

"I'm not perfect. Nobody is." Travis swept his gaze over what had become my chocolatier work area. "Does Madame Vetault know you're in here? You seem to have taken over the place."

"It's been poignant, too. Believe me." I touched my head. "See this Breton fisherman's cap? It's Monsieur's." It brought back so many good memories. "He wore it almost all the time."

"It looks good on you. That color brings out your eyes."

Was Travis flirting with me? "I'm mostly wearing it

to keep my hair out of the chocolate." I'd fashioned a speedy ponytail before donning the requisite work gloves. I was a professional, after all. Self-consciously, I shook out my hair.

Travis noticed. "I'm not flirting with you, Hayden."

Then why did I feel so flustered? I laughed. "I know that! Sure! It's just that we never talk about personal things."

"Oh yeah?" Travis arched one blond eyebrow. "'Tell me, Travis,'" he mimicked, "'what are you wearing right now?'"

I'll admit it—his purposely sultry tone worked on me.

"Good thing you've memorized that, because you've already heard it from me for the last time, remember?" I indicated his suit-and-nice-shoes getup. "Your mystique is spoiled now."

He shrugged. "Fantasy has its place." Travis demonstrated as much with his rumbly, sexy voice. "But when it comes down to brass tacks, I prefer reality. I like knowing the facts."

Right now, the facts were that I was getting distracted. I could have listened to my keeper discuss his personal philosophy of living all morning. As it was, though, I had things to do.

"All I know is, my mentor could make magic while wearing this hat. It's possible it has superpowers." I turned back to my worktable. "It makes me feel connected to Monsieur, as if I could channel his genius into this chocolate I'm working on."

Travis studied it. "It definitely *smells* amazing in here."

I preened. "Thanks. It turns out that Philippe had a couple of chocolate-tempering machines on hand. I've got a batch of dark chocolate and a batch of milk chocolate staying in temper."

He didn't ask what that meant. Instead, "Again, does Hélène know you're in here? Or did Danny teach you how to pick locks?"

"I'd rather not answer that." I sorted through some clear polycarbonate chocolate molds, choosing a few. I turned back to Travis and caught him looking at me—at my ankle, specifically.

"How's your ankle? You twisted it in the garden yesterday."

"No lasting harm done." I peered at it. It still hurt, but it was nothing that would hold me back. "I'm pretty tough."

He seemed dubious. "Do you want me to look at it?"

"Are you a doctor?"

He shook his head. A halo of sunshine had splashed through the barn window, crowning him in gold. Blonds had all the luck.

Just like the Parisian blonde with the film crew. I would have liked to get to know her better. Aside from her whooping and selfie habits, she seemed endlessly cool. Perfectly chic.

Maybe a little of that would rub off on me, I figured.

"Then no, I don't want you to look at it. Thanks."

I bustled to the other end of the worktable, newly conscious of Travis attentively scrutinizing my movements.

"You often get hurt while investigating," he pointed out. "Frankly, I've always chalked that up to Danny's negligence."

"Danny isn't negligent!"

"He is if he's your bodyguard and you get hurt." Travis glanced up to the barn-atelier's former hayloft. He rubbed his jaw, where his archenemy would have sported day-old beard stubble. My financial advisor, predictably, was as clean shaven as a model in a razor-blade ad. "He's probably busy 'checking the alibis' of all your attractive female suspects."

I almost burst out laughing. "Did you just make air quotes around 'checking the alibis'? Is this you being snarky?"

Travis didn't address that. "If the enforcer hopes to earn the generous retainer you're paying him, he should be thorough."

"Like you are?" I wasn't wild about my longtime friend being unfairly criticized. "Like you are with Mélanie Flamant?"

"When I was questioning the *policière*, you and I were still pretending not to know one another, as you suggested," Travis reminded me. "I couldn't very well shadow you like a stalker, just to prove I'm a more proficient security expert than Danny."

Aha. *That's* what this was about. My two rivalrous men.

At least Travis had a fresh take on it. He hadn't suggested Danny was by my side simply to earn an enormous paycheck.

"Well, you couldn't do both simultaneously, that's true. You're good, but you can't be everywhere at once." More's the pity. I liked Travis's company. "As far as my use of Monsieur's atelier is concerned, yes, Hélène knows I'm working in here. I asked her this morning if I could use it and she agreed."

She'd even assured me that Monsieur would have wanted me to be there. It had been touching—right up to the moment when Hélène had spied Hubert in the château's garden and skedaddled.

I thought I'd smelled whiskey on her breath, too.

"That was generous of her." Travis glanced around at my equipment: blocks of various chocolates, sugar and cream, butter, flavorings, nuts of all kinds, liqueurs, and more—plus hardware like bowls, a thermometer, molds, a bench scraper, and brushes. "This looks . . . ambitious." He pursed his lips in thought, looking more like his usual self. "The only thing missing is—"

"*Voilà.*" I interrupted to brandish a French press coffeepot. I waved it near Travis's nose, letting him breathe in the wonderful fragrance of freshly brewed java. "For you. I knew you might be a little worse for wear after last night."

I poured him a cup. He cradled it gratefully, then sipped.

"Ah." His groan of pleasure made my toes curl. "That's good." Another moan. "Thanks. The only thing missing now is—"

"*Voici.*" Here you go. I'd anticipated this, too. "Your favorite almond croissant. I liberated it from the breakfast table this morning, just for you." I placed it, on a plate, on the worktable in front of him. "Never let it be said that I don't have your back, because I do. I risked serious social censure to smuggle that out of the château for you."

His eyes lit up. "I approve of your rebellious side."

"I'm too much of a rebel to care about your approval."

I was clowning around, though, and Travis knew it. We traded an affectionate glance. After all those phone calls, it felt as though we'd been (long-distance) friends for ages.

It was nice. I didn't want to break the spell, but I

had to. "So," I began, "how did you overcome your fear of flying?"

That's right. Danny had gotten to me. So had a niggling detail that had occurred to me late last night—that Travis and I had both passed through Paris and had both taken the same train to Saint-Malo. Yet he'd encountered a strike and I hadn't. That meant that, despite my assumptions, my keeper hadn't left the States ASAP. He'd been delayed by something. But what?

Despite my newfound closeness with Travis, I wanted proof he hadn't fibbed to me. About anything, including aviophobia.

There was no time like the present to get that proof, while my financial advisor was (a little) hungover and (slightly) gullible. "So let's have it," I urged. "What's the real story?"

It turned out that the truth was unsensational, as it often is. After complaining that I'd first softened him up with coffee and pastry before hitting him up with that question (guilty, but caffeine and sugar provided confessional clarity), Travis explained that he'd spent an entire day—ten hours or so—taking an air-travel antianxiety class offered by one of the airlines.

Then, bolstered by the techniques he'd learned, he'd boarded an international flight, crossed his fingers, and left.

I laughed. "I doubt *you* crossed your fingers. You're much too practical to succumb to superstition. I bet you sat there reciting air-travel safety statistics to yourself or something."

Danny didn't call Travis Captain Calculator for nothing.

"Of course. Per annum. That seemed the best approach when I initially tried to kick my airplane phobia. But sometimes knowledge isn't enough." For a moment, Travis looked haunted. Then, he brightened. "Experience, however, is power. The class was immersive but effective, and I was motivated. I'm fine now. It helped that all the flight attendants were very kind."

I'll just bet they were. "I'm impressed. Really, good for you." I gave his shoulder a squeeze. I meant it as an "atta boy!" gesture, but it went on for a few seconds too long.

Wowsers, Travis had muscular shoulders. As far as I knew, he was a meticulous, bespectacled desk jockey. How in the world did he stay so fit? He could have given muscular, six-pack-sporting Danny a run for his money. Not that I ought to be thinking about my bodyguard's physique, either, I remembered.

We were all professionals. More important, friends.

Still, I wondered if Travis had been "motivated" to kick his aviophobia by a desire to see me. Who knew? Maybe he had.

I would have done the same for him if I'd had to.

"Finish your breakfast." I nodded at his almond croissant and coffee, momentarily nostalgic for the Nutella-filled crêpe I'd treated myself to earlier. "You're going to help me."

"Help you make chocolate?" Widening his eyes, Travis shook his head. He backed up. "I have two left thumbs in the kitchen."

"That's okay. I'll be right here. But as an alternative, you could start right away on phase two of this plan."

"Which is?" Looking relieved (and confident about the alternative), he wolfed down a bite of sugar-dusted croissant.

"You're going to pose as a businessman who's come to Saint-Malo to start a new venture. That way, you can get close to the business 'club' leader Mathieu told me about. You can pump them for info about who vetoed the *Fest-Noz* sponsorship plan, who the banner-hating redhead is, and who wanted Monsieur dead."

"Is that all?" Coolly, Travis sipped more coffee. "That's a good idea," he mused, half to himself, "except for the part where I'd have to pretend to be someone I'm not. No way. Next?"

I'd foreseen this. "Come on, Travis! You can do it."

His eyes gleamed with that earlier self-assurance— plus a slight hint of obstinacy. "Naturally, I can do it. But I won't."

"Give me one good reason."

"Women are businesspeople, too. You can do it."

I couldn't fault his nod toward equality, but . . . "I can't. I'll be busy at La Maison des Petits Bonheurs, winning Mathieu's trust and finding out all the dirt on Monsieur's neighbors."

"Then ask Mathieu who manages the business club."

"I already tried. He won't tell me, and it will seem weird if I pester him about it." I pulled out an apron, identical to the one I was wearing, and handed it to Travis. "If you think it's a no-go, I guess we'll have to come up with something else." Resolutely, I nodded. "Here you go. Put that on."

With his breakfast gone, Travis hesitated. "Either I help you make chocolates or I impersonate an out-of-town investor?"

"That's about the size of it. Do you have a better idea?"

Another pause. Maybe he did algebra in his head for fun.

"Look, it's no big deal," I told my keeper, leaving him with the apron in hand. "I only thought that, since you're here, we could try a different, smarter method of investigating. Something more businesslike and proven." On the verge of going too far, I stepped away. Breezily, I delivered my ace in the hole. "You know, something Danny wouldn't be able to pull off."

Travis narrowed his eyes. I could tell I had him.

Either that, or he'd moved on to mental trigonometry.

"It *would* be reasonable for me to scout Saint-Malo on behalf of my company," my financial advisor mused. "We have a number of international clients to serve. It makes sense."

I wanted to grin from ear to ear. I settled for, "Mm-hmm."

"I'll look into it," Travis announced. "That means you keep the apron and the chocolate making to yourself. Good luck!"

He strode toward the door, his businessman's shoes quiet against the floorboards. Outside, birds chirped. The crew of Parisians started playing Lucas Lefebvre's upcoming single over a loudspeaker. Apparently, that's how they timed their shots.

Nearly gone, Travis stopped. "Who eats all the chocolate?"

"Hmm?" Caught in the midst of spooning up some delicious-smelling melted chocolate and letting it drip back into its reservoir while checking its silky texture, I looked up. "What's that?"

"All the chocolate you make. Who's going to eat it?"

"Well, most of it is going to La Maison des Petits Bonheurs, so I can prove to Mathieu I know what I'm doing." I put my hands on my hips, deliberating. "But there are always extras. Pieces that aren't quite shiny enough or snappy enough."

Travis nearly drooled. "What happens to those?"

To his credit, he sounded pretty nonchalant about it all.

I didn't believe him, though. I knew my keeper had a sweet tooth the size of Texas. There was no way he was indifferent to the idea of "extra" chocolate to eat, any more than I would be.

You have to love your job to do it correctly, right?

I shrugged. "I suppose I could make the rounds of the château's guests. Maybe offer a few pieces to the staff."

Except Hubert. He wasn't having a single tasty morsel.

"I'll do both," Travis decided. "We have plenty of time."

I'd won. I smiled. "Let's get down to it, then."

Almost an hour later, my financial advisor and I had made a lot of progress. The barn-atelier was suffused with the sweet, irresistible aromas of two kinds of chocolate, vanilla crème filling, hazelnut ganache, and assorted cocoa butter paints.

That's right—paints. If you melt pure, creamy cocoa butter to exactly the right temperature and then tint it, you wind up with a tasty liquid "paint." I'd fashioned mine into several colors—pink, bronze, blue, black, and a dramatic green—and was currently showing Travis how to decorate clear molds with it.

You won't be surprised to learn he was a natural. Was there *anything* my financial advisor wasn't good at? I doubted it.

"That's right," I told him. "Just stipple the colors into the mold. If you need to see what it looks like, you can always lift it and take a peek through the polycarbonate underneath."

"Nah. That's what imagination is for, right?" Carefully holding his brush, Travis pushed up his glasses. His expression made me imagine him as a six-year-old in art class—you know, before all the math and statistics had gotten the best of him.

"You have to work relatively quickly," I advised, "or the cocoa butter starts to harden. It goes crumbly very easily."

I realized I was holding my breath and laughed at myself. I guess I really wanted Travis to enjoy his first chocolates.

"No problem," he rumbled. "I've always been decisive."

Attentive nonetheless, I visually gauged his paint's temperature. It would be all right. Minutes later, it was.

Travis set down his brush. Technically, it was a makeup brush. I find they keep their bristles intact better than art brushes, and they offer very fine control. Surprised? I never said I *couldn't* use a makeup brush—only that I didn't bother.

"Here goes. Now we add the chocolate. Grab that ladle."

While Travis portioned melted dark chocolate into the painted depressions, I tilted the entire mold, making sure that chocolate filled every inch. It did. Still in shiny temper, it flowed across the mold and then overflowed, just as I intended.

It was possible to do this part by machine. That

simply wasn't the way chocolates were molded in Brittany, however.

I tapped the mold to help dispel any errant air bubbles, then asked, "Would you hand me that bench scraper, please?"

Travis did. I used it to scrape the cacao-infused overflow back into its reservoir, where it churned gently. That done, I handed the mold to Travis. He balanced it in his gloved hands.

"Now what?" He eyed the filled mold tentatively. "I was following along while you made your chocolate Easter eggs, but that was at least half an hour ago. It's all a blur now."

I'd already nearly finished some intricately decorated chocolates before Travis had arrived. In France, it's not Valentine's Day that gets all the chocolate love—it's Easter. That's why I'd chosen Easter chocolates as my means to impress Mathieu. They were the most difficult and the most popular.

During *Pâques*, French families exchanged all kinds of chocolate, I knew. Molded dark, milk, and white chocolates shaped as bunnies, chickens, lambs, eggs, and especially bells are all common. That's because, for French children, Easter eggs aren't brought by the Easter bunny, but by *les cloches de Pâques*: the winged bells of Easter. Sound weird? It's actually charming and results in the same Easter egg hunts that kids enjoy elsewhere.

Then, too, some Easter chocolates sold for one hundred euros or more apiece. They were big business. If Mathieu Camara and I could bond over mine, we would be forging solidarity for sure.

"Next, just step a little closer to the tempering machine and tip over the mold," I instructed Travis. "Straight over."

He looked at me askance but did it anyway. He trusted me. "This makes no sense. Most of the chocolate is pouring out."

"It's supposed to do that. We've just made the outer shells of our chocolates," I explained as I watched the chocolate drip down. "We want to remove the excess chocolate so we can fill these with ganache or vanilla crème. After that, we'll cap the whole assortment with more chocolate, let it cool, and then—"

"Eat it." Travis nodded, still concentrating on his job. I liked the dedication he applied to the task at hand. He grinned. "Maybe I should 'accidentally' poke a hole in one of these."

"Sabotage? I didn't think you had it in you," I teased.

"That depends on the stakes." My financial advisor squinted at the upside-down mold. "I think that's all that's coming out."

"Okay. Let's set aside that one in the fridge for a few minutes"—Monsieur had a mini refrigerator expressly for this purpose—"while we work on the next set of chocolates."

We did. Or I should say, Travis did. I watched his deft movements. He caught on quickly. "You're a good student."

"You're a good teacher." He gave me a dazzling smile.

"Wait till you see what's next." I showed him how to pipe filling into each of the small chocolate hollows we'd created, watchful not to smudge any on the sides. If my cream-enriched ganache mixed with the tempered chocolate, it would ruin it. I handed the mold to Travis. "Now we pour over more chocolate."

He did, sending its rich aroma into the air between us.

I inhaled, then watched as my keeper scraped away the excess chocolate from the mold, just as I'd done. "Perfect."

"That's it? That didn't seem like such a show-stopper."

"That wasn't it. *This* is." I grabbed a big metal sheet pan and flipped it over on the worktable. I picked up a blowtorch and switched it on with a grin. "Don't try this at home, kids."

Carefully, I torched the pan to heat it. Then I motioned for Travis to hand me the first half of the giant chocolate Easter egg I'd made. I placed it on the hot sheet pan, counted to three, then lifted it. I filled its cavity with a few mini chicks, rabbits, and bells. "Now the other half of the egg."

Travis handed it to me, watching attentively.

I melted its edges on my heated sheet pan, then pressed together the two halves. "*Voilà!* Instant chocolate 'glue.'"

My financial advisor looked amazed. "I wondered how you were going to join those after filling them with the smaller chocolates. I can see why you're in such demand."

"It's all thanks to Monsieur." I'd learned this technique from him. Now I missed him more than ever. "He was very clever."

"I wish I'd met him," Travis told me. "Between listening to you talk about Philippe and staying at his château, I get the impression he was an interesting man. Diverse, certainly. His collection of antiques and artwork is actually pretty good." He paused. Then, "It doesn't quite jibe with that hat, though."

"Hey! Are you saying my mentor's favorite hat is tacky?"

My financial advisor's gaze roved over me again. I

couldn't help reliving his earlier comment. *It looks good on you. That color brings out your eyes.* But all he said was, "Let's say Monsieur Vetault's decorating sense was better than his fashion sense."

Humph. "Hélène probably did all the decorating."

"Or several of his ancestors did it. The château has been in the family for generations, right? Hundreds of years."

"Just like La Maison des Petits Bonheurs," I reminded Travis, getting back to business. "Not the hundreds of years part, but generations, for sure." I set my huge Easter egg in the fridge to solidify completely. "Time to get back to it. As soon as my chocolate sets, I'm off to see Mathieu Camara."

If my keeper was jealous of my spending time with Mathieu, it didn't show. I know, because I checked. It was silly, but I did it. I didn't guess you could spend much time around Travis and *not* entertain a fantasy or two—he was just that appealing.

"And I'm off to infiltrate the local business club."

With a cheeky salute, Travis headed off. So did I.

Just the way we always would—going our separate ways.

Eight

I was nearly chased off the grounds of château Vetault. Not because Hubert Bernard—Angry Bloody Hands Man himself—came after me again. Not because the château's resident "watchdog," Bouchon the good-natured wolfhound, did anything more threatening than sniff my (chocolate scented) clothes and wag his tail. But because I finally discovered the source of the buzzing sound I'd been noticing since my arrival: it was a professional drone cam.

I didn't realize that at first, of course. Who's on the lookout for flying video cameras on a daily basis? But when something swooped over my head, buzzing like a huge robotic dragonfly, I almost hit the deck. Heart pounding, I ducked.

Fortunately, I managed to keep my head—and protect all the elaborately decorated *Pâques* chocolates I'd made, while I was at it. Feeling a whoosh, then still air, I carefully straightened.

"*Excusez-nous! Désolée!*" the Parisian blonde called.

She jogged across the garden to make sure I was all right, wearing a smile and the chicest casual outfit I'd ever seen. It was only a T-shirt, vintage jeans, and a deep green leather jacket—plus some stylish booties and an assortment of fine gold jewelry—but on her, the whole ensemble seemed ridiculously cool.

"*Vous allez bien?*" she asked, just as Hubert had.

Coming from her, the question seemed genuine. Possibly because she *wasn't* wielding a pair of lethal gardening shears.

"*Ouah, ça va,*" I replied. Yeah, I'm fine. "*Vous filmez ici? De Paris? Je connais Lucas Lefebvre. Il est très doué, non?*"

I thought I was doing pretty well, stringing together enough French sentences to mention that her crew was filming there and I was familiar with Lucas Lefebvre, who was very talented. But just like everyone else, the blonde was onto me.

"Ah! You are American? British? Australian, perhaps?"

I blamed my vagabond travel habits for her confusion. "American." I offered her a handshake. "Hayden Mundy Moore, chocolate maker and expert drone cam dodger. *Enchanté.*"

"*Enchanté.* Also, *miam-miam!*" Basically: *yum, yum!* Her gaze dropped to my *Pâques* chocolates. She seemed confused to see Easter confections in autumn, but continued on blithely. "Sorry again about the camera. My crew is feeling annoyed today. They are behaving less carefully than usual." She leaned confidingly close to me. "Just between us, Lucas can be very demanding." A shrug. "But that is talent, *n'est-ce pas?*" She gave me a smile. "I am the person in charge of all this *pagaille*, Capucine Roux."

It did seem like a mess—a *pagaille*, if my near-miss drone-cam incident was any indication. I nodded and somehow managed *not* to search over her shoulder for a glimpse of the hunky man in question, Lucas Lefebvre. Instead, I smiled back at Capucine.

"Hanging out with Lucas all day while listening to music at a French château? I'd say you have my dream job, Capucine."

I couldn't help staring at her. I don't tend toward much artifice, but she somehow pulled off bedhead and minimal makeup flawlessly, and (sadly) to much better effect than I did. What was it with French women, anyway? They really were born chic.

She gave a dismissive sound. "Mostly it is making my crew go back to work after taking too many breaks," she demurred, "while combing the château for set decorations. Madame Vetault has generously given me the run of the place. Poor Madame Vetault. We would not have intruded here at this difficult time, except Lucas's record label has given us a very strict deadline. We have several videos to complete. Still, I am very sorry about the tragedy involving Monsieur Vetault. It is shocking, *non*?"

We traded our regrets about Philippe's untimely death. The Parisian video crew signaled Capucine to come back, but she waved them off to continue talking to me. I felt pretty special.

It was like getting to sit at the cool girls' table at lunch, all over again. I can't tell you how many new schools I've been to in how many different cities and towns in my life. It's unusual to feel that you fit in somewhere right away.

"Anyway," Capucine was saying, her big blue eyes utterly lacking in guile, "whatever I cannot find inside, I can find in Saint-Malo, at the shops there, so it is perfect for us."

"You shop for a living, too? Your job just gets better."

I was a little relieved to leave behind the subject of Philippe. Evidently, so was Capucine, because she laughed.

"I would say that *you* are the one with the dream job," she said. "Working with chocolate all day? That would be delicious!"

"If I do my job right, it is." I liked Capucine. I couldn't help it. She had a knack for making me feel included.

"I do not keep every piece of set decoration for myself, of course." Her gaze tracked Lucas Lefebvre as he lolled near a row of hedges, looking at his phone. "Everything is only on loan. It makes, for me, all the fun of shopping with none of the regret."

She glanced back and saw me watching Lucas. An insightful gleam came into her eyes. "Ah, you would like to meet Lucas?"

You would like to meet the gorgeous pop star? That ranked right up there with, you would like the double chocolate malted milk shake to go with your burger? Of course, I would!

I did my best to balk. I didn't want to seem over-eager.

Capucine only laughed and took my elbow. "*Mais, oui!* You do! Do not worry. He does not bite much." She hauled me to him.

A few steps across the garden path and one introduction later, I'd officially met my first (famous) French pop star.

I have to say, the whole encounter felt surprisingly low key. Capucine shoved me in front of her, Lucas glanced up from his phone, then I said something about liking one of his songs.

"*Merci.* That is very kind." Up close, Lucas was smaller than Danny or Travis, with dark hair and eyes to match. To say he was good-looking doesn't do justice to the effect he had on people, though. (Okay, on me.) He *did* have charisma. "You should come out with us sometime," he invited me with a warm look. "We know all the best places in Saint-Malo. You drink, *oui*? Dance?"

Lucas performed a hip swivel to demonstrate, as though he intended to hurdle the language barrier by miming a mamba.

I didn't mind. Especially not when he flashed me a flirty smile. Lucas seemed nice. He was sexy, *and* he was talented. It's not as though I have a rule that all my men be unattainable for one reason or another. It's just worked out that way (so far).

"That would be fun," I told him. "Maybe. We'll see."

Lucas gave a knowing laugh. "Hard to get. *Je comprends.*"

"That's not it," I insisted. "I have work to do."

Catching a killer. The thought snapped me back to reality.

"Now that I have met you, I will not stop asking," Lucas warned me with another flirtatious look. "Frenchmen are persistent, *chérie*. Say yes. Come out with me tonight."

I'll admit it: his oh-so-French *chérie* almost got me.

"Maybe another night," I hedged. "In the meantime . . ."

I left Capucine, Lucas, and their video crew with a few handy chocolate samples, then headed toward town. Next stop: the police station. Meeting Capucine had given me another idea.

The Saint-Malo police station was familiar turf to me by now. Fortunately, I didn't recognize the desk clerk on duty. He was not the same person who'd insisted that it would "not be possible" for me to see Madame *l'agent* Mélanie Flamant yesterday.

"*Bonjour, Madame,*" he said. "*Je peux vouz aider?*"

His bored but solicitous tone was just what I needed.

"*Je suis désolée de vous déranger, mais j'ai besoin de—*"

I'm sorry to bother you, but I need. That's as far as I got. Inevitably, the desk clerk discerned my subpar French.

"*Vous êtes américaine? Vous parlez anglais?*" Are you American? Do you speak English? "Okay. How can I help you?"

His very bluntly stated "okay" almost made me giggle. You might be surprised how often people around the world use that all-American-sounding word. *Okay!* Also, it occurred to me, no wonder my French was still so shaky. No one would let me finish a sentence, much less carry on a conversation *en français.*

"It's a very small thing, I promise." I lifted my basket full of Easter chocolates. "First, is it all right if I set this down right here?" I indicated the counter in front of his very bureaucratic-looking computer terminal. "It's very heavy."

"*Oh la,*" he clucked. "That is a great deal of chocolate!"

"*Mais oui, c'est ça.*" I explained about my job, then tilted the basket so he could have a better look. "Would you like to try some? *Juste un petit goûter?* I would value your opinion."

I wasn't sure if it was my "just a little taste" nudge or my flattery about wanting his opinion, but he finally bit.

He glanced around. The police station seemed

quiet. As I might have expected, I groused to myself, for a place that was so unenthusiastically investigating Monsieur's murder.

"*Merci.*" He chose one of the chocolates Travis and I had made that morning. He chewed slowly. His eyes lit. "*Pas mal!*"

To a French person, "*pas mal*" didn't exactly mean "not bad." It actually meant "pretty good." I was pleased with that.

Also, now I really had him. Danny had told me once that if you could convince someone to take something from you—no matter how inconsequential it was—they tended to feel indebted to you. Then you could make the most of that tendency to gain their cooperation. In my case, I needed an answer to a question.

Sound shady? Maybe. Familiar? Sure. It's the same tactic car dealers use when they offer you a "complimentary beverage" as soon as you enter their showroom. It's what cosmetics counter associates are taking advantage of when they give you perfume samples or teeny-tiny bottles of new products. In both cases, you (as the recipient) tend to feel a basic human need to reciprocate—to restore the balance between the two of you.

Preferably by buying a car or a mascara you don't need.

"I have a small problem," I began, tipping up my basket to offer him another chocolate. He accepted one of the elaborately painted varieties. "I am Hayden Mundy Moore, a friend of poor Monsieur Vetault." We exchanged muffled courtesies while he chewed. "He was my mentor. It's because of him that I know how to make chocolates like these, hand-molded in the very best tradition."

"Breton tradition." He nodded and licked his fingers. If he'd considered my mentor a *traître*, he didn't say so. "Poor Monsieur Vetault. It is good that you work so hard to honor his memory."

"*Oui*," I agreed. "The thing is—and I know this is a delicate matter—but I gave Monsieur Vetault some information a few days ago. Now I seem to have misplaced that information myself, and I need it for a certain client." I bit my lip and tried my best to look desperate. "If I don't come up with it soon, I'm going to be in big trouble, Monsieur. Is it possible to—"

"All of Monsieur Vetault's personal effects are part of our investigation," he interrupted, looking dour. "I am sorry."

I looked downcast. It was easy. I felt that way. "I understand." I rearranged my chocolates, then sighed. "Thank you, Monsieur. You have been very kind. *Bonne journée.*"

I took my chocolates and trudged toward the police station's *sortie* (exit), hoping against hope. One, two, three . . .

"*Attendez*, Madame. Wait!" *Whew.* That was close.

I turned, one eyebrow lifted inquiringly. This role would have been more convincingly played by Danny, but I did my best.

"*Oui, Monsieur?*" It was always best to be respectful.

"You say it is information you are looking for?" the desk clerk asked me abruptly. "Information you gave to Monsieur Vetault?"

I nodded, hoping he wouldn't press me for details. I couldn't describe the thing I was here for. It had been too dark. But I knew that Philippe had been holding *something* in his hand on the night I'd found him. I was hoping to see it somehow.

I was also gambling that being vague would suffice.

The desk clerk glanced behind him again. Then back at me. "There was a business card in Monsieur Vetault's hand. Is that it?"

A business card. Yes, that was probably the thing I'd seen. I sagged with relief. I nodded again, still afraid to speak.

I wasn't very skilled at subterfuge. I didn't want to be. But Travis's friendship with Mélanie Flammant hadn't yet yielded all the information we needed. I wasn't sure it ever would.

"I will show you a photo of it. You will write down the information?" The clerk helped himself to another of the chocolates I placed within reach before taking out my trusty Moleskine notebook and a pencil. "Okay! You are ready to see?"

I breathed in, steadying myself. "*Oui, merci.*"

He typed something, frowned, then typed some more. Then he swiveled his computer monitor toward me. On its screen, I saw the poorly lit image of a crumpled business card. ANTIQUITÉS MOREAU.

I must have appeared unsettled, because the clerk frowned. "This card has a special significance for you, Madame?"

His suddenly alert tone made me take a step back. I shook my head, then started scribbling all the details from the card.

"No. No, I'm sorry. It's just . . ." Feeling shaken, I pointed at the image. "I didn't expect there to be blood on it."

"*Oui, alors, qui est la mort.*" Yes, well, that is death. His sympathetic moue said it all. "*Et la vie.*" And life.

It was only a little blood—a few drops. But there

was no such thing as a little life. Especially not Monsieur's.

With that information in hand, I made my getaway—unsteadily, but I did it. "*Merci, au revoir, Monsieur.*"

The desk clerk waved me off, and that was that. I'd done it. I'd engaged in some verifiable sleuthing . . . and I kind of wished I hadn't. It wasn't fun, this murder investigation stuff.

But for Philippe's sake, I meant to carry on.

Next up: La Maison des Petits Bonheurs. At last.

When I arrived at Philippe's chocolaterie, I was surprised to see that the ugly black graffiti was gone—not because I'd cleaned it (that had been one of my missions for today) but because (ostensibly) Mathieu had given up on waiting for me.

That didn't bode well for our budding acquaintance.

I strode onward anyway, still carrying my basket of fancy *Pâques* chocolates. Between Lucas Lefebvre's video crew and the desk clerk at *la gendarmerie* (the police station), I'd depleted my supply. I still had my giant showy chocolate egg and a few of the bonbons I'd gold-dusted before Travis had joined me, though.

For now, they would have to be enough to impress Mathieu—enough to show him that the two of us had a love of chocolate in common. That we had Monsieur in common and should trust each other. I wanted Mathieu to confide in me every last detail about Philippe Vetault's relationships with his merchant neighbors.

Most particularly, about the redheaded woman who'd ripped down Monsieur's *Fest-Noz* publicity banner with such vehemence yesterday—the same woman who just happened to be leaving La Maison des Petits Bonheurs now as I tried to enter the shop.

"*Si vous ne leur dites pas, alors, je vais!*" she was shouting at Mathieu from the doorway. Then she turned abruptly.

If you don't tell them, I'm going to! was the gist of what she'd said. But I was so surprised to see her there and so busy mentally translating that I didn't move out of her way in time.

We collided in the narrow entryway. *Oof.*

"*Attention!*" she yelped at me. "*Regardez!*" Watch out!

Her voice sounded raspy—the effects of longtime cigarette smoking, I guessed, judging by the smoky odors clinging to her floral dress, accompanying cardigan, and knotted silk scarf.

She gave a very Gallic puff of disapproval, then jabbed me forcefully in the shoulder. Shocked, I stumbled backward.

Having shoved me out of her path, she made her way down the street—but only a few paces. She galumphed into the *magasin de confiture* (the jam shop) next door and then slammed the door.

Mathieu saw me and shook his head. "*Aie, aie, aie,*" he commiserated as he held open the door to allow me to enter. "I am afraid Madame Renouf is not feeling very friendly today."

"You can say that again." Shaking my head, I stepped inside the shop. The blissfully chocolaty aromas that greeted me did a lot to restore my well-being, though. Mathieu had been busy doing more than cleaning graffiti. He'd been making a variety of chocolates today, too. "Are you all right?" I examined him with concern. "It sounded as though she was threatening you."

In a town where someone had just been murdered, you couldn't simply disregard hostile behavior, could you?

"Psh. *Pas de problème.*" Mathieu waved away my worries. "Clotilde Renouf is not as important as she thinks she is. Since she has taken over the *confiserie*, she is insufferable."

Aha. "When I was training with Monsieur, there was a different woman running the jam shop. One who seemed less . . ."

"Angry? *Oui.* Clotilde's mother. But the daughter is much more ambitious than old Madame Renouf. She wants everything, including Monsieur's shop, so she can expand her own. She—"

On the verge of revealing something incriminating about Madame Renouf (I was sure of it) Mathieu stopped abruptly. He frowned.

He'd caught sight of my basket's sweet contents. Silently, he examined everything I'd brought. He stiffened. "You are making chocolate for *Pâques*? So soon? But you do this why?"

"Hey, it's never too soon, right?" I joked. "The surprise egg filled with miniature chocolates is Monsieur's specialty."

My explanation didn't exactly lighten up Mathieu. "I am aware. However, I told you before that I do not need your help."

"I know, but—" *I thought we could bond. Nope, that probably wouldn't fly.* "Did Monsieur Vetault teach you the hot sheet pan trick?"

"*Bien sûr.*" Of course. He sniffed. "I was his *protégé.*"

I was his protégée, I couldn't help thinking. *Me!*

It was silly, but it was true. Suddenly I had new insight into Travis's and Danny's ongoing rivalry.

Mathieu's relationship with Philippe didn't affect my own. Yet I wanted Monsieur's memory all to myself. Or at least I wanted to share it nicely.

Forcibly, I shook off my competitive feelings. I moved aside my basket, too. I would need a different approach with Mathieu. His encounter with Clotilde Renouf must have annoyed him. That was understandable. She seemed an unpleasant woman.

"You must be a very patient man, if you're forced to battle Madame Renouf very often," I remarked. "Are all of Monsieur Vetault's shop neighbors so combative? No wonder he wanted to retire."

It was a fishing expedition. But would I hook anything?

Mathieu exhaled gustily. He turned and flung up his arm in exasperation. "I am not supposed to deal with any of this. By now, I thought that Monsieur Poyet would arrive with his decision."

About the merger. I gave a sympathetic nod. "It must be very difficult." A pause. "Have you asked Madame Vetault about it?"

His pursed lips were all the answer I needed. But Mathieu added more, unfortunately. "No. Women cannot manage business."

Great. He was sexist, too. Maybe we weren't fated to bond over chocolate and become fast friends. Not even a little bit.

I probably shouldn't have said anything more. But Mathieu's narrow-minded statement somehow felt like a slam against Philippe. Also, against me. I couldn't let it go unchallenged.

"I happen to know that Monsieur did *not* agree with you about women in business." My mentor might have intended Nathalie to take the helm at La Maison des Petits Bonheurs, after all. But maybe Mathieu knew that—and that's why he was angry? "In the coming days, I think you'll see that." I inhaled and tried to smile. "Now, I think I need to go buy some jam next door."

Nine

The selection at Clotilde Renouf's jam shop was truly exceptional. All manner of fruit preserves were available there, from berries to stone fruits to orchard fruits, sometimes mixed together in delectable combinations. I was surprised to find that Clotilde Renouf was such an artist with *confiture*—and astonished to note that her small shop was teeming with eager customers.

How could such a disagreeable woman have cultivated such a following? I wondered as I wandered, choosing one jam after another for my private stash. Surely she drove away customers?

Yet the shop itself couldn't have been more popular. Inside its lively space, I was tempted to follow Clotilde's lead and push everyone out of my way when it came time to pay. Instead, I queued behind the other customers, studying the shop's cozy, gingham-checked interior as I waited. There wasn't an inch of wasted space inside, from the shelves chockablock with golden mirabelle jam, fig jam, and flavored honey, to the table near the *caisse* piled high with Madame

Renouf's own cookbook, to the gingham aprons embroidered with her shop's strawberry logo.

All in all, Clotilde had made quite an empire for herself. When I'd last been inside the shop, during my training with Monsieur, it had been a simple local *confiserie* (sweet shop), content to serve hungry residents and a few tourists. Now, it looked like a burgeoning jam empire, with branding and tie-ins to prove it.

If I'd been a betting woman, I'd have bet that Clotilde Renouf had spearheaded the opposition to Philippe's *Fest-Noz* sponsorship banner. She'd certainly ripped it down with gusto.

Had Madame Renouf also attacked Philippe in the dark that night? Had she scrawled that graffiti next door just beforehand?

I didn't know, but I wanted to find out. I remembered the threat Clotilde had yelled to Mathieu—remembered what he'd said about her wanting Monsieur's shop to expand her own. I could see now that she urgently needed the space to serve customers.

That was no reason to murder someone, I reasoned, but it might be motivation. Especially given Saint-Malo's restrictions against new construction in the touristy, historic old town.

When I reached the counter to pay, Madame Renouf didn't even blink. Through her reading glasses—worn on a chain around her neck—she regarded me sternly. She rang up my purchases on her shopworn cash register, then brusquely announced my total.

I had to say something to stretch out the transaction. But what? "*Votre magasin, c'est très beaux, Madame,*" I tried.

It was a compliment about how nice her shop was. It failed.

Clotilde Renouf regarded me unsmilingly and repeated the total owed. I counted out coins, searching for exact change—a maneuver that typically made me a heroine to exacting French cashiers. But Madame Renouf was the exception that proved the rule.

She snatched away the coins as soon as I doled them out, all but tapping her foot with impatience while I tallied more.

I tried apologizing for our earlier run-in. I even went so far as to take the blame for not watching where I was walking. It got me nowhere. Plus, customers were piling up behind me.

Another few minutes longer and there'd be a jam-based riot.

Growing increasingly desperate to forge some sort of alliance with Clotilde so I could question her (later) about her whereabouts when Philippe had been murdered, I looked around the jam shop. My gaze lit on something familiar. I was in luck.

"Ah, Christine Ferber, d'Alsace!" I recognized the woman whose autographed photo occupied a place of prominence behind the *caisse*. "*Je la connais.*" I know her, I told Clotilde. "*Un de mes amis utilise ses confitures dans son restaurant à New York.*"

One of my friends uses her jam at his restaurant in New York. He was no slouch, either. His place was Michelin starred.

"*Ce nést pas vrai!*" All at once, Clotilde's entire character changed. She couldn't stop smiling at me. She scooped up my jams, bagged them while gushing about "our mutual friend, Madame Ferber," then warmly hustled me down some narrow stone steps to her office—a miniature nook tucked next to the kitchen, with jam pots and long spoons hanging from the rafters. "Tell me more!"

I obliged as much as I could, doing my best to hide my surprise while I rambled on about having met the famed Alsatian jam maker a few years earlier while consulting for a struggling pâtisserie near the German border. I'd hoped to find some common ground with Clotilde Renouf, but I'd accidentally stumbled upon a gold mine. I learned, over a cup of tea and a sample of a new "in development" chocolate-almond spread intended to enhance her shop's product line, that the celebrated Christine Ferber was Clotilde Renouf's longtime idol—her model for all her business success.

"Madame Ferber has a very small shop, just as I do here," she enthused, her eyes shining at me. "But hers is recognized worldwide for its excellence. Her *confiture* is served in all the finest establishments, from Paris to Hong Kong to—as you told me—New York, *en Amérique.* My favorite is her sour cherry. You have tried it? She makes it herself there in Niedermorschwihr."

It sounded delightful, and it was. But I happened to know—thanks to my aforementioned friend—that Madame Ferber's jam-based delightfulness earned her family's company at least two and a half million dollars per year. That was a *lot* of homemade jam.

As business models went, it wasn't a half bad choice.

"It's impressive how much Madame Ferber accomplishes with such relatively modest means," I agreed. "How do you manage here?"

Clotilde gave me a blustery snort. "Not easily, I promise you! As you can see, I am so successful that I need more room."

I understood. Maybe I was wrong about her. She certainly seemed belligerent, but when met on her own terms, here in her own twee shop, Madame Renouf was actually . . . horrifyingly ruthless.

"But now that Monsieur Vetault is gone, my luck may be turning," she was boasting. She leaned confidingly nearer. "If you ask me, it was that Mathieu Camara who killed him. Mark my words."

I almost choked on a bite of chocolate-almond spread.

"No," I managed to say, eyes wide. "Do you really think so? He seems to miss Monsieur Vetault very much, and he seems so kind."

I'd already divulged some background about my work as a chocolate expert, and my training in Brittany under Philippe Vetault. Now I felt icky for saying anything at all to her.

Clotilde poo-pooed my take on the situation. "That boy wants everything to be handed to him, as smooth as butter. That is what is wrong with the young today. They want no work!"

I could verify that Mathieu worked hard. I'd tasted (okay, inhaled) the results myself. But I wasn't there to argue.

Besides, Mathieu hadn't liked Clotilde Renouf much, either.

I sipped my tea. "You say your luck may be turning?"

I felt queasy asking but did my best to sound sympathetic.

"That's right." Clotilde Renouf nodded. "Old Monsieur Vetault promised *us* that shop of his. Years ago, this was. He swore that we would have first chance to take his space when he was gone."

I hoped she meant *gone* as in *retired*, not *gone* as in *dead*.

"He knew we needed it, my mother and me," Clotilde went on, not bothering to lower her voice. She leaned closer again, her face suffused with gossipy certitude. "I think they were lovers, *Maman* and

Monsieur Vetault. No man and woman could have worked side by side for all those years without succumbing to temptation. Of course they were together! Monsieur Vetault wanted to make certain that she would be looked after, once he was gone. And now . . ."

He is, her avaricious expression said. *He's gone.*

I wanted to close my eyes and cover my ears like a child. I had no desire to learn any of this about my mentor. To me, Philippe Vetault had been like a father. Like a superhero. He couldn't be susceptible to the flaws of ordinary men. Could he?

Seeing my expression, Clotilde burst into rusty-sounding laughter. Then she had a coughing fit. She lit a cigarette.

"Do not look so distressed, Madame!" she scolded me, casually tapping ash from her cigarette. "This is the way of things. You Americans with your provincial attitudes . . . *bof*!"

Ugh. For once, I'd found a (potential) murder suspect whom I *didn't* like. I could barely tolerate Clotilde Renouf. She was aggressive, greedy, (literally) pushy, and utterly insensitive.

Somehow, I was able to keep talking. I laughed too.

"It's not that." I waved away her casual description of my mentor's infidelity—her insistence that he might have promised his family's third-generation legacy to an outsider. "I was only wondering . . . what if Monsieur's property doesn't pass to you?"

"Unthinkable." Clotilde dragged on her cigarette while her jam shop heaved with business just above our tea and chocolate rendezvous. "Monsieur Vetault and my mother had a verbal contract for that real estate. It will belong to me. The only question is how much I will have to press to make the Vetaults agree."

She eyed me coldly. "Not too far, I think. You see, I understand what has been going on between Madame Vetault and Monsieur Bernard for years now."

I gulped. If Clotilde Renouf knew about Hélène and Hubert, then maybe she was right about Monsieur. I hated admitting it.

The worst part was, *I* seemed to inadvertently confirm Clotilde's theory about Hélène's affair with her château's gardener. It was as though the jam maker had been testing me—fishing around with her suspicions—and I'd gulped down the bait.

Have I mentioned before that I have zero poker face?

I'm sorry, Monsieur, I thought. I didn't want to help the Renoufs take away Philippe's legacy, Hélène's memories, and Nathalie's birthright. Not even accidentally. I tried to rally.

"Surely none of that can be proven, though?" I asked, striving to seem approving of her. "Gossip won't be enough."

"Ah, but it is *not* only gossip," Clotilde assured me. I guessed I'd sold her on the idea that we were like-minded. Ugh. "You are forgetting the daughter, Madame Vetault, *non?*"

I angled my head, momentarily confused. Then I got it.

Nathalie Vetault was Hélène's daughter *with Hubert?*

Oh no. I wasn't sure if Monsieur had known about Nathalie's paternity. As far as I knew, Philippe had raised Nathalie as his own daughter with Hélène. But if my mentor had known the truth, it would explain a lot—especially his tolerance for his wife's ongoing "secret" affair with the gardener they both employed.

Clotilde laughed again. "I can see that, just like so

many others in Saint-Malo, you did not know the truth."

"I knew Nathalie," I argued. "She never told me anything."

"Why would she? These are family secrets . . . most of the time."

If the Vetaults wanted it to stay that way, I gathered, they would give in to the Renoufs' demands for the chocolaterie.

Judging by Clotilde Renouf's smug face, she thought she'd won. What a quandary this was for the Vetaults. For Hélène.

Maybe that's why she'd taken to tippling whiskey in the morning to go along with her copious wine drinking at night.

I doubted the Vetaults would want to see Philippe's memory besmirched by a posthumous scandal. But where did Poyet fit in?

Until I met Fabrice, Nathalie's fiancé, I wouldn't know.

"You are close to the Vetaults," Clotilde remarked. "You have known the family for a long time. If you encourage them to be reasonable about this, it would be best for everyone."

Sure. If *everyone* meant ambitious Clotilde and her mother.

I was feeling more nauseated by the moment. Unexpectedly alarmed, I glanced at my plate. The *tartine* with chocolate-almond spread I'd been enjoying suddenly seemed suspicious.

Could Clotilde have brought me down here to poison me?

My breath caught. My heart kicked up a beat. I felt flushed. Woozy. I shoved away my plate. "I have to be going."

"So soon?" Madame Renouf's face swam in my vision.

"But we were getting to know one another so well. Sit! Have more tea."

If I did, I thought I might never make it out alive.

I pushed upright, making the dishware and cutlery clatter on the tiny table we'd been sitting at. I apologized in French.

I might be dying, but I didn't want to be rude.

"*Pardonnez-moi*," I blurted. "*Au revoir*, Madame Renouf."

My passage up the jam shop's claustrophobic stone steps felt more treacherous than it should have. My legs were wobbly. Surely the stairs weren't that difficult to navigate? I reached the packed *confiserie* upstairs and stopped to get my bearings.

Everything seemed surreally ordinary. Customers shopped. Clotilde's assistant rang up purchases. The shouts of the shop's kitchen staff filtered upstairs, along with clanging pots.

I gripped my crossbody bag and veered toward the door. As I passed through it, fresh autumn air hit me in the face. Ah.

That was better. Maybe I would be all right.

The next thing I knew was . . . nothing. Total darkness.

I awakened sometime later with a jolt. My head felt fuzzy and my shoulder hurt. *Ouch.* I opened my eyes to see Travis.

Right beside him was Mathieu Camara, scrutinizing me.

Had I eaten anything at La Maison des Petits Bonheurs? I wondered abruptly. I tried to shove myself upward. In a bed?

"Whoa, easy there." Travis's rough, familiar voice

steadied me. So did his hand on my arm. *Nice.* "How do you feel?"

"What happened?" I blinked. I *was* in a bed—an unfamiliar one. Unsteadily, I regarded its quilted coverlet. Its companion night table. Its white-painted matching armoire, just to the left. Above me were old-fashioned rafters, old-fashioned crown molding, and old-fashioned paneled walls. Those were the kinds of architectural details you'd find in a very old building.

This was Mathieu's bedroom above the chocolaterie.

I jerked upright, then winced as my headache worsened.

"You fainted outside the jam shop," Travis told me.

"You were probably weak from making complicated *Pâques* chocolates seven months too soon," Mathieu added sardonically.

Reminded of his rampant misogyny, I frowned at him.

"I was having tea and *tartines* with Madame Renouf next door," I told them both. I grabbed Travis's suit sleeve and gave him additionally meaningful look—one that said, *she poisoned me!*

My scaredy-cat eyes must have done the trick, because my financial advisor took charge of the situation. He thanked Mathieu for his help and hospitality, then returned to me.

"You look well enough to get up now. Let's go."

I got the impression that Mathieu's antiwoman stance didn't sit well with Travis. Or was it an anti-me stance?

Who knew? But I remembered now that I hadn't eaten any of Mathieu's chocolates earlier. That implicated Clotilde Renouf.

She'd just zoomed to the top spot on my suspects list.

Mathieu offered token resistance to our leaving—

probably due to ingrained French *politesse*—but he gave up quickly enough for my keeper and I to get out of there without too much fuss. On the street, Travis held my arm to keep me safely upright.

I have to say, it felt pretty good. Ordinarily, I'm firmly in charge of what's going on with me. I decide where I'm going, I get myself there, I take care of business once I arrive. But with Travis by my side, I felt I could relax a little bit.

He guided me to a café table and sat me down. Solicitously, he ordered us both strong espressos and two slices of that fruity local specialty, Far Breton cake. Once the server had gone to fetch our order, Travis turned all his attention on me.

The effect was swoon inducing. I couldn't help smiling.

"This is not funny," he barked. "Don't *ever* do that again."

That brought me out of my reverie. I felt instantly indignant. "I didn't pass out on purpose, Travis." I leaned forward so no one would overhear us. "I think Clotilde Renouf poisoned me!" I smacked my lips, searching for proof. "Her chocolate-almond spread tasted fine. It must have been the tea."

Travis looked dubious. "All I know is, I was leaving Antiquités Moreau, just down the street, after meeting with Charlotte Moreau, when I saw you lying in a heap over there."

He jutted his jaw toward the jam shop's distant stoop.

"Hey, at least I had the sense to collapse in public, where you could see me and come to my rescue. Thanks, by the way."

"Again, *not* funny." He seemed beleaguered—so much so that he took off his glasses, frowned at them, then put them back on. I suspected it was a technique used to distance himself from the situation—something that might be useful when negotiating, for instance. "I realize you get hurt sometimes while doing this, but it's one thing to hear about it. It's another to live it."

"That's what Danny says. You two should compare notes."

His quelling look put the kibosh on that idea. Oh, well. One of these days, I vowed, I'd convince them to get along.

Speaking of convincing . . . I filled in Travis on everything I'd learned from Clotilde Renouf. I told him about her merciless ambition and her claim that Philippe had had a long-term affair with her mother. I described Clotilde's knowledge of Hélène's affair with Hubert and her assertion concerning Nathalie's true paternity. I concluded with Clotilde's real-estate claim on Monsieur's property and her final suggestion that I "encourage" the Vetaults to grant her ownership of Philippe's chocolaterie.

"That's a lot to take in." Travis had been enjoying his cake and coffee while I explained what I'd learned. He did not seem entirely convinced. "I'll look into all those claims."

I frowned. "Even you probably can't access Nathalie's parentage. Or all the implications of a 'verbal contract.'"

He gave me a look that said he could. Then, "How do you feel? You didn't eat all your Far Breton, and it's delicious."

His concern was touching. "I feel better. Just not hungry."

That was a minor miracle in itself. But then, that wasn't a slice of yummy chocolate cake sitting in front of me, was it?

"Do you want to see a doctor? I'll take you right now."

"The time for that might have been *before* cake and coffee," I joked. "Priorities, right?" At Travis's grave expression, I sobered. "I'm not convinced I was actually poisoned," I admitted, hoping to reassure him. "What are the odds that Clotilde Renouf routinely keeps poison on hand for visitors?"

Travis considered it, then opened his mouth.

Before he could quote statistics at me, I held up my palm.

"Let's not get paranoid, all right? Ordinarily, I'd be the first to indulge in a little drama, given the situation. That was scary! But I'm probably just overwhelmed and overtired right now, and Madame Renouf was awful. Everything suddenly got to me. Maybe I hyperventilated," I theorized. That might explain my dizziness and fainting. "I'm investigating, I'm still grieving Monsieur, and I'm pretty much subsisting on sugar these days."

"We'll get you a real dinner tonight. All the trimmings."

That sounded good. I smiled. "It's a date."

My financial advisor looked alarmed. "It's not a date."

"Don't worry. I'm not planning on forcing out Mélanie."

He laughed. "I told you, we're not an item."

I made a skeptical face. "Does she know that?" I pressed. "Because from what you've said, Mélanie is into you."

"That's because I'm a 'hot guy.'" Travis knew how to give as good as he got. "I have it from reliable sources."

"Don't let it go to your head." I watched as Travis paid for our fortifying snack. I stood. "Hey, look at me," I crowed, hoping to lighten the mood between us. "I'm fully upright!"

"Don't let *that* go to your head." My keeper took my arm for security again. "You might be convinced you weren't poisoned, but I'm not. I'll be keeping a close eye on you for a while."

"I don't need a keeper," I protested—maybe ill-advisedly, given that I flippantly referred to Travis that way much of the time. "I'm fine. If I start feeling faint or, you know, on the verge of death, I'll be sure to clue you in ASAP."

"Still not funny," my financial advisor informed me. "I really might have to call Danny and compare notes on handling you."

"Why? Can't manage the job all by yourself?" I kidded, sorry I'd planted the idea in his mind in the first place.

"This is too important for half measures," Travis informed me as we walked to my parked Citroën. "*You're* too important."

Aw. Also, this sounded a lot like the time my financial advisor and my security expert had teamed up to "protect me." I hadn't liked them exchanging information then. I didn't now.

"No worries. I'm fine! Since you went to all the trouble of carrying me up to Mathieu's bed, I thought I'd have a cheeky nap while I was there, that's all." I took out my phone and dialed. "See, look—I'm calling Danny. *You* definitely don't have to."

On the other side of the Atlantic, my bodyguard buddy picked up. "Hayden," he growled. "Next time you decide to pal around with a convicted criminal, maybe let me know first?"

"Huh?" Confused, I gripped my phone. "What are you talking about, Danny? I haven't been palling around with any criminal types." *Now that you're out of commission,* I was about to say.

He was too fast for me. "Mathieu Camara has a record."

Whoops. Out of the frying pan and into the fire.

"Was it for graffiti?" I asked. Hey, a girl had to try.

"Nope." Danny wasted no time squashing my hopes. "Not even close. I think you'd better watch your back twice as hard now."

Hmm. And he didn't even know about the possible poisoning yet. Things in Saint-Malo were getting rougher by the minute.

Ten

With the news of Mathieu's until-now hidden history of jail time on my mind, it wasn't easy to concentrate that evening. My head swam with suspects. Mathieu. Clotilde. Hubert. Hélène.

How much did I really know about any of them?

Learning about Mathieu's criminal past had spooked me. That effect had probably been helped along by Danny's ire, of course—my bodyguard buddy had pulled no punches when it came to the subject of Mathieu. I was too trusting, he'd said. Too gullible. Too prone to wanting to think the best of people, whether they deserved it or not. *I* thought that was a positive quality.

After all, in any given murder investigation I became tangled up in, everyone *except* the killer eventually wound up innocent. Was I supposed to run around accusing people blindly? Maybe hurting their chances at being trusted, being employed, being accepted by everyone around them? I didn't think so.

Danny and Travis, however, disagreed. As much as they tended to argue between themselves, on this, they were united.

I needed to be more suspicious, they insisted. Of everyone.

But I'd tried that approach in London. While it had served up plenty of potential suspects for me to investigate, round-the-clock suspicion had left me feeling miserable in the end. I didn't want to dwell on the awfulness in the world—not even while I was busy nosing around in its shadows. I *cared.*

If I became as jaded as my friends wanted, I'd lose that.

There had to be a balance. I was determined to find it. But it had been jarring to learn—contrary to my eventual impressions of him—that Philippe's trainee chocolatier had been mixed up in a number of illegal activities a few years ago. According to Danny, Mathieu had a record involving auto theft and assault—in one instance, assault severe enough to land his victim in a *banlieue* hospital in suburban Paris. After the beating he'd sustained, the man had recovered, and Mathieu had gone to jail, later being released on parole before moving to Saint-Malo.

It would have been like Monsieur to offer a troubled youth a fresh chance at life. My mentor had been generous that way. But had Mathieu repaid Philippe by stabbing him? I didn't know.

I couldn't help doubting my own attentiveness and intuition—the same qualities that usually saved my butt while sleuthing. I'd liked Mathieu at first, but he'd turned out to be secretive (at best) and dangerous (at worst). I'd hoped to give Clotilde Renouf the benefit of the doubt (because grumpiness was no crime), only to learn exactly how grasping and unkind she really was. I'd felt sorry for Philippe's widow, Hélène, who'd later given me every reason to mistrust her by sneaking around with Hubert. And as for Angry Bloody Hands Man himself? The château's gardener (and maybe Nathalie's biological father) had actually been fairly nice to me when we'd met in *le jardin.*

At this point, I wouldn't have been altogether surprised if Capucine Roux turned out to be fencing stolen drugs in the items she used as video set dressing, and Lucas Lefebvre revealed his secret activities as a French spy. Things just felt that crazy.

I'd told Danny about my "probably not a poisoning" incident at the jam shop. I didn't make it much beyond the bare details before he'd stopped me. "Put Harvard on the phone," he'd demanded.

I still didn't know what my buddy said to Travis. But from where I was standing (in the parking lot outside the Saint-Malo city walls), it looked serious. Now I was in double trouble.

Danny and Travis *united* could be pretty formidable.

I was determined to move forward, though. I couldn't let little things like Monsieur's (rumored) checkered past with the elder Madame Renouf or his (alleged) agreement to raise another man's baby daughter as his own deter me from my path. If I did, what kind of protégée would I be, really? One who gave up.

That's not me. I'm a person who sees things through—whether those things are faulty frappés or goopy ganaches or murders.

That's why, as I dressed for dinner with Travis, I ran through all my suspects—and their potential motives—in my mind one more time. I wanted my sleuthing game to be on point, no matter what happened next. So before I slipped out of my jeans-and-T-shirt getup, I pulled out my notebook and jotted down some pertinent observations. Then I put on some fresh lip gloss and mascara. Then, reminded of my initial (unsuccessful) attempt to bump into Lucas Lefebvre, I put on his music and had a quick scroll through his social media accounts. He was good at keeping them up to the minute and interesting, with photos of his video shoots and images from his earlier stints on Radio France.

Sometime later, a knock on the door grabbed my attention.

Startled, I glanced up. My château room was shadowy. The evening had darkened while I'd been perusing Lucas's accounts on my phone—and okay, daydreaming a little about his sexy, swivel-hipped mamba earlier. I had to keep my spirits up, didn't I?

"Hayden, it's me," came Travis's rumbling *basso profondo.*

Speaking of sexy . . . sadly, I wasn't dressed for company.

"I'll be right there!" I scrabbled in my wheelie bag for my (one and only) cocktail dress. Black, naturally. I shucked my utilitarian undies for something a little lacier, then wiggled into my dress. Surprised I have one, given my travel-light philosophy? The handy thing about a cocktail dress is its slinky nature. It occupies nearly no room in a bag. "I'm almost ready."

Formal meals at a French château were a big deal, I knew, especially dinner. It wouldn't do to turn up looking shabby.

I switched off Lucas, gave my *chambre* (room) a cursory check, then slipped into my sandals. I gave my hair a shake.

I opened the door. "I thought we were meeting downstairs."

"I decided to escort you." Was it my imagination, or

did Travis look especially pleased to see me? "May I come in?"

"Only if you brought dinner with you. I'm starving."

"I want to double-check your room." My keeper waited.

His expression suggested he was sure he'd prevail. "Okay."

He came inside with all the alertness and guardedness that Danny typically displayed. I thought I could deduce what they'd talked about in their (mostly one-sided) conversation earlier.

"Let me guess: Danny schooled you on security, right?"

"Something like that." My financial advisor moved past me like a suit-wearing *GQ* ninja. His bespectacled gaze swept my room and all its accoutrements. "You look nice, by the way."

His compliment didn't register right away. I was in the midst of trying to see the place through his eyes, with my soft pashmina throw, my fig-scented candle, and my framed pictures of family and friends. I might be a globe-trotter—and I never bothered to unpack—but I liked to make a room as homey as I could, whether it was in a five-star resort or a roadside cabin.

When Travis turned his gaze to me again, I swear I felt something. Probably delayed-onset poison. Right?

"Thanks." I gestured at him. "You, too. Does this place pass muster, or do you want to sweep for listening devices next?"

"It's not a laughing matter." My financial advisor stopped near the unlit fireplace. "You might have been hurt today."

"I'd hate to have kicked it before seeing *your* room," I kidded, unable to hold back a smile. "What's it like upstairs?"

He wasn't amused by the idea of tit-for-tat. "Higher."

Okay, then. "Look, don't let Danny bug you. He can be hard to take sometimes. All that cynicism, all that machismo—"

"Do you ever take anything seriously?" Travis interrupted.

His forthright gaze dared me to make another joke.

I wasn't that stupid. I like to kid around sometimes—especially when feeling under pressure—but I'm not an idiot.

"If I didn't take this seriously, I wouldn't be here." I gestured at the château—at my mentor's *home.* We were both under the roof where Philippe had lived his entire life. "The whole reason I'm doing this is that it *matters.* It matters to me if justice prevails, if reason wins out, if I understand things."

I steeled myself for an argument. I didn't get one.

"I need to understand things, too," Travis told me.

With that, the issue was closed. My financial advisor took one last peek (under the bed, for the record) for "safety's sake," then we closed the door behind us and headed downstairs.

When we arrived, several of the château's B&B guests were gathered in the sumptuous sitting room, enjoying aperitifs. The mood was swanky, the drinks were enlivening, and the décor was incredible. Floor-to-ceiling silk draperies adorned the tall mullioned windows overlooking the gardens. Through them, I glimpsed subtle lighting illuminating the topiaries and paths, fountains and flowers. A pianist plied his trade at the grand piano near the fireplace. Laughter punctuated low, polite conversations. Lest it all get *too* frou-frou, the château's wolfhound, Bouchon, padded from guest to guest, making friends from the sweeping staircase to the sofas and armchairs beyond.

Reminded by the Vetaults' dog that this was—at its heart—a family home, I felt wistful about Monsieur all over again.

Travis noticed. He gave me a smile. Then, a drink.

I sipped it while we wandered the room, admiring the lamps and mantelpieces, rugs and vases. The château wasn't a museum, but its grandeur and its history gave it a similar quality. I wondered how many generations of Vetaults had thrown parties here. How many had been born and died here. How many had drunk to excess here, the way Hélène was doing at that very moment.

The *châtelaine* weaved past me, almost stepping on Bouchon. I coaxed over the frightened wolfhound and gave it a comforting pat. The dog apparently recognized a kindred spirit, because she flopped on my sandaled feet and lolled her tongue happily at me.

Aw. Sure, this had started as a minor rescue operation, but now I was snared. Murmuring, I scratched behind Bouchon's ears.

"You made a friend." Travis hunkered down too. He had a knack with animals, I saw immediately. "You like dogs, Hayden?"

"Not exclusively, but best," I replied, distracted by watching Hélène. She seemed to be searching for something. She weaved tipsily around the sitting room, lifting knickknacks and peering behind heavy stone planters. "My lifestyle doesn't lend itself to a pet, but someday . . ." I trailed off, dreaming of it.

I must have sighed, because Travis looked sympathetic. "I'd be a different person today without my Bella, that's for sure."

Bella? I wanted to give him a hard time, but he

appeared so lovably crazy about his dog that I didn't have it in me.

Oh, wait. Maybe I did. "Bella?" I repeated, unable to prevent a grin. "Let me guess: every time you call your dog, all the women at the dog park think you're hitting on them, right?"

"That has literally never happened."

I had my doubts. I said so.

"Usually I have my nieces with me, anyway," Travis told me. "They live nearby, and they like playing with Bella."

He had nieces? That meant he had siblings, I presumed. He definitely had a dog: Bella. This was more information than I'd ever compiled about my notoriously private financial advisor.

It occurred to me that I'd been so caught up in trying to find Monsieur's murderer that I hadn't seized this obvious opportunity. My keeper was here, in person, with me. I could finally satisfy my longtime curiosity about him—*all* about him.

"It's short for Bellissima," Travis went on with a goofy endearing look on his face. "I tried calling her something else, but in the end, 'Bellissima' is all she responded to." He gave me a grin and went on petting Bouchon. "It means beautiful in—"

"Italian, I know. I'm only semi-hopeless with languages." I marveled at him. "You have a discerning dog who insists on having things exactly the way she wants them. How like you."

"It makes sense when you know the backstory," he explained with a hint of self-consciousness. "I adopted her in Italy."

"You've been to Italy, too? Travis!" I gave him a

blunt look. "Tell me the truth: your aviophobia was a hoax, right?"

Maybe Danny, ever jaded, had been correct all along.

Travis looked indignant. "No. It stems from a specific incident, years ago. It was very—" He stopped explaining. "I don't like to talk about it. Anyway, planes run both ways."

Nearby, Hélène flipped over some throw pillows—one handed, while holding a wineglass. She appeared increasingly agitated.

I refocused on Travis. "Meaning?"

"Meaning, you could easily have come to Seattle."

Something in his gravelly, seductive tone caught my ear. Was my financial advisor offended that I'd never visited him?

"I could have," I replied, "if anyone had ever invited me."

He laughed. It was a wonderful sound. "You've never waited for an invitation to do anything in your life. Admit it." Travis fixed me with a perceptive look. "You're the impulsive type."

Well . . . he kind of had me. But there was no way I'd admit it.

Possibly, that was because *I* was a little offended, too. I'd had the distinct impression, all this time, that Travis hadn't minded that the stipulations of my trust fund kept me on the road so much—that he hadn't wanted to meet me at all. I'd assumed he'd preferred to keep things all business between us.

That's certainly the way his fusty old predecessor, Mr. Whatshisname, had run things. He'd been Uncle Ross's initial appointee as my financial advisor. Once he'd retired and Travis had come on the scene, things had gotten a lot more interesting.

For a second, I lapsed into melancholy. Sweet, wild-haired, unpredictable Uncle Ross. I still missed him. In structuring his will in the unique way he had, he'd only wanted to make sure I would never settle for a "less than" life. I knew that. But in choosing Travis's financial management firm, he'd also accidentally added a heaping helping of complexity to my life.

I didn't want to travel too far down memory lane, though. I watched Hélène for a few seconds as she peeked behind a framed painting, muttering to herself in slurred French. She didn't seem to be coping very well with her husband's death. I didn't understand why she didn't retire to the private part of the château until she felt better. It would be understandable.

Travis saw me observing our hostess. He frowned.

But I wasn't interested in losing my chance to interrogate him. A while ago, Danny had dangled some hints about Travis. He'd been maddeningly short on details, though. Before Travis could derail me by offering his opinions of Hélène's erratic behavior, I got back to digging for more info about my keeper.

I sipped my drink. "So, what kind of dog is Bellissima?"

Travis blinked, distracted. "She's a golden retriever."

"I *knew* it!" I'd always pegged my financial advisor as a golden retriever type, and I'd been right. This was kismet.

I was pretty sure Danny owed me fifty bucks now.

"You knew it? You've given this some thought, then?" *Given* me *some thought*, Travis's expression elaborated as he glanced up from his hunkered-down position petting Bouchon. His eyes gleamed at me with curiosity. "What else do you want to know?"

Was he seriously offering to lay it all on the line?

"How personal are you willing to get?" I asked.

My heart was pounding, though. I love a puzzle to solve. That's the reason I enjoy the challenge of trouble-shooting chocolate. It's the reason I persist in trying to solve murders, even when my better judgment suggests that I should hang up my deerstalker hat before something *truly* drastic goes down.

"Tonight? Right now?" My financial advisor swirled his drink. He stared into its eddying amber depths as conversations hummed around us, then looked up at me. "Very personal."

Whoa. I seriously needed to get Travis tipsy more often.

"Okay." Wow. A million questions jostled each other in my mind. "Where did you grow up? Why did you go to Harvard? Do you live alone?" He couldn't be involved with anyone, could he? What kind of person would agree to Travis's workaholic schedule? "How long have you been working for your company? Do you ever wear anything except a suit? What's your dream travel destination?"

His laughter broke in. "I can see how you get people to tell you things," Travis said. "You pelt them with questions until they can't think straight, then you make them come clean."

"Sometimes I ply them with alcohol, too." I grinned.

He inhaled. "Taking these in order," he began, "I grew up—"

At the same time, Hélène wailed from across the room. She hurled an iron candelabra to the floor.

"*Non! Pas correcte. Pas ici!*" she yelled as her guests scattered. "*Non, non! Jamais!*"

I couldn't understand why a fancy candleholder had incited such fury. An instant later, Hélène burst into pitiful tears.

"She says that didn't belong there. Not ever," Travis informed me in a considerate undertone, translating quickly.

But I knew. I was already handing him my drink, then disentangling Bouchon the wolfhound from my feet. I wanted to go to Hélène. I didn't know my mentor's widow well, but I *did* know grief. Maybe I could help—especially since the château's other guests seemed to be frozen with uncertainty and awkwardness.

Well, all except one. A well-dressed man with kind features and a very expensive Swiss watch disentangled himself from the others. He beat me to Hélène by mere seconds. He comforted her.

I watched apprehensively as he encircled Philippe's wife in his arms, then gently guided her out of the sitting room. Her defeated and confused posture was enough to break my heart. That's the way I felt on the inside, albeit to a lesser degree.

Hélène may have cheated on Monsieur, but they'd still remained married for more than forty years. His loss had to have left an empty space in her life—one even Hubert couldn't occupy.

But the crisis appeared to be past. Made superfluous by that unknown man. I looked for Travis. It must be almost time to go into the dining room for dinner. My growling stomach said so.

A tasty meal (with all the trimmings, as Travis had promised) was not yet to be, though. Because next, someone called out to me. Footsteps clattered across the sleek floor.

"Hayden!" I heard in a musical French accent. "*C'est toi?*"

Hayden, is that you?

Under certain circumstances, this would have been a "now what?" moment. As it was, I wasn't at all sure what to expect.

The only thing to do was to take a few steps and find out.

Eleven

I'd lost track of my financial advisor, I realized, but I'd found Nathalie Vetault. I recognized her voice as though it was yesterday when we'd shared that disparate summer in Saint-Malo.

I turned. The mingling guests parted for a moment.

There she was: Philippe's only daughter—tall, brunette, and possessed of a rangy figure that now wore fashionable clothes as effectively as it had once made the most of a bikini and suntan.

The sight of her made me tear up helplessly. By the time I reached Nathalie, both of us were sniffling uncontrollably.

I couldn't help it. Pain is pain. It hurts to witness it.

She recovered first and leaned forward to offer me *les bises*—those French kisses on (or near) the cheeks. I inhaled Nathalie's light perfume, redolent of bitter oranges and cloves. She was all grown up now and she was trembling. Poor Nathalie.

I grasped her hands. "It's been too long. I'm so sorry about your father." I drew in a shaky breath, then tried to smile. "I can't stop thinking he'll come into his atelier and demand that I remake a raspberry ganache any second now."

"I know." Nathalie nodded, her eyes teary. "It seems only yesterday that I was up in the attic with *Papa*, sorting through family heirlooms and arguing about where to find *Grand-Mère*'s wedding dress." An unsteady smile. "He found it for me, though."

"Of course he did. Monsieur was nothing if not helpful."

I found myself staring at Nathalie's pretty face, carefully evaluating her features. Did she have Philippe's nose? His chin? His eyes? Or was that a resemblance to Hubert reflected in her grown-up appearance? I couldn't be sure. I was too familiar with her to be objective. Frankly, all I saw in her face was sadness.

Well, that and shock. I think we all still felt that.

"I had hoped that the next time we saw each other would be at my wedding," Nathalie went on. Around us, other conversations had resumed quietly. "Not under sad circumstances like these."

I agreed. "I'm so, so sorry. I could order flowers for Monsieur's memorial, or make special chocolates for afterward. Anything," I offered. "I would love to spend some time with you, too—maybe a walk by the seaside? Whatever you feel ready for."

I wanted to offer concrete suggestions—ways to help that wouldn't put undue demands on Nathalie. *Is there anything I can do?* sounds thoughtful until you're the grieving recipient of a question you don't feel prepared to tackle amid everything else.

"That is very kind of you, Hayden." She wiped away a tear with bejeweled fingers, then gave a self-conscious laugh. "It is very not French of me to cry over cocktails!" She bit her lip. Then, "Maybe we could go shopping in Saint-Malo sometime?"

"I'd like that," I said sincerely. "Is tomorrow too soon?"

"Not at all." This time, Nathalie squeezed *my* hand. "It would do me good to get out of here. Here, I . . . cannot forget."

I doubted she could forget anywhere, but I knew what she meant. Besides, it wasn't for me to decide how she mourned. We hadn't been that close, the summer I'd trained with my mentor. But given the situation, it was impossible not to feel for her.

I was searching for a response when Nathalie forged on.

"I am sorry about *Maman*," she blurted with a worried sideways glance. "I cannot believe the changes in her since I've been away. I am very busy with my job in Paris. I work for a PR company, you see, and I do not get back home very often."

I understood—and said so—but Nathalie seemed on the verge of crumpling any minute. Tearing up, she shook out her hair and then gulped some of her aperitif. Tactfully, I looked away.

Nathalie noticed and made a face. "I know, I am probably drinking too much, *non*? But one must manage somehow. Perhaps it runs in the family." She gave a humorless laugh. "I cannot cope with *Maman* when she is drinking. For that, Fabrice is much better." She cheered up. "You have met Fabrice? My fiancé?"

She waggled her engagement ring at me in that universal gesture all brides-to-be learned immediately. It looked . . . spendy.

If Fabrice Poyet was the man who'd whisked

Hélène away to comfort her, he was obviously both kindhearted *and* well-to-do.

Nathalie misinterpreted my contemplative silence. "It is terribly gauche to flash a rock like this, I know. But what can I say?" She offered an eloquent French shrug. "I love him."

"You must, to have united your families," I told her. "*Félicitations*, Nathalie. Truly." Congratulations. "I hope you and Monsieur Poyet will be very happy together. When is the wedding?"

We talked for a while about the details. It was to be a small ceremony—one that wouldn't require the same degree of planning that an American wedding sometimes did. In France, weddings tended to be small affairs, held at the city hall and celebrated with family and friends at a *petite fête* afterward.

"But you must meet Fabrice!" Nathalie insisted. She'd perked up while discussing her upcoming nuptials, even while detailing the challenges in making *Grand-Mère's* vintage dress fit her. She grabbed my hand. "He went this way with *Maman*."

"Maybe another time," I protested, stopping just short of digging my heels in the rug as Nathalie hauled me toward another room. We passed through the guests. "I don't want to intrude."

"*N'importe quoi*," she breezed. *Nonsense.* "You are like family. Papa cared for you like his very own daughter."

"*Oui*, he was very generous that way."

I realized (too late) that my response might imply something more: it might hint that I suspected Philippe Vetault had been "generous" enough to treat someone *else* "like his very own daughter." Nathalie. It might hint that I suspected he might have raised

Nathalie as his own child even while knowing that she was the result of Hélène and Hubert's affair. Whoops.

Nathalie stopped on reaching the next room. Tension stretched between us. Then it broke abruptly as she nodded.

"*Oui*, you are right about that. *Papa* was very generous."

Her reply left me none the wiser about her paternity.

Was it possible that even Nathalie didn't know the truth? If so, that would explain why Clotilde Renouf believed she had leverage over Hélène—enough to secure the chocolaterie herself.

If Hélène had kept Nathalie's paternity a secret for all these years—even from Nathalie herself—she wouldn't want it revealed now. Secrets seemed to abound in Saint-Malo. Had Hélène known about Philippe's supposed affair with Madame Renouf, too?

Had Hélène killed her husband because of it?

If she had, then it had obviously driven her to drink. Hélène still seemed smashed and distraught even in the secluded room Fabrice Poyet had brought her to, hoping to calm her down.

Nathalie introduced me to her fiancé. The youngest Poyet was earnest and blond, wearing a suit as nice as Travis's. I understood fine tailoring. I understood wealth, too. Fabrice Poyet enjoyed the benefits of both, but he seemed more concerned with making sure that Hélène was looked after. That was sweet.

After our introductions, Fabrice shot me a cautious look. He took Nathalie's arm and nudged her to a more private spot.

In French, I heard him explain to Nathalie that her mother had told him that things were missing in the château—that everything was inexplicably changed in her home. With a compassionate glance toward Hélène, he added that Hélène was upset that she couldn't find things where she expected them to be—which explained the iron candelabra incident earlier.

While I tried not to eavesdrop *too* noticeably, Fabrice theorized quietly that his future *belle-mère* imagined herself in another, happier time—a time before she'd lost her husband?

Nathalie agreed, in French, that it was possible. I translated her explanation—something to do with when Hélène had first married Philippe and taken over the role of *châtelaine*. She'd apparently rearranged the château's furniture and decorations extensively at that time. Some old things had gone down and new things had gone up—things more suited to Hélène's style. It was possible now, Nathalie said, that her *maman* couldn't distinguish between those two periods at the château.

At least that was the gist of it, I thought, given my imperfect French. I couldn't help thinking that, aside from grief, Hélène's drinking must play a role in her forgetfulness. I wasn't sure if Nathalie's mother had been sober once since I'd arrived there. Now her condition seemed worse.

Because of guilt? Or because she'd heard about Clotilde Renouf's threat to reveal the Vetault family's secrets?

"*Bonsoir*, Madame Vetault." I approached Hélène with my kindest smile. "*Vous voulez quelque chose à manger, peut-être?*"

Offering her a bite to eat was the least I could do. Maybe it would help Hélène sober up, I imagined. Plus, I'm a chocolate professional. When push comes to shove, my thoughts run toward the healing powers of brownies and double chocolate cupcakes.

"*Non, merci.*" My mentor's widow waved away my offer. Her gaze remained trained on her daughter and future *beau fils*.

If you're translating in your head, you've probably already picked up on the French practice wherein your mother-in-law is (literally) referred to as your "beautiful mother," and your son-in-law as your "handsome son." It was a charming and sweet tradition, but that didn't explain Hélène's dour look at Fabrice.

Maybe she didn't enjoy being the subject of discussion. I wouldn't have, especially not if I'd just stabbed my husband.

I couldn't stop assuming Hélène was guilty. Thanks to the trying events of the past few days, I seemed to have the attention span of a gnat. Whoever was directly in my line of sight, it seemed, appeared to be the guiltiest possible suspect.

Earlier, it had been Clotilde. Now, Hélène. Next . . . ?

Jeannette Farges, the housekeeper, stepped into view.

She entered the room from its opposite end and strode inside. In most old French châteaux, the rooms aren't arranged around a central hallway. Instead, they flow from one to the next, with each room having two passageways in and out. That explained how Jeannette happened to enter just then with a silver tray held under her arm, dressed in a classic black maid's uniform with crisp ivory cuffs, collar, and apron.

If this had been a game of *Clue*, I mused, the housekeeper would definitely be the one whodunit— possibly after having conducted a clandestine affair with the man of the château. I half expected Hélène to pounce on her rival and accuse Jeannette of spending her days *un*making beds and rumpling pillows with Philippe. But Hélène didn't seem to notice Jeannette's arrival.

No one did, except me. The housekeeper quickly recognized her intrusion. Looking alarmed, she back-tracked and disappeared from sight. I would have expected nothing less than discretion.

Especially if she were guilty of murder, I thought.

But maybe I was getting carried away. After all, I'd just proven my own point about my changeable "top" suspects. I was still far from an expert sleuth, and I was officially intruding on a sensitive family moment myself, if Hélène's reaction to my offer of a (sobering) predinner snack was anything to go by.

I made my apologies to the *châtelaine*, then nodded a farewell to Nathalie and Fabrice, still in the midst of their murmured conversation about Hélène. I didn't blame them for being concerned. The whole situation was troubling. At least they had each other to rely on, though. With a bolstering sip of my aperitif, I went to look for my own confidant: Travis.

It was time to finish questioning my financial advisor—this time, over a scrumptious multicourse French dinner for two.

If I needed any evidence that my skills at snooping were still under development, I got it that night from Travis.

I approached our dinner together with two goals. The first was to find out as much as I possibly could about my überprivate financial advisor. The second was to savor a meal served in sumptuous château surroundings. Let's just say, the second goal was easily taken care of. The first was more problematic.

Everything started off wonderfully, beginning with two flavorful *amuses-bouche* (creative, bite-size appetizers handcrafted by the chef) and followed by *entrees* (first courses) and *plats principals* (main dishes), each more delicious than the last and each paired with exemplary wines. The (even more lavish) dessert cart returned (Travis and I nearly applauded), followed by the cheese course, after-dinner *cafés*, and a final sweet: small Breton butter cookies, rich and delicate.

"Until these arrived, I was sure I couldn't eat another bite," I confessed to Travis with a grin. I nibbled off a bit more cookie. Yum. "But somehow, I'm managing, all the same."

"It's been amazing, hasn't it?" My keeper glanced around the château's dining room. Its patrons were well mannered; its ambiance, luxurious. The luminous chandeliers, tablecloth-covered tables, shining cutlery, and views of the gently lighted grounds outside were spectacular. "I've really enjoyed it."

"You've enjoyed dodging all my questions," I accused with a good-natured scowl. Our meal had taken a couple of hours. All those wine pairings were starting to add up. "Admit it: you're ducking me on purpose, aren't you? You like being mysterious."

Travis's grin suggested he did. "I'm not so mysterious."

"You are, though!" I blurted. With an apologetic glance to our fellow diners, I lowered my voice. "I'm trying my hardest, and all I've extracted from you so far are the barest details about yourself." I started recapping. "You grew up in Seattle—"

"A rare Pacific Northwest native," he agreed in a

rumbling undertone. "There aren't very many of those these days."

"You went to Harvard because you thought it was the best school, although how you afforded the tuition is beyond me."

"Let's call it . . . a grant," Travis suggested in a low voice.

See? *That* was mysterious. I decided not to pursue the details in favor of making sure I had my facts straight so far.

"You graduated with honors, took the first job you were offered, with—" Before I could name his firm, he interrupted.

"It's not all that fascinating. Let's talk about you."

"Oh no you don't." I was wise to his tricks. Danny had taught me this one. "You're not distracting me that way."

Travis widened his eyes. "I'm interested in you."

"Then check your dossier. I know you have one." I declined the *serveur*'s unobtrusive offer of another *café*. I grinned and went on summarizing. "Let's see— you live downtown, alone—"

"Except for Bella, of course."

"You work insane hours, number crunching night and day—"

"I like my work. I enjoy a challenge." Travis's meaningful look suggested he enjoyed the challenge of *me.* So did his arched eyebrow. He really was *so* handsome. Or maybe I was tipsy?

Moving on. "You aren't in a relationship right now—"

He held up his hand. Like the rest of him, it was strong, masculine, and squeaky clean. "Stop. If I'd known you were planning on putting me under a microscope, I would have—"

"Worn a different suit? I dunno, that one's nice."

I knew perfectly well what he meant, though. The thing about it was, I like sharing. I like making connections. I wanted to connect with Travis. I wanted to finally *know* him.

He smiled at me. "You look nice, too. Very nice."

No no no. I wasn't angling for flattery—only remarking that Travis typically looked ready to broker a high-end deal at any moment. Danny, on the other hand, usually looked ready to start a fight. My bodyguard's wardrobe of low-slung jeans, vintage T-shirts, and tough motorcycle boots was a good match for mine.

But what was the use comparing them? They were as different as night and day—one edgy and one steady. That was good. As much as I like chocolate soufflé, for instance, sometimes it's more trouble than it's worth. Sometimes a chocolate microwave cupcake for one is just my speed. It's fast, but tasty.

I tried another approach. "Did you volunteer to work on my account, after old Mr. Whatshisname retired?" I leaned forward, genuinely wanting to know. "Or was I assigned to you?"

Travis looked surprised. Then, "How do you know I didn't force out old Mr. Whatshisname? Induce him to retire early, just so I could wrest control of your lucrative account for myself?"

I laughed. "You're about as sneaky as a puppy, that's how."

He shrugged. "You said yourself that you don't know me very well," he reminded me. I had, just before I'd commenced grilling him for particulars. "You don't know what I'm capable of."

All of Danny's earlier warnings about my keeper and his motivations for being there in Brittany came roaring back.

I pushed them aside. "I trust my instincts. That's enough." I let drop an intentional pause. "It is for now, at least."

"So what you're saying is, you're not giving up."

"On finding out everything about you? No way."

Travis's contemplative gaze lingered on me. In the soft light and in those surroundings, he almost seemed entranced.

With me? With us? It seemed admittedly doubtful, yet . . .

Hadn't he just insisted I didn't *really* know him? For all I knew, Travis had purposely traveled to Brittany to wine me, dine me, and finally make our relationship *completely* personal.

That actually didn't sound half bad. I was partway through a wine-and-cookies-fueled reverie involving him, me, and Bella romping along Puget Sound together when his phone vibrated.

Travis apologized and glanced at it. He gave a slight frown. "It's Mélanie Flamant. I'd better get this." He got up.

Pop. There went my fantasy. I should have known better than to get carried away, especially on the heels of a deluxe dinner. I'm very susceptible to the evocative power of food. Put me across a candlelit table from a handsome man and feed us both chocolate tarts and indescribable tiered cakes, and I'm in love.

I waved away Travis and signaled for the check. With the utmost subtlety, the *serveur* brought it, then withdrew. Like everything at château Vetault, there was a prescribed ritual at work. I knew my role, thanks to years of globe-trotting—thanks to years of learning how to adapt, how to fit in, how to excel.

Just then, I had a yen to excel at making some chocolate. I signed for our meal, slipped out of the dining room while Travis took his call, and headed outside the French doors to Monsieur's barn-atelier. If there was one thing that would clear my head, it was creating something complicated, chocolaty, and delicious.

Partway up the path, all the outdoor lighting went kaput.

I was plunged into darkness, unrelieved even by the moon. Caught off guard, I stumbled. I reached out to balance myself.

I felt prickly trimmed hedges. Damp leaves. Sharp sticks.

A man's hand grabbed my arm. *Hard.* Hubert's? Who else would be able to control the landscape lighting this way, on demand?

Who else liked stabbing people in the dark? *Yikes.*

My heart shot to my throat. I yanked, got free, and ran.

Twelve

When I came down for breakfast the next morning—shaken but safe—I almost bumped into Lucas Lefebvre. The Parisian pop star was dressed for filming in what appeared to be a toughened-up version of a pirate's outfit, complete with a sword buckled at his hip. When Lucas saw me, he offered up another cheeky mamba.

Paired with the smile he flashed, it was pretty cute, honestly. In a goofy way. I returned his smile and tried out some frisky French. It was tricky, given that I hadn't had any coffee yet to jump-start my brain, but Lucas seemed to like it.

Unfortunately, Capucine called him away for filming a moment later, so our budding flirtation couldn't progress. Sigh.

Arriving beside me on the grand staircase, Travis scoffed. He'd obviously witnessed the whole exchange. "It's funny, isn't it?" he asked. "The things good-looking men can get away with?"

Ha. "That's rich, coming from you."

His expression looked angelic. "Meaning what?"

"Meaning . . ." Nope. My financial advisor didn't

need me telling him how handsome he was. He
probably heard that all the time. "What did *policière*
Flamant want on the phone last night?"

For once, I successfully diverted him. "To tell me to
tell you to stay away from the police station." Travis
pinned me with a critical look. "You didn't tell me you
went back there."

Busted. I could tell he didn't approve, unlike
Danny. My sometime bodyguard had practically high-
fived me through the phone line this morning when
I'd called to brief him.

Given the time difference, collaborating had been
tricky. My midnight was his late afternoon; my morning, his midnight.

I lifted my chin and hustled toward the croissants
and *pains au chocolat* that awaited me and Travis. "I was
planning to tell you I went to the police station." *But
interrogating you about yourself took precedence.* "But I got
sidetracked."

"I'm familiar with that." Travis aimed another
wary glance at Lucas, then refocused on me. "This is
where my friendship with Mélanie comes in handy, by
the way. Otherwise, *Madame l'agent* would be here at the
château, warning you officially."

No, thanks. That sounded scary. My few run-ins
with law enforcement while sleuthing hadn't gone
particularly well.

"Thank you for your useful flirtation." I took a seat
at the table we were shown to, then chose an apple
pastry.

My keeper sat across from me. He unfolded his
napkin. Precisely. "The *policier* who helped you has
been disciplined."

Oops. Now I felt bad. But you couldn't make an

omelet without breaking some eggs, right? "Mildly, I hope?"

A pause. Travis was making me squirm. "Yes."

The silence between us felt leaden, lightened only with sips of *café au lait* and (my) ravenous bites of apple pastry.

"Ugh. If you're going to disapprove of my tactics, do it openly, okay?" I blurted. "I can't stand the silent treatment."

There ought to be a special circle of chocolate-free hell, I figured, for people who dealt with arguments by *not* talking.

Caught in the midst of choosing a croissant, Travis paused to give me a meaningful look. "If you feel guilty, that's not my problem. It's not up to me to assuage your conscience." He selected a buttery, flaky croissant and transferred it to his plate. "I simply want you to keep me informed of your actions."

"I changed my mind. Let's revisit the silent treatment."

His level gaze met mine. "If that sounded too harsh, I apologize. I'm not awake yet. I'm not a morning person, okay?"

I gawked. How could this be? "But you're up at dawn."

"That doesn't mean I like it." Grumpily, my financial advisor spread berry jam on his croissant. He bit into it.

I recognized the strawberry logo of Clotilde Renouf's *magasin de confiture* on the jam jar. I would have expected the Vetaults to demolish every jar they had on hand, in protest.

"Also, I'm not comfortable with ethical lapses," Travis told me. "I realize that, in this situation, there's a greater good to consider. But that doesn't mean some things aren't off limits—or should be. We have to consider all the implications."

Aha. I got it. My questionable tactics with the *gendarme* had reminded him of his own—and the potential costs of both.

"*You* feel guilty about Mélanie Flamant."

Travis focused intently on his breakfast. Then, "Maybe."

I felt instantly better. "We're not so different, you and me. We'd both rather not be doing this, but since we are—"

"We want to do a good job," my financial advisor finished.

I nodded. "Yes." I'd never had this conversation with Danny. My longtime pal didn't like discussing ethics or the consequences of our decisions. As far as Danny was concerned, surviving trumped all. "We're *doing* a good job! For instance . . ."

I filled in Travis on what I'd learned, winding up with, "The business card in Monsieur's hand was from a place called Antiquités Moreau. I'm planning to visit it later this morning."

He frowned. "That's where I was yesterday, before I saw you collapse in front of the jam shop." Belatedly, he noticed the jam label. For a moment, he examined it in thought. Then, "Charlotte Moreau is the head of the local small business club."

"Then she's the kingpin! Madame Moreau must be the one who officially vetoed Philippe's plans for his *Fest-Noz* banner."

"I didn't find out that much." Travis ate more croissant.

Oddly enough, as he did, he turned inexplicably red in the face. A flush blossomed on his sculpted cheeks, then swept lower. If I could have seen through

his shirt and tie with X-ray vision, I figured I would see
him turning red all the way down.

For a heartbeat, I thought maybe my financial advisor had been poisoned—maybe the way I (maybe)
had been. I seriously considered swatting away the rest
of his breakfast, like an NFL defensive end executing
a perfect strip sack on a quarterback.

Have I mentioned the (only) sport I enjoy is foot-
ball? I'm conversant in soccer, basketball, baseball, and
rugby (all the better to make friends in the back-of-
house at a restaurant, bakery, or chocolate-processing
factory), but the NFL is *fun*.

Back to Travis. "You didn't find out if Charlotte
Moreau prohibited Monsieur's banner? What did you
find out, then?"

He cleared his throat. "Not much. More juice?"

He was acting peculiarly. "What did you find out,
Travis?"

My suit-wearing financial advisor adjusted his eye-
glasses. I'd already guessed that was his "tell." Now
he'd confirmed it.

"You're hiding something," I surmised. "What is it?"

"Nothing big." He looked straight at me—like a
man headed to the gallows. "I offered your services as
a guest speaker at the next small business club meeting. It's tomorrow at ten A.M."

Aha. I got it. "You knew I wouldn't like this,
didn't you?"

"Our interactions so far would suggest as much,
yes."

"Yet you did it anyway." I shook my head, exasperated. "I don't speak, I *do*," I reminded him. "That's my
thing! I troubleshoot chocolates—I don't talk about
them." I was already stretched thin, trying to comfort
Monsieur's family, track down his killer, and make

chocolates on the side. Plus, find out all there was to know about Travis. I shot him a stern look. "You were supposed to be scouting Saint-Malo for your company's international clients, remember? You had a cover story."

"My skills don't lie in the area of subterfuge."

"No kidding," I said drily. I glanced outside— watching the video crew setting up shots with Lucas at Capucine's direction—trying to maintain my exasperated front. But I couldn't keep it up. I looked at Travis. "That's okay. Honestly? Neither do mine."

We traded a smile. Inexplicably, it was happening. We were bonding. Over a shared fault (sort of), but still. Yay, us.

"We'll just have to keep going," I added, pulling my trusty Moleskine notebook out of my crossbody bag. I flipped it open to my notes on Philippe's murder. "We're doing the best we can."

"At least you got some pertinent information from that Antiquités Moreau business card," Travis pointed out. "Bravo."

"Yeah, about that—" Reminded of that bloodspattered proof of Monsieur's untimely death, I shuddered. "I've been thinking about it. Charlotte Moreau runs a local antiques shop, right?"

Travis nodded. We both knew *antiquités* were antiques. "Her shop has been open in that spot for that past fifteen years," he confirmed. "But her background is clean. I checked last night."

It was good to have him—and his ace research skills—on the job. I inhaled, mulling things over. "Then maybe Charlotte Moreau isn't a suspect," I surmised. "Maybe she's a clue."

My financial advisor gave me a puzzled frown. "How so?"

"Well, if Antiquités Moreau has been operating in Saint-Malo for fifteen years, then Philippe wouldn't have needed a business card from Charlotte Moreau to remind him of that."

I chose another pastry from the napkin-covered breadbasket that accompanied the jam, Breton butter, coffee, juice, fruit, and yogurt on our table's lavish spread. We would never eat all of it, but I meant to try. A girl needed brain food, right?

"But he *might* have needed a business card to remind him of something else," I went on. "Something like . . . an appointment?"

I brushed away crumbles of laminated pastry from my notebook, then showed the page to Travis. I pointed at it.

"See here? Look at the numbers, handwritten right there."

I'd sketched the business card in my notebook, striving to make the image authentic, even with the constraints I'd had.

Travis squinted, then shook his head. "Sorry. That looks like chicken scratch to me." He looked up, his face uncertain. "You're sure those were numbers? They could be almost anything."

"Are you kidding me?" I hadn't spent all that time working with my mentor without learning his handwriting. Being able to decipher the difference between 40 grams of Swiss chocolate and 400 grams of Swiss chocolate was the difference between success and failure. I pointed again. "Right here. I copied it exactly."

I'd even copied those small blood droplets, noting their size and position in case it was important. But I didn't want to dwell on those. Instead, I turned my notebook toward Travis.

"If that logo is reflective of your drawing skills, then

we're in trouble," he mused. "I've seen Madame Moreau's antiques-store logo. It looks like an old-fashioned woodcut. But *this*—"

"Forget the logo, Renoir!" I didn't need an art critique, not even from him. "It's the numbers that matter." I pointed at them with my pencil to clarify. "See? 10.09 and 15:30."

"Appointment times?" Travis guessed. "But what day? And why? Philippe was a chocolatier, not a collector—at least not as far as we know. Was he interested in buying art? Collectibles?"

"Not buying," I'd decided. "*Selling*. Selling something on the tenth of September at three-thirty in the afternoon. That's not two appointment times, it's one European-style date and time, written side by side. See the punctuation? That's got to be it. Philippe might have known all his neighbors, but he was terrible at remembering appointments—truly the worst, in fact."

Travis looked impressed. "I see it. That makes sense."

"It does, because I think Monsieur was getting ready to move on." Saying so aloud made me feel horribly wistful. I wished I'd had more time with my mentor. "I think Philippe knew his marriage to Hélène was over. With Nathalie getting married and La Maison des Petits Bonheurs passing into Poyet's hands, he had no reason to stay in Saint-Malo. His legacy was over."

"Or solidified. You could think of it that way." Travis drank more coffee, becoming visibly more alert. "Poyet is a major player. Scoring a deal with them would be a coup for any company, especially one the size of Philippe's." He looked thoughtful—probably mulling over the details. "Your mentor had reached the finish line of his profession. He'd won."

"Or he'd given up." I felt morose at the thought. It had to be contemplated, though. All possible scenarios did. "Monsieur was handing his third-generation, family-owned chocolaterie to his biggest rival. That has to hurt, doesn't it?"

"Not if you're getting a big enough paycheck in return."

Hmm. Maybe Travis *was* as cynical as Danny—if the arena was right. I couldn't accept his reasoning, though. "If it was such a big paycheck, then why sell anything to Antiquités Moreau?"

"We don't know that's what he was doing." At my mention of the antiques store, Travis's face turned a shade pinker. He went on. "Clotilde Renouf already maintains that your mentor was having a long-term extramarital affair with her mother, right?"

"Ugh! Please say 'fling,' okay? It sounds less awful."

"So you have to wonder . . ." Travis gave me a cautionary look—one that said I wouldn't like what was coming next. "What if Madame Renouf wasn't the only one?"

"You mean, what if the elder Madame Renouf wasn't Monsieur's only affair? Come on, Travis. No way. I can't believe it."

"You mean you *won't* believe it."

There wasn't much difference, as far as I was concerned. If I could keep Philippe Vetault's memory safe in my mind, I would.

"Look," I said, "when I trust someone, it's forever."

"No matter who might disagree with you? Or why?"

"No matter what. Not unless I have *proof* of wrongdoing." I had to be honest. "Maybe not even then. I'm kind of stubborn."

But mine was the *good* kind of stubborn, in my

opinion. The kind that keeps you trying, even when things look hopeless.

I stared out at the manicured *jardin*, lost in thought. At that moment, not even the *pains au chocolat* looked good to me.

When I finally glanced back at Travis, he nodded. "I get it now. Your loyalty explains a lot about you and Danny."

I guessed it did. "Good." I sat up straighter. "Maybe now you two can stop being at each other's throats all the time."

Travis looked doubtful. "I'm not sure the enforcer and I will ever see eye to eye about anything, including you."

Right. That was the part I found so difficult about their ongoing antagonism. I liked both of them. I probably always would. I wasn't wild about having so much discord in my life.

On the other hand, I wasn't crazy about being mixed up in murders, either. Yet here I was. So, on with the show, right?

"You're suggesting that Monsieur had an affair with someone else?" I wrinkled my nose. "That his 'appointment' with Charlotte Moreau wasn't really a buy-and-sell occasion?"

"More of a 'get down and dirty' occasion," my financial advisor agreed with a nod. "Madame Moreau is an attractive woman."

I considered it. Then, "Nope. I don't believe Monsieur had one affair, much less two. He was a chocolatier, not a playboy!" I sighed. "It seems much likelier to me that Philippe had official business at Antiquités Moreau—something so important that he wrote it down to make sure he wouldn't forget."

"It had to be buying," Travis mused. "Given the big

payday that was coming his way from the Poyet merger, he wouldn't have needed to sell anything. Your mentor wasn't exactly reduced to pawning his possessions to get by—although he could have, given the valuables the Vetaults have used to decorate their château."

I didn't want to discuss decorating. "How much did Monsieur stand to gain from the merger? I wouldn't have been surprised if he took less than he deserved, just to make sure the deal went forward, especially if he knew that's what Nathalie wanted."

"That's not a sensible way to run a business," Travis maintained. "If Nathalie had that much interest in La Maison des Petits Bonheurs, she should have taken over the chocolaterie herself, instead of coercing her father into a subpar deal."

"It wouldn't have been coercing *or* Nathalie's doing," I disagreed. "It would have been Philippe's. He was generous that way. Besides, running a chocolate business isn't like running a laundromat or a grocery store. To properly make chocolate, you have to have a passion for it. You have to be willing to sacrifice. You have to be called to it, in a way." I shook my head, remembering that long summer I'd trained *en formation* with my mentor. "Nathalie isn't passionate about chocolate making. But that doesn't mean she wanted to lose the family business."

"So Nathalie purposely got together with Fabrice Poyet, just to make sure her family's chocolaterie was in good hands?" Travis sounded unconvinced. "That's a stretch. Even if Nathalie could have been sure Philippe would agree to a merger with Poyet, Fabrice *and* his board would have had to agree to it."

I knew Travis had researched my mentor's more

prestigious rival. I knew he'd made several valid points, too. And yet . . .

"I'm not suggesting some sort of scenario where Nathalie seduces Fabrice to make him invest in La Maison des Petits Bonheurs." I made a face, hoping to convey exactly how abhorrent that sounded. "But what if they really *are* the Romeo and Juliet of French chocolate? What if Philippe saw how good they were together and seized his chance to cement his legacy? He must have known that Nathalie has no personal interest in chocolate." I reminded Travis of her demanding PR job in Paris. "But Monsieur was in favor of Nathalie and Fabrice's wedding. He helped them dig out *Grand-mère's* wedding dress from the attic!"

I pictured my mentor in the château's dusty *grenier* (attic), triumphantly pulling a lacy white gown from a trunk and then tenderly handing it to his daughter. It was a lovely idea.

Travis shattered it. "The merger wasn't an altruistic gesture. It wasn't a wedding gift, either." He steepled his hands and rested his chin on his fingertips in thought. "Your mentor needed that merger. His margins were razor thin."

"You just said he didn't need to pawn things to get by."

"Surviving isn't the same as flourishing. Even if Philippe had had the château's B&B income to rely on—which is slightly more tenuous, right now, than the chocolaterie's is, by the way—Philippe would still have been smart to merge with Poyet."

"Wait." I must have misheard him. "Did you just say that the château—the B&B portion of the château— is struggling?"

"Not struggling per se," Travis clarified. "But the hospitality business has fine margins, too. It's high risk and easily impacted by economic downturns and currency fluctuations that affect occupancy rates, especially in Europe."

I frowned. "Why didn't you say so before?"

"Because the château doesn't belong to Philippe," Travis explained dispassionately. "It belongs to Hélène and Hubert."

"*What?*" When I'd asked my financial advisor to run his usual check on everyone involved, I hadn't expected to learn anything new about Philippe. But I just had. "Since when?"

Travis drank more coffee, considering it. "A year ago, more or less. Although Hubert Bernard has worked there much longer."

I glanced around the château's beautiful dining room, seeing it—and the château beyond—with new eyes. Then I regarded my financial advisor. "Let me get this straight. Are you saying that Philippe allowed his wife and her lover to run this place?"

"To run it and own it. I'm sorry, Hayden, but it's true."

"I don't doubt it. I told you Monsieur was generous!"

My keeper looked at me as if I were crazy. "This goes beyond 'generous,'" he argued. "It's financially irresponsible."

"It's generous," I insisted. "Don't you see? This is perfectly in keeping with Monsieur's character. He was always giving. It makes sense he'd want Hélène to be happy." I thought of her distress over losing him. "It's obvious they had a strong connection, whatever their other problems might have been."

Travis frowned at me. "That's not rational."

"Love never is."

He seemed puzzled. "And you believe this . . . why?"

For a second, I was tempted to confide in him about

my three ex-fiancés and the stories behind them. But then I remembered that my financial advisor had access to much of my personal information. He had to know about that, too, didn't he?

"This just strengthens my theory that Monsieur was moving on," I told him instead. "Sometimes in life, you reach a crossroads, right? This was my mentor's. He knew his marriage was over—"

"It must have been over for quite some time."

"And with Nathalie's future secured with Fabrice and her life in Paris, Philippe had no reason to stay in Saint-Malo."

Travis appeared intent. "Is that what he told you?"

"No," I admitted. My heart lurched. There was a lot Monsieur hadn't told me about. "But we didn't have much time together. Only an afternoon, mostly spent with chocolate."

Travis's expression gentled. "Try to view this objectively. *You* might give away an entire château to your estranged spouse someday, but you're famously profligate with your money."

That's what Danny always said. I frowned. "Why not? I can afford to share." And I did. "I don't see you turning down the deluxe accommodations and fancy meals we've been enjoying."

"It's my job to be with you. For the moment, at least." Travis adjusted his glasses, then got back to the subject at hand. "That doesn't mean Philippe Vetault would do the same thing, purely out of the kindness of his heart." He lowered his deep, rumbly voice. "Someone *did* want to kill him, remember?"

I remembered that all too well. "All right, then maybe someone forced Philippe to sign away the château—maybe using the same leverage about Nathalie's parentage as Madame Renouf." All signs pointed to Hubert Bernard or Hélène, in that case. "Even so, that's all the more reason for Monsieur to leave town. He wouldn't have wanted to stay here, all brokenhearted."

"You're not giving up on this theory, are you?"

"Would you believe me if I said I was?"

This time, Travis almost laughed. "I can see why your muscle-bound pal finds you so tough to deal with sometimes."

"Because I'm stubborn? Hey, I have to be."

"No, because you're determined to view everything through a lens of emotion. But feelings are unreliable. Logic isn't."

I pooh-poohed. "Emotion is a better motive for murder," I told Travis. "Sooner or later, I'm going to prove it to you."

I folded my linen napkin and got ready to leave. We'd already lingered too long over breakfast. I had things to do—starting with paying an exploratory visit to Antiquités Moreau.

"Well, while you're doing that," Travis said as he, too, prepared to leave the dining room, "try to avoid taking advantage of the local *gendarmes'* gullibility, all right?"

I gave him a smart-alecky look. "I will if you will."

"Very funny. I'm not taking advantage of Mélanie."

"Hey, if you feel guilty, that's not my problem," I joked, echoing his earlier comment. "Just keep me informed, okay?"

Travis returned my smile. "I will if you will."

We parted ways at the dining room doorway—me, to finagle a trip to Charlotte Moreau's antiques shop, and him, to do further research on Fabrice Poyet and (at my request) the housekeeper, Jeannette Farges. I felt paranoid asking Travis to perform a background check on her—but less so as I spied her hurrying past the château's rear windows. Intrigued, I slipped outside.

Feeling slightly ridiculous for employing stealth against a professional housekeeper, I tracked Jeannette across the terrace. I sneaked behind a topiary and watched her light a cigarette while (obviously) on a break—*une pause,* to the French.

That's what Jeannette had been in a hurry to do. Smoke.

I was about to admit (temporary) defeat and grab my Citroën for the drive to town when, across the grounds, Lucas Lefebvre's music kicked in on the video crew's loudspeakers. I lingered to listen and maybe watch some sexy couture-pirate action, too.

An instant later, the drone camera buzzed Jeannette.

The poor housekeeper shrieked and fled, looking positively terrified. I frowned as I watched her go. Either her reaction to the drone camera was extreme, or Jeannette was anxious for another reason altogether. My money was on the latter option.

I'd already been buzzed by the drone cam. It had been startling, not petrifying. If I was right, there was more than met the eye here, with Jeannette. But before I figured out how to get to the bottom of it, I would have to figure out how to gracefully leave my hiding place. Someone had just come outside.

I peeked around the sculpted topiary. Fabrice Poyet had just stepped onto the château terrace for what I would bet was the same reason Jeannette had: to sneak a forbidden cigarette.

I didn't want to be seen slinking around from behind a topiary, but I didn't have time to dawdle. That left your favorite expert in *chocolat, Schokolade, cicolata,* and *chokora* (yep, those are all names for chocolate) only one choice.

That's right. I stepped out from behind the bushes, tossed my hair, then gave Fabrice a jaunty wave. "*Salut!*" I called.

"*Salut,*" he returned courteously, unfazed. *Hello!*

Then he resumed his forbidden smoking (I presumed), and I got on my way. Masterfully, too, I had to say. You couldn't keep a good chocolate whisperer down—not even behind some topiaries.

Thirteen

I'd arranged to meet Nathalie in Saint-Malo's *centre-ville* that morning. It only required a minor (chocolaty) bribe to convince Capucine Roux, Lucas's indie video director, to postpone filming and join us for a while to hunt set dressings—especially since, as it turned out, she and Nathalie knew one another. Their acquaintance had led to Capucine's booking château Vetault and its surroundings for Lucas's video filming.

It was a small world in Brittany. Thanks to Lucas, it even included real-life (sexy) *corsairs*, too. The two of us shared another friendly bilingual encounter after I left Travis.

French pop stars aside, though, my get-together with Nathalie and Capucine almost felt to me like a genuine morning out with girlfriends. While exploring the town with them, I could almost forget my real mission: finding out who might have wanted my mentor dead, especially in such a gruesome fashion.

In the meantime, though, there were shops to browse and shoes to try on, home furnishings to peruse and souvenirs to consider. I bought something nice to bring home to Danny; my two friends both accumulated shopping bags with a vengeance.

You would have thought that all that activity would have kept us toasty warm, but instead, I spent much of the morning freezing. My light jacket wasn't sufficient for the brisk autumn temperatures at the seaside. I shivered in one shop after another, most of which seemed only marginally heated beyond the natural insulation offered by their ancient stone walls.

Unsurprisingly enough, Nathalie and Capucine tried to help me with my "problem," but I balked. Too much shopping—at least for myself—isn't my thing. I never pack more than my wheelie bag and a duffel, remember? It's impossible to grid-skip with a lot of unnecessary clothing. Ordinarily, I dealt with fluctuating weather by layering, but that morning I'd been too distracted by Jeannette Farges' skittish behavior to grab my pashmina.

I still wondered what had the housekeeper so on edge. She didn't seem like the murderous type, but I could (now) name a few people who'd struck me the same way and had proven me wrong.

"Here, Hayden." Capucine handed me something. "Try this."

I looked at what she'd offered. A knit cap in creamy white.

"It will go well with your coloring," Capucine urged, looking just as chic as usual in her own outfit. "Go ahead."

With that recommendation, there was no way I'd say no. Offered a chance to hijack some of Capucine's French coolness, I'd have been a fool to refuse. I pulled on the hat and posed.

"*Parfait!*" Capucine decreed. "It suits you. You must

buy it, *non*? Otherwise, you will make us feel bad for spending."

At her side, Nathalie nodded. She lifted her own packed-full shopping bags. "Capucine has the excuse of getting things for set dressing, but this is retail therapy for me," she said in French-accented English. "Maybe for you, too, Hayden?"

At that reminder of missing Monsieur, I relented. I wound up much snugger, too, thanks to my knit hat. I was impatient to get to Antiquités Moreau and question Charlotte Moreau, but my two friends wanted to treat themselves first. We found a local café and sat on its terrace under a burgundy-colored awning, sipping *chocolat chaud* (hot chocolate) with soft *crème Chantilly* (sweet whipped cream) and shavings of rapidly melting chocolate.

"*Sublime!*" Capucine licked whipped cream from her lips and gave a contented sigh. "With my job, I almost never have time to spend with *mes copines*—my girlfriends. I am having such fun!"

Nathalie looked a little hollow-eyed, but she agreed. She reached over to squeeze my hand. Worryingly, she hadn't touched her own hot chocolate or the butter cookie served with it.

"*Moi, non plus*," she said. Me, neither. "This is nice."

I wasn't so sure that Nathalie's idea to go shopping had been the best strategy, given her gloomy demeanor. But she'd perked up while in the boutiques and *magasins* (stores) we'd visited.

Maybe Nathalie just didn't enjoy chocolate? It seemed inconceivable to me. "Yes, it is. Thanks for coming with me, both of you." I smiled at them. "With my work, I don't see my friends very often." They were scattered all throughout the world, living mementos of the many places I'd lived, either with my globe-trotting parents or on my own. "I do my best to stay in

touch, but texting and phone calls just aren't the
same."

I hadn't fully realized that would be one of the
costs of accepting my inheritance from Uncle Ross.
By now, some of my longtime friends were getting
married. A few were even having children. Our lives
diverged more every year, yet my life was much the
same—full of chocolate, traveling, and (now) murder.

How much lonelier might I be, if this continued?

Uh-oh. Before my occasional longings for hearth
and home could assert themselves, I changed the subject. Capucine and Nathalie and I talked about work
and the challenges involved in it, about music and
films we liked, about men and our troubles understanding them. *That* was something I couldn't bend
Danny's ear about—or Travis's, either. My guys would
have probably been sympathetic to relationship woes
or dating horror stories, but I wasn't sure I wanted our
time together spent that way.

"It *is* difficult sometimes, *non?*" Nathalie stirred her
chocolat chaud, showing no signs of doing anything
except toy with it. "Fabrice, he is wonderful, of course.
But he does not know what it is to be a woman—what
it means to *feel* as a woman."

Capucine agreed. Our conversation swerved from
emotions to racier territory and then further. These
women would have had no trouble believing that
murders were emotionally based, I thought. But there
was no way I could broach the subject.

"But some beautiful lingerie usually solves the
problem," Capucine was saying with a sassy wink as I
tuned back in to our conversation. "If I feel nice wearing it, *he* will recognize that. Not that I wear such
things for a man, of course. *Non.*"

Nathalie and I rushed to agree. In France, pretty
underthings were available at all price points. Faced

with them, I sometimes had a hard time sticking to my no-shopping guns.

Self-consciously, I touched my new knit cap. Oh well. You needed an exception to prove the rule, right? I *felt* stylish. Surely that was worth finding extra room in my carry-on bags.

Anyway, it wasn't every day you got to shop with a riotously chic French woman to advise you, was it? But we needed to get on with things, I realized, if I intended to make it to Charlotte Moreau's local antiques shop before it closed.

I finished my hot chocolate, then turned to Capucine and Nathalie. "So, where can a girl get some antiques around here?"

"Everyplace," Nathalie said dismissively. "Take your pick."

"Spoken like a true Saint-Malo native," I joked. It would have been easy to become bored with all the touristy shops.

"Only *one* place that is any good," Capucine argued with authority. "Come with me. I will show you Antiquités Moreau."

Capucine was right. Antiquités Moreau was clearly the best stocked and most discerning shop in the *centre-ville*. Whereas other antiques stores existed, they'd seemed to me more like flea markets—places that sold items of unknown provenance for low prices. At Charlotte Moreau's shop, on the other hand, the quality of the wares was evident and the prices matched that.

"Oh, la la." With that dismayed utterance, Nathalie let go of the handwritten price tag she'd been examining on a vase. "At these prices, I think I would prefer shopping in Paris."

"*Non!* It is impossible to find pieces like these in Paris." Capucine already had her arms full of a lamp and a silk shawl. She studied a necklace on display in a glass case. "Madame Moreau has been very generous in lending me items for set dressing."

I wondered what kinds of sets needed antique lamps and shawls. "Doesn't Lucas's label provide things like that?"

"Our budget is extremely limited." Capucine pursed her lips. "That is why we could not return to the château at a better time. We have to use the time we have booked." Her gaze skittered to Nathalie. "Thanks to you, Nathalie. It is so kind."

They went on discussing the château. It was odd to hear them speak English to one another, but I knew they were doing so for my benefit. That consideration didn't last our entire time inside Antiquités Moreau, however. As soon as Charlotte Moreau emerged to consult with Capucine, all pretense of helping me communicate vanished in a torrent of rapid-fire *français.*

As it turned out, that was all right with me. Being (slightly) excluded from their French conversation let me observe the proprietress of the antiques shop in my own time, with no one the wiser. There was a lot to take in, too.

I instantly understood why mentioning Charlotte Moreau had made Travis blush. The antiques shop owner was a curvaceous brunette with a coquettish manner and the clothes to match. In her perfectly fitted feminine dress and stiletto heels, she was the personification of French va-va-voom. Beside her, I felt instantaneously underdressed. At best, I gave off a tomboyish vibe in my casual clothes and sneakers. No one would have called me seductive and made it believable—not even Danny, who had a talent for (or at least a history of) credible con artistry.

I'd have liked a few encouraging words from my buddy as I officially made Madame Moreau's acquaintance, but I had to make do with trading *les bises* with her. Charlotte's magnetism was undeniable. Still, as I watched her chatting with Nathalie and Capucine a few minutes later, I reminded myself that they were all contemporaries—each in their early thirties at the utmost.

It seemed unlikely that Charlotte would have had a wild affair with Monsieur—not when he was thirty years her senior.

I chalked up Travis's theory to his own attraction to the antiques shop owner. Probably, since he found Charlotte sexy and appealing (obviously, judging by his blushing), he couldn't conceive of anyone *not* feeling the same way, including my mentor.

I still didn't want to believe that Philippe had been a rampant philanderer, sowing his wild oats throughout the town. There had to be another explanation. Maybe Clotilde Renouf was simply inventing threats to gain the chocolaterie's real estate through force. Maybe she was repeating idle gossip. Either way, I remained unconvinced she'd been telling the truth about Monsieur or about Nathalie's parentage—although she *had* been unerringly correct about Hélène's affair with Hubert Bernard.

Thinking about the château's gardener reminded me of my frightening episode last night when the landscape lights had gone out. If he'd been faster—or I'd been slower—I might have been stabbed to death with a trowel by now. I hadn't told Travis about it. Or Danny, for that matter. I was okay. It was over.

Until the next time, my sense of self-preservation whispered, but I shut it up by transferring my attention to Charlotte Moreau. There was more to her than a beautiful face, a beautiful figure, a beautiful wardrobe, and a beautiful shop.

She had a beautiful French speaking voice, too.

Kidding. You had to laugh, right?

I reminded myself that Madame Moreau was a person first and foremost, with feelings and vulnerabilities just like mine. Nobody was perfect—not even (or maybe especially) when they seemed to be. Which only served to jog loose some questions: primarily, why had Charlotte nixed Monsieur's banner? What did she really feel about his sponsorship of the *Fest-Noz*? Was she the one who'd scrawled that ugly graffiti on his chocolaterie?

Traître. Had *she* stabbed Philippe in the back because she believed Monsieur Vetault had betrayed her? Or for another reason?

The next twenty minutes' conversation convinced me that she hadn't. For one thing, I doubted Madame Moreau would have risked spoiling her outfit by scrawling graffiti in the dark. For another, she was petite—probably five feet two or so—and much too slight to have stabbed Philippe, especially at the angle someone had. For another, she'd had everything to gain by my mentor staying alive and nothing to benefit from if he died.

"*Oui*, we had an appointment," Charlotte told me genially. I'd explained that I, as a friend of the Vetault family, was taking care of a few loose ends. "Monsieur Vetault asked me to look at some pieces from his family estate and determine their value."

I tried to appear as though this was old news to me. "Which pieces were those?" I asked. "Maybe the, uh, Caravaggio?"

The Italian Renaissance artist was the first who

came to mind, probably because I'd read an article on the train on the way to Saint-Malo. One of his works had recently been auctioned for more than a hundred million euros. Danny, ever the expert, had always told me that specificity sells. When you're trying to convince someone you know what you're talking about, you have to employ some pertinent details. Freewheeling wouldn't cut it.

In this case, I apparently oversold my insider status.

"Monsieur Vetault had a Caravaggio?" Madame Moreau gawked at me.

Quickly, I backpedaled. "It's so hard to keep track of all the artists, isn't it? I'll confess, I'm not an expert."

Fabrice Poyet was. Nathalie had confided earlier that along with being wealthy, successful, caring, multilingual, and punctual, her fiancé also had been educated at the prestigious Sorbonne in Paris. I was probably fortunate he wasn't there.

I didn't need anyone else eyeing me in the pitying way that Madame Moreau was doing just then. Feebly, I waved my hands.

"I'm simply, uh, trying to take care of some unfinished business for the family," I said. "Any information would help."

"Ah, *oui*. I see. Well, I am afraid I cannot tell you anything more. I was sadly unable to keep my appointment with Monsieur Vetault, so I do not know what he was interested in offering."

I kept pushing. "Do you have any guesses? As an expert?"

Danny had also mentioned that well-placed flattery was good. I'm afraid I don't have his easy amiability, though—at least not when I'm trying to wheedle information from someone.

"As an expert? *Non*." Charlotte gazed around her flawlessly curated shop and its myriad *objets d'art*. "As a friend? *Peut-être*." Maybe. She leaned nearer to me while Capucine and Nathalie browsed her wares an aisle away. "You must know that Monsieur Vetault was planning to leave Saint-Malo, *n'est-ce pas*?"

I'd been right. I wanted to offer a celebratory fist pump. I settled for a sage, composed nod. "Of course, but . . ."

Helpfully, I left that sentence unfinished, as a prompt.

Charlotte took my starter and ran with it. "But I don't believe he was planning to bring Madame Vetault along with him. *Vous comprenez, oui*?" You understand, yes? "Yet he did not want to leave so much of his family heritage at the château. Some, he wanted to take with him. Other items, he wished to sell. Monsieur Vetault believed he had one or two valuable pieces. He did not mention to me a Caravaggio, however. I am very interested."

Whoops. Like Travis, I was terrible at subterfuge. I already regretted my improvised "detail" about Monsieur's items for sale. For all I knew, all his artwork was paint-by-number.

Or whatever the old-time equivalent of it was.

For evasion's sake, I tried some misdirection. "Do many people in Saint-Malo have valuable things to sell?" I asked, trying to appear as though my day depended on hearing the answer. "Is that where most of your pieces come from? Locally?"

"Some are local. Others come from Paris, Amsterdam, Munich, and elsewhere," Madame Moreau told me cheerfully. "All over the world. I do keep a few pieces on hand for the tourists."

She indicated some colorful Breton Quimper pottery nearby, displayed on a prominent shelf. You'd probably recognize its stylized "*petite bretonne.*" She's often shown in profile, with her traditional headpiece and aproned dress. Made in Bretagne, Quimper pottery is known worldwide and has been for centuries.

"We are all fiercely proud of our *patrimoine*, of course. But that does not mean a few pieces cannot be sold here or there, to make ends meet. I offer fair prices to everyone."

I nodded. That sense of *patrimoine* (heritage) had most likely killed Monsieur. I didn't particularly want to hear any more about it.

But Charlotte Moreau didn't require my continued interest. She was off and running by then, telling me about ancient wars fought on Breton soil—and world wars fought there, too. She spun stories about soldiers with battle spoils, grandmothers with diamond jewelry squirreled away in cake tins, and relatives inheriting fortunes. To me, it all sounded like nonsense— modern fairy tales designed to separate customers from their money, especially since I had the feeling Madame Moreau had told these stories many times before. By the time she was finished, even Capucine and Nathalie had joined us. They listened raptly.

Danny would have been the same way, I had to admit. You might not expect it, but his guilty pleasure is *Antiques Roadshow.* He *loves* it, especially when times are tough and he wants to zone out for a while. I was pretty sure he kept a few episodes downloaded to his laptop at all times for emergencies.

But even Danny would have been skeptical of Madame Moreau's stories. To hear her talk, antiques were societal superglue.

"That is why it is so critical to honor our *patrimoine,*" Charlotte was saying. "Without our traditions—without the treasured items that go along with them—we are rootless as a people. If we allow everything to change, who will we be? Once lost, the memory of the past is gone forever, *n'est-ce pas?*"

Nathalie and Capucine nearly applauded at her rousing finish, making me realize that you apparently needed a few French genes to appreciate *patrimoine* and all its subtleties.

I felt far less impressed than that—especially once it occurred to me that I still didn't know what type of weapon had killed Monsieur. I'd been assuming a garden implement, given the descriptions I'd heard, but it could have been anything.

Even something like the old tools, kitchen implements, and gilt-edged, overpriced knickknacks found at Antiquités Moreau.

I gave Madame Moreau a suspicious look and got on with my next task: lining up my speaking engagement at the next day's small business club meeting. Travis hadn't left me with much time to prepare. While I'm an acknowledged expert in *il cioccolato,* I'm not a proficient public speaker. I wanted to know what types of things Charlotte's group might be interested in learning about.

Chocolate? Traveling? Entrepreneurship? Strictly speaking, I'm a small-business owner myself, so I figured I could come up with something useful. We confirmed that the meeting was scheduled for ten o'clock in the morning—how French, to close all the shops once per month for their meeting—and then Nathalie, Capucine, and I said our *au revoirs* to Charlotte.

Outside in the bustling cobblestone street, I tried to steer the three of us in the opposite direction from La Maison des Petits Bonheurs, hoping to avoid stirring up more memories for Nathalie. But instead, Philippe's daughter seemed to deliberately veer toward the chocolaterie. Her footsteps slowed as she neared the shop. I doubted it was a conscious decision.

As it turned out, I did the same thing. That's how we all came to be standing in the shadow of an old French church, next to some potted flowers, gazing wistfully at my mentor's shop.

The scene was almost *too* idyllic. Shoppers and seaside residents went about their business, exchanging greetings of *bonjour!* Merchants stocked their wares; more flowers bloomed at the sides of the stone buildings, climbing upward on vines.

I glimpsed burly Mathieu, his bald head crowned by a cook's head kerchief, hard at work inside the chocolaterie. If Philippe had been beside him working on a fondant or dipping chocolates, this would have seemed like any other weekday in Brittany.

Next door, the jam shop's door opened. I took a reflexive step back, wary of another confrontation with Clotilde Renouf. But it was Travis's favorite *policière*, Mélanie Flamant, who emerged, notebook in hand as she jotted down what I assumed were case notes. About Monsieur's murder or another crime?

I didn't know. But I *did* know I was irked that Mélanie had only just now decided to interview Madame Renouf. I'd gotten there a full day earlier, and I wasn't a professional police officer.

Her apparent laxity didn't exactly endear her to me. I wanted the full force of the law to come down on whoever had killed my mentor. I wanted an investigation that never slept.

Madame l'agent saw us and offered a curt wave. We

all returned it, me (possibly) with slightly less enthusiasm than my friends.

"Poor Mélanie," Nathalie said as we watched the uniformed gendarme walk away. "I feel quite sorry for her, to be honest."

I hadn't expected *that*. I frowned. "Why is that?"

Maybe because she's so slipshod about her work, I thought. But Philippe's daughter had a different reason in mind.

"Because Saint-Malo is still a provincial town in many ways," she explained. "Here, progress moves slowly. Mélanie Flamant used to be a teacher in primary school, a position she left to become a police officer a few years ago. It is difficult for her to prove herself. Some of her colleagues harass her."

Oh. For the first time, I felt a glimmer of solidarity with the *gendarme*. In many ways, the professional kitchens and other places I work in are still a man's world, full of machismo and bawdy jokes. I didn't doubt the same applied to law enforcement.

"Well, she should arrest them!" Capucine stated, indignant.

"Nastiness is not a crime. *Malheureusement*." Unfortunately.

We stood across from the chocolaterie, united in our outrage. It wasn't fair that Mélanie Flamant—or any of us—weren't allowed to do our work in peace . . . which only reminded me of Mathieu's intolerant attitude toward women and business.

He glowered at us from the shop's window. We scattered.

"He is a prickly one!" Nathalie said as she tossed one final glance at Mathieu. "Now, it is time we returned to the château, *non*? Fabrice will be wondering where I am." As we walked toward the city walls, she confided, "Ever since he arrived to meet me, *mon amour* has been so kind with me."

That was sweet. I said so, feeling pleased that at least Nathalie had someone to care for her at this traumatic time.

Then, motivated by another, less altruistic impulse, I pushed further. "The two of you didn't arrive at the same time?" I strived for an informal, interested tone. "I thought you had."

Because after all, establishing alibis began with dates and times, right? I'd learned that much during my other exploits. I didn't have a police badge to help me get answers, but I had guile—and also, I reflected with regret, a bit of shamelessness.

I shouldn't have been questioning Nathalie at all. Yet she might be the key to Fabrice, as well. It was a two-for-one deal.

"Oh no. I arrived home almost immediately after *Maman* phoned me. I didn't come downstairs to mingle with our guests right away, but I dropped everything to come for poor *Papa.*"

Capucine and I murmured our regrets again. It was so sad.

"I wished I'd already been here for his retirement *fête,*" Nathalie added in a remorseful tone. She glanced at us while we dodged pedestrians near the city hall. "It is funny how quickly priorities return when a tragedy strikes. Until *Papa* died, I—"

Nathalie broke down in tears. We stopped at the edge of the street so that Capucine and I could do our best to comfort her.

A short while later, she wiped her eyes. She sniffed, then gave a weak smile. "You are both so kind. Thank you. If not for you both, Fabrice, and everyone . . . I do not know what I would do."

I hated myself for doing it, but I still wanted to know when her fiancé had arrived. "Then Fabrice is helpful for you?"

"*Mais, bien sûr!*" But of course! "That is what is so lovable about him. He has comforted me every step of the way." Her earnest gaze met mine. "The first night was difficult—"

"Without him?" I guessed in my gentlest voice.

Nathalie nodded. "But since then, and as soon as he could, Fabrice has been by my side." Another smile. "Except for shopping, of course! Like most men, he does not enjoy that!"

We all laughed and piled into my Citroën for the drive back to château Vetault. Along the way, I was able to glean a few more details about Nathalie and Fabrice—enough to convince me, at least, that neither of them had plotted Monsieur's murder.

As awful as it sounded, it had to be considered. If I suspected my mentor's wife, then I also had to suspect his daughter and his future *beau fils*, too. But since neither of them had arrived in Saint-Malo until after Philippe's death, they were both cleared. That left Hélène, Hubert, Clotilde, Mathieu (I shuddered, remembering the dark look he'd given us from the shop's window), and (maybe) Charlotte Moreau.

Travis wouldn't have agreed with my suspicion of the seductive antiques shop owner, but I knew someone who might.

It was time to call Danny and compare notes again.

Fourteen

In the hours between my shopping expedition with Capucine and Nathalie and the earliest acceptable time to call Danny (given the time-zone difference between our two locations), I did what I usually did when at loose ends: make chocolates.

I began with truffles, even though they weren't a specialty of Brittany. I felt in a Parisian state of mind after hanging around cool indie director Capucine. Let me tell you: the French capital city is bursting with exquisite chocolates, including truffles, in all kinds of exotic and scrumptious flavors. Some contained liqueur; others, hand-harvested vanilla beans or toasted hazelnuts; others, salted butter caramel. A few I dipped; others, I rolled in cocoa powder or flaked coconut.

I sampled a couple, of course—strictly for the sake of quality control—and found myself feeling better right away. Partly that was because of the inevitable rush of sugar and cacao. Partly it was because I'd put Lucas Lefebvre's music on my phone, so it was ready when I donned my headphones. Partly it was because I was working in Monsieur's barn-atelier and therefore felt close to him again, especially after I swapped my new knit cap for Philippe's favorite Breton fisherman's hat.

Feeling nostalgic, I snapped a selfie to remember it by. It would have been nicer to have a photo of me and Monsieur together, but when we'd shared that afternoon, I'd had every reason to think we'd have all the time in the world for photos.

I decided right then and there to treasure every single photo op that came my way in the future. With everyone. After all, I reasoned, you never knew when it would be your last chance to capture a moment with someone you cared about.

I double-checked my selfie to make sure it had turned out—because it wouldn't do to remember my mentor and his atelier with a blurry, useless snapshot—and noticed another notification on my phone. I'd silenced it while shopping with Nathalie and Capucine, so I hadn't realized I'd missed a text from Danny.

I opened it, looking forward to hearing from him. Aside from sharing useful information with me while I was sleuthing, Danny also often sent me funny texts—acerbic observations about whatever he was up to. My old pal had a flair for seeing through the ridiculousness of everyday life. Like me, he liked to share.

I wasn't prepared for what he shared this time, though.

It was a photo of the murder weapon in Monsieur's case—an official one, judging by the looks of it. I had no idea how Danny had gotten a hold of it. Unlike Travis, he didn't have prominent, well-connected friends . . . but he *did* have friends.

One of them—maybe someone from the bad old

days—had passed along this piece of *gendarmerie* evidence to Danny, and to me.

Beneath the photo, he'd texted two words: Any guesses?

I was startled to realize (now that I could see that horrible object in its entirety) that I *did* have a few guesses what it was—including one I was sure was right. Because the thing someone had stabbed Philippe with *wasn't* a gardening tool or an antiquated knickknack. It was an implement for working with chocolate— specifically, a huge, multipronged fork called a "chocolate chipper," used for (you guessed it) making chocolate chips from a massive, multikilo confectioner's block of cacao.

Had another chocolatier killed Philippe?

I couldn't be sure. The weapon wasn't as damning as it might seem. I, for instance, was one chocolatier who'd only used a chocolate chipper once or twice. I'd found it unwieldly and had reverted to chopping my chocolate with a meticulously sharpened chef's knife instead. But my methods weren't every chocolatier's methods. Were they Mathieu's methods? I wondered.

Had Monsieur's other protégé stabbed him that night?

At the snail's pace the *policiers* were investigating, it might be weeks before anyone found out. In the meantime, Mathieu Camara was still working in my mentor's chocolaterie, daring to toss dirty looks at Nathalie Vetault, me, and Capucine Roux. For all I knew, Mathieu was planning to target one of us next.

If he'd somehow sneaked into the château's garden last night and switched off the landscape lights, he might have been the one who'd grabbed me. That man's grip had been *very* strong.

I didn't know anyone more muscle-bound than Mathieu, except for Danny. But I stopped myself before I could get carried away.

The logical thing to do was to find out if Mathieu could even identify a chocolate chipper. It was possible that, here in Brittany, chocolate makers didn't use such tools. It wasn't a universal craft, practiced the same way everywhere. I had to give Monsieur's chosen trainee the benefit of the doubt, right?

I took another glance at that incriminating photo. Nope.

I texted Danny a thank-you note, along with a few more questions. Then, in the time it would take for my bodyguard pal to wake up and answer me, I took myself back to the walled city.

The thing about conducting an amateur murder investigation is that, well, you're an amateur. Although the word can translate variably to "admirer, fan, or enthusiast" in French, *I* wasn't a native French speaker *or* in any way a "fan" of untimely death. That meant that, in this case, I was just what you'd expect: someone who was decidedly *un*professional at something.

So I suppose I shouldn't have been surprised to wend my way through the picturesque *vieille ville* (old town) and arrive at the Vetaults' chocolaterie, only to find that someone else had gotten there before me. But if you're thinking it was Mélanie Flamant and her fellow *gendarmes*, you're a serious optimist.

It was, instead, Fabrice Poyet who'd come to La Maison des Petits Bonheurs. Like me, he was there to see Mathieu Camara—not because he suspected the chocolatier of murder (although if Fabrice had counted supersleuth among his talents, I would have easily believed it), but because he was closing the shop.

"Temporarily, of course," Nathalie's fiancé told me in his upper-crust French accent when I asked him about it. "You understand, it is best for now." He gave me a vaguely censorious look. "It upset my Nathalie to come here this morning and see the chocolaterie open for business as usual. This makes a mockery of Monsieur Vetault's death, does not it? For now, we close."

Nathalie *had* seemed distressed when we'd lingered in front of the shop earlier. At the time, I'd chalked up her reaction to Mathieu's angry glares, not distress over losing her father. But of course Nathalie was distraught about Philippe! I felt awful for not having been more sensitive. My efforts to avoid walking past the chocolaterie hadn't amounted to much. I said so.

"Still, it was very kind of you to try." Fabrice gave me a forgiving smile. I could see why Nathalie found his presence comforting. The younger Poyet seemed to expect the best from everyone—even surly Mathieu, who tromped out of the shop.

Seeing me, the chocolatier's scowl deepened. He carried what appeared to be his personal confectionary equipment, along with a couple of long aprons, a dirty head kerchief, and a box of La Maison des Petits Bonheurs molded and wrapped chocolates.

Mathieu said something to me in guttural street French—basically, the verbal equivalent of that coarse graffiti that had been sprayed on the shop's shutters. He made a rude gesture, letting me know (in case his lapse into *français* left any doubt) that he was finished being nice to me. Warily, I stepped back.

Fabrice stepped between us, his arms protectively

outstretched to shield me. He said something brusque
to Mathieu.

I'm afraid my ability to translate was on the fritz,
because I couldn't quite make out what it was. Something like Mathieu should have expected that La
Maison des Petits Bonheurs would close for a few
days' mourning. It was the only possible outcome, to
show the proper respect for Monsieur Vetault.

That seemed reasonable to me, but not to Mathieu.
I recalled the bedroom upstairs I'd awaked in after my
tartine and tea with Madame Renouf and remembered (too late) that Mathieu didn't just work at the
chocolaterie. He lived there, too.

"*Attendez, Monsieur Poyet,*" I interrupted. "*S'il vous
plaît.*" Wait. Please. I stepped from behind Fabrice's
protective arms, then pleaded with him to allow
Mathieu to stay in his home.

They both looked at me as if I were *folle.* Insane.

"*Non.*" Fabrice shook his head. "That would be
confusing for our customers, would it not? To see
Monsieur Camara coming and going?"

"Surely they would understand?" I risked a sidelong
glance at broad-shouldered Mathieu, who stood sul-
lenly nearby. "It isn't fair to make Monsieur Camara
leave home. He misses Monsieur."

Abruptly, I remembered that I'd come there to find
out if Mathieu used a chocolate chipper—if he'd
killed our mentor with one of those deadly pronged
implements just a few nights ago.

Sometimes, my natural softheartedness gets in the
way of common sense. I had to steel my resolve—and
myself—against Mathieu. If he'd murdered my mentor,
he'd find a nice home in prison soon. I intended to
do my best to make sure of it.

But Mathieu didn't need me to leap to his defense.

In fact, my attempts to help made him more resolved to leave. He yelled (in French, of course) that Fabrice could keep the chocolaterie. Then he followed up with a rude suggestion as to just what Monsieur Poyet could do with La Maison des Petits Bonheurs. I'll spare you the details. Suffice it to say, Mathieu was now unemployed.

Fabrice seemed in agreement with that—albeit in a sorrowful, well-bred way that suggested he was sorry the situation had come to this—but I couldn't be.

I still needed more information.

Mathieu turned, preparing to stomp down the street. Then he stopped and took a final glance at the chocolaterie where he'd learned his craft at Monsieur's side. I could have sworn his eyes filled with tears, just as they had when we'd met.

I'll admit it. I felt sorry for him. But not sorry enough not to try for the information I needed. I hurried over to him.

Once there, Mathieu's fearsome scowl made me quaver.

What was I doing? He might be a cold-blooded murderer!

"Oui?" he said icily. *"Vous êtes heureuse, maintenant?"*

That essentially amounted to, "I hope you're happy now?" delivered in the most sarcastic and mean-spirited way possible.

I wished I could shove Danny between us for backup. But I had only myself, so I did what I could.

"I'm sorry." I pointed to the aprons, tools, and supplies in Mathieu's arms. "But I think I left something behind at La Maison des Petits Bonheurs."

My practical knowledge of French had fled. Even my grasp of English wasn't at its finest just then, given that I seriously thought my heart might beat straight out of my chest with fear.

But Mathieu hadn't stormed off yet, so I continued with what had become a blatant fishing expedition, using our mutual memories of our mentor for bait. "It was something M. Vetault gave me, years ago," I improvised. "A metal chocolate chipper?"

At my hopeful eyebrow raise, Mathieu sneered. "*Bof!* No true chocolatier uses a 'chocolate chipper.'" His tone couldn't have been any more derisive. "I should have known *you* would have one." He beat his chest with his fist. "*Moi*, I use a chef's knife, like the professional I am. *Bah!*" He spit at the dirt.

Wow. He wasn't exactly holding back his disdain. I guess I had my answer, then. Mathieu Camara didn't use the tool that had been used to murder Monsieur. Or so he claimed. I wasn't sure.

"Then you don't have it?" I asked brightly. "For sure?"

"For sure," Mathieu said mockingly. He transferred his gaze to Fabrice Poyet, who stood watchfully waiting nearby. In French, he informed Fabrice that he had no right to close La Maison des Petits Bonheurs. Then he included me in his fiery glance. "I should have known it was *you*. Both of you!" His stilted English was for me. "You will be sorry for it!"

With that warning, Mathieu really did stomp down the street. I had the errant thought that he and Clotilde Renouf had a talent for storming off in common. She'd done the same thing.

Left alone with me, Fabrice gave an elegant gesture of regret. "It is much too bad. I am sorry, Madame Mundy Moore."

I insisted he call me Hayden. We were *tutoyer*ing

each other in no time. Have I mentioned I have a gift for making friends?

"I have heard of your work from Monsieur Vetault," Fabrice told me as we conversed outside the chocolaterie. He nodded toward it. "This place will soon become a Poyet boutique. Would you consider working at the new Poyet Maison des Petits Bonheurs?"

The name change made me blanch. At least it preserved *some* of the original Vetault family flavor, though, if not all of it.

"I'm sure Nathalie would consider it a great favor," Fabrice coaxed. "She, too, has told me of your expertise."

For a heartbeat, the notion of taking on Monsieur's legacy for myself held a lot of appeal. I was legitimately tempted.

Then, as Travis would have predicted, reason returned.

"I'm sorry." I shook my head. "I have . . . constraints . . . that prevent me from taking on long-term jobs," I explained. That was one way to describe Uncle Ross's will and its provisions. "But it's very kind of you to think of me." I decided to seize the moment. "What are Poyet's plans for the chocolaterie, anyway?"

Fabrice blew out his cheeks in a characteristically French gesture of resignation. "At one time, that was very clear. Now, though, everything is in turmoil. It is uncertain, *oui*? Without Monsieur Vetault, it will be difficult to proceed as we had planned."

I understood. Undoubtedly, the death of a principal partner in the merger would complicate things. Without Philippe and his expertise, La Maison des Petits Bonheurs was a less appealing target. His death might eventually scupper the deal altogether.

"It's heartening that you came so close," I told Fabrice as he pulled out keys and locked the chocolaterie's doors. "Without you and Nathalie, I doubt a merger would have been thought of."

"Because of the bad blood between our families?" At my nod, Fabrice laughed. "You are not *française, non*? Then you will not know that the 'rivalry' between Vetault and Poyet was a myth. Our medias made much of it, but it was never a concern—at least not to Poyet. This is what you call a 'David versus Goliath' situation, *n'est-ce pas*? Only in life, Goliath usually wins."

He had a point. I knew Travis would have agreed. Danny, too. All I knew, just then, was that I hated seeing the chocolaterie close. I nodded at it. "David will rise again?"

"Yes." Fabrice's voice was kind. So was his face, beneath his mop of blond hair. "I truly do wish to honor Monsieur Vetault. Also, it seems more and more signs point to Monsieur Camara being . . ."

He gave a vague gesture in conclusion, but I thought I knew what he meant. *Dangerous* leaped to mind. So did *murderous*.

We were both far too polite to say either word aloud.

The only trouble was, now Mathieu Camara was on the loose, unmoored from his work at La Maison des Petits Bonheurs and his small, old-fashioned apartment above the chocolaterie alike. He might go anywhere now. More important, he might get away.

I had to do something. Follow him?

"I'm sorry, but I must be going," I told Fabrice as I pulled out my phone to call Travis. "*À bientôt!*" See you later!

We traded *bonjours*. Moments later, I was officially trailing Mathieu. It wasn't exactly rocket science. As I turned around to look, I spotted him lingering near a local *crêperie*, glaring malevolently at me. I'd have sworn there was homicide in his eyes. I wondered if he'd heard Fabrice offer me a job.

Women cannot manage business. I guessed the joke was on Mathieu. I had half a mind to accept, just to prove him wrong.

The look in his eyes was too chilling for that, though. Instead, I pulled down my chic new white hat to shield me from the chocolatier's scowl and then dialed Travis to let him in on my emerging plan. Trailing Mathieu Camara might take all day.

"So I might need you to spell me later," I told my financial advisor. I'd ordered an espresso at a café close to Mathieu. In France, it was possible to nurse a six-ounce coffee for hours. So far, that's what the angry chocolatier and I were both doing. "Bring *policière* Mélanie. She can arrest him."

I'd already explained about the chocolate chipper and Mathieu's response to my asking him for one. I still thought he'd overreacted. Impugning my chocolate-making integrity went a step too far, as far as I was concerned. He could have simply said he didn't have one. But if I could prove he *had* had one. . . .

I explained as much to Travis. He wasn't as receptive as I might have hoped. "It would be incriminating for Monsieur Camara to have had the murder weapon in his possession before Philippe's death," my financial advisor agreed in his steady, rumbling voice. "However, even his possessing a chocolate chipper at La Maison des Petits Bonheurs isn't enough. It's a normal tool to have in a chocolaterie. He would have had to have had the weapon with him on the night Philippe was killed *and* have a motive."

"Right." I suspected he had both. Plus, meanness. "And?"

"And Mélanie questioned him. She came up with nothing."

I humphed. "What about fingerprints?"

"You'll have to ask your 'secret source' about that."

He meant Danny, of course. Even though I hadn't disclosed where I'd gotten that photograph, there was only one logical explanation. I frowned, keeping one eye fixed on Mathieu Camara.

"Mélanie hasn't told you if there were fingerprints?"

"We don't talk about Philippe's case much."

"Travis! That's what you're there for!" I lowered my voice to its most serious timbre. "Get some info, will you? We have to catch Philippe's killer"—*aka Mathieu*—"before it's too late."

Travis gave me one of his patented silences. This one said loud and clear (ironically) that he was being *patient* with me. Then, "The police are on the job. Maybe you should back off."

Why did someone say that to me, without fail, at least once during every murder investigation? "I would like to," I told him in an über-patient voice of my own. It was tricky while gritting my teeth in frustration. "But I can't. I owe it to my mentor."

"Philippe wouldn't want you to endanger yourself."

I pulled away my phone from my ear and gawked at it. "Are you being serious right now? Does Mélanie have you at gunpoint?"

"This is all me," my keeper said. "I want you to be safe."

Weirdly enough, it sounded as though he was *right there.*

I looked up. Duh. He *was* right there, giving me a somber look, wearing another suit and tie that made him look just as capable, serious, and brilliant as he really was. I hung up.

"Nice one, superspy. You were around the corner, right?"

Travis nodded. His expression looked grave as he searched for Mathieu, then pinpointed him. My financial advisor sat.

"If you're going down swinging, I am, too," he told me.

Aw. I melted. "That's sweet, Trav. I officially take back all the mean names I was calling you in my head a minute ago."

He laughed, then glanced at my head. "Nice hat. I think I saw one just like that someplace. Looks better on you, though."

"Let me guess: Beyoncé? *Vogue*? A super chic Instagrammer?"

"Nope." Travis crossed his arms, then ordered himself an espresso to match mine. He narrowed his eyes at Mathieu, then shifted his gaze to me. He nodded. "Tell me everything."

I guessed I wasn't finding out the source of Travis's fashion acumen. Resigned (for now) I told him what I knew.

I was up and at it bright and early the next morning, despite having spent a (rather) late night cuddled up with Lucas Lefebvre's YouTube channel. I'd taken to browsing the pop star's videos as a way of unwinding—which wasn't to say that Lucas's music was boring, because it wasn't. Quite the opposite.

I could see why Capucine needed to source so many things for her music videos. They were elaborate, full of multiple scene changes and full of inventive camera angles. I appreciated her artistry—or at least that's the story I stuck to when Travis caught me watching swivel-hipped Lucas cavorting nearly naked.

"I'm just practicing my French, that's all," I told him. "Listening to Lucas's lyrics is *très utile*." Very helpful.

If I told you he believed me . . . well, *you* probably wouldn't.

All of which was a long-winded way of saying that I wasn't at my best as I prepared to drive into Saint-Malo's *centre-ville* to speak to Charlotte Moreau's small-business group that day.

"I guess you haven't kicked your procrastination habit to the curb yet," Travis observed over *café* and *pain au chocolat.*

"I've come a long way," I protested, guiltily re-minded of how long it had been since I'd cracked open the antiprocrastination app he'd recommended.

"But not such a long way that you *don't* still create excuses for not executing." My financial advisor gave me an astute look. "After all, if you're tired from watching Lucas's videos all night, you can't be expected to perform well while speaking at the small-business meeting this morning, right?"

I resented his perceptiveness. "I didn't have much time to prepare. I had roughly twenty-four hours' notice, remember?"

"Ample time to prepare, if you manage your priorities."

I'd have liked to "manage" him into another time zone. "I suppose you always prioritize the right things, all the time?"

My keeper's eyes glimmered. "We're talking about you."

Was that the hint of a grin I detected? "Travis! Are

you suggesting that *you* have faults? I don't believe it."
I leaned forward, inhaling chocolate and pastry. "Tell
me *everything.*"

Sadly, he didn't choose that moment to bare his
soul. "If you don't hurry up, you'll need another app
to cure your chronic lateness." He pulled out his
phone. "I think I know one."

"All right, all right." I chomped my *petit-déjeuner*,
then grabbed my jacket from the back of my chair.
"I'm going."

Just to prove my (latent) efficiency, I made it to
town with time to spare. I arrived at Antiquités Moreau
half an hour before the small-business club meeting
was supposed to begin.

Even though Travis wasn't there to witness my triumph, I was proud of myself. He's not wrong about
my procrastination tendencies (hey, I'm only human),
but they don't generally cause problems with my
work. I always deliver excellent results.

It's simply that sometimes *reporting* on those results
is a little delayed. Does anybody *really* like doing
paperwork?

Given the morning's meeting, Charlotte Moreau's
antiques shop wasn't open for business yet. Instead,
Antiquités Moreau's dishy proprietress had hung a
sign on the front door stating that *le magasin* would
be *ouvert* (open) after eleven o'clock. That meant
that I had an full hour to wow Saint-Malo and then
network my way into finding out who'd graffitied
Monsieur's chocolaterie. Piece of (chocolate) cake,
right? I hoped so.

Struck by a thought, I scrutinized Madame Moreau's
handwritten sign. I wanted to discern if its style was
similar to the graffiti. *Traître.* Unfortunately, writing
with a thick marker and scrawling slurs with paint

were different. The results were inconclusive. It could have been her . . . or not.

Dressed in my only "lady boss" clothes—a pencil skirt and lightweight cashmere sweater, worn with my "fancy" flats—I raised my hand to knock, then realized the door was ajar. Hmm.

Only a fool (or someone who wasn't interested in looking for clues) would have bypassed an opportunity to snoop around. Quietly, I stepped inside the antiques shop. Its hushed atmosphere surrounded me, redolent of ancient metals, cleaning solvents, paint (aha!), and faintly musty fabrics. I noted every detail as I sneaked from one aisle to the next, then the next.

I almost bumped into Charlotte Moreau. She wasn't dead (as you might have been expecting, given the goings-on lately), but she *was* unaware of my presence. That's because she was currently caught in a heated clinch with a man. I heard a moan. Whoops.

I backtracked and stepped on a creaky floorboard. Uh-oh.

The pair separated with a jerk. Their faces turned toward me. I saw Charlotte, rumpled and flushed. Who was with her?

Fabrice Poyet, that rat. I saw him as plain as day.

Shocked, I gasped. Nathalie's fiancé was cheating on her with Charlotte Moreau? What was in the water around here, anyway? As I stared at them, Fabrice hurriedly raised his hand.

I had the sense he was about to explain—to make an excuse or otherwise tell me that things were "different" in France when it came to relationships—but I didn't want to stick around.

I was too embarrassed. Too ashamed of my own naïveté.

How could I have believed Fabrice and Nathalie were the Romeo and Juliet of French chocolate making? Their supposed epic love story was all a sham, given what I'd just stumbled into.

Unable to muster an excuse in French, I hurried out of the shop. Maybe, I decided, I should wait outside for the meeting to begin. Maybe, I elaborated to myself, I shouldn't have come in.

This was what came of being *early* to things, I decided out on the street. When I saw Travis next, he was getting an earful.

Fifteen

The first thing I did when I got back to château Vetault was officially add Fabrice Poyet to my list of suspects.

Travis seemed to think I was being unreasonable, but I didn't care. "I know what I saw! What Fabrice and Charlotte were up to in the aisle of her antiques shop was R-rated."

"Really?" My financial advisor gave me a dubious look. "Maybe you're not familiar with what film ratings comprise."

"Okay, fine. NC-17, then," I relented, unable to shake the image of my friend's deceitful fiancé locked in the arms of another woman. "They were kissing. I'm sure I saw tongue."

My keeper made a face. "How long did you watch them?"

"Hardly any time at all!" Indignant, I paced my room.

"But long enough to know that Fabrice lied afterward?"

I already regretted telling Travis the whole story. "Yes," I said firmly. "I don't care how contrite he looked when he followed me out of the antiques store. Fabrice is guilty."

Travis's skeptical expression eased. "Is it possible your view of this situation is . . . clouded . . . by personal experience?"

I stopped pacing, my enjoyable view of the château's pretty gardens ruined. I frowned at him. "You know about that?"

"About your first fiancé?" A nod. "It's a matter of public record," he was quick to explain. "You'd already registered for a wedding license before . . ." Tactfully, Travis shook his head.

I guessed he didn't want to go into detail about my own humiliating personal experience with a duplicitous fiancé.

I raised my head. "Hey, at least I tried again, right?"

In fact, I'd tried twice more to believe that love could conquer all. But I still felt mortified. It was one thing to suspect Travis knew a great deal about my personal life. It was something else again to have that suspicion confirmed in person.

"Yes, you did try again," he agreed. "You're nothing if not optimistic." He lowered his voice, purposely lulling me with its sexy timbre. "That's one of the things I like best about you."

His flattery almost worked. Okay, it did work. I gave in.

"Oh, sure. Choose *now* to restore my faith in mankind," I joked. It was *man*kind I was irked at, too. Poor Nathalie. "But your own show of integrity doesn't change the facts. Fabrice is cheating on Nathalie with Charlotte Moreau! If he'd cheat—"

"He told you that *she* came on to *him*," Travis recalled. "From what I remember of her personality, that seems plausible."

I doubted it was her personality that made my financial advisor blush, just then. "If he'd cheat on his fiancée—especially now, when she's grieving—I bet he'd do anything."

"He told you he was disentangling himself from Madame Moreau."

"Humph. Likely story."

Travis watched me pace past the fireplace, to the tall windows, then back again. He leaned on my room's antique desk, a bespectacled and suit-wearing bastion of irksome reasonableness.

"Are you going to tell Nathalie?" my financial advisor asked. "Fabrice did beg you not to, particularly right now."

Monsieur's memorial service would be scheduled soon. We were both thinking of it. I exhaled with frustration.

"No, I'm not telling Nathalie," I told him. "It's not my place. Right?" I looked to Travis for confirmation. "I mean, if you were in her shoes, would you want to know about this?"

"Would I want to know about a supposition founded on circumstance and conjecture?" A headshake. "Probably not."

It was nice of him to qualify that mouthful with a *probably* at the end. I almost laughed, despite my disgruntled mood.

"Maybe you do have a point about my personal views on this subject. I feel angrier than the situation strictly calls for, given that *I'm* not the one who's engaged to a lying, cheating—" Brightly, I glanced up. "How do you say 'dirtbag' in French?"

Travis offered a few rude suggestions. I noted each one for future use. "It doesn't matter, anyway. Fabrice is a suspect now, end of story." I searched for a justification that didn't depend on my own enmity toward him. "For all we know, Philippe happened upon Fabrice and Charlotte together, too. For all we know, my mentor threatened to tell Nathalie the truth, and Fabrice killed him rather than see his relationship end."

"Which relationship? With Charlotte? Or with Nathalie?"

"Either one!" I said. "Aren't Frenchmen famously adept at juggling wives and mistresses? Things are different here."

Travis shook his head. "You're forgetting the Vetault-Poyet merger. I doubt Fabrice would have endangered a multimillion-euro deal. La Maison des Petits Bonheurs was worth far more with Philippe Vetault at its helm. We both know it's true."

"Yes, but that's *logical.*" So I could easily dismiss it.

My keeper crossed his arms and remained silent. I could tell he thought he'd already won this debate.

"I'm talking about a much more compelling *emotional* argument," I went on. "Fabrice is entitled. He's aristocratic—at least as much as that term can be applied to anyone these days. I doubt he's ever been denied anything in his life, including, if he wanted, an affair with Charlotte Moreau."

"You're forgetting Philippe's own dalliances," Travis reminded me. "It's possible he didn't disapprove of Fabrice's indiscretions. It's likely he would have never told Nathalie."

"But if he threatened to, and Fabrice disagreed—"

I could already envision the whole sordid situation.

"By stabbing him?" Travis seemed troubled. "If that's true, then *you're* in danger now, too. You realize that, don't you? If Fabrice would kill once to maintain his secret, he might again."

All I realized was that I was finally convincing Travis. He was on the brink of seeing things my way. I shrugged off his ongoing concerns for my safety. "If *you're* correct, that doesn't matter, because Fabrice couldn't have been guilty, right? He wouldn't have endangered the merger, so, *voilà*. No problem."

I could think of several problems, actually, primarily the death of my beloved mentor. But what I needed was proof.

I still didn't have any. All I had were suspicions and hunches—mainly about Fabrice Poyet—which only proved my earlier "last seen, last suspected" theory about myself.

As recently as yesterday, my search for Monsieur's killer had centered on Mathieu Camara. Travis and I had discreetly tracked the chocolatier to a hotel near the Saint-Malo city wall, where he'd taken a room. My concerns about his potential guilty flight from justice seemed unfounded. So far. But that had left a hole in my speculations about who might have killed Philippe. After this morning, Fabrice was filling it nicely.

"Let's talk about something else," I suggested. "Let's *do* something else." I flung my arm toward the view. "We're here in a stunning French château, for Pete's sake. Let's go exploring."

Travis uncrossed his arms. Then he cleared his throat and crossed his arms the opposite way. "I'm sorry. I can't."

Danny would have been up for it, I grumbled to myself. My bodyguard pal was always up for anything. Especially if it involved the region's *bières et saucisses* (beer and sausages).

I was disappointed and not afraid to show it. "Chocolate, then? We can collaborate on more flavors. Your choice. Okay?"

My financial advisor looked away. "I'm having lunch with Mélanie today. She's knows the best place for *moules frites*."

"Fried mussels? Ugh." I made a face. Brittany was known for fresh coastal seafood of all kinds, but I'm not a fan. "You can't tell me you wouldn't rather have chocolate. Come on."

His gaze met mine. "I'm meeting Mélanie's dog today. It's a little poodle-terrier mix. Much smaller than Bella," he rushed to add, piling on a smile, "but much bigger than my fish."

I recalled his guppies but didn't feel like being humored.

"You two have bonded over dogs now, then?" Inexplicably, I felt left out. It wasn't my fault I couldn't have the canine companion I longed for. "That's so, um, sweet. I've gotta go."

I grabbed my crossbody bag and made a run for it. There was no reason for me to feel so suddenly upset, but there it was.

"Hey." Travis grabbed me before I made it halfway across the room, looking endearingly concerned. "What's the matter?"

"Right now? Your freakish speed, Flash." I nodded at his former position at the desk. "How did you grab me so fast?"

Belatedly, I realized he'd grabbed me pretty hard, too.

At the same moment, my financial advisor became cognizant of the same thing. He apologized and let me go. "I can move quickly when the situation warrants it. What's going on?"

I wanted to believe he genuinely cared about me, but part of me knew that Travis was technically there on business.

I sniffled. "I guess I just miss Monsieur, that's all."

That was partly it. Probably. But there was more going on.

I suspected Travis knew it. But all he said was, "You should come to lunch with Mélanie and me. It would be fun."

Sure. I couldn't wait to be someone's third wheel. Why was everyone else always getting lucky while I investigated murders?

"No, thanks. I'll pass." I searched for a plausible excuse—something that wouldn't make it obvious how stupidly hurt I felt about Travis's date with Mélanie. She *should* have been working on my mentor's case, after all. "I'm going into town to check on Mathieu Camara, anyway. I don't want him to get away."

While the local police enjoy moules frites *and doggie bonding,* I added silently. But I could have sworn Travis knew.

His searching glance (probably) saw everything about me.

Why had I never noticed before how closely my financial advisor watched me? It would have been flattering if I hadn't known he was interested in a different brunette altogether.

"Well, be careful," Travis warned, doing nothing to dispel my suspicions about where his priorities lay. Danny would have insisted on going with me to a stakeout. "Watch yourself."

"I will," I promised. My keeper didn't owe me anything, I reminded myself. I was fortunate he'd come there at all.

I couldn't resist a final word, though. "Don't come crying to me if you wish you'd had chocolate instead. I offered."

His smile flashed at me, full of certainty and charm.

"I have a feeling I might get both, one right after the other."

Gross. I hoped he was talking about food, not women. Otherwise, Travis was doing nothing to assuage my concerns about the trustworthiness of mankind, and by *mankind,* I meant *men.*

Specifically, the men in and around Saint-Malo that day.

Too late, Travis looked abashed. "I meant seafood followed by chocolate," he specified. "Just so we're clear on that."

What was with him and reading my mind, anyway?

"Still sounds like poor decision-making to me." With a nod toward his phone, I joked, "Maybe there's an app for that?"

Then I gave him a cheerier wave and got myself out of there, bound for the cobblestone streets of the seaside *ville.*

Once ensconced at a bookstore across the street from Mathieu Camara's *petit* hotel, I quickly learned that there was nothing more boring than extended surveillance. Not waiting in line at the DMV. Not buying fiddly *billets* (tickets) for the Paris *métro* from the RATP's problematic machines. Not even watching paint dry. I hung around anyway, waiting for my fellow chocolatier to somehow incriminate himself in Monsieur's murder.

Monsieur Camara didn't leave his hotel room once. If he was plotting anything in there, I was none the wiser for watching.

Feeling defeated, I studied the area around the hotel. Maybe Mathieu could sneak out another way? Maybe he'd slipped past me somehow? I couldn't cover the entryway and the alley.

I made up my mind to check all the angles. I had to be thorough, right? Midway there, though, I heard something.

I hurried to the other corner and peeked around the side of a bank—a branch of BNP Paribas that wouldn't have been out of place in Paris or Lille. Across the square, three police cars had parked in front of Madame Renouf's jam shop. *Gendarmes* were moving in and out of the *magasin de confiture* with authority.

Uh-oh. I had a bad feeling about this. The *policiers* had the somber demeanor of officers who'd been called to a crime scene. Some executed a crowd control protocol; others went in and out of the shop, speaking to each other in subdued voices.

I'd seen things like this before—things that raised goose bumps on my arms and left me sick to my stomach, just the way I was then. Without meaning to, I headed in that direction.

I passed a few residents and nodded to them. Judging by the *gendarme* who'd corralled them together, they were witnesses.

Had something happened to Clotilde Renouf?

The jam maker hadn't been at the small-business club meeting this morning, which had taken place despite the awkwardness that now existed between me and that (supposedly) irresistible vixen, Charlotte Moreau. At the time, I'd assumed Madame Renouf had skipped attending because I wasn't her hero, the Alsatian jam maker. Now, though, I had to rethink everything.

Who *had* been at the meeting? I pondered as I neared the barrier the *policiers* had erected. I reviewed the faces and names of the Bretons I'd met that morning, trying to determine if any of them stood out as dangerous. The answer? Not really.

Curious neighboring merchants blocked my path. I excused myself and slipped past them, nearing the jam shop's entryway. Though it, I glimpsed more officers at work but still couldn't tell what was going on. Despite my (sometime) antipathy toward Clotilde Renouf, I was worried about her. Sure, she was a top suspect in Monsieur's murder. Sure, she might have stabbed my mentor with a chocolate chipper. But if she was hurt somehow—

"Clotilde Renouf is dead," Travis said.

He was right beside me. Huh? I turned to face him. "*What?*"

"Mélanie was called to the scene while we were at lunch." My financial advisor had a leash in one hand. At the other end of it was the cutest, curly-haired little white dog I'd ever seen. Evidently, Travis had been pressed into dog-sitting duty for the *policière's* sweet-faced poodle-terrier mix. "One of the shop's employees phoned the police about half an hour ago."

I couldn't believe it. "Clotilde is *dead*? Really?"

A grave nod. "The shop was closed for the small-business club meeting. If not for one of the employees having forgotten her cell phone inside, no one would have discovered Madame Renouf until tomorrow morning, at the earliest. The employee became concerned when no one answered her knock or her phone call."

"I guess she really wanted her phone?" That's how people are these days, though. Their phones are their lifelines—no pun intended. I narrowed my eyes, hoping to pinpoint which employee had found Clotilde Renouf. My keeper pointed her out as one of the people I'd seen being questioned. "What happened? Was it"—I lowered my voice and searched Travis's face—"another *murder?*"

I hoped not. My queasiness intensified. If Clotilde had been killed (partly) because I'd failed to find out who had attacked Monsieur at the *Fest-Noz*, how could I live with that?

Under the circumstances, I felt sorry that I'd suspected Madame Renouf. She'd been unpleasant and hostile, but she hadn't deserved to die. It now seemed unlikely she'd killed anyone.

"No one is sure yet if there was foul play involved or if it was just an accident," Travis told me. His gaze scanned the crowd—searching for Mélanie Flamant? "It looks as though Madame Renouf fell down some steep stone stairs inside her jam shop."

I shivered, remembering those treacherous steps. They'd felt none too safe to me when I'd been trying to escape my own tea-and-tartines rendezvous with gossipy, greedy Clotilde.

"Fell?" I repeated. "Or was pushed?"

My skeptical tone made Travis look at me. "Hold on, now."

"Hold on, why? My mentor was murdered, remember? Monsieur didn't trip and fall backward onto that chocolate chipper all by himself."

"But Madame Renouf might have. She was middle-aged and none too spry. Those stairs were old and poorly lit. It may have been hours between when she fell and when she was discovered. It's not inconceivable that she could have died during that time."

"Wait a minute—did you just say 'poorly lit'?" As far as I knew, he hadn't visited the shop. "You've seen the stairs?"

Travis hesitated. Then, "Mélanie and I were very close by at the *moules frites* restaurant. We were first here." He bent to give the dog a reassuring pat. "I might not have heard Mélanie telling me to stay outside with Fleur. I saw the stairs and—"

The body. I didn't want him to have to say it. It was horrible enough that my keeper had witnessed it at all. Leaving aside the matter of his "might not have heard" comment—and all it implied about his burgeoning stealthiness—he still looked pale to me. On a closer look, his hand shook on Fleur's leash.

Poor Travis. There was only one thing to do. I opened my arms, stepped closer, and hugged him. I wanted to comfort him.

Take it from me—it's not easy witnessing a crime scene. It's the kind of thing that sticks with you. My financial advisor—*my friend*—appeared pretty stoic, but he was shaken.

The way his formerly rigid posture softened as I held him told me everything. Our hug only lasted a few seconds, but it was long enough for me to remember that Travis was human. No matter how precise, brilliant, or annoyingly perfect he might seem to be, he was just as prone to fear and pain as anyone.

He felt like granite in my arms. I ended the hug and took a step back. "Wow, the city wall has nothing on you," I said in my most cheerful, mood-bolstering voice. "Do you work out or what?"

He laughed, and everything was back to normal—everything, that was, except my perception of him. We were buddies now.

"I do what I can. I don't want Danny to get the jump on me." Travis regarded me with equability. "Sometimes I get the sense that your bodyguard bears me some serious ill will."

Danny. I had to call him. He needed to know about Clotilde Renouf. At this point, I doubted her death had been accidental.

"Don't worry. It's unlikely the situation will devolve into out-and-out brawling," I reassured Travis. I eyed his suit-wearing self, feeling impressed. He was more than brains—he was brawn, too. "But if it does, I think you'll hold your own."

"In a fair fight?" My financial advisor's face suggested that wasn't what he expected from Danny. "Absolutely, I would."

Despite our banter, both of us were drawn back to the jam shop and what was going on inside. I felt hideously aware that one more person's life had ended prematurely. But how? Why?

Quietly, I offered up some conjecture. "You know, Madame Renouf's death probably nullifies her claim on Monsieur's shop. I mean, her mother could still argue that she had a verbal agreement for the real estate, but Clotilde seemed like the one who was keen to get a hold of Philippe's chocolaterie."

"The elder Madame Renouf is eighty-two and has suffered from mental decline for years," Travis said. "It's safe to say that the issue of who gets your mentor's chocolaterie is closed."

"Except for Poyet, of course."

"Of course. The merger is still up in the air."

I stepped closer to be sure we wouldn't be overheard. Cute little Fleur made a nice excuse for my movement. Aw. She was so fluffy! "Then who would benefit from Clotilde's death?"

"Hélène Vetault." Travis's reply was instantaneous. "Philippe's will leaves everything to her and Nathalie unless there are opposing claims, like the one Clotilde Renouf made."

"Or Hubert Bernard?" I could easily imagine him sneaking into the jam shop and pushing Clotilde Renouf to her demise.

"No." Travis shook his head. "He's part owner of the château, but Hubert has nothing to do with La Maison des Petits Bonheurs or its valuable real estate. Presumably, he has no motive to attack Madame Renouf, except on Hélène's behalf."

Travis was consistent, I'd give him that.

"Unless Clotilde saw Hubert kill Philippe," I surmised. "If she was a witness, Hubert would have wanted her out of the way."

"If Madame Renouf saw anything, she didn't tell the police."

"Hmmph. Did the police ask?" I inquired pointedly, still irked at the *gendarmes'* slow investigation of Monsieur's death.

"Of course, they did." Travis straightened, leaving leashed Fleur wiggling for more of his attention. His superserious expression leveled me. "Mélanie is conducting a reasonable investigation. I won't listen to any more complaints that the police aren't doing enough to solve your mentor's murder."

Whoa. I raised my palms. "Sorry. I'm not an insider like you are. I can only report on what I see, and that's not—"

Enough. The sight of two officers emerging from the jam shop with a wooden crate carried between them stopped me cold. I recognized what was in that crate. First, Monsieur's *Fest-Noz* banner—the one that redheaded Clotilde Renouf had ripped down so unceremoniously a few days ago. Second, several cans of paint.

Black paint. Paint that might have spelled out *traître*.

I was still reeling at the implications of that when Mélanie Flamant emerged in the officers' wake.

She saw Travis and me, standing there with Fleur

the dog, and headed straight over to us. She was dressed for duty in her *gendarme* uniform, reminding me (belatedly) that I'd seen her leaving Clotilde Renouf's jam shop yesterday, when I'd had my girls' day out with Nathalie and Capucine. That must have been when Mélanie had questioned the jam maker. Her uniform also let me know that Mélanie's *moules frites* lunch with Travis hadn't exactly been a hot-and-heavy date. Maybe they were . . . friends?

Inconclusively, they greeted each other with *les bises*. When everyone kissed in France, how was I supposed to know what was really going on between my keeper and the *policière*?

Mélanie thanked Travis for looking after petite Fleur. Then she turned to me, her gaze somber and clear beneath the brim of her white knit hat. It was an unorthodox addition to her official uniform but an understandable one, given the weather.

I smiled, finally understanding something Travis had said.

"Nice hat," he'd told me when he'd seen my new one. "I think I saw one just like that someplace. Looks better on you, though."

I couldn't gloat about my triumph in the hat-wearing arena, though. Because beneath her clear and intelligent eyes, Mélanie Flamant sported a black eye and a bruised cheek. She'd taken stitches to her jaw, which was lumpy and frighteningly purple. She walked with noticeable caution, too. She was injured elsewhere, I guessed, either her ribs or her shoulder.

Maybe both. "What in the world happened to you?" I blurted out.

The *policière* and Travis shared a knowing look. I couldn't believe either of them was being so lackadaisical about this.

I gave my financial advisor a disapproving smack to his arm. "You might have told me about this *first*," I said.

"Madame Renouf's condition was more serious," he informed me.

Well. *That* calmed me down. But I still shook my head at Mélanie Flamant in bewilderment. "Are you all right?"

"I will be fine," she said. "I am tougher than I look."

Studying her, I didn't doubt it. I was awestruck by her fortitude. Also, disturbed by the injuries she'd suffered.

Was *this* the kind of "nastiness" Nathalie had been talking about when she'd explained that Mélanie had been harassed at work? If so, it was much more serious than I'd envisioned.

"I'm so sorry this happened to you." I looked around for a bench. "Maybe you should sit down. Would chocolate help?"

Mélanie gave Travis another meaningful look. "You were right. She is exactly as forthright and pushy as you said."

Pushy? "Hey! I'm only trying to help," I protested.

"I know. Me, too." Mélanie smiled, then sobered again. "This is what Travis has made me see about you. This is why, well . . ."

She hesitated. So I jumped in. "Whatever you need."

"Maybe it is time that we joined forces," the *policière* suggested. "I suspect that if we share information together—"

"Yes! I'll do it." How could I not? If it helped bring Monsieur's killer to justice, I was in. I glanced at her knit cap again. "How could I say no? We're hat twins. Let's go."

Sixteen

I didn't tell Danny everything Mélanie Flamant confided in me that afternoon about her investigation into Philippe's murder. After all, the *policière* had told me those details in confidence. I was honor bound not to betray her trust—exactly the way, it turned out, that Travis had been, a time or two.

But when my muscle-bound pal and I had our usual phone debriefing that evening, I *did* remember to ask how he was doing, spurred by my recollections of Mélanie's awful injuries.

I'd been checking with Danny daily until now, naturally. But today, my inquiries about his condition held new concern.

"What's the status of the eyeball situation?" I strived for a carefree tone, despite my worry. It was unsettling to know that Danny—always so strong, competent, and helpful—was just as mortal as Travis was. He could be hurt, too, even if I didn't remember another time when he had been. "Did you intimidate your retina into reattaching yet?" I pressed with a smile. "Are you a medical miracle now? Is your doctor suitably impressed?"

My buddy's laughter traveled reassuringly over the line.

"I've always been a quick healer," he told me. "I'd rather be there, though." *With you,* his warm tone added. "What's up?"

I heard him loud and clear. Danny didn't want to discuss his (temporary) frailty. Okay, then. I could go along with that.

"Betrayal. Infidelity. Murder. You know, the usual."

His tone sharpened. "There was another murder?"

He swore. It was a good thing I didn't have him on speaker phone—and Travis wasn't in my château room—because none of what Danny said about my financial advisor's inability to protect me was flattering. It wasn't even printable. Danny was mad.

I knew that was partly because he felt helpless. So I let him blow off steam, then said, "Let's go back to the betrayal."

I wanted his take on the Fabrice-Charlotte-Nathalie situation. I didn't know anyone who more effortlessly "pulled" (as the Brits would say) in the dating department than Danny. He had no ties at the moment, but he had in the past—and in most things, my bodyguard buddy was as cynical as they came. Surely he'd agree with me that Fabrice was a cheating, lying rat.

"Nah, if he told you Charlotte came on to him, maybe he's telling the truth," Danny said when I'd finished relating the morning's sleazy situation. "Why would he bother lying to you? Just because the guy looks guilty, doesn't mean he is."

"He'd lie to me because I might tell Nathalie."

"If he's that skilled a liar, he could handle that," my (onetime) conniving friend pointed out. "He could easily cajole Nathalie into forgetting one minor indiscretion. Frankly, the person most likely to overlook his cheating is his girlfriend."

No way. I shook my head. "That can't be true!"

I sensed his answering shrug. "The wronged woman rarely wants to know the truth. If I were you, I'd stay out of it."

I humphed. "You're just saying that because you're a man."

"Yes?" His tone had turned silky. Dangerously so. "And?"

"And you've probably cheated on dozens of women." I paced anew, just as I had when confronting Travis earlier. Outside in the château's *jardin*, guests were strolling the paths. It was the B&B's usual wine hour, when everyone tried regional *vins*. "So of course you'd side with Fabrice here. It's only natural."

Silence. Then, "Sure you don't want to rethink that?"

I'd been too direct. I backpedaled. "You're right. I'm not aware of any times when you were personally a lying dirtbag."

"That's because there aren't any." He sounded testy.

"But just in general, men are prone to cheating, right?"

"If I said something that nasty about women 'in general,' you'd tar and feather me." Danny seemed to be holding his temper in check. "Are you sure this isn't personal for you?"

Great. He'd chosen the same tactic Travis had—to throw my checkered romantic past in my face. Why wouldn't anyone share my indignation? I was only upset on Nathalie's behalf. She was nice. She had enough to deal with after losing her father.

I said as much to Danny. He actually gave a wry chuckle.

"Whatever you need to tell yourself." He paused.

"Just out of curiosity, what did Harvard have to say about all this?"

It figured. I'd inadvertently stumbled upon something Danny and Travis could both agree upon: that men *weren't* inescapably predisposed to sleeping around with anyone wearing a skirt.

"It doesn't matter. Let's talk about Mathieu Camara."

Another chuckle. "I get it. The Human Calculator and I *do* agree on something. Huh. Interesting." My longtime friend lowered his voice. "Be sure to tell him that. Take pictures. I want to see Harvard's expression when you tell him we agree."

"Ha, ha. Very funny. Anyway . . ." I told Danny how Mathieu had denied using the chocolate chipper—how he'd reacted to La Maison des Petits Bonheurs' closing. "You can't really blame him," I mused. "I mean, Mathieu did live above the chocolaterie."

It was a common arrangement, especially in the old town.

"Now he's out a job and a place to live," I explained. "It's understandable he'd be bitter. I thought he'd leave town, but so far, he hasn't." I told Danny about Mathieu's hotel standoff. "I'm convinced he's just trying to throw me off his trail. It would make the most sense to leave, so he's not."

"He can't leave. He's on parole."

Oh yeah. I'd forgotten about that relevant detail. But I wasn't done yet. "Did I tell you what he said about women?"

"I can't wait to hear," Danny said drily.

I decided to overlook his sarcasm in favor of relating my encounter with Mathieu from a few days ago, when the chocolatier had made that snide comment about women being bad at business.

"He made a generalization based on gender?"

Danny asked when I'd finished. "No way! Nobody ever does that anymore."

Whoops. "Fine. I get your point. Not all men are cheaters. But women definitely aren't hopeless at business—not by a long shot." I still resented that comment. "I got the last word, though. I told Mathieu that Monsieur hadn't agreed with him."

I summed up the situation, ending with a fiery reenactment of my comeback: "In the coming days, I think you'll see that!"

I couldn't help feeling proud of my passionate defense of my mentor's views. I still expected them to be validated by Philippe posthumously granting control of La Maison des Petits Bonheurs to Nathalie or Hélène. But I didn't exactly get the "you go, girl!" applause that I wanted from Danny. On the phone, across two continents and an ocean, my security expert friend was quiet. Then he came at me with something I hadn't expected.

"You know, that might have sounded like a threat."

"A threat? From me? I was just setting Mathieu straight," I disagreed. "I couldn't stand that he thought Monsieur was an antiwoman bigot—someone who might have agreed with him."

Danny didn't comment on that, but he did muse further about the state of affairs at the chocolaterie. "It's possible Mathieu would have been out of work anyway. Maybe Poyet bought your mentor's chocolate shop purposely to close it down. Have you thought of that? Those bigtime CEOs love shutting down a competitor by buying them out. No muss, no fuss, clean hands."

"It wasn't a buyout," I argued. "It was a merger."

"Says the guy who stood to lose his job when Poyet cleaned shop. The first thing anyone does when taking over is bring in their own people—people they trust. Unless he's more of a bozo than you described, I'm guessing Mathieu Camara knew that."

I was still boggling over my bodyguard's foray into the business world. "He never said anything about any of that."

"Why would he?" Danny came back at me. "You're his rival. He'd rather die than look weak, especially in front of you."

I shuddered. Another person dying was an all-too-real possibility. "Let's not get carried away with hyperbole."

But Danny wasn't finished yet. "I know you're the sunshine and rainbows type, but we have to be realistic here. To Mathieu Camara, *you* were public enemy number one. You still are. Not counting Philippe, since he's out of the picture now. Just *you*."

I disagreed. It was no use. My buddy was on a roll.

"You were Philippe's favorite trainee—his golden girl," he reminded me. "You were the one he couldn't stop raving about."

I remembered the picture Monsieur had hung of me in his shop—the one with the cracked glass. "I suppose, for Mathieu, that could be hard to take. But he seemed to like me at first."

"Sure, he did. He wanted to save face. But trust me—to him, you were the competition. He wanted to annihilate you."

"Wow, competitive much? I'm worried for Travis now."

"It's a figure of speech," Danny said. "Mostly. The point is, you only know your side of the story. Maybe, while you were busy trying to wow Mathieu with your Easter chocolates and your knack for making friends, *he* was realizing he'd been replaced."

"By me?" I laughed. "I already told you—I turned down Fabrice's job offer. I can't stay in Saint-Malo. You know that."

For once, he didn't lapse into a tirade about my trust fund. "It's *months* too soon for Easter chocolates," he reminded me. "For all Mathieu knew, you'd already started taking over. You'd already started making plans for the big-money season."

"But I wasn't! I wouldn't have. This is way off base."

Usually, my favorite bar-crawling buddy agreed with me about things. I felt uncomfortably off-kilter at that moment.

"Taking over," Danny repeated, "and expecting Mathieu to be happy about it. Because what it looks like from the other side is some jerk comes in to steal your job *and* wants to be pals."

"So I'm the 'jerk' in this scenario? No. I was being nice. I felt sorry for Mathieu. We had chocolate in common." I hauled in a deep breath for patience. "I was investigating, too."

"Okay, let's come at this from another angle," my buddy suggested. "If Easter chocolates are so expensive and critical, the way you told me, then who usually comes up with them?"

Argh. He had me. "The boss. Monsieur made all the designs."

I got it. Suddenly, it was impossible not to see my interactions with Mathieu Camara in a different light. To him, I was an interloper, not a potential friend. How could I have been so blind? Just because I was secure in my position with my mentor didn't mean that Philippe's *other* trainee felt the same.

"But Mathieu is a skilled chocolatier," I argued, unwilling to go down without a fight. This discussion felt a lot like the other times Danny had told me I was "too nice" for giving someone the benefit of the doubt. "He had no reason to fear me."

"Really? There's a reason Poyet made you that job offer." Danny's tone was firm. Proud? "You're a world-famous, highly sought-after, well-paid chocolate expert. You don't see how you're competition to a hard-luck type like Mathieu Camara?"

"But you see everything through the lens of competition." I didn't want to be that way. "Just the same way Travis sees everything as an excuse to be logical. That doesn't make either of your opinions any more valid or more true than mine are."

"Yeah, it kinda does. Because you're still too nice."

There it was. I gritted my teeth and paced to the window.

"You don't want to see the truth," Danny insisted. "Not about Philippe and his affairs, not about Nathalie's real dad, not about Mathieu. You can't stand that he didn't like you—"

"Stop right there." Mathieu did like me. Once. I felt reasonably sure of it, because I'd liked him. "This isn't about me."

"Isn't it? Who else is tracking a murderer and overlooking the single mostly likely person in town to want *her* dead?"

I imagined Mathieu grabbing me in the château's dark *jardin*. Maybe it had been him out there, the other night.

"Mathieu Camara isn't your friend. He's an ex-con."

"Yes? And?" It was my turn for a piercing retort, like Danny's earlier. "You're always telling me not to judge people by their pasts, especially not people who've been in trouble."

"In trouble" was code for "in jail," of course. Like Danny.

"I never meant you should overlook what's right in front of your face." He gave a frustrated sound, making the phone speaker crackle. "First, Mathieu needed that job. With his record, work isn't easy to come by," my buddy recapped. "Second, you turned up just when the future of the chocolate shop was uncertain—"

"Because of the Poyet-Vetault merger, not me."

"—and started showing off all your chocolate expertise," Danny went on. "Expertise Mathieu specifically told you he didn't want. Then you showed up to gloat about him getting shafted by Fabrice—stood there watching him being ousted."

"It wasn't like that! I didn't know that's what Fabrice planned to do. He only arrived here a day or two ago."

"And now you're surprised Mathieu's shot you a few dirty looks? I have news for you, Hayden. You're lucky if he doesn't try a lot worse. He's probably the one who killed Philippe. As far as Mathieu knows, your mentor purposely set him up to have his whole life ruined—all so Philippe could rake in a bundle of cash from Poyet. Then *you* blew into town to pick up the pieces."

Yikes. That sounded like a motive for murder, even to me.

I winced, feeling blasted by Danny's pointed outburst. It was true that my longtime pal was ludicrously competitive, but he wasn't prone to flights of fancy. If he thought there was something here, there probably was. I paced to the fireplace.

I wished I could sink onto my cushy four-poster

bed and forget the whole thing. Mathieu, Hélène, Clotilde . . . everyone.

"I didn't call you to argue," I said in a conciliatory tone. I didn't want us to be at odds. Especially not with so much distance separating us. Fortunately, Danny seemed to agree.

"Me either. I've had more than the usual amount of time to think," he admitted in a rough voice. "Being laid up sucks."

At his aggrieved tone, I sympathized. Then, "You really think Mathieu saw me as competition?" Danny emphatically said that he did. "Because even if that's true, it doesn't matter anymore. Not now that he's un-employed. He quit on his own."

"Fabrice forced the issue by closing the shop. If you didn't see that coming, then Mathieu must have been blown away."

"Not in a good way, either." I thought about it. There he'd been, working as usual at La Maison des Petits Bonheurs, when Fabrice had turned up to take control of the place. Even though Nathalie's fiancé had only wanted to close the shop for a few days—out of respect to Monsieur—it had to have been jarring for Mathieu to have been forced out of his home, even temporarily.

Mathieu was pretty sensitive—at least if the tears he'd shed over our mentor's unexpected death were anything to go by.

On the other hand. . . . "Travis told me that the Poyets were footing the bill for Mathieu's hotel room. He looked into it. That's not what you'd do if you wanted to obliterate Mathieu. It's all aboveboard. Maybe we're wrong about a few things."

"Maybe you're not thinking clearly. It's difficult to investigate a murder," Danny commiserated. I thought of him, immobilized facedown while recuperating, and knew that neither of us had it easy. "Think about it," he urged. "Mathieu told you he didn't hear anyone doing that graffiti on the shop, right?"

I nodded. "He said he was sleeping the whole time."

"How likely is that? Even with those thick stone walls? He *had* to have heard something going on. Maybe *he* even did it."

I held my tongue, reminded of the paint I'd seen the *gendarmes* carrying out of Clotilde Renouf's jam shop today. It seemed most probable that *she'd* made that graffiti. Or that someone wanted the police (and me) to believe that she had.

I couldn't help suspecting Charlotte Moreau of that.

"But Mathieu seemed so earnest when I met him." Still reluctant to think the worst of the chocolatier, I paced to the desk where Travis had leaned earlier. I thought I caught a whiff of his spicy aftershave. Mmm. "He gave me a nickname! He wasn't even mad when he knew who *I* was, but I didn't know who *he* was." *Monsieur did not mention me? Never?* Mathieu had looked discomfited, but he hadn't blamed me. I told Danny as much.

"*You* see it that way. He probably saw it another way."

I tried to put myself in my (hypothetical) rival's shoes. I couldn't quite get there. "Honestly? I was so busy trying to find out what he knew, I couldn't pay attention to much else. La Maison des Petits Bonheurs was my first stop in investigating."

"How do you know *he* wasn't investigating you, too?" Danny asked. He never hesitated to tackle the blunt questions. "If I were in his shoes, that's what I'd be doing—trying to measure up my competition, then figuring out how to take her down."

"But that's so mean!" I blurted.

"We're talking about a potential murderer, remember?" There was familiar humor in my old pal's voice, though. Thankfully. "You're both amateurs, so neither of you was good enough at sneaking around to notice what the other one was up to."

If that was true, we were in good company—right along with Travis. I could understand better what my financial advisor saw in Mélanie Flamant, now that we'd talked further. They were both analytical, both intelligent, both determinedly straight-arrow.

I no longer wondered why Travis hadn't extracted more useful information from the *policière*. I could see now that Travis—knowing he wasn't skilled at subterfuge, either—had instead focused on building a bridge between Mélanie and me, hoping we would eventually collaborate. He'd succeeded, too.

"Does the chocolate shop have a surveillance system?" Danny broke into my thoughts with one of his typically security-minded questions. "If it does, I'd lay odds there's footage somewhere of Mathieu Camara chucking your damn photo against the wall." He gave a low snicker. "Care to make the fifty bucks I owe you for Travis's golden retriever bet double or nothing? I'm in."

"I'll just bet you are. You lost." I laughed, too, despite everything. I was chilled at the idea of Mathieu hurling away my photo in a rage, though. That didn't sound . . . healthy. I bit my lip, considering it. "You really think Mathieu resented me?"

Maybe I had reason to be concerned. I trusted Danny.

"You can be pretty insufferable," my buddy joked.

I couldn't very well take offense. "There *is* a crime

wave going on in Saint-Malo." I told him about Mélanie
Flamant.

The attack on the *policière* was unforgivable. Predictably, my security-expert friend immediately agreed
with me about that.

"Does she know who did it? Some scumbag she works
with?"

"Maybe." If so, that would leave Mélanie little re-
course, I knew. It would be tough to sic the police on
the police. I felt sorry for her. "She was walking her
dog near the city wall when someone jumped her—
someone bigger, taller, and stronger."

"Police officers make a lot of enemies."

"Try to sound a little less blasé, will you?"

"Hey, I know *you*. That's it. Not Mélanie Flamant,
not Mathieu Camara, and not Travis. I want *you* to be
careful."

"I am being careful. And you don't need to warn
me about Travis." I sighed. "You might as well give up.
I trust him."

There was a short, fraught silence. Then, "So what's
this nickname Monsieur Chocolate gave you, anyway?
You like it?"

It was the closest he'd come to an apology. I appreciated the effort, however minimal. "*Chouchou.*" For
laughs, I put a little extra Frenchiness into it. "Mathieu calls me *chouchou.*"

"'Choo-choo'?" Danny mimicked. "Like a train?
Weird."

"No, *chouchou*, like . . ." I stopped short of scratch-
ing my head in bafflement. "I'm not actually sure what
it means. Maybe I'll ask Mélanie the next time I see
her. We're getting together tomorrow to discuss
the case. I think she's doling out info to me slowly, in

case I turn out to be slightly less trustworthy than Travis says I am. I'm lucky he vouched for me at all."

Danny's response to that was a surly mumble. I guessed all wasn't quite simpatico with the two of them—at least not yet.

"Whatever you do, watch out for Mathieu," he advised after a few moments' thought. "He's not going to be placated by a few nights in a cheap hotel. He's out a job and a place to live."

"Maybe I could hook him up with one of my former chocolate consultees? I've worked in France before. I know people who might be able to help him." *Despite his criminal record,* I added to myself. "Provided he's not a killer, of course."

"Of course. Help the guy who thinks he has *you* to blame for all his troubles." Danny sounded exasperated. "What was I just saying about you being too nice? Mathieu might be out for revenge. If he's already whacked your mentor because of this—"

"Because of *me*, you mean?" Gulp. "Danny, be serious."

"I'm being deadly serious. If Mathieu killed Philippe because he wanted to squash the merger, or because he knew his boss was planning on replacing him— maybe with *you*—after the Poyet thing went down, then he won't hesitate to come after you now. Logically, you're next on his list." Only Danny used a much coarser term than that for Mathieu's "list." "Think about it."

I didn't want to. It was pretty frightening. But I had to.

"Logically, it's all coming to a head," Danny pushed. "Now, Mathieu has nothing left to lose. That makes him dangerous."

My buddy was right. Fabrice's closure of the shop could have been just the inducement Mathieu needed to take action.

Just the inducement Mathieu needed to kill. Maybe *again*.

Reminded of what had happened to Clotilde Renouf today, I told Danny more about the situation. We brainstormed for a while, but as far as we could discern, the jam maker had had no real connection to the chocolatier. Yes, Clotilde had wanted Monsieur's real estate for herself, but aside from that, her life hadn't overlapped much with Mathieu's. There was no motive.

That meant that if Clotilde *had* been murdered—and hadn't simply fallen to her death unintentionally—it probably hadn't been Mathieu Camera who'd done it. The realization was a lot less comforting than it might have been. Were there *two* murderers on the loose in friendly, picturesque Saint-Malo?

"So, still no luck on the murder weapon?" Danny broke in.

"Not really." I'd already told him that Mathieu Camara had (staunchly) denied using the implement. "I'm still hoping Mélanie will tell me she has fingerprints. I'm planning to look into other local chocolatiers, just in case, but so far, the chocolate chipper isn't just a useless tool—it's a dead end."

"How many chocolatiers had booths at the *Fest-Noz* thing? That would be someplace to start—with people who were already there and already had the tool. Proximity means a lot." I heard a macabre smile in Danny's voice. "You'd be surprised how lazy criminals can be. As a rule, they're not really go-getters."

I grinned. "Hmm. I know someone who breaks that rule."

I meant *him*. Former him, at least, before he'd gone straight, turned his life around, and earned two degrees.

"Really? Sounds like an annoying twerp to me."

"I'll be sure to tell Travis you said so." He'd like that.

"You wouldn't." A pause. "So how about that bet?"

I recalled it. "A hundred bucks says Mathieu smashed my picture on purpose? Nah. I don't even know how you'd prove it."

Our original bet had been for five dollars. That should tell you how many times the two of us had let it double down.

"*I* know how you'd prove it."

With the shop's security-camera coverage, I presumed.

My smile broadened. "You'd have a hard time finagling that footage without being here in person." I knew how he worked. "I'm guessing it's tough to work your magic over the phone?"

"Oh yeah?" His voice deepened. "Is that a challenge?"

I knew better than to dare him. At least I should have.

I waved to Lucas Levebre from the window. He seemed to be finished filming videos for the day. "So what if it is?"

"Game on." Danny sounded intrigued (as usual) by any challenge. "I'll let you know what I find out."

"All right, you do that." I wasn't afraid of Danny and his unorthodox methods. Not when he was on my side—and he always was. "In the meantime, I've got a wine tasting to attend."

And a French pop star to meet up with, I added to myself as Lucas gave me a long-distance mamba from the château's grounds.

All this talk about murder, motives, and people who (might) want to see me dead (preferably within the next several hours) had left me seriously spooked. For a few minutes, at least, I needed a little R & R—and I knew just the place to get it.

Seventeen

My just-for-fun interlude with Lucas Lefebvre was short lived, but it was just what I needed to recharge my batteries before kicking my investigation into my mentor's death into high gear. I spent the rest of that night coaxing Hélène into giving me a tour of the château's private spaces, including the attic, where I didn't see much beyond boxed-up mementos, dusty artwork (dark and depressing, if you asked me), and spiders (shudder!).

Ultimately, I didn't have the heart to spend much more than an hour or so with the despondent, wine-quaffing *châtelaine*. It was just too heartrending to see Hélène scurry from room to room in her luxurious home, chatting in a frenzied way about items that used to be here or had been moved there or had otherwise (according to Hélène) gone missing. It seemed evident that Philippe's death had pushed his widow over the brink somehow.

I wasn't even sure that Hélène remembered who I was.

"The making of an insanity plea?" I asked Travis,

unsure if the French courts allowed such a defense in a murder case.

My financial advisor promised to find out, leaving me with the memory of Hélène nearly weeping as she looked behind a credenza and *didn't* find whatever she'd been searching for.

She howled about having to find it no matter what. I did my best to comfort her, then vowed not to repeat that experience anytime soon. The next day, I slipped out to watch Hubert gardening. Despite my concerns about Mathieu, Hélène, and even Charlotte and/or Fabrice being motivated to murder Monsieur, several signs still pointed to the bloody-handed man I'd actually *seen* holding the weapon that had killed my mentor.

To me, Hubert seemed terrifyingly adept with sharp tools. He hefted them with ease, too, despite his advancing years. While I loitered around the *jardin*, pretending to admire the plants and vines and orderly paths, Philippe's old friend (and Nathalie's potential birth father) sharpened his cutters and whacked down errant tree branches. At one particularly chilling moment, the gardener-turned-unlikely-B&B-owner turned up his pruner, tested the lethal blade with his thumb, and nodded with evident satisfaction. The notion of him having done the same with that deadly chocolate chipper left me nauseated and cold.

I *had* to find out who'd killed Philippe Vetault, and I had to do it very soon. But even when I forced myself to return to Antiquités Moreau and try to mend fences with Charlotte Moreau, I didn't seem to make as much progress as I needed to.

"I am sorry that you witnessed what you did the other day," the kittenish antiques shop owner told me, dressed for the occasion in another feminine wrap

dress and heels. "Monsieur Poyet was here to discuss
an item he wishes to arrange an auction for—"

"You really don't need to explain," I interrupted,
not buying a word of her excuse. Who could refute
her, after all?

"But I wish to!" Charlotte's eyes widened. "I would
not want you to think poorly of me because a clumsy
man pawed me."

Wow, she pulled no punches. I had to hold in a
grin.

"I imagine that Monsieur Poyet might see things
differently?"

She seemed irked at that—but enlightened. "Let
me guess: he told you that *I* was the one who—"
Charlotte broke off, surveying the chichi items in her
shop with impatience. "Oh, la la. I am friendly with a
few men in Saint-Malo and now I am a loose woman?
No. No, I say!" She put her hand familiarly on my
arm, then gave me an appealing look. "You must believe me. Do you?"

For a moment, I was tempted. I was all for feminine
solidarity, wasn't I? Plus, she seemed awfully beguiling.

Damningly, that only lent fuel to Fabrice's fire.

"Let's just put this behind us, all right?" I suggested.

"Yes!" Charlotte looked relieved. She gave me a
canny look. "Perhaps you came to discuss that Caravaggio you mentioned?"

Whoops. I was in too deep with my previous cover
story. I made up an excuse involving the Vetaults'
crowded attic, then skedaddled. I wanted to complete
my roundup of my suspects—which left Mathieu
Camara and Fabrice Poyet to account for—but before
I could do that, I had another rendezvous with Mélanie
and Travis to keep. We were meeting at the Saint-Malo
weekly market. We hoped to make our get-together

appear friendly and casual—you know, unrelated to our investigation into Philippe's murder.

The *gendarme* was concerned about tipping off her primary suspects; I was wary of seeming to give official information to the authorities by hanging out at the police station. I didn't want to push Mathieu (for instance) into making a fatal move that I (most of all) would deeply regret, just because he thought I knew too much and was sharing it with the *policiers*.

Whether our strategy would be useful remained to be seen. Before I could drive to the town square where the market was being held, I first had to extract my Citroën from the château's small graveled parking lot. When I reached it, my compact car had been blocked in by two others, parked higgledy-piggledy.

I looked around for help, but no one was in the immediate area. I headed back inside the château. Its marble floors echoed with my footsteps—that's how much the place had emptied out since breakfast. With the *Fest-Deiz* still in full swing and all the many attractions of Brittany within reach, most of the guests had left for the day. I checked the desk area where I'd originally met tipsy Hélène Vetault, but she wasn't there.

Hmm. Despite its overall luxuriousness, the château didn't have valet service. It was far too small to offer porters. In many European accommodations, the owners themselves serve those functions, which is usually fine with me as a light traveler. But now those conventions had me trapped. The clock was ticking. Literally. There was an ornate grandfather clock in the château's entryway, counting off the minutes until my meeting.

I climbed the stairs and kept looking for someone to help, jangling my keys in my hand as I traversed the fancy hallway and arched windows overlooking the *jardin*. Years ago, I'd been dazzled by those features of the house. Today, I still was.

I spotted someone in a traditional maid's uniform at the end of the hallway and broke into a trot. It was Jeannette Farges, the housekeeper. Finally, I was saved. It was possible she would know to whom the cars in the parking lot belonged.

My money was on someone on the kitchen staff, or possibly another housekeeper. But I didn't want to simply barge into the château's kitchen and demand to have those cars moved—especially not with my admittedly limited *français*. I hurried toward Jeannette, grateful she wasn't on a cigarette break just then.

She heard me coming and jumped with fright. Whoops.

"I'm sorry, I didn't mean to scare you," I called.

Jeannette's blank look reminded me that she might not understand English. While I did my best to rephrase my apology in French, the housekeeper finished what she was doing, which was, essentially, hurling clean towels at one of the guests.

She muttered an apology—to Fabrice Poyet, I saw— then gave him a stilted curtsy and turned away with worry in her eyes.

I imagined, since I didn't like him, that Fabrice was a demanding guest. Either that, or he'd propositioned Jeannette, too. Someone like Fabrice obviously didn't respect boundaries, whether they were between fiancés, antiques dealers, or people who worked for the family he was about to become a part of.

More likely, though, the housekeeper was simply worried about keeping me waiting. What if I were another demanding guest? I tried to be especially kind and considerate as I explained my predicament to

Jeannette. I went on to describe the car that had blocked me in: a battered blue Peugeot sedan.

"*Avec un autocollant*—a sticker?—*pour Les Bleus?*" she asked.

With a bumper sticker in support of the French national soccer team, known as The Blues? she wanted to know.

"*Ouai.* Yes." I nodded, relieved that she recognized it.

"*Je la connais,*" she told me with a smile. I know it. "*Si vous attendez un instant, s'il vous plaît, je vais vous aider.*"

She wanted me to wait a moment, then she would help me.

I offered a grateful *merci*, then took out my phone to text Travis and tell him I'd be a few (unavoidable) minutes late. I couldn't miss Fabrice, though, frowning at Jeannette and me from his château room door, held open just a sliver. As soon as he saw me looking, though, Monsieur Poyet frowned and slammed the door.

Striving to be even-handed, I reminded myself that being unlikable wasn't a crime. Neither was cheating or lying—or even using the excuse of "honoring Monsieur Vetault" as a reason to toss out the rough-around-the-edges parolee working at your (future) chocolaterie. I still suspected that's what Fabrice had done when he'd closed Monsieur's shop so abruptly. Given how selfish he seemed, I doubted he cared that

Nathalie had been upset. He must have known that delivering ultimatums to Mathieu would push him to quit. My fellow chocolatier was a proud man. He wouldn't have wanted to kowtow to Fabrice's demands—although he had taken his money, so what did I know? I wasn't an emotive Frenchman.

Down the hall, Jeannette beckoned me. I followed her downstairs, and within a few minutes, my problem was solved.

Before driving away, though, I grabbed a few petite boxes of handmade chocolates—I always carry samples with me in my crossbody bag—and gave them to the housekeeper and to the fan of *Les Bleus* soccer who'd inadvertently boxed in my Citroën.

They accepted the chocolates with multiple *merci*s and smiles, prompting me to remember as I waved and left the château that, most of the time, my work as a chocolate whisperer is rewarding. I love it—when it doesn't involve murder, at least.

With my mind (regrettably) on exactly that, I drove along the pastoral French back roads to the Saint-Malo town market.

You know I'm a food professional, so there's not much I enjoy more than an opportunity to suss out the local food scene wherever I go. I make it a habit to visit restaurants, grocery stores, food carts, and open-air markets like the ones held in most small European towns, immersing myself in the regional culture in the most delicious way possible: with its food.

Not that markets were (necessarily) limited to food; most featured a variety of items. You'd expect artisanal jams, cheeses, and breads, or freshly picked flowers, or produce from resident farmers. You might not expect clothing from small designers, pottery and artwork, candles and soap, or musical instruments for sale, but you'd be likely to find all of them.

I met Travis and Mélanie (and Fleur the dog) at the edge of the town market, then we wandered into its midst as a trio. I volunteered to walk Fleur, and couldn't help imagining myself as her actual human companion as I took her leash. I really wanted a dog of my own. So far, I seemed destined to have doggie dates only while working on consultations (and investigations).

Today, from where I stood, the *policière's* bumps and bruises had only gotten worse. Knowing Mélanie as I did now, I felt awful for her. As we stood there in our matching hats, I gave her a commiserating face. "How are you feeling today?"

"Determined." She swept the crowd with an intense gaze—one that should have withered the intentions of any wrongdoers. "If I knew who did this to me, I would have them prosecuted."

Whoa. "Remind me not to make you angry," I joked. "Not that I can blame you. You were walking Fleur when it happened?"

Mélanie nodded. "Someone jumped me from behind. Started to hit me. Yelled obscenities at me." She shuddered. "I fought him."

"Good for you," I encouraged. Honestly, I felt at a loss for what else to say. As women, we were particularly vulnerable, and we both knew it. I was fortunate nothing similarly dangerous had happened to me during my travels. "You really *are* strong."

The *gendarme* gave me a Gallic pursing of her lips. "Do not fool yourself that I survived because I fought him. It was not so simple. My attacker wanted to hurt me and scare me, but that is all. That is to say, I do not think he wanted to kill me."

The matter-of-fact way Mélanie said that gave me chills.

"I can't believe you have to put up with harassment in this day and age," I told her. "Can't your supervisors do something?"

She shook her head. "Who can say it is not them at fault?"

Ugh. That was even worse. But before I could say so, Travis stepped between us women. "Hey, we're here to enjoy ourselves," he cajoled. "Maybe we can talk about this another time?"

"Of course." Mélanie shot me a conspiratorial look. We had agreed to meet at the market to exchange information, but Travis either didn't want to acknowledge that or chose to overlook it.

Maybe witnessing Clotilde Renouf's accident had affected my financial advisor more than he wanted to admit. To look at him—wandering amid the market's many sellers, examining just-picked green pears and a dizzying array of fresh apples—anyone would have thought Travis really was enjoying a fun market morning.

I relented—especially since I spied Fabrice and Nathalie at a stand nearby, discussing its vibrant green, orange, and yellow winter squash. I didn't want to reveal my collaboration with the police, so I turned to my keeper and asked him to help pick out some ripe figs for us. Maybe we'd have a picnic lunch later?

"Absolutely," Travis agreed. He started a fast, amiable conversation in French with the seller, pointing and nodding.

If you're ever at an open-air market in France, provincial or Parisian or otherwise, you should know that there's a protocol at work. It's not a grocery store or a corner bodega. It's not a self-serve situation. To prevent customers from rummaging through each seller's wares—bruising and ruining produce as they inexpertly make their selections—each customer is expected to describe to the seller what they want, how much they'd like, and any relevant details—when the item will be served, for instance. That way, the seller can choose a perfect apple, bunch of leafy greens, or (today) some figs. Everyone leaves happy—often after the (expert) seller has recommended some additional serving suggestions or helpful cooking ideas.

With our figs in hand, Mélanie, Travis, and I made our way across the market. We chose a crusty baguette next and some soft local cheeses for our spontaneous picnic lunch, then stopped at another vendor to select some oval, reddish-purple plums. They looked amazing. If I'd had a bottle of red wine and a tasty chunk of quality dark chocolate to cap off our meal, I'd have been delighted. I glanced around the market, wondering if any of the local chocolateries I was familiar with had stalls there.

As I did, something buzzed in the air, inches from my hat-covered head. I clapped my hand on my noggin in surprise, then looked up to see Capucine's drone cam whizzing around the market. Her crew was there, too—sadly, without Lucas Lefebvre.

"We are capturing local color," Capucine explained when she caught up to me, hastily apologizing if she'd startled me by playfully buzzing me with her camera. "It is helpful for editing together my footage if I have a lot of choices to pick from."

I understood. Doubtless the old market *was* awfully scenic. Its expert artisans, vibrantly colored fruits and vegetables, idiosyncratic customers, and a distinctive French old town square would form an excellent backdrop for one of Lucas's videos.

I told Capucine that I didn't mind, then asked her (as a favor) if she might be able to grab some shots of Travis and me together. I didn't know when I might be spending a day with my financial advisor in person again. I wanted to seize the moment.

Capucine understood—or at least, she thought she did. The indie director gave me a wink. "*Oui*, I will get you keepsakes."

Her intimation was clear: she thought I was interested in Travis—*romantically* interested. Before I could correct her or otherwise promise *not* to sappily moon over whatever footage she gave me, Capucine was on her phone, giving quick directions to the crewmember who was manning the drone cam's controls.

Feeling slightly silly, I sidled up to Travis and tried to appear knowledgeable as he discussed the plums. We were waiting for our turn to buy some, but I—knowing we were being filmed—felt suddenly awkward. Where to put my hands? How to smile?

As it turned out, it didn't matter. Just as the drone cam swooped in for a close-up shot of us, the whole thing plummeted.

It crash-landed, diving to the earth amid some surprised marketgoers. They dispersed. In the process, several of them stepped on the drone cam. In the end, Fabrice Poyet emerged with it. He made a sad face as the complicated, plastic-and-metal device hung from his grasp with multiple parts snapped off.

"*Ah, non.*" Sorrowfully, he shook his head. "*Elle est cassée. Quel dommage.*" Roughly, oh no! It's broken—what a shame.

At least he'd retrieved it. That was one point in his favor. I'd have almost expected Fabrice to stomp on it himself.

"*Bien que c'est bien.*" With a concerned expression, Capucine took the mangled camera from him. "*Vous inquiétez pas.*"

It's all right. Don't worry. She was handling things with equanimity, but I knew how tight her budget and schedule were.

I exchanged glances with Travis. He'd noticed the same things I had. What's more, he knew me. I gave him a subtle nod.

By this time tomorrow, Capucine and her crew would have a replacement drone cam, courtesy of me (and Uncle Ross's money).

"I'm sorry about this, Capucine," I told her. "I feel responsible." I nodded at Travis. "I shouldn't have asked you."

"It was not your fault." She smiled at me. "I will send you the footage we *did* get, okay? You still want it, *n'est-ce pas?*"

I assumed she was still hoping to extract some footage from the drone camera somehow. I nodded and thanked her, feeling all too aware of the people milling around us, Mélanie Flamant included. I didn't want anyone to overhear our conversation.

It was bad enough I'd basically enlisted Capucine and her crew to make a personal video of Travis and me shopping. I didn't need the whole world to know how sentimental I could be.

Fortunately, my keeper chose that moment to distract me with what seemed to be a question. I promised to catch up with Capucine later and turned to him, expecting a query about what model of replacement drone camera I wanted to buy the film crew.

Instead, Travis said, "I've been telling Mélanie about Mathieu Camara's nickname for you. What was it again?"

Aha, that's right. I'd wanted a translation from her. "*Chouchou.* Mathieu calls me *chouchou.* I have no idea why, but—"

I was brought up short by the somber glance Travis and the *policière* exchanged. I was missing something significant here.

"Why?" I pushed. "What's going on?"

Mélanie frowned. "*Chouchou*? You are sure?"

I nodded as the three of us moved farther away from the market-going crowd. The sounds of melodious French faded a bit. I imagined a bird's-eye view as Capucine's drone cam would have seen the scene, if it had survived—tall, blond, bespectacled Travis in his coat and dapper scarf, and shorter, brunette Mélanie and I in our jackets and matching white knit caps.

I had a premonition of what she was going to tell me.

"*Chouchou* is slang," the *policière* said. "It means . . . in English, I suppose that one would say, 'teacher's pet'?"

I got goose bumps. *That* wasn't an affectionate nickname.

"*Oui*, and?" I crossed my arms, determined to hang tough.

Mélanie's expression became even graver. "And it is what my attacker called me. 'Go back where you belong, *chouchou*,' he said, cruelly, with every blow—*en anglais*, in English." The *gendarme* winced. "I thought it was because he was trying to disguise his voice—because he did not want me to recognize him. My colleagues, other people in town, they want me to quit work."

I understood more than I wanted to. "It was Mathieu Camara. *Mathieu* was the one who attacked you." *Who beat you savagely.*

I couldn't say so, but we all knew it. When I glanced at Travis, he was studying my hat—the very same hat as Mélanie's.

"Hayden, he thought it was *you*," my financial advisor told me, his usually seductive voice husky with worry. "He thought he was attacking *you*. He thought he was telling *you* to go away."

Danny had been right. I felt cold to the core—especially once I remembered my very first meeting with Mathieu Camera at La Maison des Petits Bonheurs. When he'd found me taking snapshots of the graffiti on Monsieur's chocolaterie, Mathieu had been aggressive. Then I'd lowered my phone, he'd seen my face, and he'd confessed that he'd thought I was someone else.

You have hair like hers, the chocolatier had said then.

I'd thought he'd been ham-fistedly flirting with me. Especially once he'd followed up with, *Only it is your smile that is the much prettier one.* But I'd been horribly wrong.

"There are things that you do not know about my investigation." In a firm voice, Mélanie Flamant took charge. "I suggest we share everything, now, before it is too late."

Eighteen

The next several hours were fraught with tension. It didn't take long for Mélanie to confide in me the rest of what she hadn't shared—and for me to do the same. We all noshed through our fruit, bread, and cheese picnic as we did. I don't think any of us tasted it. At that point, it was fuel—something to keep up our energy while we talked about the attack on Mélanie, the things I'd seen at the *Fest-Noz*, the suspects that Travis and I had compiled, and the research we'd all done.

From everything she told me, Mélanie *had* been conducting a thorough investigation. That much was evident, exactly as Travis had assured me. I felt sorry for having doubted her. Seeing her sense of resolve that afternoon, I knew that the investigation into my mentor's death could not have been in more competent hands. Despite her detractors, Mélanie Flamant was an expert *policière*—and she had much more information than she'd revealed.

Unfortunately, though, that information did not include enough proof to arrest Mathieu Camara for Monsieur's murder. The deadly chocolate chipper, implicating as it might have seemed, had not carried any fingerprints or other forensic evidence.

"The killer wore gloves," Mélanie explained ruefully. "It was chilly that night. Such attire would not have been unusual."

I silently cursed the Breton weather and wondered aloud about Hubert Bernard, too. His bloody hands still haunted me.

"He was attempting to help—to remove the weapon," the *policière* told Travis and me. "He and Monsieur Vetault were longtime friends. Monsieur Bernard was distraught and drunk. He did not know that it was already too late to do anything. He meant no harm."

Then Hubert truly *hadn't* remembered finding Philippe's body, I surmised, recalling my conversation with the château's gardener when he'd surprised me in the *jardin* that day. It must have been awful for Hubert to have awakened, miserable and hung over in jail, only to learn that his childhood friend was dead.

Although Monsieur's death *would* have left the way clear for Hubert and Hélène to be together, I mused. But, by all accounts, Philippe hadn't objected to his wife's relationship with Monsieur Bernard. My mentor had left them with ownership of the château B&B, after all. If that wasn't generous, I didn't know what was.

Maybe, since Philippe expected to get a big payout from the Vetault-Poyet merger, he'd felt he could afford to be giving.

"Are you going to arrest Mathieu Camara for attacking you?" I asked Mélanie. "I'd be happy to give a statement. Whatever you need." Troubled, I examined her bruised face. "I'm so sorry."

"It is not your fault. Monsieur Camara is an angry

man," the *policière* said. "And yes, I will arrest him. But because it is still possible that he is the one who killed M. Vetault, I do not want to be too hasty. I must do everything very carefully."

Travis agreed with her. "If you need evidence, we can look for it. If you want help, we're ready to give it. Anything."

The two of them shared an affable look. It wasn't quite smarty-pants-in-love territory (which I felt relieved about, actually), but it was definitely . . . something. Mutual admiration?

"See, Hayden? I don't know why you and Danny are always trying to go it alone." Travis gave me a scolding look. "The police are ready, willing, and able to help in these cases."

Well . . . they hadn't been in San Francisco. Or in Portland.

In London, Detective Constable Satya Mishra had been slightly more capable, but I'd still run into serious trouble.

Travis hadn't been there. Long-distance assistance wasn't the same. But I decided to let his misapprehensions slide. If another opportunity ever arose for my financial advisor to help in a homicide-related capacity, then we'd talk frankly about it.

I still hoped I was finished with murder and mayhem.

"Thank you." Mélanie nodded, then began gathering her things. She reclaimed little Fleur by taking the leash from me, too. Our less-than-idyllic picnic was over. "It is necessary that you two return to château Vetault and stay there." Her gaze transferred to Travis, then softened slightly. "Be careful. I will phone you when the appropriate actions have been taken."

Travis nodded—but not me. I couldn't agree. "We're

supposed to just wait around, then?" I shook my head. "No way."

I was sorry that poor Mélanie had been attacked, but I couldn't forget that it should have been *me* sporting bruises.

"There must be something else we can do," I went on, keeping my voice low. The town market must have ended. More people were strolling past us now, most of them carrying flowers and produce and bread in their market baskets. "We could keep an eye on Mathieu Camara and make sure he doesn't get away."

"And if the murderer is someone else?" Mélanie arched her brows. "You will be . . . I believe it is called sitting ducks?"

"We'll be no less 'sitting ducks' at the château!"

Travis touched my arm. "Not if we stay in our rooms."

I scoffed. Danny would never have suggested hiding. I wished he were there. I could have used his handy impulsiveness.

"I could arrest you on suspicion and keep you in a jail cell for safety," Mélanie offered. "That would be very secure."

Hmm. Suddenly, house arrest in a wonderful French château didn't sound so bad. Besides, I still wanted to think about all this on my own—to review my notebook of observations and ideas.

Some (or most) chocolatiers and professional bakers maintain notebooks. The difference is theirs are extensive collections of recipes, formulas, and percentages, compiled over years of experience. Mine has become a compendium of reasons to murder someone and how to (potentially) get away with it.

Honestly, I'd rather have been tracking cacao

butter percentages and chocolate varietals or recipes for cookies.

My personal favorite is chocolate chip, aka the king of cookies. But I'm amenable to peanut butter, snickerdoodle, a nice oatmeal-cranberry-pecan cookie with white chocolate chunks . . .

"Fine. We'll stay in until you give the all-clear," I said.

Was it wrong that I was daydreaming about cookies? I must have been stressed, because I couldn't stop mentally creaming butter and sugar, adding vanilla and salt, spooning in flour . . .

"I'll make sure of it." Travis burst my mental bake-off bubble just as I reached for the cocoa powder and semi-sweet chocolate morsels needed for triple chocolate chunk cookies.

I shot him an unhappy glance, wishing I had a strategy that *didn't* involve lolling around waiting to be ambushed. I'd been planning to follow up in person on Danny's tip about the importance of proximity (and criminal laziness) when it came to chocolatiers who might have had access to the chocolate chipper on the night of the *Fest-Noz* when Monsieur had been murdered.

I doubted a phone call would pack the same punch. Not to mention, my French was probably too poor to extract useful information—not without the help of hand signals and smiles.

"*Très bien.* I will be in touch," *policière* Mélanie said.

With that, I was stuck. I drove my Citroën back down the winding autumn roads to the château and prepared to wait.

* * *

In the end, waiting had to wait. Because as I entered
the château and headed for the front desk to claim
my *chambre* (room) key, I ran into Hélène. Not altogether surprisingly, the *châtelaine* had a full wineglass
in one hand and (shortly thereafter) my room key in
the other. I could see she'd been drinking for a while.

Patiently, I waited for my key while Travis parked
his rental car. It was easy to be relaxed about the delay,
knowing that I'd defiantly sprinted into the château
after finding my own parking space, unwilling to
be overprotected by my financial advisor. Travis
had seemed determined to guard me, going so far
as to walk me (arm in arm!) to my car after leaving
Mélanie.

I didn't think our "house arrest" kicked in the
moment we lost sight of the *policière*, but Travis had
disagreed. He'd tailgated me the whole way back
from Saint-Malo, a suit-wearing guardian angel who
navigated French traffic roundabouts like a pro. Of
course I'd felt compelled to duck him for a few seconds once we arrived. I needed a little breathing
room, didn't I?

"*Voilà! Voici, votre clé!*" Hélène brandished my key
with a triumphant smile. In many older European
hotels, room keys are kept at the front desk, to be re-
linquished, and claimed, when guests come and go.
Mine was on an ornate gilded key fob with silk fringe.
Just then, Hélène held it tantalizingly out of my reach.
"*Vous voulez une petite visite de la maison, peut-être?*"

She was asking if I wanted a little tour of the house,
as though I hadn't already toured the place with her
multiple times. Poor Madame Vetault. I felt sorry for
my mentor's wife all over again. "*Peut-être,*" I replied.

Maybe. "*Bientôt.*" Sometime soon. In the meantime . . . "Did you find what you were looking for?"

At my switch to English, Hélène blinked. She frowned.

"*Ah, non.* No." Her eyes filled with tears. "I promised that I would look for it, but I must have misplaced it." Her gaze grew dark. Apprehensive. "So many things are missing to me."

Like her husband, I couldn't help imagining, morbidly.

I couldn't be sure she hadn't had some sort of mental break. She definitely didn't seem stable or well. Would finding out who'd killed Philippe really be enough to help Hélène?

She swigged more wine, then gave a tipsy salute to the wall behind the reception desk. The nook didn't occupy much space, but what existed appeared to be noticeably bare—especially as compared with the rest of the château's extravagant furnishings.

"*Il aurait dû être là!*" she wailed as she studied that bare wall behind the desk. "*Je ne peux plus le trouver maintenant.*"

It should have been right here! I can't find it anymore.

Before I could formulate a response that went beyond "I'm sorry," Travis barged in. He shot me a beleaguered look, then crossed the marble-lined foyer and strode past the stone stairs.

When he reached Madame Vetault, his demeanor softened. He must have heard part of our conversation, because he jumped right in and did something that hadn't once occurred to me—not for days.

I'd been so busy feeling sorry for Philippe's widow

that I hadn't thought to ask the most (sorry to say) logical question.

"*De quoi est-ce que vous cherchez, Madame?*" he asked in his deep, rumbly, considerate voice. "*Peut-être je peux vous aider.*"

What is it that you're looking for? Maybe I can help you.

Hélène responded immediately. "*Le peinture de ma famille.*"

Aha. Of course. My mentor's wife was looking, I translated, for a family portrait that had been misplaced. I had an idea.

"I'll check with Nathalie," I told Travis. "Be right back."

I was willing to bet that Philippe's daughter had taken the family portrait upstairs to her room sometime, possibly to keep her company in her grieving. She, too, might have been too grief-stricken to pointedly question her mother about all the "missing" items Hélène kept going on about. Nathalie had told me that she found her mother's drinking difficult to deal with.

Trailed closely by Travis's tight-lipped misgivings, I headed upstairs to the room I'd seen Fabrice in earlier. He and Nathalie had to be sharing accommodations, I reasoned.

My beach going friend from that long-ago summer of training with Monsieur answered my knock promptly. "Hayden, hello!"

Behind her, I glimpsed her fiancé bustling around the room. I must have been staring at him (probably with animosity, given his dalliance with Charlotte Moreau), because Nathalie frowned.

"Fabrice has been called back to Paris on urgent

Poyet business," she explained softly. "He will miss Papa's memorial, but I will remain here in Saint-Malo for some time, of course."

I nodded, but I couldn't help wondering if Nathalie was slightly less easygoing when it came to Fabrice's business priorities than she seemed. It looked as though they'd argued.

Fabrice put some clothes into a suitcase, then glared across the spacious room. Irritably, he snapped his fingers. The housekeeper, Jeannette Farges, timidly came into view with more items. Fabrice barked at her to hurry up. He was insufferable.

"I'm sorry to disturb you," I told Nathalie. "You must want to spend your time alone together before Monsieur Poyet has to leave."

"*Pas de problème.*" No problem. "You wanted something?"

"*Oui!* Yes. I'm sorry." I snapped back to my friend's face, leaving aside the issue of her deceitful, tyrannical fiancé for now. "I was wondering . . . it seems that your mother is looking for a family portrait that she's lost? One from the château's front desk? I promised her I would try to help her find it."

Nathalie frowned in thought. "There has always been a photograph on the desk," she said. "But it remains, I think."

"Then you didn't . . . maybe . . . borrow it?" I asked delicately.

"*Bof.* If Maman cannot find her things, she should stop drinking." Now Nathalie seemed harassed. "I cannot help you."

Wow. She really was upset by her mother's drinking. Fabrice strode to the entryway and glowered at me with his hand on the door. "It is time that you leave, Madame."

In the middle of the room, Jeannette Farges watched the whole tableau unfold with an inscrutable expression. Most likely, she simply wanted to get away from Fabrice Poyet.

That made two of us. "I'm sorry, Nathalie. We'll talk later." I gave Fabrice a dismissive look. "*Adieu, Monsieur.*"

It was rude of me, and I knew it. But I just couldn't help myself. In most cases, *au revoir* or something casual is used to say good-bye; *adieu* is reserved for instances when you never expect to see the other person again. At that moment, it fit.

Fabrice was stone-faced . . . all except for his nostrils. I saw them flaring with angry hauteur and almost laughed out loud.

He might have been able to fool Nathalie, but not me.

Inside the room, the housekeeper piped up. "Monsieur?"

That was my cue. I nodded another silent good-bye to Nathalie, then headed down the hallway. I wished I could have easily solved Madame Vetault's dilemma, but so far, I hadn't.

A door slammed behind me. Then opened. Then slammed again.

"*Madame, attendez!*" Jeannette called out. "*S'il vous plaît!*" Wait, please! I heard her footsteps hurrying behind me.

They were muffled by the deluxe carpet, of course. We were still in the Vetault's fancy château, after all. I stopped.

I mustered a smile for her. "I'll bet you're not sorry

Monsieur Poyet is leaving," I joked. "One less guest to try to please?"

Jeannette gazed at me, possibly in confusion. I wasn't sure how much (if any) English she spoke. It occurred to me that I had never experienced anything less than exemplary service from the housekeeper, though. Fabrice definitely stood alone in his annoyance with her. Why was he always so curt with her, anyway?

"Thanks for breaking the tension back there," I added in my friendliest tone. I nodded toward Nathalie and Fabrice's *chambre*, then mimed her pert query. "'*Monsieur?' Merci à vous.*"

"*Ah, de rien.*" You're welcome. The housekeeper curtsied.

That was uncomfortable. Embarrassed, I stopped her. "If I can just ask," I said slowly, watching her face to determine if she understood, "how do you deal with someone like Monsieur Poyet?"

All Jeannette comprehended was Monsieur Poyet. Her eyes filled with tears. Her lips blubbered. Her former composure vanished.

Oh no. What had I done? I tried again in French, my query mingled with apologies for upsetting her. I'd only wanted to congratulate her on a job well done. Instead, I did something else: I reminded the housekeeper of something distressing.

Jeannette apologized in French, then added something more. I didn't understand. She gestured for me to follow, then let us both into an unused *chambre de château*—a guest room—where we could (I presumed) speak privately. She drew in a deep breath.

"*J'ai très peur. Aidez-moi, Madame. S'il vous plaît.*"

It was worse than I thought, I realized as I translated.

I'm very afraid, the housekeeper had said. *Please help me.*

There was no way I could placidly go under house arrest now. I nodded and reassured her. "*Je vais. Je vous promets.*"

I will. I promise, I'd said. And I meant it, too.

Nineteen

When I got back downstairs after helping Jeannette, Travis had secured my room key and his own. We went to his room to pick up a few things, then headed to my (slightly larger) *chambre.* Once we were inside, that was it. The waiting game was on.

Have I mentioned that I detest waiting? I'm someone who likes to be always on the move—to be always *doing* something. Just then, being stuck sitting around felt excruciating.

Fortunately, Capucine Roux had messaged me about the film footage she'd promised at the market. She'd given me temporary access to her film crew's Internet "cloud" account, where they stored their work online. It wasn't edited, the director told me, apologizing for the excess material, but it was complete.

Well, if anything could distract me from waiting for *policière* Mélanie to arrest Mathieu and give us the all-clear, it was shots of Travis and me together—not to mention uncut images of hunky Lucas Lefebvre singing, dancing, and being all-around irresistible. While Travis wedged shut our room's door with a

straight back chair and then paced near the fireplace,
I pulled out my laptop to get a clearer view of Capucine's film.

Viewing it was more challenging than I'd expected.
I felt antsy and preoccupied, distracted by thoughts
of everything that had gone on recently. Fabrice's animosity bothered me; so did Nathalie's seeming
sudden annoyance with me. I wished I could have
talked things over with my mentor's daughter, but
with her fiancé lurking around behind her, that had
been impossible.

I wished I could have located Hélène's lost family
portrait, too. No wonder she'd been so consumed
with finding it. I would have wanted all the images I
could have of my departed husband, too, I thought
as I stared distractedly at the video coverage that
Capucine and her crew had captured for me. Travis
and I looked natural together on film, but our appearance had been (unsurprisingly) cut short by the drone
cam's crash.

Mindlessly, I scrolled backward through time, viewing more footage. I saw Lucas smile and dance,
hamming it up. I saw shots of the Breton countryside,
images of the château and its gardens, film of the
churning ocean and its rocky shore. It was clear that
Capucine and her crew had done their homework
before coming to Brittany, because they'd captured all
the most perfect local color to serve as background
for Lucas's music videos.

The next chunk of footage looked darker. Night
filming. I realized with a start that I'd reached the seg-
ments they'd taken days earlier, before Monsieur's
death. I slammed shut my laptop's lid and looked
away, not wanting to see it.

Travis noticed. "Are you all right?"

His voice sounded kind. Too kind. I teared up. "Uh-huh."

My financial advisor wasn't buying it. He heard my scratchy voice and knew I was upset. "Hayden, tell me what's wrong."

I hate waiting, I considered saying. *Or, let's do something!*

"Do you really think Hélène was looking for that family photo?" I asked him instead, hoping to distract myself. "The framed photo on the front desk that Nathalie mentioned to me? Madame Vetault didn't seem thrilled when I pointed it out to her."

"We can't expect 'thrilled' from a widow. She's struggling right now."

That was putting it mildly. "I was hoping she'd be happy." I frowned, knowing I was purposely delaying viewing the footage from the night of the *Fest-Noz. Hello, procrastination, my old friend.* "Nathalie didn't mention any other family portraits."

"We can't be sure that's really what's bothering Hélène," Travis pointed out. He'd started pacing again. "It might be that the family portrait is only the latest item she's thought of."

"It's weird that she's so obsessed with finding things," I mused, then shrugged. "I guess that's grief for you, though."

Both of us believed that Hélène truly missed Philippe.

I glanced down at my laptop. I ought to view that film.

"On the other hand," I said, "maybe we're missing the obvious explanation. Maybe there's *another* family portrait somewhere." I set aside my laptop. "Let's go look for it."

Travis shut me down with a glance. "We're not

leaving this room. Not until we hear from Mélanie that it's all clear."

"But that might take days! We can't just hide in here."

"We can, we will, and we are," my keeper insisted. His gaze wandered to my laptop. "Putting off writing some reports?"

His know-it-all tone got my dander up. "No," I huffed with undeniable self-righteousness. "I would never do such a thing."

Travis suppressed a grin. "Not anymore, you mean."

"Exactly." Gritting my teeth, I made a show of whipping open my laptop again. I pointed to my screen. "See? No problem."

My maneuver worked—to a point. My helpful financial advisor quit nagging me about my procrastination tendencies. The only trouble was, now I was faced with Capucine's *Fest-Noz* footage.

If Danny had been there, he would have told me to look for the chocolatiers we'd talked about earlier— the ones I'd planned to interview in person but hadn't after my market meeting with Mélanie had taken a turn for the criminal regarding Mathieu.

My muscle-bound pal had a point about opportunity being almost as important as motive when it came to murder. Someone had had access to that chocolate chipper that night. Someone had cornered my mentor and stabbed him with it. If Capucine and her crew had accidentally captured any of that with their drone cam . . .

On the verge of viewing it, I hesitated. Surely, given the circumstances, Capucine would have searched her footage for anything useful, or the police would have commandeered it and done the same. But if what *policière* Mélanie had told me was as complete as she'd sworn it was, no one had thought of that.

I had to look. But my heart was racing, and so was my mind. I definitely didn't want to see my beloved Monsieur stabbed to death in front of my eyes. I exhaled, then grabbed my phone.

A double-check of my messages confirmed it. Capucine hadn't edited any of the footage. She'd been focused on getting as much as she could before her crew's time in Brittany had run out.

Okay, then. I screwed up my courage and ran the footage.

From the drone cam's perspective, I saw Saint-Malo and the *Fest-Noz* as I never had. The walled city looked majestic and moody, minimally illuminated by those hanging light strings and full of *fête*-goers. The small camera swooped over trees and down among them, soared above the old rooftops and along the winding cobblestone streets. To my surprise, no one seemed to notice its presence. The camera hadn't been very big, but it had made an audible sound. Most likely, the live Breton *bagad* band and the raucous crowd had drowned out any telltale noises from above.

I estimated only a few minutes had gone by since Travis and I had sequestered ourselves in my château room, but it felt like ages to me. On the footage, I glimpsed police cars and emergency vehicles surrounding Philippe Vetault's fallen body. I felt a mournful lump rise in my throat. I swallowed hard and then moved the footage slider to the left, rewinding quickly in time.

I wound up at an earlier point in the *Fest-Noz*, after the vendors had set up their stalls and after most of the residents had arrived for the celebration, but before

Monsieur's death. It was still dark out—spookily so, given what I knew would happen.

I searched the film for people who looked threatening, for one of my suspects, for anyone who might have wanted to hurt my mentor. No one appeared to be doing anything malicious. I even saw myself, wandering amongst the stalls, small and unknowing.

A chill passed through me. I wished I'd known somehow what was going to happen—wished fervently I could have prevented it. As it was, all I could do was keep searching the footage while Travis strode beyond the chair where I was curled up to do so.

At the edge of the frame, a furtive movement caught my eye. I backed up, then zoomed in. On the digital footage, I caught sight of another stall—a chocolatier's stall. It wasn't La Maison des Petits Bonheurs', but there was someone familiar there, lurking just at the edge of the nearest light string.

I recognized Fabrice Poyet, wearing a wool overcoat and leather gloves, eyeing the crowd as he edged closer to the stall. With one quick movement, he snatched something from the chocolatier's worktable, then tucked it beneath his open coat.

The chocolate chipper. I knew that's what it had been.

I had the luxury of rewinding. I backed up and confirmed it. I moved on, unable to breathe as I watched Fabrice move stealthily through the crowd. He skirted the edge of the *fête*, keeping away from most of the lights, but it was definitely him.

I felt queasy. I realized my finger was hovering over the stop button. I curled it away and made myself keep on watching.

Quickly enough, it had happened. Fabrice didn't attack my mentor on camera, but he came close enough. The Parisian film crew's footage plainly showed Monsieur Poyet tracking down Philippe, having a confrontation with him, then pushing him down. Hard.

The last image I saw of my beloved Monsieur was as Philippe stumbled, wide-eyed and outraged. An instant later, Fabrice bore down on Philippe from behind. Just before he struck, the drone cam moved lazily away. Its faraway operator couldn't have known until later what horrible images it had captured that night.

A tear trickled onto my cheek. I understood that I was crying, but I felt strangely numb, too. I finally knew what had happened to Philippe Vetault, and thanks to Hélène, Charlotte Moreau, and Mélanie Flamant, I thought I knew why.

But while I was doing this, my mentor's murderer might be getting away. I closed my laptop and shoved it under the bed.

"All done?" Travis heard me. "See? That wasn't so bad."

My financial advisor turned, presumably to congratulate me on conquering my antireport-writing procrastination. Instead, he saw my petrified expression and frowned.

"What's wrong? What happened?" His gaze skittered to the underside of my room's four-poster bed, where I hoped to keep my proof of Fabrice Poyet's guilt secure until I reached Mélanie.

I was already dialing my phone, hoping I wasn't too late.

The phone rang and rang. No luck. I swore under my breath.

"Hayden?" Travis looked surprised and worried. "Tell me."

Quickly, I did. To his credit, Travis took the news in

apparent stride, with no time wasted on arguing or naysaying. He didn't bother trying to tell me I was overreacting or demand to see Capucine's film footage for himself. He believed me.

Would anyone else? Another *gendarme?* I didn't know.

It was an all-too-real possibility that, given the Poyet family's wealth and influence in France, Fabrice would not face criminal charges. Not unless the evidence against him was sound.

"Fabrice must have known that Capucine's drone cam might have captured footage of him at the *Fest-Noz*," I told Travis. "He might not have realized it until he saw it buzzing around the market, but once he had a chance to destroy it, he did."

I bet he *had* stomped on the fallen drone cam, just as I'd supposed he would at the time. Too bad I'd dismissed the idea.

"At least he tried." Travis looked concerned. Full of focus. Supersmart. Thank goodness. "He must not have known the video crew would have a cloud-based backup on the Internet."

Silently, I gave thanks for technology. But none of it would do us any good if Fabrice escaped. He'd been packing to leave earlier. Obviously, he hadn't been sticking around Saint-Malo for Monsieur's memorial service. He intended to miss it, despite Nathalie's disappointment and disapproval.

I thought I knew what he'd been waiting for. It involved Hélène Vetault . . . and the mysterious item she'd been searching for.

"It's not a family portrait that Hélène's misplaced," I told Travis on a surge of inspiration. "I translated her French wrong." I leaped from my cozy chair and

hurried to my room's *petit* antique desk. As quickly
as I could, I sorted through the information there,
bypassing booklets about Breton attractions to grab
the one I wanted: a glossy brochure about château
Vetault and its history. "Hélène meant 'family painting,'
as in, a painting that belongs to her family, not a family
portrait."

I flipped open the brochure and pointed to the
second page.

Travis looked at the image I'd indicated. "That's
Hélène and Philippe at the château, standing at the
B&B's front desk."

"Right. And what's that hanging on the wall behind
them?"

Travis squinted. "If I don't miss my guess, that's a
Caravaggio. It's not a large painting, but if it's real—"

"It *has* to be real." My mind raced with the possibil-
ities. "Charlotte Moreau *was* telling the truth. Fabrice
Poyet wanted to set up an art auction with her. For
this." I stabbed my finger on the image of the painting. "But first he had to find it."

"Which was why Hélène was in a tizzy all the
time," Travis surmised. "Not only was she drunk and
distraught, she was under threat from her future
son-in-law. He wanted that painting."

I nodded. But my financial advisor wasn't finished
yet.

"But that brochure is years old," he estimated.
"Look at the details. This was taken when the château
became a B&B."

"Right. Which was when Hélène became *châtelaine*—
when she redecorated the whole place in preparation
for opening it to the public. See the lamps? The knickknacks? The curtains? I saw a bunch of that stuff up in

the attic, on one of Madame Vetault's house tours. I know I did!" I paced. "I bet that's where the painting was stashed, too—forgotten until Nathalie and Fabrice went with Philippe to look for *Grand-Mère's* wedding dress."

When Nathalie had shared that story, I'd envisioned my mentor retrieving a lacy white gown and tenderly giving it to his daughter. What I'd missed had been Fabrice nearby, eyeing the valuable Caravaggio that Hélène had unknowingly stashed. To Nathalie and Philippe, the painting would have been just another family heirloom, as dark and depressing as the others. But to Sorbonne-educated Fabrice Poyet, it would have been a gold mine.

I couldn't believe I'd finally run into a long-lost-art story—and it had turned out to be much too real for my liking.

"You're forgetting one thing," Travis said. "If your mentor was as generous as you're always saying, why wouldn't he have just given the painting to Fabrice and be done with it? Philippe obviously wasn't interested in having the artwork on display."

I guessed my financial advisor *could* be as cynical as Danny. "I said Monsieur was generous, not that he was an idiot. It's not the same thing, you know." I made a face, then paced some more. "Plus, art is subjective. Just because Philippe didn't want to display that Caravaggio doesn't mean he wanted Fabrice to have it. Maybe he didn't like Fabrice." It would be a reasonable position. "Maybe he wanted better for Nathalie."

"Maybe he wanted to sell it himself, once he saw Fabrice's interest in it," Travis hypothesized. "Maybe that's why he made that appointment with Madame Moreau at her antiques store."

It all fit. "But while we've been talking, Fabrice

could be getting away." I grabbed my phone to call Mélanie again.

Travis did the same. Neither of us was successful. Oh no.

I bit my lip, then looked out the window. "It's possible Mélanie is busy booking Mathieu Camara and hasn't noticed us calling. I couldn't blame her if she's taking extra time to press charges against the man who brutally attacked her."

My financial advisor nodded. "I'm not sure we can wait."

That was more like it. I brightened, despite the circumstances. It always makes me feel better to take action.

If I could remember that pearl of wisdom when tempted to procrastinate on something, I'd *really* have my problem licked.

"We've got one more ace up our sleeve." I told Travis about my earlier encounter with the housekeeper, Jeannette Farges. "She wouldn't have said anything, ordinarily. She's been so scared—scared of Fabrice. But Jeannette changed her mind today."

Funnily enough, the reason for that had been my rude send-off to Fabrice Poyet, after he'd ordered me to leave Nathalie alone. *Adieu.* Remember how I'd remarked it was bad-mannered? As a Frenchwoman, the housekeeper had recognized as much—and she'd been impressed by that. She'd admired my unknowing strength.

In carefully worded French, Jeannette had explained that I'd been the only one whom she'd ever seen standing up to Fabrice and his bullying. She'd thought that I might be able to help her, if anyone could—and that's why she'd followed me down the hall. That's why she'd sneaked us both into that unused château room and confessed that she'd *seen* Fabrice on the night of Monsieur's murder. He'd threatened the housekeeper with dismissal (or worse) if she told anyone he'd arrived early "as a surprise for his fiancée." It hadn't been until later—when Fabrice had pretended to arrive on Travis's delayed train— that Jeannette had realized the consequences of what she'd seen.

Specifically, Fabrice Poyet, skulking around the château, trying to secure the painting for himself by any means possible.

That was why Jeannette had been so skittish around Fabrice, flinging towels at him and looking scared. It was why she'd been startled on the terrace during her cigarette break—not because of the film crew's drone cam, but because Fabrice had shown up.

"The painting must have been moved," I guessed, "sometime between when Fabrice first saw it and when he killed Monsieur. He could have gotten away, but he needed the painting first."

"It's too valuable to ship," Travis agreed. "No one is going to mail a painting worth tens of millions of euros. Even though it's small, it would be difficult to transfer covertly, without prompting too many awkward questions." My financial advisor thought about it some more. "I don't think Fabrice was meeting with Charlotte Moreau to set up an auction. I think he wanted to find out if Philippe had done so—if he'd realized the value of the artwork yet. It sounds as though he hadn't."

"Because Fabrice killed him before he could. That must be why Fabrice chose the night of the *Fest-Noz*, before Monsieur could keep his appointment with Madame Moreau." I felt nauseated just thinking about the horrible events that had led to my mentor's death.

"But if Jeannette Farges testifies that she saw Fabrice *here*, a whole day before he claimed to have arrived—"

"Combined with that video footage of Fabrice stalking Philippe," Travis went on, "*and* Clotilde Renouf's statement—"

"Then we've got him," I finished. "But only if we can get Mélanie Flamant here before Fabrice gets away." I fretted, walking to the window to look outside. It was getting darker. Autumn evenings were made for elusion. "Jeannette promised to go straight to the police in Saint-Malo—not even finishing her shift first—but if she loses her nerve, we're in trouble."

Remember how I mentioned that I didn't tell Danny *everything* I'd learned from the *policière* during our phone call? One of the things I neglected to discuss was the statement that jam maker Clotilde Renouf had given to Mélanie before she died.

In it, Clotilde had confessed that, like Jeannette, she'd *also* seen Fabrice Poyet in Saint-Malo a full day before he'd claimed to be there. Those were twenty-four critical hours. They were the difference between my mentor's future son-in-law having arrived after Philippe's death or (incriminatingly) before it.

But Clotilde hadn't admitted as much the first time she'd been questioned by the police. It hadn't been until Mélanie had returned, doggedly certain that the jam maker had more to reveal, that Clotilde had described seeing Fabrice headed for the *Fest-Noz*. She'd known exactly when it had been, because she'd been returning to her shop after having scrawled graffiti on the shutters of cute little La Maison des Petits Bonheurs.

That's right. Disagreeable Clotilde Renouf *had* resented my mentor enough to paint *traître* slurs on his chocolaterie. Her bitterness had placed her in a unique position to notice Fabrice. The possibility that he'd killed her because of it had crossed my mind. So far, Mélanie believed Clotilde's death had been accidental, likely caused by a heart attack and fall.

It was all laid out in black and white. All that remained was stopping Fabrice before he got away—something he'd plainly been preparing to do earlier. We couldn't wait any longer.

"We've got to make a move," I told Travis as I headed for my château room's door. "I can't wait here while he escapes."

"No." My financial advisor trailed me. His hand reached the chair just as I prepared to yank it from under the doorknob. It felt, all at once, comically ineffective. "Hayden, you can't."

"I have to!" I felt tears welling again and blinked them back. This was not the time. I had to be strong. "He killed Philippe! I can't just let him get away with it."

I pulled on the chair. It came away much too easily.

I blinked. Travis had let go in favor of calling Mélanie again. Ever sensible, he held up his palm for me to wait.

Danny would have done this my way, I knew. He would have slowed down Fabrice wrong-side-of-the-tracks style, if he had to—with his bare hands. My bodyguard was hard-hitting that way.

I, unfortunately, didn't have the option of brute strength.

In the few seconds that elapsed, I thought I might lose my mind. I trusted Travis, but sitting tight? Now? It was too much.

This time, though, my keeper got a hold of the *policière*. I could tell from my side of their hurried conversation that Mélanie and her fellow *gendarmes* were finally on their way.

"If it's too late, I'll never forgive myself," I worried.

"It won't be too late." For some reason, Travis looked as though he'd slipped an *extra* ace up his sleeve. "I did hear you, you know, about your reservations about Fabrice's character."

"Yeah?" I was chomping at the bit. "And?"

"And that's why I parked right behind his rental car," my financial advisor said. "I mean, *right* behind him in that small lot. I boxed him in but good. If Fabrice thinks he's driving away without a fuss, somehow taking that unwieldy multimillion-euro painting with him, then he'd better think again."

I couldn't believe it. "Travis! You were finally sneaky!" I could have kissed him for it, too. "That's good. It gives me just enough time to slow down Fabrice until the police get here." I set down the chair and opened the door. "Let's go."

Twenty

If you're thinking that delaying a known murderer is somehow easy, then I'm not sure how you're defining *easy*. Because it's not. Before confronting Fabrice Poyet, I first had to get my mind right. It wouldn't do to come face-to-face with the man who'd cold-bloodedly stabbed my cherished, gray-haired Philippe Vetault and then crumple to bits in a torrent of tears.

With me, that was always a possibility. I'm notoriously soft-hearted—or at least that's what I've been told.

That evening, though, as I prowled the hallways of château Vetault, nearing the room where I'd last glimpsed arrogant, ruthless, unforgivably greedy Fabrice Poyet, I felt downright relentless. You know, *eventually*. It took me a few minutes to move past my understandable fear (he was a murderer) and find the strength to purposely go looking for him (possibly foolishly).

As it happened, though, in the end, Fabrice made himself perfectly, conveniently, and audibly obvious to me. That's because he was doing the one thing most patently Fabrice Poyet (short of homicide): having a temper tantrum at Hélène Vetault.

When I reached the bottom of the sweeping stone staircase, Nathalie's fiancé was shrieking in French at Monsieur's widow.

The sight of him mistreating Hélène made my blood boil.

I strode straight to Fabrice and shoved him. *"Hé! Laissez la tranquille! Que faites-vous? Quel est votre problème?"*

Basically (in order), hey, leave her alone! What are you doing? What's your problem? Imagine that said in the most hostile tone a chocolate whisperer could muster, and you had it.

Conveniently, my understanding of French was okay for the moment. I guessed fury, fear, and fortitude were good for my multilingual aspirations. I was determined not to back down.

I used my newly excellent *français* to address Hélène, asking if she was all right. She waved off my concern, her gaze fixed fearfully on Fabrice. If I guessed correctly, he'd finally run out of patience with her. He wanted that painting. Now.

I faced him again, trying to seem as though I'd simply stumbled upon his argument with the *châtelaine* and didn't approve of his rough behavior. *"Vous n'avez aucun droit."*

I'd accused him of having no right to behave the way he had. I was trembling, though. I hoped Fabrice couldn't see.

He blew out his cheeks with characteristic impatience.

"Leave us." His distinct, clipped English included

me and Travis, right behind me. "This does not concern you. Go away."

Fabrice flicked his hand as though we were bothersome pests. Even if I *hadn't* known he was a murderer, that would have incensed me. I straightened to my full height and squared off.

There was a patented antimugger move coming from me to him any second now. I knew it was effective. I was aching to use it.

I'd used it for the first time in Barcelona. I could vouch for its ability—if used correctly—to drop an attacker cold. At this point, Danny and I had even developed a shorthand for it.

But my dependable bodyguard pal wasn't there. Travis was.

He stepped forward, hands out in a peacekeeping gesture. Whatever he said to Fabrice Poyet (in French, naturally) made the murdering dirtbag pause. He gave me a calculating look.

I'd thought we were making progress. I'd planned to corner Fabrice someplace far from Hélène Vetault. I'd hoped to delay him long enough for Mélanie and the *gendarmes* to arrive. If that failed, my backup plan involved one of the château's heavy iron candelabras, my no-weakling luggage-lifting arm, and Fabrice's skull. I'm not talking murder . . . just a robust delay.

But that's when the château's grand front door burst open. In spilled Capucine Roux, her Parisian film crew, and Lucas Lefebvre, their arrival an unwitting reenactment of the day I'd arrived in Brittany to celebrate Monsieur's retirement *fête*.

I wished with all my might that I could return there.

"Madame Roux! Madame Roux!" Hélène appeared

relieved. She rushed over to the cool indie director and spoke to her in French. They conferred a few minutes. Then my mentor's widow turned back.

"Madame Roux knows where the painting is," Hélène told Fabrice, her voice full of heartrending mingled fear and relief. "She saw it a few days ago, while looking for set dressing. She will take you to it, right this minute. Do not worry."

I was so hyped up that it took me a few seconds to realize that she'd spoken in English, not French. There was no time to puzzle out why. An obviously innocent Capucine was already coming nearer, her pretty face full of sincere helpfulness.

All I knew was that I didn't hear sirens outside yet.

If Fabrice got what he'd been waiting for, he'd leave. For all we knew, he'd already discovered (and dealt with) the parking-lot trap Travis had devised to slow him down.

Now what? While the Parisians gave Capucine a hard time about "working" instead of doing more partying with them, Hélène edged closer to me. The *châtelaine*'s gaze focused on mine.

The startling thing was, her eyes looked absolutely clear.

"My husband always said you were clever," Hélène said in an undertone. "I hope that you will show it now. For his sake."

I was too astonished by her apparently instantaneous return to sanity and soberness that I could only gape. Had Hélène been *pretending* all this time? Could *she* have been sleuthing, too?

If so, she deserved a *César*—the French version of an Oscar.

"Painting?" I repeated brightly. I strode forward.

"Do you mean the Caravaggio?" I asked Fabrice. "I saw it this morning."

While Travis shook his head at me—I guessed there was no repressing his natural sense of caution—I gave Monsieur Poyet a laugh.

"You should have said that's what you wanted," I told him in my breeziest, most upper-crust tone. Didn't know I had one? Hey, I've traveled the whole world, remember? I can be posh when I have to be. Just then, I did. "I'm more partial to abstract art, myself. Delaunay, Mondrian, Léger . . . anything non-figurative. I mean, a trust fund is incomplete without investments. I might as well enjoy what I'm looking at while I'm parking my money."

Fabrice frowned at me. I think he was surprised.

I'm no slouch when it comes to fine arts, either. I just don't enjoy making judgments about someone else's creativity.

Isn't that what most conversations about art come down to?

"But I suppose radical naturalism has its admirers, like you," I went on. I was pretty sure Travis was gawking at me now. I was happy I'd boned up on art-world lingo before visiting Madame Moreau's antiques shop. "I'll show you where the painting is. While I do that, you might be interested in my consulting work."

I glanced backward at Travis, hoping his mind-reading skills were up to snuff. He'd always been able to guess what I was thinking. Right now, I was thinking my financial advisor would need to lead the police to me and Fabrice pretty soon.

I took Fabrice's arm, forcibly encouraging him to come with me while I chatted on about my in-demand skills as a chocolate expert. Thanks to Danny and his recent praise of my work (as compared with Mathieu Camara's, at least), my assets were right on the tip of my tongue. I wanted Fabrice Poyet to believe that, aside from being an art-collecting dilettante (just his kind of person), I was also a scheming self-promoter who would stop at nothing to secure a new chocolate-whisperer consultation.

"Especially with an esteemed, successful company like Poyet," I gushed as we ascended the stairs to the attic.

In spite of everything, Fabrice seemed just self-serving enough to listen to me. Touching him made me feel queasy, and leaving behind Travis, my security blanket, doubled my sense of doom. What if Fabrice strangled me at the top of the stairs?

What if he copied my candelabra idea and brained me?

My knees felt like jelly as we reached the ornate stone landing. Below us in the entryway, the Parisians headed en masse to the château's dining room, apparently in the mood for a meal.

I imagined Hélène and Travis down there. I channeled my financial advisor's steadying influence and somehow kept going.

Once I got started, keeping up my chocolate patter was easy, even if being in the presence of a scary murderer wasn't. Danny always complains that I don't like to promote my services, but that evening, I had no trouble prattling on to Fabrice Poyet about product enhancements, pioneering flavors, and strengthened profits. I thought of Monsieur's praise of me, just days ago.

You have not lost your feel for le chocolat, Philippe had said with the gruff fondness that I'd loved in him.

You were a natural talent. I gave you a direction to follow, nothing more.

I'd cared for Philippe. I still owed my mentor everything.

For his sake, I found a way to continue. We climbed higher.

"A company as old as Poyet, even one so respected, must always remain on guard against losing its edge," I advised Fabrice. "Product lines must stay current through innovation."

As I rattled on, I realized that I still didn't know where the painting was. Sooner or later, Monsieur Poyet would call my bluff.

On the other hand . . . I felt a hand land on my derrière and realized that perhaps Fabrice was interested in something else.

Ugh. It took everything I had not to recoil in disgust. My priority had to be keeping Philippe's murderer from getting away. If that meant letting him grope me . . . well, I had renewed empathy for Charlotte Moreau and her antiques-store rendezvous.

"Monsieur Poyet! How dare you!" Playfully, I swatted away his hand. "Is this the way business is always conducted in France?"

I knew it wasn't, but I was at a loss for banter. I couldn't meet his unkind eyes as I tried to stay one step ahead.

He laughed. "We both know *you* are not interested in business." On the next landing, he backed me into a corner. "Your friend told me what *you* are really interested in."

Fabrice's breath blasted my forehead. He was tall. His shoulders blocked my view of the staircase and the safety below.

I wished Nathalie would wander down the hall and interrupt. I also wished she wouldn't. She was in for enough heartache when she learned her fiancé was a pitiless killer. She didn't need to add multiple instances of creepy lecherousness to that, too.

"My friend?" Silently, I swore to give *Travis* the "Barcelona" treatment when I saw him next. What had he told Fabrice about me, anyway? "He wasn't supposed to tell you that."

Whatever it was. I was getting in much too deep now.

"I am glad he did." Philippe lowered his gaze to my (nearly nonexistent) cleavage. It was hardly shown to advantage in my T-shirt, but that didn't discourage him. "I like a bold woman."

"Oh, good. That's me." I tried to sound seductive, like Charlotte Moreau. I probably sounded as though I'd just come down with bronchitis. "I like a . . . bold man," I said lamely.

Gross. At least we weren't talking about the painting. If I survived, I would need a thousand showers to feel clean again.

"Unfortunately, I am in a rush this evening." Fabrice's harsh mouth turned down at the corners. "Perhaps you would meet me in Paris?" He mentioned a "nice" hotel on Avenue George V.

I thought I knew the hotel he was referring to. If so, rooms there started at 1,000 euros per night—and I doubted Fabrice would be content with a standard room. He didn't need to steal a multimillion euro painting. He hadn't needed to kill to get one, either. Remembering that strengthened my resolve.

"What about Nathalie?" I protested. "Won't she object?"

"She will not need to know about this." Fabrice

stepped nearer and put his hand on my hip. His gaze dropped to my lips. I had the revolting sensation he was about to kiss me. "She will be busy for some time, thanks to the funeral of her father."

At that, Monsieur Poyet actually *grinned*. He was loathsome.

I nearly lost my wits with rage. His despicable face swam in my vision, making me feel dizzy. "I . . . don't know what to say."

"Say yes," he urged, looming nearer. "Say *oui. Oui, oui—*"

His breathy tone finally made me snap, just moments before his mouth landed on mine. "No!" I gave him a hard shove.

He reeled backward. Then he grinned again. "I like this."

Were his eyes sparkling at me with glee? I couldn't believe it. I dropped my pretense. "I thought you wanted the painting."

Fabrice tilted his head. "I will get it. Very soon now."

It was a command. When I didn't immediately comply by taking him to the Caravaggio, Monsieur Poyet regarded me seriously.

I detected exactly the moment when he recognized my ruse.

His face contorted with fury. "You do not have it."

I couldn't pretend anymore. "I wouldn't give it to you if I did." Where were the *policiers*? Surely, enough time had elapsed for them to arrive, even via Saint-Malo's rural roads. "It doesn't belong to you. It belongs to Monsieur and his family."

"*Bof.* They did not even recognize its true value. *I* did." Fabrice made a boastful digression into explaining his fine arts expertise, his overall intelligence, and his family's status. Then he shrugged. "If Monsieur Vetault had simply given me the painting when I asked him for it, none of this would have happened."

I trembled harder than before. "And by 'none of this,' you mean . . . ?" *Killing Philippe.* I needed him to say it. To admit it.

He gave a cruel laugh. "If you think I am confessing . . . no." His rueful headshake dashed my hopes. "I am not so much a fool."

"You were, though," I shot back, knowing how dangerous it was to provoke him but unable to avoid it. I had to stick to my plan. I had to delay him. "You were seen. You left evidence."

For a moment, uncertainty clouded Fabrice's face. Then, "Anyone who knew anything is dead now."

He had to mean Clotilde Renouf. Nausea washed over me. Had he really killed the jam maker, hoping to cover his tracks?

"If anyone else comes forward, no one will believe them."

He gave another contemptuous gesture. I realized that he was referring to Jeannette Farges—and hoped I'd convinced the housekeeper to conquer her fear and go to the police earlier.

"You're forgetting me. *I* was there. I saw you," I bluffed. It was partly true. I'd seen the footage. "Tell me," I added in a voice that undoubtedly quaked with fear, "what would you have done if that chocolate chipper *hadn't* fit inside your coat?"

Fabrice's eyes widened. He knew I had him.

Then, an instant later, he had *me.* He grabbed me. "I am afraid that the stairs here are very slippery." He pulled me by the elbow toward the edge of the landing. From there, it was a long way down to the château's ornate entryway. "I will be very sad when you fall. We could have had fun together in Paris."

I pushed back, but he was too strong for me. Sure, I'm able to heft heavy bags of cacao beans and tote my own luggage, but this was different. When push came to shove, I was helpless.

We struggled, grunting and scuffling on the landing. The château's baroque furnishings swung wildly in my vision. I wanted to scream for help, but I didn't have the breath for it.

Fabrice jammed his arm around my throat. I saw stars.

Heart pounding, I twisted. I still couldn't get free. I wasn't in position for anything else, so I kicked backward. My sneaker connected with Fabrice's shinbone. He yelped in French.

Thankfully, his grasp loosened just enough. I went limp in his arms, forcing Fabrice to drop me in a heap. I landed with an *oof!*, painfully bashing my hands and knees on the ancient stone.

Fabrice wasn't so lucky. He lost his balance on the top step and fell. I looked up just as he plummeted. Philippe's killer didn't pinwheel his arms for a few dramatic seconds. He didn't swear to get revenge on me. He didn't even cry out.

He just fell. But the sound his head made on the stone would haunt me forever, I knew. I didn't want to look, but I had to make sure he wouldn't reach up and drag me down with him.

Wild with adrenaline and fear, I crawled to the edge of the landing. My arms wobbled, barely able to support me as I peeked.

I should have known someone as evil as Fabrice Poyet was too strong to be killed so easily. He was waking up, dazedly, as *policière* Mélanie Flamant and her colleagues slapped on cuffs.

My mentor's killer would obviously live to stand trial for his murder. I guessed that was justice—the best I could get.

A few seconds later, Travis was there. He climbed past the official *gendarme* hubbub and crouched beside me with concern.

"It's bad enough you're investigating murders as a hobby," my financial advisor told me in his deep, seductive growl. "You probably shouldn't start committing them yourself now, too."

His reference to Fabrice's fall made me laugh. Weakly.

"That wasn't my intention." I grabbed Travis's arm, intent on getting to my feet. Whoops. I swayed, still too amped to support myself. But Travis had me. "What took you so long?"

"Well . . ." My keeper looked hesitant, but he came through in the end. "You seemed pretty close to extracting a confession. Mélanie hung back on purpose for a few minutes, just in case."

I shook my head with disbelief. "No wonder her coworkers are mad at her," I joked. "She could have gotten me killed."

"I wouldn't have let that happen. I was ready to charge up there myself and rescue you. Mélanie had to have me restrained."

I chuckled, then realized he was serious. "Really?"

"She's smart. She didn't want me to risk the case."

"No, I mean . . . really? You wanted to save me that much?"

Travis looked abashed. He nodded. "Sometimes you're—"

"Too nice?" I interrupted. "Stupidly softhearted?"

"No." My keeper's gaze settled on me. Affectionately. "I mean, yes, you're both of those things sometimes. But also—"

"Full of procrastination? Annoyingly antsy?"

"Brave," Travis said at last. "Really, really brave." He hugged me close—possibly to keep me from witnessing the emotion I heard in his husky voice. "You saved the day, Hayden."

Below us, the *gendarmes* were dealing expertly with Fabrice.

"That is correct," Mélanie agreed. She was busy arresting Monsieur's killer, but she was close enough to have overheard us. "Madame Farges has given a statement. Travis told me about the film footage. We already had bank records showing that Monsieur Poyet stayed in a hotel close by in Dinard on the night Monsieur Vetault was killed." The *policière's* attention rested on my financial advisor for an instant, letting me know that those records had likely come from him. "But without your delaying Monsieur Poyet, he might still have gotten away." She nodded. "Very well done."

Even woozy and wired, I managed to smile. I was glad it was over. But I had another question. "Did you get Mathieu Camara?"

Mélanie nodded. "Monsieur Camara will be going back to jail."

"Then he won't be able to hurt either of us anymore." I looked at the *policiere's* head, where she still sported her white knit hat. Mine was packed. I was sorely tempted to toss it, but I couldn't. It was a reminder of all we'd accomplished.

For Monsieur, I'd wear it proudly. And I'd remember him.

"If you need me, I'll be happy to give a statement or anything else," I told Mélanie, watching as more officers arrived to treat Fabrice's injuries. I wanted him able to stand trial—to go to jail forever. "In the meantime, there's something else I have to do." I gestured to Travis. "Come on, tough guy. You're just the man I need for this job."

Twenty-one

It took my sultry-voiced financial advisor a while to comb through all the details. But in the end, he emerged triumphant.

I'd known he would, but his success warmed my heart anyway—possibly because of how pleased with himself Travis looked as we handed the resulting (necessary) documentation to Hélène Vetault and Nathalie. The two of them stood united in front of La Maison des Petits Bonheurs a few days after Fabrice Poyet had been arrested, charged, and booked into jail for Monsieur's murder.

According to Mélanie, a conviction and lengthy sentence were all but guaranteed. She had everything she needed to make certain of that. "Partly thanks to you," she'd assured me.

I didn't know about that. But I knew that—for the sake of *patrimoine*, justice, and everyone who loved delicious treats—my mentor's chocolaterie had to reopen. That's why we were there.

It had taken a diligent effort to unravel the canceled Poyet-Vetault merger, examine Philippe's will and other personal papers, and make all the correct decisions. But Travis did it.

He was different from Danny, that was true. He was different from *me*. But he was uniquely helpful and dedicated.

He handed the chocolaterie's keys to Hélène and the attendant ownership documents to Nathalie. They accepted both.

"Monsieur would have wanted you to have the shop," I told them sincerely as we all stood gazing at its charming exterior. "I hope you'll be able to reopen very soon. I can suggest a few chocolatiers with the relevant experience and expertise."

Three pointed gazes swung straight to me. I balked.

"Who *aren't* me," I hurried to add, "even though I wish I could stay." I was tempted. If I didn't leave Brittany, maybe I wouldn't run into another homicide. I could hope, couldn't I? "I'm afraid I can't do that, though. I need to get home."

Home. I couldn't miss Travis's questioning look. He knew as well as I did that I didn't have one of those. Not really.

Maybe someday. Moving on . . . "Although I *have* been pretty busy over the past few days." I'd worked through my grief and trauma by pouring all my energies into making chocolate in Monsieur's barn-atelier, creating from dawn to dusk, stopping only to attend Philippe's poignant memorial service. "I think I've left you with enough inventory to last until you hire someone."

Hélène nodded, clear-eyed and sober. Her drinking *had* been a trick—a tactic designed to prevent Fabrice from leaving before someone could prove he'd killed her husband. The *châtelaine* hadn't been able to find that proof herself—not even with Hubert trying to help—but her future son-in-law's intense interest in the painting had tipped her off that something was amiss.

For her daughter's sake, Hélène had done her best, moving things around the château in the middle of the night and then pretending not to be able to find them the next day. We could only assume that Philippe had accidentally kicked off the idea by hiding the painting until he could have it expertly assessed.

For Nathalie's part, she'd been understandably devastated by her fiancé's heinous act. She hadn't been entirely surprised, though, having had her own misgivings about Fabrice's behavior.

"When he refused to attend Papa's memorial, that was the end," my French friend had told me. "I was through with him."

There in front of La Maison des Petits Bonheurs, Travis put together his hands. He regarded the two Frenchwomen we'd come to know so much better over the past several days. He smiled.

"Has Madame Moreau contacted you regarding the auction?"

The painting had indeed been a lost Caravaggio, estimated to be worth more than fifty million euros. The Vetaults had unwittingly preserved it as a family heirloom for centuries without knowing its true value. Charlotte Moreau had been beside herself when she'd finally seen and authenticated it herself.

I, of course, had been busy apologizing for doubting her claim that Fabrice Poyet had pawed her against her will.

Hélène nodded. "She believes it will do well at auction."

"Are you sure you don't want to keep it?" I asked.

"Very sure." It was Nathalie's turn to nod. "Papa intended to sell that painting. Madame Moreau confirmed as much. He'd told her he wanted to assure the château's future before leaving Saint-Malo." Her mournful gaze lowered to the chocolaterie key in her hand, then lifted to her mother's face. She smiled. "He knew the B&B was struggling. He had lost hope of reconciling with Maman, but he wanted to leave her with one final gift."

That was the generous Monsieur I knew. I raised my brows at Philippe's widow. "What does Monsieur Bernard think of all this?"

"Hubert understands," Hélène told me. "At one time, our partnership was . . . more, but it has waned. We are now joined only by business. That is enough." She gave me the ghost of a smile. "Some things are most desirable when forbidden, *n'est-ce pas?*"

I knew she meant her forbidden *amour* with Hubert, but I didn't want to linger on the past. "Forbidden, like chocolate?"

In demonstration, I raised the boxes of molded *chocolat* I'd brought with me. Travis and the two Vetaults laughed happily.

"*Oui, c'est ça,*" Nathalie agreed. Yes, that's right.

I couldn't help wondering what *she* thought about Hubert Bernard. Were the rumors true? Was the gardener really her birth father? Most likely, Travis and I would never know for certain.

I supposed I'd have to be all right with that. Together, we'd captured a killer—with the help of Danny's far-flung assistance, of course. That meant it was now time to move on.

We said our good-byes to Hélène and Nathalie. We even exchanged warm *bises.* Then I took a lingering look at the chocolaterie. This was where I'd learned my craft. With Monsieur by my side, I'd discovered something wonderful about myself.

I'd learned something amazing about the world that summer, too. I'd learned that it could always be made more delicious.

Feeling sentimental, I turned away. But Travis saw me.

He always did, didn't he? Even (somehow) long-distance. That was why he'd conquered his fear of flying to be with me.

Companionably, my financial advisor slung his arm over my shoulders. "Cheer up, Hayden. You can always visit later." He smiled at me as we made our way through the winding cobblestone streets of the *vieille ville* (old village). "Maybe you can convince Hélène and Nathalie to begin a chocolatier-in-residence program for you."

I appreciated his efforts. However . . . "Don't try to sweet-talk me now. I'm still mad at you." I cornered him near a café. "What did you tell Fabrice that day? He wouldn't get off me!"

I shuddered, remembering Monsieur Poyet's groping and leering.

"Well . . ." Travis bought time by eyeing a tray of pastries being brought out from the café's kitchen. His sweet tooth was no excuse, though. "You know that Poyet is a public company?"

"This isn't the time for a lesson in corporate structure."

"That means that Fabrice Poyet might have been in charge of certain things, but he had a board of directors to satisfy."

His explanation was rapidly devolving into boredom central. Plus, those pastries *did* look pretty tasty. Yum. "So?"

"So, Monsieur Poyet had had multiple sexual harassment claims filed against him over the years, several still pending. He'd gotten to be a serious problem for the company. If not for the promising Vetault-Poyet merger keeping his career alive, he'd already have been ousted for his sexist, predatory behavior."

"Sounds like him." That meant that Fabrice wouldn't only be criminally prosecuted—he would likely lose a huge chunk of his personal fortune, too. "Which means you said to him that . . . ?"

It had been in French. If not, I'd have already known.

"I told him you were hot-to-trot for him," Travis confessed eventually, speaking quickly. "Not in so many words, of course. As you know, most colloquialisms don't translate precisely."

"Travis!" I swatted him. "How could you?"

"I knew he'd go for it. He was just that arrogant," my financial advisor explained. "We needed him to go with you."

"So you pimped me out to a killer?" I gawked at him, then drew in an indignant breath. "Danny would *never*—" I began.

I stopped abruptly. Then I studied Travis more closely.

Actually, Danny *might* do something like this. That meant . . .

"The two of you have been collaborating again, haven't you?" I demanded to know. "That 'hot-to-trot' thing was *his* idea, right?" I smacked my forehead, incredulous that I hadn't realized it before. "If you two aren't sworn enemies anymore—"

"Then we can do a more efficient job of helping you."

At Travis's enthusiastic tone, I shook my head. This could only mean one thing. "This is going to be a nightmare."

They both knew so much about me—but from vastly different angles. Between my sexy-voiced financial advisor and my rough-and-ready security expert, I'd never know a moment's peace.

I moaned as much to Travis. He had the audacity to laugh.

"It's going to be fine," he said. "The enforcer isn't so bad." His grin broadened. "Not once you get to know him better."

I envisioned "the enforcer" and "Harvard" teaming up to "keep me safe" on some future amateur murder investigation.

I groaned again at the implications. They might think they could work together amicably, but I knew better. I *knew* it.

There was only one thing to say. "No big deal," I told Travis blithely as I reached for my phone to confront Danny. I didn't care how drastic the time difference was. We needed to have this out. "It's a good thing I won't be needing your help anymore, since I'm finished with all this sleuthing stuff."

My call to Danny rang and rang while I glared at my financial advisor. He appeared completely unaffected by my concerns.

"You don't really believe you *won't* run into another murder, do you?" Travis inquired. "Statistically speaking, it's unlikely. However, since you're already a statistical anomaly—"

I'd been wrong. There were *two* things left to say.

Especially if Travis was going to lecture me about statistics. Ugh. I like my math confined to baking. That's it.

I spied the café's waiter passing by with those sugary, scrumptious pastries. I raised my hand and beckoned him over.

"*Oui, Madame?*" he asked. "*Vous désirez?*"

Roughly: yes, miss? What would you like?

I could think of several things I wanted just then. Peace. Quiet. The freedom to snuggle up with a golden retriever of my very own. But I settled on the one thing I knew would satisfy me most.

"*Oui, merci,*" I said. "*Avez-vous du chocolat?*"

You've probably already guessed the translation.

I needed some chocolate, and I needed it fast.

Recipes

FRENCH YOGURT CAKE
(with chocolate)

1 container yogurt
2 containers all-purpose flour
1 container granulated sugar
2 eggs
1½ teaspoons baking powder
½ teaspoon salt
1 teaspoon vanilla extract
½ container vegetable oil
1 container chocolate chips

GET READY: Preheat oven to 350° and have ready a medium-size, greased loaf pan.

MAKE CAKE: Empty yogurt into a medium-size mixing bowl. Rinse and dry the yogurt cup, then use it to measure the remaining ingredients. Add everything to the mixing bowl except oil.

Mix well, smoothing out any lumps with a whisk. Add vegetable oil; whisk till combined. Stir in chocolate chips.

BAKE CAKE: Pour batter into loaf pan. Bake for 25-30 minutes, until cake is light golden brown and a toothpick inserted just off center comes out clean. Let cool for 10 minutes, then remove from pan and let cool completely. Slice and enjoy!

Notes from Hayden

In France, easy yogurt cakes like this one are a popular children's *goûter* (snack), but you don't have to be a *gamin* (kid) to appreciate a cake that doesn't even require measuring cups! Just use your yogurt container to measure, and *voilà*!

This recipe works no matter what size yogurt container you use, since the ingredient proportions remain the same (although you might need to adjust baking times). Don't use nonfat yogurt or yogurt containing gums and thickeners—best results come from using delicious, creamy, full-fat French-style yogurt!

MICROWAVE CHOCOLATE CAKE
FOR ONE (for Danny)

4 tablespoons all-purpose flour
3 tablespoons granulated sugar
2 tablespoons cocoa powder
¼ teaspoon baking powder
pinch of salt
4 tablespoons milk
2 tablespoons vegetable oil
splash of vanilla extract
1 tablespoon chocolate chips (optional)

GET READY: Have ready a *microwave-safe* mug, ramekin, or small bowl. It should hold approximately 12-14 ounces.

MAKE THE CHOCOLATE CAKE: In a small mixing bowl, whisk together flour, sugar, cocoa powder, baking powder, and salt. Pour in milk, oil, and vanilla; whisk thoroughly to combine.

Stir in chocolate chips, if using.

"BAKE" THE CAKE: Pour batter into mug, ramekin, or small bowl. Microwave on full power for 45-70 seconds (time will depend on your microwave's strength), until cake is barely set. Carefully remove from microwave, let cool for 5 minutes, then enjoy warm!

Notes from Hayden

Think of this as a Danny-size cupcake—it serves one
(hungry) person! It's fast and easy to make, too. Just
make sure you watch the "baking" time carefully—it's
easy to overdo this one.

You can serve this tasty chocolate cake with whipped
cream, Nutella (for that European touch) or ice
cream (or even gild the lily with chocolate sauce!) but
it's also nice on its own.

LE CHOCOLAT CHAUD
(French-style hot chocolate)

2 cups whole milk
5 ounces top-quality bittersweet chocolate,
   finely chopped
2 tablespoons granulated sugar (optional)
dash of vanilla extract
½ cup freshly whipped heavy cream
chocolate shavings (optional)

GET READY: Warm milk in a medium saucepan over medium heat. Carefully whisk in chopped chocolate and sugar (if using—if your chocolate is sweet enough for you, you might not need additional sugar). Continue warming *chocolat chaud* mixture, whisking often, until chocolate is fully melted and the hot chocolate steams lightly. It should become slightly thicker and smell delicious.

TO SERVE: Add vanilla extract, stir well, then pour *chocolat chaud* into demitasse cups (for small servings) or coffee cups (for larger servings). Serve with whipped cream and (optional) chocolate shavings for a luxurious, chocolatey delight!

Notes from Hayden

This scrumptious take on hot chocolate is *everywhere* in France. It's fast and easy to make, too. It's much richer and thicker than American-style hot chocolate—

that's why it's typically served with fluffy whipped cream on the side . . . so you can create exactly the velvety consistency you prefer by stirring in more whipped cream or just putting a spoonful on top. *Miam-miam*!

This recipe makes 4 "Parisian size" or 2 "American size" servings. Since *chocolat chaud* is so luxurious, you might be content with a smaller serving, especially if you're enjoying whipped cream (and chocolate shavings on top), too.

HAYDEN'S (stress relieving) OATMEAL-CRANBERRY-PECAN COOKIES WITH WHITE CHOCOLATE
(small batch version)

3 tablespoons brown sugar
2 tablespoons granulated sugar
1½ tablespoons milk
1 teaspoon vanilla extract
2 tablespoons vegetable oil
½ cup all-purpose flour
¼ teaspoon baking soda
⅛ teaspoon salt
½ cup old-fashioned oats (uncooked)
2 tablespoons dried cranberries
2 tablespoons chopped toasted pecans
¼ cup good-quality white chocolate, chopped

GET READY: Preheat oven to 375°.

MAKE COOKIES: In a medium bowl, stir together brown sugar, granulated sugar, milk, and vanilla. Add oil; mix until well combined. Add flour, baking soda, salt, dried cranberries, pecans, and white chocolate; mix until no floury streaks remain.

SHAPE & BAKE COOKIES: Scoop rounded spoonfuls of cookie dough onto greased or parchment-lined baking sheets, spacing each about two inches apart. (A #20 portion scoop—which holds 3 tablespoons—is handy here.) Flatten cookies slightly. Bake for 9-11 minutes, until just set. Cool and enjoy!

Notes from Hayden

These are my go-to "stress cookies," guaranteed to make anyone feel better right away! This makes a small batch of cookies—I'm always too eager to make something new to have *too* many of the same cookies around, but you can easily double this recipe.

The trick here is to use the best quality white chocolate you can find—no "confectioner's coating" allowed! Look for cocoa butter near the top of the ingredients list (along with sugar and milk powder). If cocoa butter isn't at or near the top, keep searching for another brand! Chocolatiers like Barry Callebaut, Merckens, and Valrhona make white chocolate chunks, chips, and *fevres* (oval disks) that are tasty enough to enjoy on their own.